HUNTED

A SEVENTEEN SERIES NOVEL

A.D. STARRLING

COPYRIGHT

Hunted (A Seventeen Series Novel) Book One

Fifth print edition: 2018

First published as Soul Meaning: Seventeen Book One in 2012

www.ADStarrling.com

ISBN-13: 978-0-9572826-6-7

Editor: Invisible Ink Editing (www.invisibleinkediting.com)

Cover: Deranged Doctor Design (www.derangeddoctordesign.com)

DEDICATION

For my family

PART ONE: DEATH

PROLOGUE

MY NAME IS LUCAS SOUL.

Today, I died again.

This is my fifteenth death in the last four hundred and fifty years.

CHAPTER ONE

I WOKE UP IN A DARK ALLEY BEHIND A BUILDING.

Autumn rain plummeted from an angry sky, washing the narrow, walled corridor I lay in with shades of gray. It dripped from the metal rungs of the fire escape above my head and slithered down dirty, barren walls, forming puddles under the garbage dumpsters by my feet. It gurgled in gutters and rushed in storm drains off the main avenue behind me.

It also cleansed away the blood beneath my body.

For once, I was grateful for the downpour; I did not want any evidence left of my recent demise.

I blinked at the drops that struck my face and slowly climbed to my feet. Unbidden, my fingers rose to trace the cut in my chest; the blade had missed the birthmark on my skin by less than an inch.

I turned and studied the tower behind me. I was not sure what I was expecting to see. A face peering over the edge of the glass and brick structure. An avenging figure drifting down in the rainfall, a bloodied sword in its hands and a crazy smile in its eyes. A flock of silent crows come to take my unearthly body to its final resting place.

Bar the heavenly deluge, the skyline was fortunately empty.

I pulled my cell phone out of my jeans and stared at it. It was smashed to pieces. I sighed. I could hardly blame the makers of the device. They had probably never tested it from the rooftop of a twelve-storey building. As for me, the bruises would start to fade by tomorrow.

It would take another day for the wound in my chest to heal completely.

I glanced at the sky again before walking out of the alley. An empty phone booth stood at the intersection to my right. I strolled toward it and closed the rickety door behind me. A shiver wracked my body while I dialed a number. Steam soon fogged up the glass wall before me.

There was a soft click after the fifth ring.

'Yo,' said a tired voice.

'Yo yourself,' I said.

A yawn traveled down the line. 'What's up?'

'I need a ride. And a new phone.'

There was a short silence. 'It's four o'clock in the morning.' The voice had gone blank.

'I know,' I said in the same tone.

The sigh at the other end was audible above the pounding of the rain on the metal roof of the booth. 'Where are you?'

'Corner of Cambridge and Staniford.'

Fifteen minutes later, a battered, tan Chevrolet Monte Carlo pulled up next to the phone box. The passenger door opened.

'Get in,' said the figure behind the wheel.

I crossed the sidewalk and climbed in the seat. Water dripped onto the leather cover and formed a puddle by my feet. There was a disgruntled mutter from my left. I looked at the man beside me.

Reid Hasley was my business partner and friend. Together, we co-owned the Hasley and Soul Agency. We were private investigators, of sorts. Reid certainly qualified as one, being a former Marine and cop. I, on the other hand, had been neither.

'You look like hell,' said Reid as he maneuvered the car into almost nonexistent traffic. He took something from his raincoat and tossed it across to me. It was a new cell.

I raised my eyebrows. 'That was fast.'

He grunted indistinct words and lit a cigarette. 'What happened?' An orange glow flared into life as he inhaled, casting shadows under his brow and across his nose.

I transferred the data card from the broken phone into the new one and frowned at the bands of smoke drifting toward me. 'That's going to kill you one day.'

'Just answer the question,' he retorted.

I looked away from his intense gaze and contemplated the dark tower at the end of the avenue. 'I met up with our new client.'

'And?' said Reid.

'He wasn't happy to see me.'

Something in my voice made him stiffen. 'How unhappy are we talking here?'

I sighed. 'Well, he stuck a sword through my heart and pushed me off the top of the Cramer building. I'd say he was pretty pissed.'

Silence followed my words. 'That's not good,' said Reid finally.

'No.'

'It means we're not gonna get the money,' he added.

'I'm fine by the way. Thanks for asking,' I said.

He shot a hard glance at me. 'We need the cash.'

Unpalatable as the statement was, it was also regrettably true. Small PI firms like ours had just about managed before the recession. Nowadays, people had more to worry about than what their cheating spouses were up to. Although embezzlement cases were up by a third, the victims of such scams were usually too hard up to afford the services of a good detective agency. As a result, the rent on our office space was overdue by a month.

Mrs. Trelawney, our landlady, was not pleased about this; at five-foot two and weighing just over two hundred pounds, the woman had the ability to make us quake in our boots. This had less to do with her size than the fact that she made the best angel cakes in the city. She gave them out to her tenants when they paid the rent on time. A month without angel cakes was making us twitchy.

'I think we might still get the cakes if you flash your eyes at her,' mused my partner.

I stared at him. 'Are you pimping me out?'

'No. You'd be a tough sell,' he retorted as the car splashed along the empty streets of the city. He glanced at me. 'This makes it what, your fourteenth death?'

'Fifteenth.'

His eyebrows rose. 'Huh. So, two more to go.'

I nodded mutely. In many ways, I was glad Hasley had entered my unnatural life, despite the fact that it happened in such a dramatic fashion. It was ten years ago this summer.

Hasley was a detective in the Boston PD Homicide Unit at the time. One hot Friday afternoon in August, he and his partner of three years found themselves on the trail of a murder suspect, a Latino man by the name of Burt Suarez. Suarez worked the toll bridge northeast of the city and had no priors. Described by his neighbors and friends as a gentle giant who cherished his wife, was kind to children and animals, and even attended Sunday service, the guy did not have so much as a speeding ticket to his name. That day, the giant snapped and went on a killing spree after walking in on his wife and his brother in the marital bed. He shot Hasley's partner, two uniformed cops, and the neighbor's dog, before fleeing toward the river.

Unfortunately, I got in his way.

In my defense, I had not been myself for most of that month, having recently lost someone who had been a friend for more than a hundred years. In short, I was drunk.

On that scorching summer's day, Burt Suarez achieved something no other human, or non-human for that matter, had managed before or since.

He shot me in the head.

Sadly, he did not get to savor this feat, as he died minutes after he fired a round through my skull. Hasley still swore to this day that Suarez's death had more to do with seeing me rise to my feet Lazarus-like again than the gunshot wound he himself inflicted on the man with his Glock 19.

That had been my fourteenth death. Shortly after witnessing my unholy resurrection, Hasley quit his job as a detective and became my business partner.

Over the decade that followed, we trailed unfaithful spouses, found missing persons, performed employee checks for high profile investment banks, took on surveillance work for attorneys and insurance companies, served process to disgruntled defendants, and even rescued the odd kidnapped pet. Hasley knew more about me than anyone else in the city.

He still carried the Glock.

'Why did he kill you?' said Reid presently. He braked at a set of red lights. 'Did you do something to piss him off?' There was a trace of suspicion in his tone. The lights turned green.

'Well, broadly speaking, he seemed opposed to my existence.' The rhythmic swishing of the windscreen wipers and the dull hiss of rubber rolling across wet asphalt were the only sounds that broke the ensuing lull. 'He called me an ancient abomination that should be sent straight to Hell and beyond.' I grimaced. 'Frankly, I thought that was a bit ironic coming from someone who's probably not that much older than me.'

Reid crushed the cigarette butt in the ashtray and narrowed his eyes. 'You mean, he's one of you?'

I hesitated before nodding once. 'Yes.'

Over the years, as I came to know and trust him, I told Reid a little bit about my origins.

I was born in Europe in the middle of the sixteenth century, when the Renaissance was at its peak. My father came from a line of beings known as the Crovirs, while my mother was a descendant of a group called the Bastians. They are the only races of immortals on Earth.

Throughout most of the history of man, the Crovirs and the Bastians have waged a bitter and brutal war against one another. Although enough blood has been shed over the millennia to fill a respectable portion of the Caspian Sea, this unholy battle between immortals has, for the most, remained a well-kept secret from the eyes of ordinary humans, despite the fact that they have been used as pawns in some of its most epic chapters.

The conflict suffered a severe and unprecedented setback in the fourteenth century, when the numbers of both races dwindled rapidly and dramatically; while the Black Death scourged Europe and Asia, killing millions of humans, the lesser-known Red Death shortened the lives of countless immortals. It was several decades before the full extent of the devastation was realized, for the plague had brought with it an unexpected and horrifying complication.

The greater part of those who survived became infertile.

This struck another blow to both sides and, henceforth, an uneasy truce was established. Although the odd incident still happened between embittered members of each race, the fragile peace has, surprisingly, lasted to this day. From that time on, the arrival of an immortal child into the world became an event that was celebrated at the highest levels of each society.

My birth was a notable exception. The union between a Crovir and a Bastian was considered an unforgivable sin and strictly forbidden by both races; ancient and immutable, it was a fact enshrined into the very doctrines and origins of our species. Any offspring of such a coupling was thus deemed an abomination unto all and sentenced to death from the very moment they were conceived. I was not the first half-breed, both races having secretly mated with each other in the past. However, the two immortal societies wanted me to be the last. Fearing for my existence, my parents fled and took me into hiding.

For a while, our life was good. We were far from rich and dwelled in a remote cabin deep in the forest, where we lived off the land, hunting, fishing, and even growing our own food. Twice a year, my father ventured down the mountain to the nearest village, where he traded fur for oil and other rare goods. We were happy and I never wanted for anything.

It was another decade before the Hunters finally tracked us down. That was when I learned one of the most important lessons about immortals.

We can only survive up to sixteen deaths.

Having perished seven times before, my father died after ten deaths at the hands of the Hunters. He fought until the very last breath left his body. I watched them kill my mother seventeen times.

I should have died that day. I did, in fact, suffer my very first death. Moments after the act, I awoke on the snow-covered ground, tears cooling on my face and my blood staining the whiteness around me. Fingers clenching convulsively around the wooden practice sword my father had given me, I waited help-lessly for a blade to sink into my heart once more. Minutes passed before I realized I was alone in that crimson-colored clearing, high up in the Carpathian Mountains.

The crows came next, silent flocks that descended from the gray winter skies and covered the bloodied bodies next to me. When the birds left, the remains of my parents had disappeared as well. All that was left was ash.

It was much later that another immortal imparted to me the theory behind the seventeen deaths. Each one apparently took away a piece of our soul. Unlike our bodies, our souls could not regenerate after a death. Thus, Death as an ultimate end was unavoidable. And then the crows come for most of us.

No one was really clear as to where the birds took our earthly remains.

'What if you lived alone, on a desert island or something, and never met anyone? You could presumably never die,' Reid had argued with his customary logic when I told him this.

'True. However, death by boredom is greatly underestimated,' I replied. 'Besides, someone like you is bound to kill himself after a day without a smoke.'

'So the meeting was a trap?' said Reid.

His voice jolted me back to the present. The car had pulled up in front of my apartment block. The road ahead was deserted.

'Yes.' Rain drummed the roof of the Monte Carlo. The sound reminded me of the ricochets of machine guns. Unpleasant memories rose to the surface of my mind. I suppressed them firmly.

'Will he try to kill you again?' said Reid. I remained silent. He stared at me. 'What are you gonna do?'

I shifted on the leather seat and reached for the door handle. 'Well, seeing as you're likely to drag me back from Hell if I leave you high and dry, I should probably kill him first.'

I exited the car, crossed the sidewalk, and entered the lobby of the building. I turned to watch the taillights of the Chevrolet disappear in the downpour before getting in the lift. Under normal circumstances, I would have taken the stairs to the tenth floor. Dying, I felt, was a justifiable reason to take things easy for the rest of the night.

My apartment was blessedly cool and devoid of immortals hell-bent on carving another hole in my heart. I took a shower, dressed the wound on my chest, and went to bed.

CHAPTER TWO

A PERSISTENT RINGING BROUGHT ME OUT OF A DEEP SLEEP. I blinked away dreams of avenging angels, rolled over, and peered at the clock on the bedside table. It was ten am. Sunlight streamed into the room between the curtains opposite my bed. The sky beyond was a vivid cerulean blue.

I slid to the edge of the mattress and picked up the new cell from the floor.

'Yo,' said Reid.

'Uh-huh.' I rubbed my eyes.

'The address Haus gave you was a dead end. So was the phone number. I did however find someone by that name staying at the Parker Hotel.' Cain Haus was the immortal who had contacted our agency two days previously, and who more recently had stuck a sword through my heart. 'How do you wanna play this?'

I yawned. 'Pick me up in twenty.'

Thirty minutes later, we were sitting in a corner booth in Betty's Cafe.

Betty's opened forty years ago in what is now a prime location in Roxbury. It was around the corner from the Mission Hill station and had become the unofficial haunt of the cops who worked there. Betty's husband was a retired member of the Boston PD. Eight years ago, the couple retired to Florida and left the coffee shop to their son, Joe. Apart from adding a fresh lick of paint to the front of the building, Joe never changed the decor; the honey-colored wall paneling still contrasted nicely with the linoleum floor, while the weathered black and red Formica tables gleamed in the soft light of the lamps hanging from the wooden-slatted ceiling. Even the menu had remained untouched; these days, if you asked for a latte in Betty's, you still got a funny look.

Reid nodded at old acquaintances while we waited for our orders. 'So, what's the plan?' he asked.

I dragged my gaze from the busy street beyond the window and studied my partner. Despite living through a divorce in the time that I had known him, Reid had not aged much in the last ten years. There were a few more wrinkles around his eyes and a deepening of the cynical twist that hovered almost constantly near his lips, but he had otherwise retained the sturdy build that had made him such a good Marine and cop.

'I think we should tail him first, find out whether there are others with him,' I said with a shrug. 'Hunters normally work as a pack.'

'And how do you intend to kill him?' said Reid.

I avoided his stare. We had had this conversation enough times for me to know exactly how the next few exchanges would go.

'You need to get a gun,' said my partner.

'I don't like guns.'

He scowled. 'You're a first-class shot.'

I sighed. 'That doesn't mean I have to carry a gun.'

There was a calculated pause. 'What about a sword? You're good with swords.'

I looked at him steadily. 'Where do you propose I keep it? Besides, I've told you before: I don't like violence.'

'Unfortunately, violence likes you,' said Reid doggedly. 'How many people nursing a bottle of whisky on the end of a pier and grieving the death of their best friend get accidentally shot in the head by a random gunman?'

Another sigh left my lips; my partner was being unusually vocal today.

'And what about that drug dealer in New York, the one who stabbed you in the back?' His eyes narrowed. 'Oh, and let's not forget Rudy.'

I grimaced. Rudy Lomax was a fifty-year-old accountant who used to work for a large international merchant bank in Boston's financial district. Despite owning a penthouse in Back Bay with views over the Charles River and wearing thousand-dollar suits, Rudy had defaulted on his alimony on more than one occasion. When the collection agency retained by his ex-wife hired us to tail him, the accountant became enraged at this breach of his privacy and ran me over with his Lexus.

'To be fair, he only broke my leg,' I muttered into my coffee. 'And I was fine by the end of the week.'

'Really?' Reid countered with a sneer. 'What about Louisiana?'

I looked away from his accusing gaze and shifted in the seat.

Even I had to admit Louisiana had been an ugly affair. We had gone looking for a missing fourteen-year-old girl called Carly Jennings, a bright-eyed and vivacious child. Jennings had met a man through an internet chat room a few months before her disappearance. The trail led us to the southern state of Louisiana via New York and DC, where we uncovered a child prostitution ring with connections to South America and the Far East.

Things started to go wrong when the Feds got involved. By the time the gun smoke cleared, two agents had died, and I had been shot twice. Jennings was found scared but unscathed at the bottom of a ship's cargo hold bound for Mexico.

'Louisiana was a fluke.' I looked at the pancakes that had just landed before me, thanked the waitress, and reached for a fork.

Reid grunted. 'Lots of things in your life are flukes.' The conversation was thankfully cut short by the arrival of a serving of artery-clogging fried food. He ignored my disapproving tut-tut and dug into his eggs.

We left the cafe a quarter of an hour later and drove across town to the Parker Hotel. The sky remained bereft of clouds. A few seagulls circled high above, white shapes flecked with gray. The Hancock Tower gleamed in the distance to the left.

Reid pulled up behind a hot dog vendor and went inside the building. He returned within minutes and settled in the driver's seat.

'Haus is still inside. Doorman said he arrived two days ago. Alone.'

I frowned at his words. This was unusual behavior for a Hunter; from the multiple attempts on my life over the centuries and inside knowledge provided by a couple of very close friends, I knew the minimum number of assassins assigned for an execution-style mission was normally two. Both the Crovir and the Bastian Orders had strict rules on these matters, and any member going beyond their remit was severely punished, usually by a death. Was Haus acting by himself?

I had wondered briefly that morning which side he belonged to. Then again, it hardly mattered. I was only surprised that the immortals were after me following almost a century of silence. It was becoming apparent that at least one faction still wanted me dead.

At four o'clock, Haus had still not left the hotel. The hot dogs had proven to be sickeningly greasy, and three cups of coffee were burning a hole in my stomach. Reid was on his fifth cigarette. At this rate, I was going to die from second-hand smoking.

The sudden purr of the engine finally jolted me from a semi-comatose state.

'Is that him?' said Reid.

I looked across the street. A pale, thin man with ash-blond hair and a black overcoat had walked out of the hotel and was hailing a cab.

'Yes,' I murmured. 'That's the man who murdered me, all right.'

Reid twisted the steering wheel and merged into the peak-time traffic. Twenty minutes later, we had barely moved two blocks. The cab finally crawled onto Interstate 93 and headed toward the Zakim Bridge and the Charles River. It soon pulled off the highway and turned onto a side road. Reid slowed the Chevy and followed.

We drove through a series of increasingly rundown neighborhoods. Snatches of hip hop music drifted in sporadically through the car's half-open windows. Hobos scoured the alleys behind shops and stores, some of them pushing their worldly belongings in broken shopping carts. We stopped at a set of traffic lights and earned a battery of hostile stares from a group of teens standing next to the intersection.

Less than a mile away, sunlight glinted on the steelwork of the Tobin Bridge. We were not far from the water.

The roads became deserted. Stretches of disused land appeared on our right, graveyards for the corpses of burnt-out cars and broken white goods. By the time we entered the maze of derelict buildings that bordered the Mystic River, Reid had put the Chevy into a crawl.

Red taillights flashed up ahead. The cab pulled to a stop next to an abandoned warehouse. Haus climbed out and stood watching as the car drew away. He spun on his heels and disappeared in an alley at the side of the building.

The Chevy rolled to a standstill. Reid turned off the engine. We glanced at each other before exiting the car.

Sandy loam crunched softly beneath our boots as we made our way toward the alleyway. The blares of car horns carried on the wind from the toll bridge. In the blue skies above, a seagull screeched and whirled smoothly on invisible currents.

I heard the crack of the bullet a heartbeat before it hit the ground next to us. Reid swore as I yanked him into the lee of a building.

'I thought you said he had a sword.' He took the Glock out.

'Hunters are trained in the use of a range of weapons,' I replied quietly.

Another bullet whizzed out of the alley. It was followed by a wild cackle.

Reid raised an eyebrow. 'Why is he laughing?'

'I don't know. I asked him the same question last night. All he did was laugh louder and call me a half-breed.' I grimaced. 'It doesn't sound like healthy laughter to me.'

'I know what you mean,' muttered Reid. 'It kinda reminds me of that Jack Nicholson movie.'

'"One Flew Over the Cuckoo's Nest?"'

'No, "The Shining",' said Reid. Another cackle followed. 'Now what?'

Before I could muster a reply, Haus's words drifted on the breeze toward us. 'Come out, come out, wherever you are!' he shouted from the alley.

Reid pursed his lips. 'He does a bad Nicholson impression. Just for that, he deserves a bullet.'

I touched his shoulder and silently indicated the roof of the adjacent building. He nodded. We turned and headed for the broken side door we had walked past earlier. There was a tortuous creak of metal as we squeezed through the gap between the frame and the doorjamb.

The inside of the warehouse was unusually warm. The air

was fetid and smelled of death. We strolled past the rotting carcass of a raccoon and moved toward the rickety stairs at the southwest corner of the building. Broken bottles, crushed cans, and dirty syringes littered the corridors on the upper floor. Beyond a roomful of damaged mannequins and rust-covered sewing machines, a door opened out onto a fire escape. It was a short climb to the roof.

The wind had picked up. It brought with it a range of smells: the organic stench of the river, the rank odor of oil from a nearby refinery, the chemical stink of the tannery half a mile away. The acrid reek of gunpowder.

I pulled Reid behind an air vent just as the bullet ricocheted off the hot asphalt yards from our feet.

'He's a smart bastard,' grunted my partner.

'Uh-huh.'

'Northeast corner of the roof?'

'Yes,' I murmured.

'I can smell you, half-breed! You stink higher than a skunk!' shouted Haus from the neighboring rooftop.

Reid looked at me and cocked an eyebrow.

'I showered this morning,' I said, deadpan.

He shook his head, rose to one knee, and fired two rounds at the opposite building. An answering volley scored cracks in the rooftop five feet from where we crouched.

'He's either a crap shot or he's playing with us,' muttered Reid.

'I'm pretty sure it's the latter.' Neither Order forbade their Hunters from playing with their prey. In fact, the Crovirs were quite famed for it.

'If we sit here any longer, he's gonna shoot us like fish in a barrel,' said Reid. 'What say we get the hell out of here?'

I nodded. He let off another five rounds. Before the last bullet left the muzzle of his gun, we were up and running toward the next vent.

'Why isn't he shooting—' Reid started to say as we neared the metal tower.

The ground suddenly gave beneath us as a section of the roof collapsed. In hindsight, it had been a pretty obvious trap.

We landed in the room with the mannequins with a thunderous crash. Above the noise of the falling debris, I heard a harsh grunt from Reid. I dug my way out of a pile of inanimate figures, wincing at the sharp stabs radiating from several cuts and bruises, and turned toward him.

He was lying stiffly next to the bank of industrial sewing machines. A forty-inch-long steel rod rose through his left thigh and pinned him to the floor.

Alarm darted through me. 'That's not good,' I said, meeting his eyes. He gritted his teeth in response.

A dull thud drew our gazes to the ceiling. Haus had cleared the gap between the two warehouses. Rapid footsteps sounded above our heads and a shadow appeared against the patch of blue sky visible through the jagged hole in the roof.

'Found you, you dirty half-breed!' hissed the immortal.

My eyes widened as I looked past the barrel of an M9 Beretta pistol into the face of a madman.

'Go!' shouted Reid.

The deafening noise of the semi-automatic filled the confined space. I sprinted across the room, deadly shards erupting around me. Blood bloomed on the back of my left hand. I reached the far wall, hit the fire door with my shoulder, and emerged into bright sunlight. Haus's wild cackle reached my ears as I sailed over the railing of the fire escape and dove into the river.

Bullets riddled the water behind me when I cleaved the dark surface. I swam further into the murky depths and twisted around until I floated in the eddies. Shots scored the choppy currents above once more; by the look of things, Haus had loaded another magazine into the Beretta.

A dull roar echoed in my ears as I debated my options. The Hunter would not kill Reid. This I was certain of. Instead, he would use my partner as bait to lure me out.

That's what I would do if I were in his shoes.

I turned with the faintest of misgivings and let the current carry me north.

It was two hours before I got back to the apartment. Night had long since fallen across the city. The driver of the cab that I eventually managed to hail sniffed at me suspiciously before allowing me into his car. His disposition did not improve when I handed him a wad of soggy dollar bills at the end of the journey.

After checking the rooms for signs of forced entry, I showered and redressed my wound. I then did something that would have surprised Reid had he been able to see me.

I headed for the painting of Monet's 1906 "Water Lilies" that hung above the mantelpiece in the living room.

I stopped beneath the canvas and gazed at the mesmerizing shades of blue for silent seconds. Of all of Monet's works, this was the one I found the most soothing. It had taken several years and a considerable amount of money to convince the artist to make another copy for me.

I took down the painting and laid it on the couch before turning to face the wall once more. I touched a section of the cool white plaster and keyed in a code in the small electronic pad that emerged beneath my fingers. A ten-inch-wide partition slid open next to the pad. I pressed my right hand against the fingerprint recognition screen and looked into the retinal scanner above it. Seconds later, the entire wall retracted by a foot with a ponderous noise.

A metal panel descended from a hidden recess in the ceiling.

No one knew that I owned the apartment complex. Ten years ago, following the death of my best friend at the hands of the Hunters, I set up a company made up of twenty fictitious shareholders and named it Baldr Inc. I bought the building and the freehold for the land it stood upon. Over the years—at times using independent contractors, but mostly doing the work myself—I modified the tower block for my own personal use. Prospective tenants to the building all underwent detailed background checks. As it was, the apartments on the ninth and eleventh floors were never leased. Mine was the only apartment in use on the tenth floor.

I considered the display of weapons that now occupied what had once been the east wall of my living room. Although I abhorred violence and opted not to carry a gun, my life as an immortal had taught me that weapons were a necessary evil. I hesitated before selecting a Glock 17 and a Smith & Wesson .45 ACP. I tucked the guns inside the holsters on my thighs and loaded a handful of magazines in the belt at my waist. My gaze was finally drawn to the center of the panel.

In the first half of the seventeenth century, during the early Edo period, I spent several formative years in Japan; I had been traveling through Asia at the time and had come across an interesting rumor concerning a man called Miyamoto Musashi. Miyamoto was a samurai who hailed from the then Harima Province of Japan and was reputed to have won all the duels he had ever participated in, beginning with his first one at the age of thirteen. To this day, he is still considered one of the most famous sword masters in Japanese history.

It took me an entire year to convince Miyamoto to take me on as an apprentice. During that time, I became proficient in the country's language and its various dialects, and immersed myself into its strange new culture. Once under Miyamoto's tutelage, I learned the art of Niten Ichi-ryu, a two-sword fighting style he had perfected using a long blade, the katana, and a shorter blade, the wakizashi; in combination, the two blades were known as the daisho. Miyamoto was a hard taskmaster and it was almost a decade before he came to be satisfied with my technique, and this only after I defeated him in a duel. When I left Japan, he had a daisho made for me as a leaving present. Carved into the blade of the katana was an identical copy of the intertwined alpha and omega birthmark over my heart.

I lifted the ancient swords from their stands in the middle of the metal panel, grabbed a long coat from the closet in the hallway, and headed out of the apartment. At the end of the corridor, a keypad-operated door opened onto a private lift that took me eleven floors down to the basement of the building. I stepped out into a dark void, turned, and flicked a series of switches on the wall to my left. Light flooded the large subterranean space before me.

The basement was off limits to the other tenants. Bar the lift access and the virtually invisible security doors that opened out onto a back alley, there was no other way in or out of the lower floor of the apartment complex.

As I crossed the concrete floor, my steps echoing off the distant walls, my thoughts turned to the events of the last twenty-four hours. One question overrode all others in my mind. Why were the Hunters on my trail again? I wondered briefly whether I had crossed their territory in some way and brought myself to their attention once more. I discarded the notion straight away; if the Hunters had wanted to find me, they could have done so with maddening ease in the last hundred years.

The more I pondered the matter, the more I felt the urgency to know the answer. I was not usually one for premonitions, but I could sense storm clouds gathering on the horizon.

I stopped in front of a sleek machine that looked like it had been built for speed. The GSX1300R, known simply as the Hayabusa, is a 1299 cc, four-cylinder, 16-valve engine hyper sport bike that can do zero to sixty mph in two-point-six-seven seconds. It was, and still is, the best motorbike ever made by

Suzuki and the fastest two-wheeled vehicle I have ever handled.
I was one of the lucky few who had managed to get their hands
on a limited-edition midnight-black version.

Moments later, the Hayabusa roared through the streets of
the city. It was raining again. I ignored the wet spray rising from
the asphalt and headed swiftly across town. The roof of the
Cramer building soon appeared between the maze of dark office
blocks that crowded the stormy skyline; as the scene of our last
battle, I had no doubt that Haus would be waiting there for me.
I grimaced. He probably thought it was poetic justice or
something.

The alley behind the tower was blessedly empty. I braked to
a stop and switched the engine off. The low growl of the
Hayabusa whined into silence. I parked the bike behind the
dumpsters, walked back to the middle of the alley, and studied
the fire escape several feet above my head. I took a couple of
steps back, ran, and jumped. The fingers of my right hand
closed on the lowest rung of the ladder. It slid down smoothly
to the ground.

I started to climb.

Dark skies loomed above me when I neared the top of the
steps. I stopped and crouched against the side of the building,
my hands closing on my guns while I strained my ears. Other
than the harsh patter of rain, the clamor of traffic from the
avenue, the rumbling of distant thunder, and the dull thrum of
blood in my skull, I could hear no other noise. I raised my head
slowly above the concrete parapet.

'Welcome, half-breed,' said Haus from somewhere in the
darkness.

A gasp left my lips as I was abruptly lifted from the stairwell
by a pair of unseen hands and hurled through the air. By the
time I landed on my back and skidded halfway across the water-
slicked rooftop, I had fired half the rounds in both guns.

They all hit their target.

'Hey, Cain, you never told me he was this puny,' said the giant in front of me in a thick Eastern European accent. He looked down and fingered the holes in the fine wool, roll-neck sweater stretched across his chest.

I caught a glimpse of the bulletproof vest beneath it before focusing on the weapon he held in his right hand.

It was an impressive single-edged Chinese sword, a dao. A flash of lightning illuminated the sky and caused the curved blade to gleam in the rain. The canted hilt looked small in the grip of the man who held it.

The giant was a much taller and wider version of Haus. Muscles bulged across his shoulders and rippled under his tailored trousers. His small, red-rimmed eyes displayed the dull glimmer of an arrogant bully on steroids. He was also very fast.

In all my years as an immortal, I had only come across a handful of Hunters who had surprised me as swiftly as he had.

I saw Haus sneer out of the corner of my eyes.

'What did you expect? After all, he *is* a half-breed.' The Hunter's expression hardened beneath his pale skin. 'Finish him, Abel,' he ordered.

I looked behind Haus.

Reid sat against an emergency door at the far end of the rooftop. There was a bandage around his thigh and a fresh bruise next to his mouth. His right hand was cuffed to a bolt in the doorframe.

'Cain and Abel?' I said wryly as I rose to my feet.

Reid shrugged. 'And they're brothers as well,' he said with a weak grin. 'Go figure.'

The words had barely left his lips when the giant bellowed and charged.

My feet glided across the concrete rooftop as I drew the daisho from my waist. The wakizashi blocked my attacker's sword. I moved the katana once and stepped back smoothly.

Blood gushed out of the Hunter's chest in a crimson flow; as

I had suspected, the vest had not been stab-proof. A puzzled expression dawned on the larger man's face. He fell backward slowly and hit the ground hard.

He would not rise again.

'How—' Haus mumbled, eyes widening in his ashen face.

I watched impassively while the immortal's last breath left his lips and his face sagged into the waxen expression of the dead.

It had taken two centuries for me to understand the real reason why the immortals hated me so. It was not, as I had originally presumed, because of racial bigotry or repugnance at the bloodlines being tainted in some way.

The principle reason they loathed me and their single-minded motivation for wishing me dead came down to one thing and one thing only. Fear.

As far as I knew of our extensive history, I was the only immortal who had the ability to truly kill another immortal. It did not matter whether it was their first or their sixteenth death. If the weapon I wielded bore a direct physical connection between my body and their heart, they would lose their immortality instantly and be unable to regenerate and live again.

It was as if I could shatter their entire soul in one strike, like Azrael, the Angel of Death.

Haus raised the blade in his right hand and came at me across the rooftop, his mouth open on an unintelligible scream. I blinked water from my eyes, gripped the daisho, and shifted in the fighting stance taught to me by my Edo master. Our swords clashed under the pounding rain just as a bolt of lightning streaked across the dark heavens.

It took but seconds for me to realize Haus was the better fighter of the two brothers; I narrowly missed decapitation twice. In the end, however, the daisho proved stronger than his blade.

A roll of thunder tore the skies when the katana finally slipped past his guard. Haus froze. His chin dipped and he gaped at the sword protruding from his chest.

I never looked at his left hand.

Reid's shout reached my ears at the same time the bullet punched through my ribcage, trailing a river of fire into my body.

Haus chuckled and gasped. 'Olsson was right. You're weak, half-breed!' A grimace distorted his features. The gun and the sword clattered out of his grip. He slid to the ground, his unblinking gaze turned toward the heavens.

I felt my heart slow down. My vision dimmed. My knees gave way beneath me. My last thought before darkness claimed me was the name Haus had spoken with his final breath.

≈

I GASPED AND OPENED MY EYES. IT WAS STILL RAINING. A crow spiraled out of the night sky and landed on the rooftop.

'Yo,' said Reid.

≈

CHAPTER THREE

THE DOWNPOUR CONTINUED INTO THE NEXT DAY.

'I can't believe you died twice in the space of forty-eight hours,' said Reid.

I took a sip from the cup of liquor-laced coffee in my hand and chose to maintain a diplomatic silence. It was difficult to tell whether my partner's voice held disgust or admiration. Somehow, I suspected it was the former.

We were in our office in Mission Hill.

After my fourteenth death at the hands of Burt Suarez, Reid had spent an entire month stalking and, for want of a better word, hounding me until I finally capitulated and accepted his offer to become my business partner. It was that or shoot him. Since I had never killed anyone in cold blood, I was left with little choice but to agree to his proposition.

I asked him once why he had been so determined to work with me. To this he replied, 'I had a feeling things would always be lively around you. Besides, the homicide unit was starting to wear me down.'

I decided to take this as a compliment. We changed the name of the detective agency I had originally formed with my best friend and moved to smaller premises across town. The other place held too many painful memories for me.

The previous night, a young ER doctor enthusiastically expounded on how the steel rod that had pierced Reid's thigh had missed his bone and artery by a mere inch. He sounded faintly disappointed it hadn't done so. He went on to ask about the bullet wound in my chest and finally faltered in the face of our stares. Reid refused the crutches offered to him by a nurse and made a half-muttered promise to return for a follow-up check. The woman's face filled with doubt at his words. She perked up when I told her I would bring him back for the appointment, dead or alive.

We rode to the docks earlier that morning to retrieve the Chevy. Bar some bird droppings, the car had remained untouched. Reid never asked about the Hayabusa.

I sat on our second-hand leather sofa, closed my eyes, and leaned against the backrest. I heard Reid press the answer button on the phone. The subtle scratch of pencil across paper followed as he wrote down the messages from the previous day.

Our landlady had called about our overdue rent, her tone somewhat cool. A hesitant Mr. Novak wanted to know how much it would cost to provide photographic evidence of his wife's infidelity. A soft-spoken and elderly sounding Miss Kaplinsky had phoned about a missing cat. A salesman from Ink R Us promised a fifteen-percent discount if we ordered thirty ink cartridges by the end of the day. A Mr. Price from Maine Investment Corp wished to talk to us about investigating one of his employees.

The last message was from several days ago. I opened my eyes and studied the ceiling as the words of a dead man rolled out of the speaker.

'Good morning. My name is Cain Haus. A friend recommended your agency to me. I would be grateful if you could ring me back to arrange a meeting.' There was a small lull. 'I particularly want to meet with Mr. Soul. The matter I wish to discuss is a delicate one and I believe he's in the best position to assist me.'

The beep of the machine was loud in the hush that followed.

'There's a voice we won't be hearing anytime soon,' murmured Reid. There was more silence. 'Wanna talk about it?' he said finally.

I rose, strode to the filing cabinet that served as our drinks tray, and reached for the bottle of bourbon. I poured another measure into my coffee.

'That bad, huh?' said Reid.

'Mikael Olsson.'

He looked at me blankly.

'That's the name Haus mentioned last night,' I explained in a leaden tone. 'It's also the name of a friend who died ten years ago.'

Rain drummed against the window. On the street below, people milled along the sidewalks, umbrellas bowing under the force of the heavy autumnal shower.

'Was he the one you were mourning when Suarez shot you?' said Reid.

I nodded mutely.

He knitted his eyebrows. 'Any chance Haus knew him from way back then?'

I shook my head. 'I don't think so. Mikael disliked the Hunters as much as I did.'

A door slammed somewhere in the corridor outside. We shared the second floor of the building with several other offices. Elevator doors opened with a faint 'ping'. Voices rose and faded in the distance.

Reid grunted. 'So, what are you saying?'

I turned from the window. 'I think he might still be alive.' I hesitated as the words sank in. Now that I had actually voiced them, they felt more real. 'And I think he faked his own death, somehow.'

It was the only logical conclusion I had reached. I could not, however, fathom the why.

I first met Olsson in England, in the late nineteenth century; at the time, I was living in London and working as a reporter for The Times. In those days, the broadsheets were full of frenzied news about The Whitechapel Murders and the puzzling identity of the serial killer who would eventually come to be known as Jack the Ripper. Olsson wrote for the Morning Post. London's East End was our beat and we often found ourselves sharing pints of ale and gruesome stories in the local pubs. We became firm friends but drifted apart ten years later, as friends sometimes do. It was not until I met him again in New York in the 1960s that I realized that he was an immortal. Olsson was similarly shocked. We kept in touch and eventually went on to form our detective agency in 1990. As immortals who had yet to meet their soulmates, having another immortal companion to pass the years with was a great solace.

Then, one night ten years ago, everything changed. I received a frantic call from Olsson and reached his house to find the front door forced open and a trail of blood leading all the way to the backyard. Though I searched for weeks, I never found his body.

'There was nothing in the house to suggest the identity of his killer?' said Reid skeptically.

'No.'

'And the cops never found out who did it?'

I shook my head.

Reid drummed his fingers on the desk. 'Did he have any enemies?'

I sighed. 'If he did, he never told me about them.'

He frowned. 'You suspected the Hunters?'

I shrugged. The immortals were the only ones who could

have executed such a smooth assassination. Although I had no proof of this, I had been pretty certain that Bastian or Crovir Hunters had been behind Mikael's disappearance.

'Was it to get to you?' Reid asked.

I ran a hand through my hair. 'I don't know. If they knew about Mikael, then they must have been aware of our association. But they never came after me.'

Reid studied me for a while longer before rising from his seat. 'Well, the rent ain't gonna pay itself if we just sit here playing twenty questions.' He shrugged into his coat and headed for the door. 'I'll call Novak and Price. You take Kaplinsky.'

I narrowed my eyes. 'You're giving me the cat?'

Reid gestured at his wounded leg. 'Do I look like I'm fit to chase felines up trees? Besides, we need the money.'

We didn't really, but that was a subject I had yet to broach with Reid; I was pretty certain he would adamantly refuse any financial help I offered. I also sensed I would jeopardize our friendship if I did suggest it.

I pursed my lips. 'Admit it. You just dislike cats.'

Reid scowled. 'Yes, I do. They're smug and they always look like they're up to no good.'

Miss Kaplinsky was a retired school teacher who lived in a quiet neighborhood in East Boston. Her cat, a silver tabby, had gone missing two weeks previously. Despite actively canvassing the streets and advertising for a reward in the local paper, she still had not heard any news about the absent feline.

Reid dropped me at her address before driving off to meet with Price.

Golden Leaf was a retirement complex built in the early 1970s. The four tired-looking, redbrick, garden-style buildings were arranged around a central courtyard lined with sycamore trees and rhododendrons. Sunlight streamed through the

swaying branches and cast dappled shadows on the walkway as I
made my way across the grounds.

Apartment 12B was a first-floor corner unit with views over
the park across the road. The retired teacher greeted me in a
respectable tweed skirt and a long-sleeved cream blouse. The
apartment was small and neat, the air redolent of vanilla.

'He never usually strays, you know.' Miss Kaplinsky showed
me to a seat. 'He's a good cat.' A sigh escaped her lips. 'I do
hope nothing bad's happened to him.'

I glanced at the shelves and sideboards in the front room.
They were crowded with picture frames depicting dozens of
smiling children in uniform standing and sitting in orderly rows.
The color in most of them had faded.

'Would you like something to drink?' said the retired
teacher. I shook my head. She crossed the floor to a writing
desk and removed something from a drawer. 'This is a recent
photograph of him.' She took the seat opposite mine and
leaned across the narrow coffee table. Hands covered in paper-
thin skin and fine, spidery veins touched the glossy print.

The shot had been taken in the courtyard below. The cat
was sitting in the shade of a tree and appeared half-asleep. It
looked like it was grinning.

'We'll do our best to find him. Can I have this?' I indicated
the picture. She smiled and nodded.

I took my leave. Predictably, a search of the buildings and
the courtyard yielded no results. I questioned the neighbors
and explored the adjacent streets before coming full circle. I
paused on the sidewalk outside the retirement complex and
studied the park across the road. Miss Kaplinsky had already
visited it on several occasions and found no signs of the missing
cat. I called Reid.

'How're you doing?'

'Not bad,' he replied. 'Price suspects one of his employees
has been playing with the numbers. He wants to hire us.' His

voice was almost drowned out by the city traffic in the background.

'I'm going to the park to look for the cat.'

'Uh-huh,' said Reid.

I frowned. 'Are you laughing?'

'No,' came the strangled reply.

I sighed. 'Come get me when you're done.' I ended the call, crossed the street, and entered the shadows beneath the trees.

The park was divided in four sections. There was a play area for kids, an artificial lake with ducks and other waterfowl, an extensive expanse of lawn, and several wooded areas. I explored the open spaces first before heading for the woods.

I personally did not mind cats. They used to be worshipped as gods, were fastidiously clean and territorial, preferred their own company, and could generally take or leave humans. They were said to be a lot smarter than dogs, although probably not as loyal.

I pulled a packet of catnip out of my pocket; I was hoping this particular feline had the intelligence of the average Labrador.

Half an hour later, I had completed my search of the park. Several squirrels and strays had shown interest in the bag in my hands. Of the silver tabby, however, there was no sign. I was about to call it a day when a range of tower blocks to the north caught my eye. A series of dark alleys ran between the derelict looking structures. I studied them thoughtfully before crossing the road to the closest passage.

The alley gave birth to a network of backstreets crowded with fire escapes, heating vents, industrial-sized dumpsters, and the occasional tent of cardboard boxes lined with dirty cloths and a sleeping bag.

The first inquisitive meow sounded moments later.

A ginger tom peered at me from under a metal skip. By the time I reached the next intersection, other cats had emerged from the gloom. I stopped and looked over my shoulder. The cats froze in their tracks and watched me with large, solemn eyes. There was not a single silver tabby among them.

I sighed. It was too much to hope that I would find the missing cat on the first day.

I turned to retrace my steps and reached for my cell phone. There was a flash of black and white at the edge of my vision. I stopped and looked up.

Some twenty feet above the ground to my left, a silver cat perched on a ledge next to a fire escape. I removed the picture the retired teacher had given me from my jacket and stared at it. There was no mistaking the pattern of stripes; it was the missing feline.

I moved carefully toward the metal staircase. Behind me, the strays followed the scent of catnip. I stopped beneath the ladder and gazed at the cat. It observed me with unblinking, round, golden eyes.

'Here, kitty,' I said self-consciously.

There was resolute silence from above. I waved the catnip around and made further encouraging pleas; this failed to produce a reaction from the cat. I bit back another sigh and put the bag away. There were no two ways about it; I was going to have to climb. I glanced over my shoulder. The strays had sat down in anticipation of the upcoming show. They looked like they were grinning.

The silver cat watched me warily while I made my way up the fire escape. Less than a minute later, I reached the landing next to the brick shelf. The cat sat at the other end. Its golden gaze remained unwavering.

'Okay, we can do this the easy way or we can do this the hard way,' I stated firmly.

The cat looked unconvinced by this threat.

I retrieved the catnip from my rear pocket and brandished

it in the air. The golden eyes widened in interest. The cat rose on its front legs.

The ring of my cell phone shattered the fragile balance. The cat shot up and disappeared in the shadows above me. The strays scattered down below. I pulled the handset from my jacket and stared at the number on the display. I did not recognize it.

I pressed the answer button and barked, 'Yes?'

Soft breathing travelled down the line. It was followed by a voice from the past. 'Hello, Lucas.'

My fingers clenched on the phone. 'Mikael?' I whispered.

He chuckled. 'As good as always, I see. I didn't think you'd recognize me after all these years.'

I suddenly felt exposed. 'What do you want?' I asked coldly, my gaze shifting to the dim passage beneath my feet. The strays had stopped a respectable distance from the fire escape and were watching me curiously. There was no one else in the alleyway.

I looked up and scrutinized the opposite building. Industrial-sized windows occupied most of the rear facade of the deserted tower block. I could not make much of the gloom behind the dirty, cracked glass.

'Come now, is that any way to greet an old friend?' Olsson drawled.

'You might as well get to the point,' I retorted. 'Haus already told me about you.' I put the phone on speaker, hooked it on my shirt, and started to climb.

'Did he now?' said Olsson. His words crackled with static from my movements. His voice was no longer friendly. 'And what exactly did Haus say?'

'He mentioned your name before he killed me.' Several stories up, I came across the silver cat. It balanced on a ledge next to the fire escape and studied me guardedly.

I climbed over the railing and took a cautious step toward it.

'Oh,' murmured Olsson. 'So, he *did* manage to kill you before he died.'

Motion below drew my gaze. The strays disappeared, sleek shadows fading in the gloom. A loud hiss erupted in front of me. My head snapped up.

The silver tabby was crouched on all fours, its back arched and its golden gaze focused unblinkingly on a point an inch past my left shoulder.

I grabbed the startled cat and jumped back on the landing. Fragments of metal and brick clouded the air as bullets scored a line in the brick wall next to me. Out of the corner of my eyes, I saw figures appear at the end of the alley. I turned and raced up the stairs.

Glass shattered somewhere above me. A falling shard caught my cheek. Above the splintering and cracking noise, the stutter of a machine gun rose from the rooftop of the opposite building.

Heat bloomed on the back of my hand. For a second, I thought I had been shot. I glanced down and saw the silver tabby clinging to me grimly; its claws had drawn blood. I gripped the cat and dodged a further spray of bullets.

The metal steps suddenly juddered beneath my feet. Two men in black suits were climbing the fire escape. One of them leaned over the railing and raised a black object. I heard a distant twang and felt the draft of an arrow as it whizzed past my shoulder.

'Hang on!' I gasped. The cat's claws dug in further.

I skidded onto the next landing and jumped. My fingers closed on the bottom rung of a ladder. I drew my legs up and arched my body over the empty space beyond the railing.

There was a fleeting moment of weightlessness. A heartbeat

later, I crashed through a window and landed hard on a floor inside the building. I rolled and leapt to my feet.

The machine gun roared as I started to run. Bullets ricocheted off the ground, raising chips from the concrete. An indignant yowl accompanied the dull thuds. I winced; the cat was trying to scratch bare bone.

I bolted from the room and started down a dingy corridor. My phone beeped. I grabbed the cell and glanced at the display. It was an incoming call from Reid.

'Where are you?' I barked into the mouthpiece.

'Outside the client's building,' he replied. 'What's the matter?' he added, his voice stiffening. 'You sound breathless.'

I ducked past an open doorway and narrowly avoided another volley of bullets. 'Get to the north entrance of the park! Hurry!' I shouted before ending the call.

I darted across a series of intersections, my eyes frantically scanning the desolate halls for an exit. An emergency door finally materialized at the end of a passage. Glass tinkled somewhere in the building. Distant footsteps followed.

I hit the door at a run and almost went over the metal banister on the other side. A gloomy stairwell opened up beneath me. I turned and started down the steps.

I was ten feet from the ground floor when the door at the bottom of the stairs suddenly opened. A man entered the building in a flood of daylight. He blinked at the shadows and raised his gun just as a crash reverberated from above; the suits had found the emergency exit.

I tightened my grip on the cat, grabbed the handrail, and stepped up against the wall. A crossbow bolt hissed past my ear as I vaulted over the banister. It missed my shoulder by a hairbreadth and thudded into the concrete floor.

The gunman's eyes widened a second before my feet landed on his chest. A grunt left his lips and he flailed backward, the gun clattering out of his hand. I elbowed him in the throat, scrambled to my feet, and headed for the exit. The cat glanced around at the sound of choked gurgling. Footsteps pounded the stairs behind us.

I emerged in a narrow passage between two tower blocks. A squeal of tires rose up ahead. I caught a glimpse of the Chevy as it shot past the mouth of the alley. I sprinted toward it.

Bullets struck the ground close on my heels when I emerged from the alleyway.

'Hey! Over here!' I yelled, waving wildly with my free hand.

Reid spotted me in the rearview mirror, slammed on the brakes, and put the car into reverse. The Monte Carlo screeched to a halt at the curb. I opened the passenger door and dove inside headfirst. A dull thud erupted from the rear of the vehicle.

'Go!' I shouted. 'They'll aim for the tires!'

Reid pulled away and floored the accelerator.

'What the hell's going on?' he said with a scowl. He glanced sideways as I straightened in the seat. 'And what is *that?*'

I looked down. I had forgotten about the cat. The silver tabby's golden eyes were locked on my face, its claws still firmly hooked in my flesh.

'It's Miss Kaplinsky's cat.'

I carefully detached the animal from my arm. It relented and switched its grip to my jeans.

Reid maneuvered the Chevy around the mid-afternoon traffic and looked in the rearview mirror. He drew in a breath sharply. 'Is that an arrow?'

I looked over my shoulder. A crossbow bolt was embedded in the trunk of the car. 'Uh-huh.'

'Unless our client has some seriously fearful enemies, I presume those were Hunters again?' he asked, his mouth a thin line.

'Yes. It was—'A sudden burst of static interrupted me. The cat twitched; the claws stabbed in further.

I grimaced and looked at the dashboard. Reid had inherited an old police radio scanner with the car. It had proven useful on many of our previous investigations.

My blood grew cold as I listened to the words pouring out of the speakers of the black box.

'Control, this is C-16 on Concorde. Have responded to the disturbance at Golden Leaf. Calling in a 10-54 Code 1 at 12B.'

'Copy, C-16. Go ahead.'

'Victim is resident at the address, white female, late seventies. Bullet wound to the head, DOA. Witnesses point to suspect being a white male, mid-thirties, six-foot two, one seventy, black hair, blue eyes, wearing a black leather jacket and jeans. Suspect is on foot and may be armed.'

'Copy, C-16. Will dispatch EMT and notify Patrol and Operations.'

'Copy, Control.'

'Lucas?' Reid said quietly.

I looked blindly ahead while I recalled the scent of vanilla and a room crowded with faded memories.

CHAPTER FOUR

THE EAST BOSTON POLICE PRECINCT WAS HOUSED IN AN imposing, neoclassical brick and granite structure on the corner of a busy commercial junction not far from the harbor.

Contrary to its stately outer appearance, the inside of the building could have been any other station in the city. The wide corridors and grand ceilings failed to mask the scruffiness of the place and the people who worked within its walls, while the smell of sweat, coffee, and cigarettes permanently imbued the air, which had acquired a yellow to smoky, brown haze.

The interview room on the first floor offered a rare glimpse of Boston's downtown skyline. The setting sun had turned the waters of the bay crimson and bathed the austere walls of the chamber with an orange glow.

The homicide detective assigned to Miss Kaplinsky's murder was a bear of a man by the name of Meyer. He dwarfed his partner, a much younger sergeant detective called Pratt. Pratt was skinny, virtually devoid of facial hair, and had a bobbing Adam's apple that could have sunk the Titanic; Meyer appeared to be the type to grow a five o'clock shadow ten minutes after a shave. Pratt's suit was smooth and wrinkle-free, his tie crisp, and his shoes shiny with fresh polish; Meyer looked like he shopped at the Salvation Army and sported well-worn, scuffed Doc Martens. Despite these flagrant discrepancies, they made a good team.

It was only Reid's reputation that had kept them from formally interrogating me as the prime suspect in the case.

Meyer studied the notepad in his hand. Not that he needed to check the facts; he looked like the kind of cop who'd memorize everything about a person in a flash.

'You said you left the victim's apartment at around thirteen hundred?'

'Yes,' I replied.

'Where did you go?' said Meyer.

'I spoke to a couple of her neighbors, a Mr. Harrison from 8B and Mrs. Garcia from 10A.'

'Why?' said Pratt in a hard voice.

Despite the anger thrumming in my veins, I allowed a faint smile to cross my lips.

'I wanted to ask them about the cat.'

Pratt's gaze shifted to the shape on my lap.

'Is that the feline in question?'

Bored by the proceedings, the silver tabby had gone to sleep; its claws were still resolutely ensnared in the denim fabric of my jeans.

'Yes.'

Meyer closed the notepad with a snap. 'What'd you do after that?'

'I searched the neighborhood and the park across the road.'

'How long did that take?'

'About an hour twenty.'

Meyer rose from the table and strolled to the window.

'And you found the cat? Just like that?' he said, gazing at the fading light.

I kept my expression neutral. The older detective was a

difficult man to read, which made him the better cop; I couldn't tell whether his rigid stance denoted skepticism, tiredness, or both. Pratt on the other hand had not quite mastered the art of hiding his emotions; if he had his way, I would be under lock and key before I could breathe the word "lawyer".

'The catnip helped,' I volunteered.

Meyer returned to his seat.

'You said in your statement,' he glanced at the paperwork before him, 'that you didn't recognize the men who were after you?'

'That's correct,' I answered truthfully.

Silence followed.

'Does this kind of thing happen to you often?' said Meyer.

I pretended ignorance. 'What do you mean?'

Meyer sighed and waved a hand vaguely.

'The bullets. The arrows. The random strangers trying to kill you.'

I wondered how he would react if I told him the truth.

'No,' I said steadily.

The older detective's eyes narrowed. 'We haven't got the official reports from ballistics yet, but the rounds from the alley are a close match to the one found in the victim's body.'

I remained silent.

'Do you have a gun, Mr. Soul?' said Pratt.

'No.'

The two cops glanced at each other. I could tell they were not buying this barefaced lie.

'I recall Reid telling me that you were an excellent shot,' said Meyer.

I let the smile dance on my lips once more while I silently cursed my absent partner. 'He has a tendency to exaggerate.'

Meyer cocked an eyebrow. He obviously knew Reid better than I thought he did.

Pratt sneered. 'You mean to tell us you've never fired a gun while working as a private investigator?'

'I don't like guns.'

'That's not an answer!' snapped the younger detective.

Meyer scowled. 'Enough.' He stood and pushed the chair under the table. 'That'll be all for today, Mr. Soul. We'll be in touch again in the next few days. Make sure you're available for questioning.' He paused. 'And we'd appreciate it if you didn't leave town for the foreseeable future.'

Reid was waiting in the station's reception. We left the building without exchanging a word and strolled to the Chevy. Leaves rustled in a nearby sycamore tree as a cold gust blew through the parking lot. I took a deep breath and exhaled slowly, glad for the fresh air after the stuffiness of the precinct.

'What did Meyer say?' Reid asked once we were inside the car.

'The bullet that killed our client matched the shell casings the Hunters left in the alley.' I unclenched my fingers, still struggling to quell the ice-cold rage threatening to overwhelm me.

'Well, that should help your case at least. Did he say anything else?'

'Yeah. He told me not to leave the city.'

Reid pulled out of the parking bay. The beams from the Chevy's headlights washed across the dirty asphalt as he headed for the river.

'What're you intending to do with that?' he said after a moment's silence. He indicated my lap with a cocked thumb.

I gazed at the sleeping cat. 'Miss Kaplinsky had no next of kin. I guess it's staying put for the time being.'

A resigned expression dawned on my partner's face. 'Has it got a name?'

I hesitated. 'It's—Cornelius.'

Reid's eyebrows rose. 'You're kidding, right?'

I shrugged noncommittally.

'What I don't get is why the Hunters would murder a defenseless old lady,' he said eventually, his gaze focused on the road ahead.

'I don't know the answer to that either.' This was a half-truth. Deep down, I suspected I knew the reason why. And if I was right, things would only get worse.

'This is the third time in three days they've tried to kill you.' Reid glanced at me. 'Why now?'

'I don't know. I didn't exactly get time to ask questions.' I leaned against the headrest. 'Maybe they're under new management.'

Reid grunted. 'That's a helluva lot of don't knows.'

I sighed. 'I know.'

Another minute elapsed. 'So, what're you gonna do about it?' he challenged.

I smiled faintly at his words; he knew me well. I looked out of the window, stalling for time.

We were headed down the Sumner Tunnel. Traffic was light for the time of day. A fire engine came up behind us and overtook the Chevy in a roar of sirens and flashing lights. The cat woke up and yawned. I looked down to find its golden eyes staring at me unwaveringly.

'I'm going to New York,' I said finally.

Reid was quiet for a while. 'What's in New York?'

'Someone who has answers, or knows where I can get them.' I stroked the cat's head. A low rumble of approval erupted from its belly.

A blast of static and garbled words escaped the radio scanner as we drove out into the North End. The fire was on the east-side dockyards. An orange glow smudged the skyline ahead and to the left.

'Meyer told you not to leave the city,' said Reid, his tone neutral.

'He did.'

There was a short lull. 'I'm coming with you,' he stated, adamant.

I turned a steady stare on him. 'This *will* get ugly.'

Reid shrugged. 'I'm already involved.' He glanced at me and scowled. 'I'm not going to change my mind about this, so don't give me that look. And don't say another word!'

'I wasn't intending to.' Once Hasley decided something, it would take nothing less than an act of God to steer him from his intended path. 'What about Price?'

'Price can wait,' Reid retorted dismissively.

I looked at the cat. Its golden eyes were still fixed on my face; it seemed to be awaiting my decision as intently as Reid.

'Okay,' I said finally. 'But we need more weapons.' My gaze shifted to the dashboard. 'And a new set of wheels.'

'What's wrong with the Chevy?' Reid protested.

'Trust me, right now all the Hunters on the east coast know about the Chevy.'

He hesitated. 'How many of them are there?'

'Hundreds.'

He appeared to be mulling over something. 'You have a car?'

I closed my eyes. 'Yes. Several, actually.'

Reid's apartment was a short drive from our office in Mission Hill and a half hour from the suburb where his ex-wife and children lived. Though small, the condo's austere black and white decor complemented his character and former lifestyle as a Marine.

I kept a lookout while he packed some essentials in a large rucksack. The cat followed him around the apartment, throaty purrs escaping its belly as it rubbed its head against his ankles.

I smiled. 'He likes you.'

Reid grunted something unsavory. He reached under his bed

and pulled out a crate secured with heavy-duty military padlocks. He unlocked it and flipped the lid up. The cat sauntered across the floor to investigate the contents of the chest.

'Leave those,' I said.

'I thought you wanted weapons.' Reid's hand hovered over the small arsenal inside the container. He had served with the 3rd Battalion 6th Marines at Camp Lejeune, in North Carolina, had participated in Operations Desert Shield and Desert Storm in the Persian Gulf, and Operation Just Cause in Panama. He knew his firearms.

I hesitated. 'Do you hold a license for the guns?'

Reid nodded.

'Then definitely leave them. And take your passport.'

His eyes narrowed.

'Just in case,' I said with a shrug.

Fifteen minutes later, we walked into the lobby of my building and took the lift to the tenth floor. No one had followed us.

The hallway outside the apartment was deserted and the rooms were as I had left them that morning. I grabbed a couple of duffel bags from a closet and packed some clothes in one of them.

Reid was sitting on the couch when I headed into the living room. The cat lay next to him. They watched silently as I strolled to the fireplace and took down the Monet. Moments later, the metal panel holding my collection of weapons dropped from the recess in the ceiling.

Reid finally rose to his feet and joined me. The cat jumped on the floor and followed.

'How long have you had these?' His fingers traced the contours of a Beretta PX4 Storm pistol.

I paused in the act of loading firearms and magazines into the second bag. 'A few years.' I indicated the guns. 'Take what you can carry.'

The last item to go in the bag was the daisho, each blade securely sheathed inside a leather scabbard. I reached behind the panel and pulled out a large, rectangular package taped to the back.

Reid looked on wordlessly while I ripped open the cellophane wrap and emptied several passports and wads of different currencies onto the coffee table. I closed the wall panel, took a piece of paper from a notepad, and wrote down a series of numbers.

'These are the codes for my accounts. Memorize them.' I passed the sheet across to him. 'The one in the Cayman Islands holds bonds for half a dozen financial institutions. The bank in Zurich has a deposit box under my name. There's enough there to buy you and your family security for life.' I avoided his probing gaze and packed the money and passports inside one of the bags. 'I've given Bergman and Sacks your details.'

'The solicitors?' said Reid.

I nodded.

'Why are you telling me this?' He studied the numbers on the paper.

I smiled faintly. 'Because I have a feeling I'm going to die.'

Reid grunted and struck a match. The flame caught the edge of the sheet. He dropped the burning ashes in the fireplace.

'You never really needed the job, did you?' he said, his tone faintly accusing.

I watched him steadily. 'Life as an immortal would be tedious without one.'

He still looked thoughtful when I took him to the private elevator that led to the basement. Seconds later, I turned on the lights in the underground garage. Reid stopped in his tracks. I crossed the floor to a black Toyota Land Cruiser with white racing stripes and smoked windows, and loaded the bags in the rear.

He strolled to a blue 2008 Dodge Viper ACR SRT10 and inspected the rest of the basement with a cocked eyebrow. 'This is quite a collection.'

In addition to the Hayabusa, the Land Cruiser, and the Dodge Viper, the garage housed a GMC Yukon Denali, a Porsche Carrera GT, two Mercedes-Benz SLR McLarens, a Dodge Charger SRT-8, a Yamaha YZF-R1, and a Ducati Supermono.

I climbed behind the wheel of the Land Cruiser.

Reid took the passenger seat and slammed the door shut. 'Why have I never seen you drive any of these before?'

I hesitated before murmuring, 'You'll find out soon enough.'

I pressed the remote control on the key ring. Lead-lined steel doors glided open at the head of a ramp. I put the cruiser into gear and drove out into the alley at the back of the building.

Reid looked over his shoulder. 'We're not taking the cat with us, are we?'

Cornelius had assumed a sphinx-like pose on top of the ammunition bag. The golden gaze switched to Reid. The cat yawned.

'We're dropping him off at the landlady's,' I replied while I negotiated the lanes behind the block. 'I called her when we were at your place.'

Mrs. Trelawney lived in a crowded 1960s condominium within shouting distance of our office. She shared her three-bed, fourth floor apartment with her daughter Izzie, Izzie's husband Pepe, their three children, Theo, Max, and little Isabelle, two dogs, three cats, five goldfish, and a hamster. Mr. Trelawney had passed away from lung cancer twelve years previously.

Little Isabelle opened the door. She took one look at the silver tabby, shrieked, and ran back inside the apartment. Cornelius bestowed a wary look upon me.

A figure appeared in the corridor. 'There, there, you're acting like you've never seen a cat before, girl,' grumbled Mrs. Trelawney. She wiped her hands on a dishtowel and frowned at her granddaughter.

The warm smell of cinnamon and caramel drifted from the woman as she drew closer. Little Isabelle clung to the back of her grandmother's dress and peered shyly at us.

'Oh.' Our landlady stopped and inspected the silver tabby. 'Why, he's a handsome specimen, isn't he?'

Cornelius made an approving sound.

I handed the cat over and placed an envelope on the table in the hallway. 'This is for taking care of him.'

Mrs. Trelawney hefted the bemused feline in one arm and opened the brown package. Her eyes widened. 'This is a lotta money.' She paused. 'In fact, I'd wager there's enough here to cover your rent for the next five months.'

I sensed Reid's hot gaze on the back of my head.

Our landlady hesitated. 'You boys ain't in some kinda trouble now, are you?'

'Not anymore than usual,' I said.

Mrs. Trelawney watched us for silent seconds. 'Wait here.' She disappeared down the corridor and returned with a cake tin in hand. 'I baked this today.' She shoved the container in Reid's unresisting arms. 'Now, get out of here. And take care of yourselves.'

Reid was silent on the way back to the SUV.

'You would have refused if I'd suggested paying the rent.' I maneuvered the Cruiser into the nighttime traffic before glancing at him.

'That's not what I'm thinking about,' said Reid. 'And yes, you're right; I would have refused.'

I looked at the rearview mirror. 'What is it then?'

Reid studied the tin box. 'This is a lot of cake.'

I grinned. My eyes shifted to the side mirrors. I stiffened, fingers clenching on the steering wheel.

'What?' said Reid. He peered over his shoulder.

'You got your seatbelt on?'

'Yeah, why?'

'We're being tailed,' I said grimly. 'Hang on.'

~

CHAPTER FIVE

THE CLOCK ON THE CENTRAL CONSOLE READ MIDNIGHT WHEN we reached the outskirts of New York City.

It had taken a quarter of an hour to lose the two SUVs tracking us. Somewhere off Interstate 90, Reid helped me remove the racing stripes from the Land Cruiser and change the number plates.

Despite the lateness of the hour, the Henry Hudson Parkway was packed. I drove past the George Washington Bridge, exited onto Riverside Drive, and joined 12th Avenue. Moments later, I crossed Park Avenue and turned right onto Lexington.

"Solange" was a small, exclusive jazz club situated in a leafy street off 3rd Avenue. With a maximum capacity of a hundred heads, it was off the beaten track of the city's busy nightlife. Entry was strictly by invitation. The owners liked it that way.

The doorman eyed us coolly when we strolled up to him. He scrutinized my business card before unclipping the black velvet rope from one of the gold-colored stanchions guarding the entrance. We moved past him and headed down a dimly lit spiral staircase.

The walls were lined with scarlet silk padding and adorned with old black and white photos depicting the club's long history: Louis Armstrong, John Coltrane, Miles Davis, and Charlie 'Bird' Parker were among some of the names featured in the pictures. At the bottom of the steps, a pair of polished mahogany doors opened onto a wide, sunken floor.

The room was drowned in deep reds, dark purples, and rich earth tones. The furniture was Brazilian cherry wood, with elegant lines, plush velvet upholstery, and satin cushions. Discreet booths overhung with black rococo curtains afforded privacy to those that needed it, although the muted lighting provided enough of that as it was.

A woman in a shimmering crimson cocktail dress stood on a raised podium to the far left. She was crooning a French song in a deep, sultry voice, her eyes closed and her glossy, ruby lips glistening in the mellow spotlight. Behind her, cymbals vibrated gently, a piano tinkled, and a saxophone hummed.

Reid followed in my footsteps as I headed for the bar on the other side of the room. I stopped by a tall, black leather and cherry wood stool and observed the figure behind the counter.

'Hello, Pierre,' I said quietly.

The man finished polishing the wine glass in his hand and turned around slowly.

Pierre Vauquois had always reminded me of a very solemn Great Dane. Although the years had added padding to his body and silver lines to his hair, giving him a distinguished look worthy of Capitol Hill, his face remained as inscrutable as ever. He glanced at Reid, untied the apron around his waist, and handed it to a waiter hovering close by.

'We're not to be disturbed under any circumstances, understood?' Vauquois instructed firmly. The waiter nodded, Adam's apple bobbing.

The older man set a bottle of 1980 Krug Clos du Mesnil on ice and loaded the tray with four champagne flutes. He turned and disappeared through a door hidden behind a thick, purple curtain. Reid and I stepped behind the bar and followed.

Carpeted stairs led to a three-story townhouse above the club. We walked through a second pair of mahogany doors and entered a hallway with a polished parquet floor. Vauquois stopped and placed the tray on a gilded French console table. He closed the doors, turned, and embraced me in a tight hug.

'Lucas.' He patted me gently on the back before examining me with a critical eye. 'You look awful.'

My lips parted in a small smile. 'I've been better.'

Vauquois looked to my right. 'You must be Reid.' He held a hand out to the former US Marine.

Reid hesitated before shaking Vauquois's hand. 'I'm afraid you have the advantage of me.'

'Ah. I see Lucas is being secretive as always,' murmured Vauquois. He collected the tray and led us down the hall to a beautifully decorated drawing room with a tall, vaulted ceiling. We settled in the period seats arranged around a low table while Vauquois poured the champagne. He handed us a glass each.

Reid studied the bubbles in the flute. 'This looks expensive.'

'It is,' said a voice from the doorway. It was the woman in the red cocktail dress. 'The nineteen-eighty Krug? You're spoiling us.'

She crossed the room, kissed the cheek of the smiling Vauquois, and took the glass he proffered. She watched us carefully over the rim of the champagne flute while she sipped the golden liquid.

'My name is Solange Vauquois,' she said finally. 'Pierre and I own the club.'

She moved behind Vauquois's chair and leaned on the headrest, her hand on her husband's shoulder.

'You are Reid?' A faint trace of her birth accent modulated her voice as she gazed at my partner.

Reid nodded.

A smile lit up Solange Vauquois's face. 'Lucas speaks very highly of you.'

Reid's eyebrows rose. 'He does?'

The woman grinned. She looked at me. 'Did you drive?'

'Yes,' I replied.

Solange turned to Reid, a sympathetic grimace twisting her lips. 'Was it awful?'

'It was one of the scariest experiences I've ever had,' Reid admitted with a heartfelt grunt. 'I thought I was going to die.'

Solange burst out laughing, the sound clear and musical.

I shifted in the chair. 'It wasn't that bad,' I mumbled.

Reid scowled. 'You were like a stuntman on the Nürburgring. I'm surprised a patrol car didn't pull us over.'

'I'm afraid he's always been one for fast things,' said Solange, her eyes sparkling.

Reid scrutinized the couple. 'You're immortals, aren't you?' he said after a while.

Solange's expression sobered. She glanced at Vauquois.

'Yes, we are,' she replied quietly.

I first met Solange and Pierre in Paris in the late sixteenth century, not long before I began my travels through Asia. In those days, I was a homeless, unruly, and willful mutt who lived on the streets of the not-so-fair city and was forever in trouble with the law. One winter night, at the end of a long day drinking cheap liquor distilled in the backyard of a friend's home, I got into an ugly fight with one of the patrons of Pierre and Solange's tavern. Instead of hauling me to the closest gaol and leaving me at the hands of whichever bastard sergeant was in charge of the prison that day, a fate I no doubt deserved, they offered me food and a bed for the night. In my short immortal life, I had only ever known compassion from my parents. It took a while for my mistrust to fade.

It was Pierre who encouraged me to go on a voyage to foreign ports, to "broaden your mind and your views of the world" as he put it. Upon my return two decades later, they realized I was an immortal, as I did them. From then on, Solange and Pierre adopted the roles of surrogate parents and mentors; their two children, François and Claude, had died from the Red Death in the late fourteenth century, and they themselves had been afflicted with the curse of infertility. When I left Europe after the end of the Second World War, they followed me to New York.

'I see,' Reid murmured after Solange explained the circumstances of our meeting. 'Does that mean you knew Olsson?'

'We never met,' said Vauquois. 'But we knew of him.' The older man looked at us quizzically. 'What's going on?'

'Mikael's alive,' I said. Shock and surprise dawned on the couple's faces. 'And for some reason, he's joined forces with the Hunters who're after me.'

I gave them a brief account of the events of the last week.

'Oh, Lucas! Your sixteenth death?' Solange whispered, her face ashen as she lowered herself to the seat next to her husband.

I avoided her eyes, aware that this knowledge brought her great pain.

'Have you heard anything unusual recently?' I asked Vauquois.

Although they kept mostly to themselves these days and rarely associated with other immortals, the Vauquoises had contacts who regularly apprised them of significant events in both the Bastian and the Crovir societies; having been spies during the Seven-Year War, the French Revolution, and most recently members of the French Resistance, it was a hard habit for the couple to break.

My heart sank as I observed Vauquois's troubled expression.

'A secret meeting attended by several members of the Crovir First Council took place in Washington a few weeks ago,' the older man said finally. 'I don't know the exact details of what was discussed, but whatever it was, it's stirred things up.' He hesitated. 'Our friend inside the Second Council told me the Crovirs are on the move. Not only here, but in Europe as well.' He rolled the neck of the flute between his fingers. 'It's the largest mobilization of Hunters we have seen since the immortal wars. They're looking for something. Or someone,' he added gravely.

Reid glanced between us. 'The First Council?'

'The immortal societies are ruled by nobles who form the Councils,' said Vauquois. 'The First Council is the most senior, made up of the Heads of seven Sections. The Order of the Hunters, the Counter Terrorism group, Human Relations, Commerce, Immortal Legislations and Conventions, Research and Development, and Immortal Culture and History.'

'The Second Council is the Assembly,' Solange continued. 'It consists of the Regional Division directors under each Head of Section. Below them is the Congress of the Council, who function as local authority chiefs.'

'The Head of the Order of the Hunters is the most powerful member of the First Council. This applies to both Crovirs and Bastians,' said Vauquois. 'The Hunters are essentially the assassins, bodyguards, policemen, and soldiers of the immortal nobles.'

'So, it must be the Crovirs who're after you,' said Reid, his gaze shifting to me.

I sighed. 'I don't understand why I've become a priority again after all this time. The last attempt on my life was in nineteen ten.'

'Whatever or whoever they're after, they're getting desperate,' said Solange, her tone somber. 'I have rarely known them kill a human in such an open fashion.'

Reid's eyes never left my face. 'On the other hand, if you were to become a suspect in an ongoing homicide investigation, it would slow you down considerably, and make it easier for them to get to you. That's what it was about, wasn't it?' he said slowly.

I nodded, my hands fisting on my lap. The same thought had crossed my mind after our client's murder. The Hunters must have grasped the opportunity when they came across it.

Silence fell across the room.

'I hate to ask this of you, but do you think you can find out more?' I asked Vauquois.

'No,' he replied. '*I* can't.' A faint smile crossed his face. 'But our contact might be able to point you in the right direction. Excuse me.' He rose and disappeared through a door at the end of the room.

'What will you do?' Solange asked quietly while we waited for his return.

'I don't know.' I placed the empty champagne glass on the tray. 'Try to stay alive until I get to the bottom of this, I guess.'

Vauquois finally reappeared with a piece of paper in his hand. 'Our friend was reluctant, but I convinced him to give us a name at least.' He passed the note across.

I studied the name and address scrawled on it. 'Who is this?'

'Someone high up in the Crovir Councils.'

I raised my eyebrows. 'Will he help?'

Vauquois chuckled. 'I doubt it. But you might find something useful at his place.'

I tucked the note inside my coat and rose to my feet. 'Let's go,' I said to Reid.

'Won't you spend the night? It's been so long since we last saw you.' Solange crossed the floor and stopped in front of me.

I leaned down and kissed her gently on the cheek. 'I don't want the Crovirs to track us here. If anything was to happen to either of you, I would never forgive myself.'

A sad smile flitted across her face. We said our goodbyes and left the building through the back door.

'They're nice people,' Reid said when we got in the Cruiser.

'Yes, they are.'

He stretched his shoulders and yawned. 'So, where to now?'

'We're going to Washington.'

Reid made a face. 'Straight into the lions' den, huh?'

I shrugged. 'Put your seat belt on.'

He stiffened, eyes moving to the rearview mirror. 'Why, we being tailed again?'

'No.'

Reid frowned. 'I think I should drive.'

We took turns behind the wheel, stopping for a few hours' sleep outside Trenton. We had a generous portion of Mrs. Trelawney's angel cake for breakfast and made the outskirts of the District of Columbia by six am.

The address Vauquois's contact had provided was in Capitol Hill, in a leafy suburb just south of Lincoln Park. I pulled over several doors down from a large, detached Victorian residence and switched the Cruiser's engine off. Lights were on behind the wide bay windows on the second floor.

I leaned back against the headrest and closed my eyes briefly. The events of the last days were finally catching up on me; I had rarely felt so exhausted. Still, the question of why the Crovirs wanted me dead would not go away. Even more puzzling was how Olsson fitted into any of it.

An hour later, a black chauffeured Lincoln town car stopped at the curb. The front door of the house opened and a man in a gray wool coat stepped out. He locked the door behind him and strolled down the steps to the tiled path crossing the short fore-garden, a cell phone to one ear and a brown leather briefcase in the other hand. He acknowledged the driver of the Lincoln with a brief nod and got in the back of the car. The chauffeur closed the door after him, climbed in the front seat, and drove off. I put the Cruiser into gear and followed.

The Lincoln headed south and merged with the morning traffic on the I-295. It moved to the I-395 freeway, crawled past the Washington Monument Memorial on Maine Avenue, and turned onto 17th Street. It went by the Ellipse and the White House before pulling into an underground garage below a dark glass and steel tower on Pennsylvania Avenue Northwest.

I stopped the Cruiser on the opposite side of the road and studied the building. There were no visible nameplates on the facade.

'Investment bank?' hazarded Reid.

'Lawyers?' I said.

Reid shook his head. 'Lawyers don't go around in chauffeured Lincolns. Not in DC, anyway.' He glanced at me. 'Well, we won't get anywhere just sitting here. What do you wanna do?'

I dragged my gaze from the imposing sky rise and looked at the clock on the console. It had just gone eight. 'Who do we know in town?'

The man who joined us for an early lunch was an Intelligence Analyst for the FBI's Criminal Investigative Division. A second generation Italian-American born and raised in New York, Bob Solito still sported a heavy Brooklyn accent despite having lived in DC for fifteen years. We first met him during the Louisiana incident and had since crossed paths on a number of other joint investigations.

'This personal business?' he said after he placed his order.

I nodded.

Solito sighed. 'Thought so. You guys normally go through official channels for this kind of intel.' He popped a white tablet in his mouth and winced as he chewed on it. 'The wife said she'd leave me if I didn't quit smoking,' he muttered by way of explanation at our stares. He pulled an envelope from his coat and slid it across the table. 'That's all I've got at the moment. You guys didn't exactly give me a lot of notice.'

'Thanks.' I flashed a grateful smile at him, opened the package, and spread the contents on the table.

'Frederick Rudolph Burnstein is the President and CEO of GeMBiT Corp,' said Solito. 'He has no past records or convictions on any criminal database in the world, including NCIC and Interpol.' The FBI analyst scratched his head. 'This guy is as clean as a whistle. He doesn't even have a speeding ticket to his name.'

I inspected the copy of an article from the Washington Post. It was a review of a recent production of 'Les Misérables' held at the National Theatre. At the bottom of the page, a black and white photograph depicted the principal actors and the director posing with famous local patrons of the Arts.

Our guy from Capitol Hill stood out from the crowd. Burnstein's eyes gleamed with a strange, visceral intensity as he gazed into the camera, his crooked nose giving him the appearance of a hawk. His lips were parted in a cold, artificial smile.

'GeMBiT?' said Reid. He leafed through the fact sheets that came with the article.

'Genetic and Molecular Bioinformatics Technology,' Solito explained. 'The company was first registered in DC in nineteen seventy. Most of its shareholders are in the US and mainland Europe, and it has close affiliations with universities leading research in molecular biology and genetics on both sides of the Atlantic.' He rubbed his chin thoughtfully. 'At the last count, GeMBiT has pledged four hundred million dollars in research grants this year alone.'

Reid let out a low whistle while he studied the printouts. 'What are they trying to do, exactly?'

'Cure cancer, among other things,' Solito replied.

Reid's eyebrows rose.

'Their principal areas of interests are oncology, tissue growth and repair, infectious diseases, and immunology,' said Solito. He shrugged at our stares. 'Hey, I'm just quoting all this stuff. I wouldn't know anything genetic or immunological if it bit me in the ass.'

I scrutinized the blueprints on the table. 'Are these the floor plans for the house in Capitol Hill?'

Solito nodded. 'He had the place renovated five years ago. I'm afraid you're gonna have to give me more time if you want the ones for the building on Pennsylvania Avenue. I couldn't find any copies filed with Building and Land Regulation. '

'Thanks. These will do for now,' I said.

'What's this about anyway?' said Solito. Lines puckered his brow at our expressions. 'Forget I asked,' he muttered. 'I'll let you know if I find anything else.'

He called an hour later. 'Seems Burnstein loves the opera as much as theatre. He's got tickets for tonight's opening performance of La Traviata at the JFK Center. Show starts at six fifteen.' There was a lull at the end of the line. 'Oh, and Soul?'

'Yeah?'

'There's a temporary felony want out for you in Boston. You've got forty-eight hours until I call it in.' Solito hung up.

I stared at the cell phone.

'What?' said Reid.

'Meyer's going to issue a warrant for my arrest.'

Reid lapsed into thoughtful silence. 'Well, we knew it was coming,' he said finally. 'So, what's our next move?'

I smiled at his tone. 'We're breaking into Burnstein's place tonight.'

Reid narrowed his eyes. 'Won't the man object to us just waltzing into his place?'

'That's the beauty of it. He won't be there.'

Burnstein left for the opera at 5:10. We waited until darkness fell before leaving the Cruiser and approaching the house. According to Solito's intel, the GeMBiT Corp CEO's home security system was state of the art and had been installed in the last three months. It took us eight minutes to disable it.

A few steps inside the house and I could tell that Burnstein was a keen art collector; I had not seen so many original paintings and sculptures outside a national museum for some time.

A search of the ground floor and the upstairs bedrooms revealed nothing of interest. An enormous study with triple aspect views occupied most of the third floor. The walls were lined with bookcases and filing cabinets. A mahogany Edwardian pedestal writing desk sat beneath the bay window facing the manicured gardens at the rear of the property.

I closed the blinds and switched on the desk lamp. Reid started poking through the contents of the bookcases and cabinets while I turned my attention to Burnstein's home computer.

It took several minutes to hack into the operating system. Halfway through, Reid came up behind me and peered curiously over my shoulder.

'Do I even wanna know how you learned to do that?' he muttered, watching my fingers fly across the keyboard.

I paused and thought of the MIT guys who had taught me my skills and who were now the heads of the largest computer and security consultancy firms in the world. 'Not really.'

A thud drew my gaze to the other side of the room a moment later. Reid had dislodged a painting on the wall. He picked it up gingerly, stared at the small chip in the corner of the frame, and placed it back on its hooks.

'Do you think he'll notice?'

I shrugged. 'Probably. That's an original Rembrandt.'

Reid looked at me blankly. 'It is?'

'Yeah.' I turned back to the desk. 'It's worth about half a million dollars.'

He inhaled sharply. 'You're kidding, right?'

'No.'

'Who the hell keeps that kind of thing in their house?' he exclaimed.

I glanced at his disgruntled expression and resolved there and then never to tell him about the Monet in my apartment.

Burnstein's computer defense software was better than his home security. I had just cracked the safety codes to access the files when a thoughtful 'Ah' made me look around.

Reid had reached the last filing cabinet. It had opened to reveal a strongbox. He glanced at the lock pick set on the floor next to him. 'Somehow, I don't think this is gonna do the trick.'

I rose from the desk and joined him.

'It's a high-security composite safe.' I crouched and ran my fingers over the cold metal door. 'Inner and outer steel plates. High-density fire-resistant body. Drill-resistant frames. Chrome-plated steel locking bolts and a spring operated detent system. It probably has a tempered glass relock mechanism as well.'

'I worry about you,' Reid said with a wooden expression.

I grinned. 'Luckily, it has an electronic combination lock.'

Reid sighed. 'Somehow that doesn't make me feel any better.'

'Help me bring the computer over.'

Fifteen minutes later, I pulled the safe door open.

'Wow. I thought that was only possible in movies.' Reid looked slightly impressed.

'If you have the right software and a couple of wires, anything is possible,' I said, studying the contents of the strongbox.

In addition to several pouches of high-quality diamonds, five gold bars, and a number of passports, the safe held a dozen document wallets. Eleven of them contained information about Burnstein's private investments and GeMBiT Corp.

The last folder was the thickest of the group and was filled with copies of research papers published in the last fifteen years by a number of universities in Europe. The recurring subject matter appeared to be cell cycle control and DNA transposition. One name in particular, a Professor H.E. Strauss, appeared as a common contributor in most of the publications and had been highlighted in red ink.

I turned to the computer and typed 'Strauss' in the search box. A single jpeg file and an email reference came up under the results. I directed the arrow over the jpeg file and clicked the mouse.

An image slowly filled the screen. It was a black and white photograph of a man and a woman, taken at night. They were sitting next to a large bay window inside a restaurant. The man was caught with his back slightly turned and in profile. He was leaning across the table toward the woman, whose face was fully illuminated by the chandelier above their heads.

Her hair was dark and tumbled in soft curls past her shoulders, framing a pair of almond-shaped, smoky eyes. The light glistened off her full lips and glinted on the thick, intricate sun cross pendant at the base of her throat. She was smiling at the man.

'This the person they're after?' said Reid.

I stared at the woman in the picture, an unfamiliar emotion stirring deep within me. I had to force my gaze away from her face before looking up the email.

It was from Burnstein and had been addressed to an encrypted account on a remote server somewhere in Europe. Dated several weeks ago, the message was brief: "Arrange Council meeting. Strauss is the key. Must secure at any cost."

A soft tinkle sounded somewhere downstairs. Reid and I looked at each other. I rose to my feet just as one of the windows shattered, raining glass shards inside the room. A second later, a smoke grenade sailed through the broken pane and clattered onto the floorboards.

CHAPTER SIX

THE CROVIR HUNTERS CAME SILENTLY, GUNS FITTED WITH suppressors. We were almost at the first landing when a volley of bullets whined past us and struck the wall. Shadows shifted at the bottom of the stairs. Muzzles flashed in the gloom.

I reached for the swords at my waist.

Bodies fell before me as we were forced up the steps. The blades shuddered in my hands, blocking round after round. Reid fired the Glock repeatedly at the Hunters streaming down a first floor corridor toward us. We stepped over the men he had shot and headed for the master bedroom at the front of the property. I slammed the door shut, locked it, and helped Reid push a dresser across the threshold.

I walked to the window and stared at the empty yard below. 'You go first,' I said briskly. 'I'll hold them off.'

Reid glared at me. Unspoken words filled the silence between us. I didn't have to state the obvious fact; in a battle with the immortals, he stood at a serious disadvantage.

There was a thud outside the room. The dresser shifted slightly.

'You owe me for this,' he said between gritted teeth. He

lifted the sash window, climbed over the sill, and turned to catch the keys of the Cruiser. A second later, he disappeared in the night.

The door crashed open, the dresser scraping across the floorboards with a shriek of tearing wood. I turned to face the men who crowded inside the room. Some held swords. The ones who didn't had guns.

'Be careful,' one of the Hunters warned. 'This is the half-breed.'

The other immortals glanced at each other uneasily.

I had hoped Olsson would be among them; there were some burning questions I needed to ask my old friend. Still, I had no doubt our paths would cross again if I survived this night.

My breaths slowed as I silently repeated the mantra taught to me by my Edo master, my feet moving to the basic starting stance of kendo.

Eyes narrowed on the other side of the floor.

'Gentlemen,' I said quietly.

The next sixty seconds were a blur of light and shadows. A bullet missed my head by an inch. Another one scorched a red track across the back of my right hand. The acrid smell of gunpowder filled the room and spent rounds clattered to the ground while the katana danced and weaved through the air, spilling blood across the walls and the floorboards. Throughout it all, I breathed steadily.

The last Hunter begged for his life.

'Please, this will be my seventeenth death,' he whispered hoarsely at my feet, staring in wide-eyed horror at the blade poised above his heart.

Memories of a vanilla-scented room rose in my mind. I closed my eyes briefly. 'I'm sorry.'

Sirens blared in the distance when I came out of the house. Wings fluttered above my head as crows gathered on the rooftop of Burnstein's home.

The Cruiser screeched to a halt in the middle of the street when I reached the sidewalk. External lights came on along the road and dim figures appeared on doorsteps. Burnstein's neighbors looked at me curiously while I climbed in the SUV.

Reid pulled away swiftly. 'You're bleeding.'

I looked at my hand. 'It's only a flesh wound.'

I clenched my fingers distractedly, feeling strangely numb. It had been some time since I last killed so many men. I took a deep, shuddering breath and tried to ignore the smell of death clinging to me.

'How's your leg?' I said.

Blood had seeped through the bandage around Reid's wound and stained his trousers.

'I'll live,' he replied gruffly.

A patrol car raced past us, lights flashing in the night. Another followed close behind it. We headed away from Capitol Hill.

'They all dead?' he said after a while.

'Yes.'

I cursed my own foolishness; we had probably triggered a silent alarm in Burnstein's house. I suspected it had been inside the safe.

The blare from my cell phone broke the silence that followed. It was Solito.

'I heard there were shots fired at that house in Capitol Hill,' the FBI agent said stiffly. 'Tell me it wasn't you guys.' A babble of conversation and music echoed in the background behind him.

'I would be lying if I said we weren't involved,' I murmured. Solito swore.

I waited a couple of seconds. 'I need another favor.'

There was a frozen beat. 'You're kidding, right?'

We met the FBI agent in an alley behind a bar in Dupont Circle; he had been out celebrating the retirement of a field officer and was still dressed in his work suit. His eyes kept straying to the blood on my hand while I explained my request.

'I've been listening to the scanner. The cops have reported four bodies at the property. They're saying there was a lot of blood in the place, which makes them suspect there were even more bodies than the ones they've found.' Solito ran his fingers through his hair. 'No doubt they'll call us in.'

A group of people walked past the mouth of the alley, drunken voices raised in song.

'I know this probably doesn't mean a lot to you at the moment, but they weren't good men,' I said.

'And we might as well warn you now,' Reid added with a grunt. 'You're probably not gonna be able to ID any of them.'

Solito chewed his lip. He let out a sharp exhale and removed a notepad from his back pocket.

'This is the last thing I'm gonna do for you guys,' he muttered while he scribbled on the paper.

'Thanks, Bob,' I said gratefully.

The address Solito gave us was for a house in Chinatown. I took the wheel, drove down Massachusetts Avenue, took a right on 5th, and parked along a side road. A narrow, nondescript, two-story building stood sandwiched between an electrical store and a restaurant a couple of doors down. Lights were still on in the store. The restaurant was dark.

We left the Cruiser and walked to the house. I climbed a short flight of concrete steps and pressed the buzzer.

'Why are we here again?' said Reid with a puzzled frown.

The door creaked open before I could reply. A small, wizened man peered at us through the crack.

'Can I help you?' he said in thick Mandarin, squinting in the glow cast by a nearby street lamp.

'We're here to see Yuan Qin Lee,' I replied in the Zhongyuan dialect.

The old man brightened. 'You speak Han Chinese?' he exclaimed in broken English.

'A little bit,' I said with a faint smile.

'Come in, come in.' He beckoned us inside the building with a sharp wave of his liver-spotted hand and closed the door.

We were faced with a cramped corridor filled with the smell of cooking and cheap disinfectant. Curious faces appeared in an open doorway to the left. The old man gestured frantically and shouted harsh words in Mandarin. The faces disappeared.

I glanced at the toys littering the passageway. 'Are you the patriarch?'

'For my sins,' grumbled the old man. 'They all useless, the lot of them. Only one who make money is Qin Lee.'

We followed him to an alcove at the end of the hall. He pulled aside a curtain and revealed a door that opened onto a dimly lit staircase spiraling down to the lower level of the house.

The basement was large and extended well beyond the boundaries of the property. I spied a second door at the rear of the room.

Banks of computer monitors lined benches along the walls, their screens flickering oddly under the harsh light from the half-dozen fluorescent tubes crowding the low ceiling. A low hum emanated from the hard drives on the left, dark monoliths in the otherwise bright room. Wires crawled between the cable organizers dotting the concrete floor.

A young man with horn-rimmed spectacles and shiny black hair sat hunched over a drafting table in the middle of the room. The frames around his eyes glinted under the spotlight screwed into the desk.

'Qin Lee?' I called out. The young man's head came up sharply. Almond-shaped eyes narrowed behind the lenses. 'Solito sent us.'

He observed us for a couple of beats before carefully

putting down the document he had been working on. He removed the latex gloves from his hands, rose from the chair, and spoke a few words to the old man. The latter glanced at us with a troubled expression, nodded once, and left.

Qin Lee waited until the door closed at the top of the stairs before turning to us with a frown. 'What do you want?'

I indicated Reid. 'I need some passports for him, among other things.'

'I already have a passport,' Reid protested.

'You need new ones,' I retorted.

He held my gaze for a couple of seconds before sighing; he knew not to ask for the reasons why. Yet.

I listed the additional items I required.

Qin Lee crossed his arms and pursed his lips. 'This will cost you.'

'Money's not an issue. When can you have the documents ready?'

He shrugged. 'Day after tomorrow, at the earliest.'

'We need them tonight.' I ignored his shocked expression. 'Like I said, money isn't an issue.'

Two hours later, we walked out of the house with three fake passports and a document wallet.

'It would help if I knew what was going on behind that thick skull of yours,' Reid muttered once we were inside the Cruiser.

I started the engine. 'What do you want to know?'

'Well, for one thing, why the hell did you just fork out a fortune for those forgeries?'

'Because I suspect we're going to need them before the week's over.'

'Why? Where are we going?' said Reid.

'France.'

His brow furrowed. 'Any particular reason?' he said after a beat.

'The last paper Strauss published was from UPMC, the Université Pierre et Marie Curie, in Paris,' I explained. 'I want to know why Burnstein and the Crovir First Council are so interested in this person.'

Reid studied the road for a while. 'You sure about this?' he said finally.

I hesitated. 'It's the only clue we've got.'

He sighed. 'When do we leave?'

I took out the cell and dialed the Vauquoises' number. 'Hello, Pierre? It's Lucas.' I listened. 'We're fine. Look, we need to get to Paris. Can you help?...No, commercial flights are out of the question. This has to be discreet.'

There was a longer interlude while I waited for Vauquois to return to the phone. I pulled a pen and paper out of the glove compartment and wrote down the address he dictated.

'Thanks, Pierre. Give my love to Solange.'

We headed north of DC and reached the private airstrip Vauquois had directed us to outside Baltimore around midnight. The only plane on the tarmac with its lights on was a white Cessna 750. I parked the Cruiser inside the hangar next to it and followed Reid to the aircraft.

A tall, trim, middle-aged man with silver-streaked brown hair came down the steps to meet us when we entered the shadow of the plane.

'Are you Pierre's friends?' he said in an amiable voice.

'Yes, we are,' I replied. We shook hands.

'I'm Jim, your pilot.' He glanced at our bags. 'Will this be all?'

I nodded.

'Good,' he said. 'Come aboard.'

Thirty minutes later, we were airborne. As the east coast fell away beneath us, I turned to the documents I had printed at Qin Lee's place; before the Crovirs surprised us in Capitol Hill, I had forwarded the photograph from Burnstein's computer to a fake email address on a separate server. The research articles by Strauss and generic information on the UPMC had been freely accessible on the internet.

'Wake me up when we get there.' Reid reclined his seat and closed his eyes.

I spent the next two hours poring over the information in Strauss's papers. Occasionally, my gaze would stray to the black and white print of the man and the woman in the restaurant.

Why was a senior member of the Crovir Councils so concerned with a scientist involved in genetics and molecular biology? Sure, Burnstein was the head of a biotechnology corporation, but the security measures surrounding the information on Strauss suggested the President and CEO of GeMBiT Corp had a more vested interest in the professor than pure academic curiosity. More importantly, what did it have to do with the Crovir Hunters' renewed attempts on my life? The timing of the events was too close for this fact to be a coincidence. And where did Olsson feature in all of this?

Somewhere over the Atlantic, I was lulled into a troubled sleep by the drone of the Cessna's engines.

Eight hours after we left Baltimore, we landed on a deserted airfield thirty miles outside Paris. The local time was fifteen hundred.

'Pierre called,' Jim told us when he opened the cabin door. 'He said he would arrange transportation for you.'

We unloaded our bags and bade the pilot goodbye. As we stood on the tarmac and watched the Cessna dwindle to a speck on the skyline, on its way to Le Bourget Airport to refuel, the distant backfiring of engines alerted us to approaching vehicles. We turned and gazed down the strip.

A black Jaguar XK120 roadster was making its way rapidly across the tarmac toward us. Not far behind it was a dusty, mustard-yellow Citroën 2CV; French hip-hop music blasted out of its open windows.

The roadster braked to a stop some three feet from us. An energetic young man with blond hair and blue eyes leapt out of the driver's seat.

'*Bonjour! Vous êtes* Lucas?' he said with a blindingly white smile.

'*Oui*,' I replied distractedly, my eyes roaming over the familiar Jaguar.

He threw the car keys across to me. '*Compliment de Monsieur Vauquois!*' he shouted and jogged over to the 2CV.

The bearded youth behind the wheel of the Citroën nodded a brief acknowledgement and pulled his shades down. We watched the car do a screeching U-turn and hurtle erratically down the runway. The rap lyrics faded in the distance.

Reid studied the roadster with a grimace. 'Do all immortals have a thing for nice cars, or is it just you and the people you know?' He dropped our bags in the boot and climbed in the passenger seat.

'What can I say? We like the classics.' I slipped behind the wheel and ran my fingers lovingly over the dashboard and the gearbox.

Pierre and Solange had left the vintage car with friends in Chantilly when they moved to New York; they still used it whenever they visited France. It had been a while since I had driven the antique.

Despite the heavy Saturday afternoon traffic and Reid's occasional acerbic comment on my driving, we made Paris in just under an hour; the old back roads had not changed much in the few decades since I had last been to the capital. I crossed the *Boulevard Périphérique* near the *16ème arrondissement*, went over the *Place du Trocadéro*, and headed for the *Pont d'Iéna*.

'Nice,' said Reid moments later. Up ahead, the Eiffel Tower rose majestically at the head of the *Parc du Champ de Mars*.

Traffic slowed when we hit the *Boulevard Garibaldi* and the *Rue Froidevaux*. By the time we reached the *13ème arrondissement* and pulled over opposite an apartment building halfway down a side street, the sky was starting to redden. A smile curved my lips when I spotted the well-preserved green Renault 5 Super-mini taking center stage in the allocated parking space in front of the edifice.

I climbed out of the roadster, crossed the sidewalk to a pair of oak doors, and pressed the buzzer for apartment 3A.

A gruff voice barked a disgruntled '*Oui?*' through the speakerphone seconds later.

'*C'est* Lucas.'

There was a pregnant pause. 'Lucas?' Surprise elevated the pitch of the man's voice. '*Nom de Dieu!*'

Heavy footsteps sounded on the other side of the doors after a minute. They slammed open. The figure on the threshold gaped before engulfing me in a bear-like embrace.

'My word, Lucas! You haven't changed at all! What's it been, ten, twelve years?'

I grinned at the short, portly, middle-aged French man with the thick mustache. 'About that.'

Gustav Lacroix was a retired detective who used to work at the headquarters of the French National Police; he was one of the few mortal friends the Vauquoises and I had maintained contact with since we left France. Although the Frenchman often joked that we had discovered the secret whereabouts of the Fountain of Youth, I had a feeling he suspected our somewhat unearthly origins. Still, he never asked us questions.

I glanced at the Supermini. 'I see you've still got the old car.'

'Pah! I wouldn't trade it for any of these new fancy-schmancy contraptions.' Gustav's eyes glinted when he saw the roadster. 'On the other hand, I wouldn't mind getting my fingers on that little beauty.' He greeted Reid like an old acquaintance and ushered us inside the building.

'So, what brings you to Paris?' he said once we were inside his apartment.

'We have business in town.'

A wry smile dawned on the old detective's face. 'Ah. I see.' He placed a tray of freshly brewed coffee on a low table in the sitting room. 'I take it it's the kind of business you can't talk about?'

I nodded.

He sat in a large, padded armchair. 'Well, if there's anything I can do to help, don't hesitate to ask.'

'Thanks.' I reached for one of the porcelain cups and took a gulp of the hot, fragrant liquid; the familiar taste flooded my mouth, bringing back memories of lazy summer days spent in the French capital. 'Actually, I do have a question.'

Gustav looked at me expectantly.

'Have there been any—unusual incidents in the city of late?'

A bemused expression washed across the retired detective's face. 'In Paris?'

I smiled. 'Sorry, that was a stupid question. What I meant was, something out of the ordinary, mysterious—unnatural even?'

Gustav thought for a moment before shaking his head. 'No. Not that I've heard of anyway. But, tell you what, my nephew works at the DCPJ, *la Direction Centrale de la Police Judiciaire*. You haven't met him before. He just moved to Paris from Lyon. He's coming over for dinner tonight.' The old detective shrugged. 'He might know something.'

Christophe Lacroix turned out to be a much taller and slimmer version of his uncle. It became rapidly evident that his warm, chocolate-brown eyes and loose demeanor belied a sharp intelligence.

'You've known my uncle for long?' he said curiously while we sat at the dining table and sipped wine from a fine bottle of Cru Beaujolais.

'Yes.'

'Gustav mentioned you wanted to know of any strange events that may have occurred in the city recently?' he asked.

'Uh-huh,' I said with a noncommittal nod.

Christophe Lacroix leaned back in his chair. 'What do you do for a living?' he drawled, watching us over the rim of his glass.

'We're private investigators,' Reid replied, his tone carefully blank.

The French detective's eyes moved to my face. 'Oh? And what exactly, may I ask, are you investigating in our lovely *Ville-Lumière?*'

Reid and I exchanged glances.

'It's a missing person's case,' I said levelly.

Lacroix raised his eyebrows, a sardonic twist distorting his mouth. 'Really? Why don't you tell me more? I might be able to help.'

I smiled. 'I'm afraid that's impossible. Our clients are very particular. They would like to keep this as low-key as possible.'

Lacroix frowned.

Gustav entered the room and lowered a large casserole dish in the middle of the table. He lifted the lid. Steam billowed out, followed by the fragrant aroma of slow-cooked meat and vegetables. 'Voila! My famous *Coq au Vin*. Dig in!'

The conversation turned to more mundane matters. Gustav's nephew took his leave just after ten, blaming an early start the next day. He stopped in the apartment doorway and studied us carefully.

'In response to your earlier query, no, there haven't been any unusual incidents in the city of late. None that has attracted the attention of the DCPJ anyway.'

'Thank you,' I murmured.

We rose from the table and headed for the door a short while later.

'Here, this is the spare key for when you get back,' said

Gustav, handing me a door key. 'I'm afraid one of you will have to sleep on the sofa. The guest room only has a single bed,' he added apologetically as he let us out of the apartment.

Earlier that evening, I had looked up the H.E. Strausses listed in Paris in the retired detective's White Pages. There were five of them. Although the CGM, the Center for Molecular Genetics research lab where Strauss was assigned, was located on the Gif-sur-Yvette campus some twenty miles southwest of the French capital, my instincts told me that the professor quite likely kept a place in the city. I ruled out the Strausses who lived too far from the center and the addresses that were not within walking distance of a train station or metro. That left only three H.E. Strausses; one in Montreuil and two within the *Boulevard Périphérique*, in the *11ème* and *7ème* *arrondissements*.

We took the roadster and headed east past the *Pitié-Salpêtrière* Hospital and the *Quai de la Gare*. I crossed the River Seine at the *Pont de Tolbiac* and turned right onto the *Quai de Bercy* before joining the *Boulevard Périphérique*. Eight minutes later, we entered the suburb of Montreuil.

The first address was a detached house in a small road not far from the metro station. Lights were still on behind the ground floor windows when we pulled up some fifty yards from the property. After watching the place for ten minutes, I left the car, crossed the shallow fore garden, and knocked on the front door. It was opened by an elderly gentleman.

'*Est-ce que je peux vous aider?*' he said in a frail voice, blinking in the porch light.

'I apologize for bothering you at such a late hour,' I replied in French. 'I was passing through and thought I'd look up an old university friend, a person by the name of H.E. Strauss?'

'Oh. I'm terribly sorry, I'm afraid I'm the only Strauss living at this address,' he said with a weak smile.

I thanked him and strolled back to the car.

'Any luck?' said Reid.

'No. Let's try the next address.'

Traffic had thinned out considerably and the drive to the *11ème arrondissement* took less than ten minutes. The address was an apartment located in an old neoclassical building halfway down a quiet cul-de-sac. I parked the car at the entrance of the street and we sat watching the block. The curtains were drawn and the lights were off behind the large French windows on the second floor. They remained so for the next half hour.

'Wanna check out the last place?' Reid suggested. I nodded.

The apartment in the *7ème* was owned by a Hélène Eveline Strauss, a teacher at a local elementary school. Her voice sounded thin and harassed on the speakerphone and the high-pitched screams of children rose in the background.

'Sorry to bother you,' I said hastily after confirming her details. I returned to the car.

'No luck here either?' muttered Reid.

'No. Let's go back to the *11ème arrondissement*. I have a feeling that's the place we want.'

We headed across the river and I pulled into the empty parking space we had previously occupied. The apartment on the second floor was as dark as when we had left. Minutes after I turned off the engine, the front door of the building opened. A man stepped out with a dog on a leash. He glanced curiously at the car when he walked past.

'Fancy a stroll?' I said to Reid.

He shrugged. 'Sure. It beats sitting here the whole night. Besides, the friendly neighborhood watch might call the cops on us if we hang around here much longer.'

We left the roadster and headed down an alley at the side of the building. It led to a gate behind the property. We scaled the wooden palisade and landed quietly in a short, walled garden.

Lights from the first and fourth floors bathed a brick patio in a golden glow. Flowerpots dotted the edges of the terrace and a set of four ornate metal chairs sat around a small cream table. Outlined starkly against the back wall of the apartment block was an elaborate, iron spiral fire escape. The lack of rust suggested it was a fairly new addition to the otherwise grand and faded facade.

We negotiated the metal steps carefully and stopped next to an old sash window on the second landing. The soft tinkle of a piano drifted from somewhere above, while the smell of freshly brewed coffee and the babble of conversation rose from the floor below.

Reid removed the lock pick set from his jacket and carved a hole in the glass with a small, circular diamond cutter. He reached through the opening and thumbed the internal lock. There was a soft click.

It took both of us to lift open the heavy wooden frame of the sash window; several layers of paint had glued it solidly to the casing. The cords and counterbalances creaked faintly in the night when the pane finally moved in its runners. We climbed through the narrow gap and entered the building. We straightened and remained still while our vision adjusted to the darkness.

A security light illuminated a common stairwell to our left. On the other side of it, a passage ran parallel to the corridor we stood in. There were four apartments on each floor, two at the front and two at the rear of the building. We headed for the one that faced onto the cul-de-sac.

As we passed the apartment on our right, the door opened quietly on well-oiled hinges. An old woman in a white night-dress appeared on the threshold and squinted at us.

'Is someone there?' she said in a frail voice, her tone hesitant. 'Is that you, Hubert?'

Reid and I froze on the landing. I held my breath, aware that she only had to raise her hand to touch my face. Tense seconds passed. The old woman finally released a sigh and closed the door. We carried on down the corridor.

Silence greeted us outside Strauss's apartment. I tried the door handle. It twisted easily in my grip. I glanced at Reid. He was already reaching for the Glock. I slid the wakizashi from its scabbard and pushed the door open with the tip of the blade.

The interior of the apartment was inky black and still as a tomb. The air was stifling and overlaid with a faint stench of decay. We stopped just beyond the threshold.

The low, rectangular outlines of furniture appeared in the gloom. To the left, the grand, ceiling-high French windows loomed behind sets of heavy, brocaded curtains.

Reid switched on a pen torch. Dust motes danced in the beam as he swept it across the vast space.

A drawing room occupied half the width of the apartment. Tastefully decorated with an eclectic collection of old and opulent furnishings, it boasted a beautiful vaulted ceiling and a stone fireplace. French doors at the rear opened onto a kitchen diner.

We traced the smell of putrefaction to a garbage holder and the half-open fridge; the internal light cast a pale glow on the linoleum floor and partially illuminated the kitchen cabinets. Inside, the shelves were well stocked. A glass of rancid orange juice stood forlornly on the countertop.

On the other side of the drawing room, a corridor led to a master bedroom, a bathroom, a study, and a small second bedroom.

Although the apartment bore a general air of untidiness to be expected of a busy scientist, it also showed signs of having been searched. The hard drive of the computer in the study had been wiped clean. Documents lay scattered within wallets and folders inside the drawers of the writing desk and the filing cabinets that lined the walls. The tomes in the bookcases had been put back haphazardly. Even the messages had been deleted from the answer phone in the drawing room, while a digital camera with its internal memory erased lay on the coffee table.

'You notice the pictures?' said Reid.

I nodded, anxiety knotting my stomach.

Dotted around the apartment were dozens of photo frames. They were all empty. Only the paintings had been left untouched.

'Lucas.'

We were inside the master bedroom. I looked to where Reid had directed the torch beam. On the rear wall of the chamber, next to an oil canvas reproduction of Degas's 1888 "Dancers", was a spattering of dried blood.

A small, perfectly round hole had been punched into the plaster scant inches from it. It looked very much like the entry point of a bullet.

'Crovir Hunters?' said Reid.

'Probably.' My gaze shifted from the crimson droplets to the Degas. I crossed the floor to the bed and lifted the painting off the wall. There was a small, faded rectangular mark on the rear of the gilded frame. I traced it with the tips of my fingers, my mind racing.

Something had been taped to the back of the painting.

I peered at the space behind the headboard. It was empty. I put the painting back on the wall, knelt, and looked under the bed. Reid dropped down on the opposite side and shone the torch across the floorboards.

The light glinted off a small object half obscured by a dust-covered suitcase. I reached for it.

My fingers closed around something hard and cold. I lifted it to the light. It was a key attached to a strip of adhesive tape. Bloody fingerprints covered the metal. Beneath them were engraved the letters CNRS and the numbers 129.

CHAPTER SEVEN

WE LEFT THE APARTMENT AND TOOK THE STAIRS TO THE ground floor. A row of letterboxes flanked the wall just inside the front doors of the building. There was mail inside H.E. Strauss's box.

It was past one in the morning when we returned to Gustav's place. I switched on a table lamp in the drawing room and we went through the handful of letters we had collected from the *11ème arrondissement*. They were all addressed to *Monsieur* or *Professeur* Hubert Eric Strauss. Most of them were bills. There were a scattering of invitations to forthcoming international symposiums and conferences on molecular genetics.

Something slipped out from the pile of correspondence and fell on the floor. I picked up a small, rectangular board.

It was a postcard from Italy. Dated twelve days ago, it depicted the Faraglioni rock formations off the Amalfi coast and was signed "*A*". The message read *See you soon* in neat, feminine writing.

'No phone calls have been made from Strauss's apartment in the last month,' said Reid, studying one of the bills. 'Before that, there were twelve calls made to the same number in the space of a week.'

I studied the figures that preceded the telephone number. 'That's a Swiss dialing code.'

One of the letters was from Strauss's bank. It confirmed that a sum of 100,000 Euros had been transferred to an account in Zurich, as per the professor's instructions. The transaction had taken place four weeks ago.

Reid raised an eyebrow. 'Does this mean he's in Switzerland?'

'I don't know.' I took out the key we had found in Strauss's apartment and studied it thoughtfully. Judging from the bullet hole and the blood, the professor was in more than a little trouble. I had been hoping to find some answers in Paris. Instead, I only had more questions. 'I think we should take a look at the Gif-sur-Yvette campus tomorrow.'

Having decided it would be best to leave Paris before Sunday traffic clogged up the arteries of the city, we caught a few hours' sleep and were up again at dawn.

'Are you sure you can't stay longer?' Gustav asked while he cleared the breakfast table. The Frenchman looked despondent at the news of our early departure.

'I'm afraid not,' I replied with an apologetic smile. 'The trail will get cold if we leave it any longer.'

We bade goodbye to the retired detective and left the *13ème arrondissement* shortly before eight. I drove west across the River Seine and soon joined the N118 highway. Twenty minutes later, I pulled up outside a 24-hour cafe with internet facilities. I searched for maps of the CNRS campus while Reid looked up the NCIC database and Interpol's website.

'Well, you haven't made the wanted lists yet,' he muttered after a while.

'Glad to hear it,' I said.

Located in the Science Valley of the Yvette River some

twenty miles south-west of the French capital, at the gateway to
the *Parc de la Vallée de Chevreuse*, the town of Gif-sur-Yvette was
home not only to the *Centre Nationale de la Recherche Scientifique*
but also the CEA, *Commissariat à l'Énergie Atomique*, *Supélec*,
L'École Supérieure d'Électricité; the LGEP, *Laboratoire de Génie Élec-
trique de Paris*; the *Centre Nationale d'Études*; and the National
Police Academy. The CNRS campus was on a one-hundred-and-
sixty-acre estate located within the boundaries of the town
itself. At nine in the morning, the grounds were practically
deserted.

I parked the car under a row of trees and we crossed a lawn
toward a four-story edifice that housed the laboratories of the
CGM. It took a couple of minutes to override the security
system at the rear of the building. Once inside, we found an
administration office on the ground floor. A staff board on the
wall indicated that Strauss worked in a laboratory two levels up.
We took the stairs and soon entered a corridor tiled in white
and smelling strongly of antiseptic.

'This kinda reminds me of a hospital,' said Reid as we
walked down the cool, clinical hallway.

'Uh-huh,' I said, glancing at the names on the doors.

'I hate hospitals.'

'Sure,' I murmured.

'Why do I get the feeling you're not really listening to me?'

We turned into a side passage. A door bearing a nameplate
engraved with the words "Prof. H.E. Strauss" stood at the end.

A lab lay beyond it. Bar the complex machines that crowded
the cluttered worktops and the humming fridge cabinets lining
the walls, it was empty. A dry whiteboard filled most of the
back wall; it was covered with complicated numbers, diagrams,
and equations joined by interlinking arrows and question
marks. Next to the board, a second door opened onto a small
office.

Paper overflowed from the in-tray on the desk. There was a

print of Gustav Klimt's "The Kiss" on the wall, with a year planner overrun with memos hanging lopsidedly to the right of it. An empty picture frame rested next to a cactus plant on the windowsill.

A search of the drawers and filing cabinets produced nothing useful; there was no mention of CNRS 129 anywhere. Loose wires on the floor and a faded rectangular area on the desk indicated Strauss had had a computer in the office.

'This key has got to be for something here,' I said, staring around the room.

'Well, whatever it is, it ain't in this place,' Reid retorted with a shrug.

We left the lab and explored the rest of the building. A corridor on the ground floor led us to a staff changing room filled with rows of lockers. My steps quickened as I strode along the aisles, eyes scanning the closets for the number 129.

I found it halfway down the third row. The door hung loosely from its hinges. It was glaringly empty.

Reid stopped beside me. 'Looks like someone beat us to it.'

I frowned. Something about the door did not look quite right. I traced the metal numbers with a finger.

'What is it?' said Reid.

I studied the faint, fresh marks in the heads of the screws that secured the middle number with rising excitement. 'This isn't the right one.'

We found locker 139 in the next aisle.

I tried the key, my heart thumping in my chest. The lock opened with a faint click. 'He swapped the numbers around.' I opened the door and reached for the slim, brown package taped to the roof of the locker.

'Smart guy,' Reid said with a grunt. 'He must have known they were after him.'

The envelope contained a memory stick and a journal. There was an inscription on the inside page of the diary.

'"*Hope this brings you inspiration*", signed "*A*",' I quoted.

'This the same "*A*" from the postcard?' said Reid.

'Handwriting looks the same.'

The first entry in the journal was dated two years previously. I leafed through the well-thumbed pages.

The diary was a chronicle of Hubert Strauss's work over a period of twenty months. It also seemed to be a reflection of the scientist's state of mind and life during that time; numerous red-inked annotations and diagrams crowded the margins, with memos, letters, and email printouts stuck randomly between the sheets.

A metallic clink sounded outside the door of the locker room. It opened a second later. The sound of shuffling feet and the squeak of wheels followed. Someone started to whistle under their breath.

I motioned Reid around the aisle. We circled the room until we reached the open doorway and saw a janitor mopping the floor to the right, his back to us. We left silently and exited the building through the rear door.

In the hour since we had arrived at the campus, the place had come to life. Peals of laughter and the chatter of conversation rose toward the blue skies; a group of students had laid picnic baskets under some elm trees and were making the most of the autumn sun.

We turned and headed for the car. It took a few seconds to detect the men tracking us.

'I make four,' I said in a low voice, hands hanging loosely at my sides. I could feel the weight of the guns under my coat.

We were still some hundred and fifty feet from the roadster.

'There's a fifth guy behind the oak tree up on the left,' Reid observed casually.

Tension hummed through my limbs. I kept my expression neutral. 'They must have been watching Strauss's office.'

'How do you wanna play this?' said Reid.

I shrugged. 'Divide and conquer is always a good plan.'

His shoulders stiffened. 'On the count of three?'

I nodded.

We parted ways seconds later and headed briskly in opposite directions.

The Crovir Hunters' bullets cracked through the air close on our heels. We turned and exchanged fire.

Shouts of surprise and alarm rose from the bewildered students. More gunshots echoed under the trees. Panic gripped the campus.

By the time the screams started, Reid and I were racing toward the car.

I skidded behind a tree and stood rock still while rounds thudded into the other side of the trunk. Reid sank to his heels in the lee of a van to my left.

'Cover me!' I shouted.

He nodded, dropped to one knee, and let out a volley of shots.

I bolted for the Jaguar. Bullets peppered the ground behind me, splatters of soil striking the back of my legs. I leapt over a low crash barrier, landed on my feet, and kept running. A figure appeared to the right. I raised my gun and squeezed the trigger, still sprinting toward the roadster.

I was about twelve feet from the vehicle when a whistling noise suddenly rose behind me. I glanced over my shoulder.

The world exploded in a wave of bright light and deafening sound.

The blast from the rocket-propelled grenade lifted me in the air and hurled me onto the hood of the car. I felt a couple of ribs crack on impact and lay stunned for seconds, a shrill buzz roaring in my ears while I slowly blinked at the blue skies.

Reid's voice finally made it through the noise in my head.

'Get up! *Move!*' he barked.

I felt him drag me off the Jag and push me inside the car. I shook my head dazedly while he cleared the bonnet and vaulted into the passenger seat.

'*Drive goddamnit!*' he shouted.

A spray of bullets scored the ground next to the tires. One round ricocheted off the wing mirror. I turned the key frantically in the ignition and looked out the window. Something glinted in the grass several feet away.

It was the memory stick.

'Where the hell are you—' Reid yelled behind me.

I was already out of the door and lunging for the silver rectangle. My fingers were inches from it when a bullet slammed into the ground next to my hand.

Reid leaned out of the passenger window and returned fire over my head while I scrambled backward into the driver's seat. Somewhere to the right, a panicked scream was abruptly cut off.

I blinked sweat and blood from my eyes, engaged the transmission, grabbed the steering wheel, and floored the accelerator. Flames flashed up ahead a second later. I spun the car to the left.

Reid cursed as he slammed into the door.

The second explosion blasted a young tree from its roots and lifted the roadster's rear tires several inches off the blacktop. The suspension groaned as the vehicle slammed down onto the asphalt. I shifted gear and headed toward the north exit of the campus.

Reid arched an eyebrow. 'That was fun.'

'They're getting reckless. Whatever's in there, they want it bad.' I indicated the journal by my feet.

'You're probably right.' He looked over his shoulder. 'By the way, not that I'm rushing you or anything, but it looks like they're closing on us.'

I glanced at the rearview mirror. There were two black SUVs on our tail.

'Hang on,' I said grimly.

The Jag was doing a hundred and forty kilometers per hour when we hit the road. The tires screamed as I took a sharp right, narrowly missing a caravan in the opposite lane. A horn blasted the air, followed by a litany of colorful language. Flocks of birds took off from the trees that flanked the carriageway, their wings thumping the air noisily.

The SUVs shot out onto the asphalt behind us.

Something pinged off the trunk of the roadster seconds later.

Reid frowned over his shoulder. 'Are they shooting at us?'

I swerved around a horse trailer and looked at the wing mirror. 'Uh-huh.'

He sighed. 'Damn it. I hate shooting in the wind.' He rammed another magazine into the Glock and leaned out the window.

The SUVs were forty feet behind and closing fast. Reid steadied the gun in both hands and squeezed the trigger twice. A distant bang rose behind us. 'Gotcha!' He grinned and slid back in the seat.

The blown-out front tire destabilized the first SUV. It spun, flipped over twice, and crashed into the guardrail with a harsh shriek of tearing metal. The second SUV swung around the wreckage with a high-pitched screech of tires. It teetered on two wheels, righted itself at the last second, and resumed its deadly pursuit.

A couple more bullets struck the trunk of the Jag. I winced.

Reid hung out of the window and emptied the Glock. 'Can this thing go any faster?' he said conversationally.

My eyes dropped to the speedometer. We were already doing one hundred and ninety kilometers per hour. 'Not really.'

'That's a shame. They just lifted the rocket launcher out through the sunroof.'

I stared at the rearview mirror and saw the black mouth of

the weapon on top of the pursuing vehicle. My knuckles whitened on the steering wheel. 'That's not good.'

'No, it sure ain't,' retorted Reid.

My gaze shifted to the road ahead. We were coming up to a roundabout. To the right of it lay the entrance to Soleil Synchrotron, a scientific facility co-owned by the CNRS and the CEA and dedicated to advanced research on sub-atomic particle acceleration. I shifted gears and swerved sharply.

The grenade missed the roadster by a couple of feet and took out the Synchrotron signboard, a huge chunk off the grassy knoll in the middle of the junction, and part of the road beyond it. Clumps of soil rained down around us and clouded the windshield. I switched on the wipers.

Reid absent-mindedly dusted dirt off his arm. 'At this rate, if they don't kill us, *you* will.' He looked behind. 'So, you got any other bright ideas? 'cause these guys ain't going anywhere fast.'

I studied the layout of the road, heart pounding in my chest. A peek in the rearview mirror showed the SUV thirty feet behind and closing.

'Yes. Put your seat belt on.'

Five seconds later, I crossed the central reservation and accelerated toward a truck in the opposite lane. The driver's eyes widened behind the windscreen of his cabin. He gaped and spun his steering wheel to his left.

The roadster raised a cloud of dirt and gravel as it skidded into the lay-by. The tail of the truck swung perilously close to the Jag's front bumper before spinning lazily through a one-hundred-and-eighty-degree turn. Bales of hay fell off the flatbed and scattered across both lanes.

The truck tilted on its wheels before coming to a juddering halt in the middle of the road.

The SUV hurtled into one of the haystacks, skidded wildly, and smashed head on into a utility pole. Flames erupted from beneath the hood and engulfed the front of the vehicle. The doors opened and dark-clad figures stumbled out.

I steered the roadster onto the road and drove off.

Reid observed the chaos behind us before turning to me. 'That was a bit wild.'

I shrugged. 'It worked.'

'You're bleeding again.' He indicated his right temple.

I wiped the blood dripping down the side of my head and winced at the stabbing pain radiating from my broken ribs. I merged with the traffic heading south on the N118 moments later and headed east on the A5 motorway.

It had just gone noon when I pulled into the town of Troyes. We grabbed something to eat and went in search of a cyber cafe. The incident at Gif had already made national news.

'One student has been shot dead and three more were seriously injured on the campus of the CNRS in Gif-sur-Yvette, following an incident earlier this morning. According to the police, gunfire erupted during an apparent altercation between a number of unidentified men just after nine-thirty. Judging from the scenes of devastation around us, the use of some sort of incendiary device or bomb has not been excluded by the authorities. The men implicated in the disturbance subsequently fled the scene in separate vehicles. Two black Freelanders with unknown registrations have since been recovered within a two-mile radius of the campus. Both have been involved in crashes. One police source reports that although a significant amount of blood was evident at the sites of the accidents, no bodies have been recovered from the vehicles.'

The live feed had been shot on the Gif campus. The building housing the laboratories of the *Centre de Génétique Moléculaire* dominated the background. Behind the female presenter, a police cordon enclosed a large area of the lawn. Two coroner officers were zipping a body into a bag under the elm trees.

'Police are still looking for the third vehicle involved in this incident, thought to be a black vintage Jaguar. So far no information is available on its possible whereabouts.' The female presenter faltered. Her hand rose to her earpiece and she listened intently for several seconds. Her eyes widened. 'I have just received some breaking news from my colleague in Paris,' she continued excitedly. 'The body of internationally renowned scientist Professor Hubert Eric Strauss was discovered in his apartment in the *11ème arrondissement* two hours ago. Professor Strauss, who worked at the *Centre de Génétique Moléculaire* on this very campus behind me, is thought to have been the victim of a botched burglary. The police in Paris have confirmed that one of the professor's neighbors reported seeing a black vintage car at the scene of the crime late last night.'

We watched the images on the computer silently.

'Hunters put the body there?' said Reid finally.

'Probably.'

I gazed blindly at the elm trees on the screen. The immortals were more than desperate; the mounting body count was proof of this. The anger simmering in my gut flared at the thought of Olsson.

'I don't get it,' said Reid. 'If he's the one they were looking for, why kill him?'

I tapped a finger on the cover of the late professor's journal. 'Maybe it wasn't him they were after.'

Reid looked at me blankly.

'I think whatever they're searching for has something to do with his work.'

He rubbed his chin. 'Well, we've got his journal.'

'Yeah. But we lost the memory stick,' I said with a grimace.

'I still don't see what any of this has to do with you.' A sigh of frustration left his lips. 'Where's the connection?'

I frowned. Things were getting more dangerous by the hour. Yet, I felt I was still far from finding any answers.

The monitor in front of Reid flickered. He studied it for a couple of seconds. 'I'm afraid I've got more bad news.'

I stiffened. 'What?'

He indicated the display. 'Looks like we both made the wanted lists.'

I leaned across and studied the fuzzy mug shots on the NCIC and Interpol pages. 'We always look that disreputable?' I said, arching an eyebrow.

Reid shrugged. 'Depends on the time of day, but yeah, mostly we do.'

A name on the Interpol site drew my eyes. The agent assigned to our case was one Christophe Lacroix.

'I don't know whether to call it coincidence or irony,' said Reid flatly.

I glanced at him. 'Do you need to tell Sam?'

Samantha was Reid's ex-wife. Despite their divorce five years ago, they still got along well. I suspected they would get back together at some point in the future.

'No, it'll only make things worse,' he muttered. 'Besides, they might trace the call.' He struck a match and lit a cigarette.

I looked past Reid at the bearded colossus behind the cafe's reception desk. 'I don't think you're allowed to smoke in here.' I flashed a smile at the man; his brow knitted into a scowl.

Reid inhaled and blew smoke rings toward the ceiling. 'It's been a busy day. Anyone who wants to stop me from having a light is gonna have to kill me first and pry this from my cold, dead fingers.'

The bearded giant had rounded the desk and was heading our way like an unmoored tugboat.

I shut down the computers, rose, and dragged Reid off the chair. 'Come on, let's get out of here. We need to find a new set of wheels. And I've got a call to make.'

I found a public phone booth two streets down from the cafe and rang Gustav Lacroix.

'What's going on?' said the old detective in a troubled voice. 'Are you all right?'

'I'm sorry. We never meant to cause you any trouble.' I hesitated. 'Tell your nephew that not everything is as it seems.' I disconnected, a pang of guilt stabbing through my chest.

We bought a secondhand Audi A4 from a dealership just outside Troyes. Reid followed me in the new car as I headed down a series of small country roads in the Jag. I left the roadster under a dusty tarpaulin in an abandoned barn tucked in some woods at the end of a rutted lane. I would call Vauquois at our next stop and tell him of its whereabouts.

'Where to now?' said Reid once we were back on the motorway.

I glanced at him, my grip light on the steering wheel of the Audi. 'We're going to Zurich.'

Silence followed. 'We checking out Strauss's bank?' he said finally.

'Among other things.' I gazed at the road. 'The number Strauss was calling is also in Zurich.'

'You think this "*A*" person is there as well?'

'I'm betting on it.'

~

CHAPTER EIGHT

WE DROVE THROUGH BASEL AND FOLLOWED THE LIMMAT River to Zurich, reaching the city late in the afternoon.

Known as the cultural capital of Switzerland, the political center being Berne, Zurich started life as a tax collection point on the border of the Roman Province of Gallia Belgica, in the first century AD. It passed through the hands of several Holy Roman Emperors during the ensuing centuries before finally becoming part of the independent Swiss Confederation in 1291. Immortals had a heavy hand in molding the future of the country, as they did in so many others throughout the history of mankind.

I exited the motorway west of the river, crossed over the Wipkingerstrasse, and pulled into the parking lot of a hotel on the Limmat Quai. The room we booked faced over the water, the windows offering a glimpse of the lake as well as sweeping views of the Limmat and two of the city's most famous churches, the Fraumünster and St. Peter. Reid went in search of cigarettes while I used the hotel's internet room to access an online reverse search database. Minutes later, I had an address for the Zurich phone number Strauss had called repeatedly over a month ago. It was in Riesbach, an affluent district on the banks of the lake.

We left the hotel shortly after six and headed east on the Uto Quai.

The drive to the Bellerivestrasse was short and uneventful. The harsh cries of black-headed gulls and the piping calls of terns echoed across the lake in the crisp evening air. To the south, fading sunlight glistened on the distant peaks of the Alps.

The house was a fairytale, three-story Swiss cottage, complete with shingled roof, bracketed eaves, gables, and decorative wood trimmings. Located on a low rise at the end of a residential street, it had spectacular views over the water.

Night soon fell and traffic slowed. The shores of the lake came alive with the lights of the city. The cottage remained dark and lifeless.

We left the car at eight and ascended the slope at the rear of the property. Hazel bushes and honeysuckle shrubs formed a hedge around the yard, and the air was rich with the sweet smell of late-blooming flowers.

Lights came on in the neighboring house as we stepped onto the edge of the lawn. We waited in the shadows and watched an elderly man close the curtains on the ground floor. Seconds later, we were on the steps of the rear porch. A pair of sturdy walking boots and a lone umbrella stood on the wooden deck.

Reid slipped the lock pick out of his pocket and went to work on the door. Beyond it, we found a kitchen full of vivid autumnal colors. The countertops were tidy and clean. A single, cold mug of black coffee stood by the sink. From the mould coating the inside, it had been there for days. The cupboards were well stocked, while the fridge and bin stood empty.

The rest of the house was decorated in pale pastels. Oil paintings dotted the walls and corridors. An eclectic collection of antique furniture crowded the rooms, their dark lines broken by a scattering of bright throws and cushions. On the second floor, a large, black, French Rococo bed dominated a distinctly feminine bedroom. The wardrobe and drawers were full of women's clothing, and the air smelled of oranges.

A study lined with bookcases looked out onto the lake, an imposing antique Louis XVI desk occupying the space in front of the main window. A careful search of the drawers and wall cabinets provided no clues as to the identity of the owner of the house. There was a letter on the doormat inside the front door. Addressed generically to the owner of the property, it confirmed that all the post had been diverted to a private mailbox in Geneva.

Of the dozens of picture frames that crowded the windowsills, walls, and console tables around the house, not one contained a single photograph.

It was Reid who found the metal and glass casing wedged in a gap between the floorboards in an upstairs closet.

'This looks old,' he said, handing it to me.

My lips curved in a faint smile as I traced the antique plating with my fingers.

'Yes, it is. It's a daguerreotype.' I looked up into Reid's blank face. 'It's a style of photography dating back to the early nineteenth century,' I explained.

It had been several decades since I had last seen one of them. I turned the frame over and studied the picture under the glass. Though the image had faded with the passage of time, I could still make out the two figures in the photograph.

The first one was a tall, thin man with graying hair. Dressed in a double-breasted frock coat worn over a buff waistcoat and trousers, he had a top hat on his head and held an ivory-headed cane in his hand. The second figure was a little girl in a pale, high-waisted gown, complete with pelisse. Dark curls peeked out from beneath her bonnet and framed a pair of pale, wide eyes. She was holding on tightly to the man's left hand.

They stood in front of a half-finished St.Vitus Cathedral, within the grounds of Prague Castle.

'This original?' said Reid.

'Yes.' I examined the man and the little girl for silent seconds before slipping the frame inside my coat.

Although I was certain I had never met either of them before, a strange sense of recognition hovered at the edge of my consciousness.

We left the house and returned to the hotel. Once in the room, I took out Strauss's journal and laid it on the coffee table. We had not had time to study it yet.

'Do you understand any of this stuff?' said Reid after we had pored over it for half an hour.

'Not really,' I replied, dismayed.

The pages of the journal were filled with scientific jargon. Occasionally, a series of exclamation marks followed a particularly complex paragraph. To complicate matters further, the last pages of the journal had been encrypted. Neither of us could decipher the code.

'This is interesting,' said Reid minutes later. He held out a copy of an email.

It had been sent two years ago by the President and CEO of GeMBiT Corp and was addressed to Strauss at his UPMC mailbox. The content was brief: Burnstein was offering his congratulations to Strauss on successfully securing a research grant worth ten million dollars for his project on advanced cell cycle control and DNA transposition.

Reid whistled softly. 'That's a lot of money.'

I stared at the figure. 'Yes, it is.'

We found another email from Burnstein near the back of the journal. This one was dated three months ago. The message was short and conveyed an undeniable element of urgency:

Burnstein was requesting an immediate meeting with Strauss to study the latest results of his research and had demanded access to the laboratory samples that the scientist had been working on.

Strauss had forwarded the email to a third party on a separate server. The internet address of the mail recipient consisted of a series of numbers followed by the letters *fgcz.uzh.ch*. Above Burnstein's message, the scientist had written, "The Americans are getting restless. We need to talk."

The reply to the email was encrypted.

'Isn't this a Swiss email address?' Reid asked, brow puckering.

The letters looked vaguely familiar. I reached for the document wallet containing copies of Strauss's research papers and leafed through the contents.

'It stands for the Functional Genomics Center of the University of Zurich.' I showed Reid the article featuring the FGCZ logo. There was a name next to it.

It was Prof. A.M. Godard.

'So, we now know who the elusive "A" is,' murmured Reid. 'Isn't the University of Zurich close to here?' He rose and brought the map on his bed over to the table.

'There's another campus in Irchel Park, to the north of the city.' I indicated another section of the map. 'Let's see what we can find at the bank first.'

The next day, we left the hotel early and went to buy some suits.

Strauss's bank was located on the Bahnhofstrasse, one of the most exclusive shopping avenues in Europe. At almost a mile long, it was also home to the Zurich Hauptbahnhof, Switzerland's largest railway station. We observed the bank from a newspaper kiosk across the road before crossing the busy avenue and stepping through revolving doors.

The bank's decor was pale and fairly clinical. An armed

guard stood unobtrusively next to a potted palm tree to the left of the airy lobby. He scanned us briefly before resuming his stoic inspection of the street life outside.

The woman behind the reception desk looked up with an inquisitive smile when we crossed the cream marble floor toward her.

I smiled back. 'We need to see the director please,' I said in Swiss German.

'Do you have an appointment?' she asked pleasantly.

'I'm afraid not.' I removed a badge from the inside pocket of my suit and showed it to her. 'This is a police matter.'

The woman's smile became strained as she studied the insignia. She lifted a telephone handset and spoke softly in the mouthpiece. A short conversation ensued. She placed the receiver in its cradle and indicated an artfully arranged circle of seats to the right of the vestibule.

'If you would please take a seat? The Director will be with you immediately,' she murmured politely.

"Immediately" turned out to be a quarter of an hour later. By then, Reid had loosened his tie and paced around the lobby several times.

'I need a smoke,' he explained at my stare.

'You had one an hour ago.'

He gave me a blank look. 'What does that have to do with anything?'

I sighed and smoothed out the wrinkles in my coat. Just as I was about to rise from the seat and approach the reception desk, a musical ting sounded from the end of the foyer.

'I am extremely sorry. I was in an important meeting,' said the man who walked out of the lift to greet us. 'My name is Florent Mueller. I am the Executive Director of the bank. How may I be of assistance?'

Muller was short and dapper. He had a firm handshake and smelled faintly of menthol.

'I am Agent Petersen of Swiss Interpol. This is FBI Agent Barnes.' I indicated Reid. 'We're investigating the murder of one of your clients, a Professor H.E. Strauss. He transferred a substantial sum of money to your bank a fortnight ago. We would like to study the details of the account. We're especially interested in any transactions that may have transpired on it since then.'

Mueller glanced at Reid's rumpled suit and carefully studied our identification.

Qin Lee had done a first-rate job; the IDs were as good as the real things.

The director hesitated. 'I take it you have obtained the appropriate legal document to access the account?'

I reached inside my coat and produced a perfect forgery of a lifting order by the Prosecutor-General, granting Swiss Interpol access to the bank accounts of Professor H.E. Strauss; I had had Qin Lee fax it through to the hotel last night.

Mueller inspected the paper and turned to speak to the receptionist briefly. He indicated the lift. 'After you.'

We stepped out onto the fifth floor of the building a moment later. A man stood waiting for us inside the director's office.

'This is Gustav Allenbach, our Head of Accounts,' said Mueller in heavily accented English. He turned to Allenbach. 'These gentlemen are from the International Police. They would like some information on one of our clients.'

Allenbach made a copy of the lifting order before opening a laptop on the desk. He typed and clicked on the keyboard and pad before swiveling the screen around for us to look at.

'I'm afraid there's not a lot to see,' he said apologetically. 'Hubert Strauss opened an account with us two months ago, with an opening balance of two hundred and fifty thousand Euros. He transferred another one hundred thousand Euros into the account four weeks later. No further transactions have been made since then.'

I glanced at Reid with a sinking feeling. It looked like this was going to be another dead end.

Allenbach frowned as he studied the monitor. 'I do, however, note that the safety deposit box was accessed by the co-account holder last Friday.'

'The safety deposit box?' I repeated, staring blankly at the man.

'Yes. It was opened at the same time as the account,' said Allenbach.

'Who's the co-account holder?' said Reid.

I knew the name before Allenbach said it. 'Professor A.M. Godard.'

A light rain was falling across the city when we exited the bank a short while later.

Reid hunched his shoulders against the cool autumnal wind sweeping down the avenue. 'Want to check out the university?'

'Yeah.'

A quick internet search that morning had confirmed that the Functional Genomics Center was on the Irchel campus. We took the tram toward Stettbach and got off in Milchbuck. From there it was a short walk across the park to the university.

A site map showed the location of the FGCZ on the first floor of a building to the north of the grounds. The entrance foyer was busy and no one paid us any attention as we headed for the stairs. One flight up, a glass security door appeared in our path.

A couple of students sauntered down the steps from the floor above. They glanced at us curiously as we hesitated on the landing.

'We can't exactly open this one without being seen,' Reid muttered, his eyes following the pair disappearing toward the ground floor. 'We could always break the fire glass.' He indicated the alarm on the wall.

I touched his arm. 'Wait.'

A young woman was approaching the security door from the other side. She had a stack of folders in her arms and was reaching distractedly for the access badge at her waist. The door beeped and swung open. We moved silently aside as she crossed the threshold, head cast down.

I took a step toward her.

A gasp left her lips. The files fell from her arms.

'Oh, I'm sorry. I didn't mean to startle you,' I murmured apologetically. 'Let me give you a hand.' I smiled and hunched down to help her gather the scattered folders.

The woman flushed and stammered a quick 'Thank you!' in Swiss German before dashing down the stairs. I watched her until she vanished from view.

'Charming,' Reid muttered. The access card he had lifted off her waist dangled from his hand.

We swiped through the security door and entered a wide corridor. Twenty feet in, a floor-to-ceiling glass wall appeared on our left. Beyond it was a large laboratory. Figures in white coats sat behind the crowded worktops.

A door with the nameplate "Godard" affixed to it stood at the end of the passage. It was locked. Reid had just slipped the lock pick set from his coat when a voice called out behind us.

'Can I help you?'

I turned and studied the speaker. It was a woman in a white coat. She stood in the doorway to the lab, a suspicious expression on her face. A tall man with blond dreadlocks came up behind her and blinked at us through thick bifocals.

'We're looking for Professor Godard.' I held up the badge and took a few steps toward her.

The woman studied the ID. 'And this is with regards to?' she said, unfazed.

'It's a rather delicate matter, I'm afraid. We're investigating the death of a scientist in France, a Professor Hubert Strauss. We believe he was a friend of Professor Godard.'

The woman glanced at the man with the dreadlocks. A troubled expression flashed in their eyes.

'I'm sorry,' she said. 'We haven't seen or heard from Anna in a fortnight.' She bit her lip. 'We know she had traveling plans, but she should have been back in the lab this week.'

Unease trickled through my mind at her words. 'Is this normal behavior for Professor Godard?' I said, keeping my tone neutral.

The woman shook her head. 'No. Anna is very conscientious. This is most unlike her.' She hesitated. 'Do you think her absence is linked to the death of that French scientist?'

'I'm afraid I don't know,' I replied truthfully.

A rumble rose behind the woman. I looked at the man with the dreadlocks.

'Hmm, I just saw her assistant, Helena,' he muttered.

'Helena was here?' the woman squealed. 'Why didn't you tell me?'

The man flushed and pushed the bifocals up his nose. 'I didn't think it was important.'

'When was this?' I asked.

He shrugged. 'Not that long ago. Ten, fifteen minutes maybe.'

'Did she say anything?'

The man shuffled his feet and looked at the woman for reassurance. She nodded encouragingly.

'She mentioned she was going to meet with someone at the Hauptbahnhof,' he murmured. 'She said not to tell anyone she'd been here today.' The last words came out in a guilty mumble. 'I think she took something from Anna's office.'

Unease turned to alarm. 'What does Helena look like?' I said urgently.

'She's tall, slim, with long blonde hair. She was wearing a cream coat and hat,' he replied. 'And she had on her green scarf today.'

We bade our goodbyes and left the building swiftly.

'You thinking what I'm thinking?' said Reid as we jogged across the park.

I nodded. 'She's probably meeting with Godard.'

We now had a name for the elusive "A". The house in Riesbach had to belong to her.

It took us twelve minutes to get to the Hauptbahnhof on the tram. The clock face on the station's stone facade read five minutes to noon when we entered the central hall.

The place was packed; visitors and locals milled across the crowded floor, some browsing the arcade that lined the vast space while most rushed to and from the tall archways that led to the platforms.

We were halfway across the concourse when Reid stopped and indicated the opposite end of the atrium. A blonde woman in a cream camel coat was disappearing inside a glass lift. There was a flash of green at her neck when she turned to face the closing doors.

We hurried over to the escalator. By the time we reached the bottom of the rolling steps, the woman had exited the lift and was heading briskly north along a wide passage in the shopping mall beneath the station. We fell into step behind her.

She stopped outside the window of a confectionary shop and looked around furtively before removing a cell phone from her handbag. She dialed a number and waited several seconds before starting to talk.

'Can you make out what she's saying?' I said quietly as we strolled past.

Reid could lip-read. It was a skill that had come in handy in many of our past investigations.

'Not in the language she's using,' he murmured after a while.

The woman ended the call. She stood frowning at the phone for a moment and slowly retraced her steps.

We followed her past the lifts to the other side of the shopping mall, where she turned at a junction. A flower shop came into view a short distance from the next intersection. She was about twenty feet from it when a figure stepped out from behind a pillar next to the boutique.

I caught a glimpse of soft, dark curls framing a pair of smoky eyes and felt a sudden tightening in my chest.

The woman in the camel coat lifted a hand and waved, her steps quickening. She reached inside her bag and removed a short, gray flask.

The bullet struck the center of her right temple soundlessly. Her head jerked sideways. She dropped to the ground with a thud and lay still.

A trickle of blood coursed down the side of her face and spilled into her open, unblinking eyes. The flask fell out of her limp fingers and rolled a few inches across the polished floor.

The figure next to the pillar froze.

'Helena!' she screamed a heartbeat later. An elaborate, thick, gold sun cross pendant fell out from the open neck of her black coat as she lunged forward.

Bullets whined through the air and scored the ground around her.

She darted across the floor, grabbed the metal flask, and scurried backward, a wince distorting her features as she gripped her left shoulder.

Hunters materialized from behind the concrete columns and escalators that punctuated the mall. They raised their guns and fired at the woman crouching in the shelter of the pillar, raising a cloud of chips and plaster dust from the stonework.

Reid and I started to run.

'I'll take the left!' he shouted, drawing the Glock.

I nodded and raced across the hall, the katana in one hand

and the Smith and Wesson in the other. The sound of gunshots echoed to the roof of the shopping center. Shouts of alarm and panicked screams followed within seconds.

A harsh cry suddenly erupted from my right, drowning the background noise.

'Anna!'

Another figure was making its way toward the wounded woman behind the pillar, an ivory-headed cane in hand. My eyes widened.

It was the old man from the daguerreotype.

A sharp sting suddenly bloomed on my face. I turned and fired at a Hunter on the stairs to my left. A volley of shots thudded into the floor next to me. I released the katana, grabbed the Glock 17, and raised both guns at the immortals on the opposite side of the concourse.

Smoke and the sour smell of gunpowder filled the air as we exchanged fire, empty cartridges clattering to the ground around me.

There was a flash to my right. I ducked and narrowly avoided the blade aimed at my neck. I let go of the guns and reached for the katana. I saw the Hunter's sword swing down out the corner of my eyes.

I dropped and rolled, heart thudding against my ribs.

The tip of the blade struck the ground next to my ear, raising sparks from the floor. I leapt to my feet.

The immortal hesitated, the sword raised above his head.

'The half-breed,' he hissed, recognition dawning on his face.

My lips parted in a grim smile. I moved.

Seconds after I delivered the killing blow, something struck my left leg. I looked down. A bullet had grazed my thigh. I sheathed the katana and grabbed the guns from the floor.

'Hey, I'm running out of ammo!' Reid shouted urgently on my left.

I pitched a couple of magazines across the floor toward him

and raced toward the flower shop. By the time I reached the pillar, the woman and the old man had disappeared. I looked around wildly and spotted them thirty feet from where I stood.

They were making their way swiftly toward the opposite side of the mall. A series of flashes erupted on the ground next to them.

'Get down!' I yelled.

They ducked as more bullets thudded into the polished floor inches from their feet.

I spotted the two Hunters on the other side of the concourse, took aim, and fired. The men jerked and fell against a wall.

'*Go!*' I shouted.

The pair straightened and started to run. The old man glanced over his shoulder. He froze in his tracks when he saw me and turned around.

'Lucas?' he said hoarsely. The figure next to him twisted on her heels.

I saw her face fully for the first time and felt heat flare inside my chest.

Even though pain clouded her features, there was no mistaking her; she was the woman from the black and white photograph on Burnstein's computer. I closed the distance separating us, tension and that strange feeling of recognition coursing through my veins.

'Do I know you?'

The old man opened his mouth to reply. Just then, more Hunters appeared from around the mall. Bullets crisscrossed the air between us. The gunfire drowned out his words.

The woman dragged the old man toward the escalator leading to the upper level. I followed on their heels, laying down cover fire while they struggled through the mass of people swarming for the exit. Daylight framed the opening to a bustling street at the top of the stairs. I yelled out a warning as they rushed through the doorway and merged with the teeming crowd outside.

I swore and raced after them, emerging on the thronged pavement seconds later.

The whine of an engine rose from the right. I turned and saw a black four-by-four pull out of a parking space. It maneuvered around the heavy traffic and headed for the running pair.

Instinct took over. I bolted across the sidewalk, slid over the hood of a passing car, landed on my feet in the middle of the road, and raised both guns. A clang of bells erupted behind me. I looked over my shoulder. My heart stuttered in my chest.

I caught a glimpse of rising panic on the face of the driver of the tram heading inexorably toward me and dove over the safety barrier on my right. A grunt left my lips as my hip struck the metal railing.

The four-by-four shot past me, mounted the pavement, and turned right into the 'No Entry' zone on the Bahnhofstrasse, on the heels of the old man and the woman.

The crowd on the busy strip scattered, panicked shouts soaring toward the sunny skies.

Bullets suddenly shattered the rear window of the vehicle and drew sparks from its bumper. It swerved sharply, its wing mirror grazing a lamppost. I glanced to the left.

Reid had emerged from another escalator and was racing after the four-by-four, Glock in hand.

I vaulted over the handrail, darted across the road, and kept pace with him along the opposite pavement. Blood pounded in my ears and my breaths came in short, sharp bursts.

The old man and the woman dove out from the pavement and barely missed the front bumper of the four-by-four as it weaved toward them. A second engine gunned into life behind me. I turned.

Another SUV was racing up the packed avenue toward the

couple. Tinted windows rolled down and two men leaned out of the vehicle. Muzzles glinted in the sunlight.

Time slowed. I skidded to a stop, leapt over a bench, rolled into the middle of the strip, and rose to my feet. I dropped the Glock and lifted the Smith and Wesson in both hands. Bullets flashed past my head and shoulders as the Hunters fired. I squinted, aimed, and squeezed the trigger twice.

The front right tire of the SUV blew out. The vehicle veered wildly in a squeal of burning rubber and flipped. A gasp left my lips. I threw myself to the ground.

The dark shape of the SUV passed a couple of feet above me before crashing onto the asphalt some dozen yards away. It slid on its roof in a shower of sparks and ground to a halt against a lamppost.

I pushed myself to my feet, turned, and rocked back on my heels as a hot gust of compressed air blasted down the avenue. The ground trembled beneath me. I stumbled and leaned against the bench.

One of Reid's bullets had pierced the tank of the first four-by-four. I ignored the burning wreck in the middle of the Bahn-hofstrasse and scanned the crowds through the blood dripping past my eyes.

The old man and the woman had disappeared.

There was movement beside me.

'Whoa.' Reid gazed into the muzzle of the Smith and Wesson, hands raised defensively.

I lowered the gun and fought to control the tremor in my hands.

'I think we got most of them.' He holstered the Glock. 'On the other hand, seeing as we're dealing with supernatural beings here, they'll quite likely start to pop up like daisies some time soon,' he added with a grimace. Sirens rose in the distance. 'What say we get the hell out of here?'

My heart pounded dully inside my chest. I turned and looked in the direction of the train station. I started to run.

'Hey, where're you going?' Reid shouted behind me.

I entered the main hall of the Hauptbahnhof seconds later and darted through the crowds toward the main tracks.

I found them boarding a train on the last platform.

It was pulling away when I reached it.

'Stop!' I shouted, banging on a window.

The old man turned at the sound. His eyes widened. He crossed the aisle and pushed the window down.

'Don't follow us!' he ordered harshly.

I heard Reid call out behind me. I stumbled and almost lost my footing.

'Why are the Hunters after you?' I yelled, struggling to keep pace with the moving train.

The old man did not reply immediately.

I sprinted along the platform, the gap separating us growing larger by the second.

'Please, for your own good, don't come after us,' he said finally, his words almost inaudible above the noise from the tracks. 'I could not bear to lose both of you.' His blue eyes glistened brightly in the light filtering through the glass atrium overhead.

Then, he was gone.

~

CHAPTER NINE

WE LEFT THE CHAOS AT THE HAUPTBAHNHOF AND HEADED swiftly back to the Limmat Quai. The blare of sirens filled the air behind us. Emergency vehicles raced past on the Bahnhofstrasse, flashing lights reflected in the shop windows. We kept a low profile and stayed inside the crowds.

The hotel receptionist stared when we entered the lobby a short time later; although I had done my best to clean the blood on my face, there was no masking the dirt stains on our suits.

Our room was as we had left it. I dressed the wound on my leg and we checked out moments later.

'The cops won't be far behind,' Reid warned as we drove away from the hotel. 'There were CCTV cameras all over the place.'

I remained silent and pulled into the heavy afternoon traffic.

Reid's heated gaze drilled into the side of my face. 'So, you wanna tell me what that was about back there?'

I maneuvered the car around a coach. 'The old man at the station was an immortal. I think he's a Bastian.'

Reid raised an eyebrow. 'And you know this how?'

I reached inside my coat and handed him the daguerreotype.

He studied the photograph for several seconds. 'You mean, he's the guy in the picture?'

'Yes.'

A short silence followed.

'He acted like he knew you,' said Reid. 'Have you met before?'

'No.' I hesitated. 'Most of the immortals who know of me are Hunters.'

He mulled this over. 'You think he's one of them?'

I recalled the tears in the stranger's eyes. 'I honestly don't know,' I answered truthfully.

'What about the woman?'

I glanced at him. 'I think she's the little girl in the picture.'

'Which would make her an immortal as well,' Reid stated after a beat. 'Does this mean Strauss was also an immortal, or at least aware of their existence?' He drummed his fingers on the antique photograph. 'The Crovir Hunters are after you and this woman. What's the link?'

I shrugged, a wave of lassitude washing over me.

The same questions had been going round in my head for the last half hour. I was still nowhere near grasping the possible answers.

Reid looked up from the daguerreotype and gazed out the window. 'Where're we going, anyway?'

'Vienna,' I replied. 'That's where the train was heading.'

He frowned. 'What makes you think they'll be there? They could have gotten off anywhere.'

'There's a large population of immortals in Vienna. There will be safe houses where they can hide.'

He studied me for several seconds before pulling a packet of cigarettes from his pocket. 'All right, Vienna it is then,' he muttered under his breath and struck a match.

'Look at it this way. It's been a while since we've been on a road trip.'

He looked less than impressed with this statement.

We drove east along the Alps, past Munich and Salzburg, and reached our destination in the late evening.

As one of the oldest cities on the continent, Vienna had been a popular settlement for immortals since Roman times, when it guarded the frontier of the Empire against the Germanic tribes of northern Europe. It was the capital of the Holy Roman realm in the fifteenth century and became famous for being a center of international espionage while occupied by the Allies at the end of the Second World War.

I had only been to Vienna once before. Unfortunately, my visit coincided with the Ottoman Empire's second attempt to capture the city in 1683, which ended with the Battle of Vienna following a siege that lasted two months. It was there that I first learned how to use a pistol and suffered two of my deaths in somewhat gruesome fashions. Despite its breathtaking beauty, the place still held unpleasant memories for me.

We checked into a rundown inn in Landstrasse under our fake passports and caught up with international news in a small internet cafe around the corner. The Hauptbahnhof gunfight had already made the headlines.

'Following the incident at the main railway station in Zurich today, which resulted in two deaths and several minor injuries, the City Police are searching for two male suspects in their late thirties to early forties who left the scene shortly after the disturbance,' said the evening newscaster. 'One of the victims, a female in her late twenties, has been identified as Helena Baschtanhaus, a research assistant at the FGCZ, the Functional Genomics Center of the University of Zurich. Miss Baschtanhaus died from a single gunshot wound to the head. The local police and Interpol are currently studying CCTV images from the station and from around the city close to the time of the incident. So far, there have been no official comments made on rumors that this event may be linked to yesterday's brutal attack on innocent students at the CNRS campus in Gif-sur-Yvette, in France.' The screen filled with a grainy video clip of the inside of the Hauptbahnhof. 'Another aspect of today's incident that is said to be baffling all involved in this investigation is the collection of images captured by the public on their camera phones. These show several men who had fallen after apparently suffering multiple fatal gunshot wounds rise again minutes later and walk out of the station. One source suggests that the men may have been wearing bulletproof vests, although this theory does nothing to explain the amount of blood found at the scene. And lastly, to add even more mystery to this already puzzling affair, a flock of crows seemed to have invaded the Hauptbahnhof minutes following the incident and disappeared just as rapidly moments later.'

'They don't seem to care that they've been caught on camera,' said Reid in a hard voice. 'Are immortals really that much above the law?'

'Yes, they are,' I said after a short silence. My hands were fisted tightly on my lap and my jaw ached from clenching my teeth.

Reid put a hand on my shoulder. 'You can't undo what's been done. Let's just get to the bottom of this thing before those bastards kill any more people.'

We left the cafe and boarded a rapid transit metro into the city. Moments later, we got off at Schwedenplatz.

The plaza was abuzz with activity, the street lamps and lights from the nearby bars and restaurants casting a bright glow on the waters of the Danube. A large crowd of revelers strolled along the pier, raised voices echoing in the crisp evening air.

I crossed the square and led Reid down a nondescript side street. We reached a junction and took a left into a cramped passage a few hundred feet from the canal's edge. Pockets of darkness populated the alley. The upper tiers of the buildings crowded the skyline on either side, adding to its claustrophobic feel.

Halfway along the path stood one of the oldest pubs in the city. I stopped outside the establishment and studied the oak sign above the lintel; bar a lick of paint, the facade had not changed much in the last three hundred years.

I pushed open the thick, iron-plated door and stepped across the threshold. The hubbub inside died down.

Soft lighting painted the interior walls of the tavern in muted shadows. A walrus of a man stood polishing glasses behind the bar, his head bent toward a pair of wizened figures hunched on low wooden stools. Smoke wreathed the air and hovered in a pale blanket near the low ceiling. Dozens of pairs of eyes watched us through the yellow haze.

'Are they always this friendly?' Reid muttered as we crossed the floor to a corner table. The low murmur of conversation resumed around us.

I shrugged. 'Last time I was here they used to shoot first and ask questions later, so I guess this is an improvement.'

A woman came over to take our order. 'What will it be?' she said, tucking a lock of hair impatiently behind her ear.

'Two Stiegl, please,' I replied. The level of noise dropped fractionally so that my next words practically echoed across the tavern. 'The original beer.'

The woman's eyes narrowed. 'The original Stiegl? I'm afraid it's no longer in production.'

'Really?' I smiled. 'How strange. I happen to know the owner of this place can still get his hands on them. An old stock of sorts?'

A tense silence had fallen across the tavern. Reid shifted in his seat and placed his hand lightly on his leg, inches from the Glock.

The waitress scowled and had just opened her mouth for what was likely going to be a sharp riposte when a shadow suddenly loomed behind her.

I looked up into the large, bearded face of the bartender.

'It's okay, Maria,' the man said in heavily accented English.

The woman pursed her lips and stormed off.

The bartender waited until she disappeared from earshot before turning to us with a grin. Gold teeth glinted in the gloom. 'May I help you, gentlemen?'

I studied him while the chatter of the tavern's patrons started up around us once more. 'Like I said to your barmaid, we would like two bottles of the original Stiegl.'

The man's smile did not shift. 'I'm afraid that beer is no longer in production, sir.'

Although his tone remained pleasant, I detected the flash of wariness in his gaze.

'That's strange.'

'What is it that you find strange, sir?' said the bartender politely.

'I seem to recall a substantial collection of the stuff hidden in your cellar in 1683.' I smiled. 'I believe even Commander Starhemberg knew of it.'

Count Ernst Rudiger von Starhemberg was the army commander who held Vienna with a garrison of a few thousand men against the much larger and more heavily armed Ottoman contingent during the famous siege. In acknowledgement of his accomplishments in saving the imperial capital, Leopold I, the Holy Roman Emperor at the time, promoted him to field marshal and made him a Minister of State.

The bartender went still at the mention of the commander's name.

'You're an immortal,' he said after a short silence.

I nodded.

He glanced at Reid. 'He's not,' he stated, matter-of-fact.

'It's the eyes, isn't it?' said Reid. 'There's something about the eyes.'

The bartender grinned. 'Oktav Grun, at your service.' He offered his hand.

I shook it and stifled a wince at his bear-like grip.

'We don't often see new faces around here,' the man continued in the same light-hearted tone. 'Why, this place is normally only full of old *schlingels*.'

'Rogues,' I translated at Reid's puzzled expression.

Raucous laughter rose from the shadows around the tavern.

'Maria, bring us three bottles of Stiegl!' Grun barked over his shoulder. He grabbed a chair and dragged it across the floor to the table. 'So, you were here during the Ottoman siege?' he said, sitting down heavily. The wood creaked in protest beneath his bulky frame.

'Yes, I was,' I replied with a faint smile.

Oktav nodded. 'Those were tough times.' He rolled up the sleeve on his left arm and showed us a faint, jagged scar that ran almost all the way around his biceps. 'That was from a Turkish saber. And this,' he extended one leg, 'was from the sappers during the first siege.'

The Turkish soldiers had dug extensive tunnels under the city's walls during the Ottoman siege. These underground passages had subsequently been filled with gunpowder mines and detonated in an attempt to destroy the extensive fortifications that surrounded Vienna at the time.

I observed the shallow indentation in the bartender's calf. 'You were here during both sieges?'

The Ottoman Empire's first attempt to capture the imperial Roman capital took place in 1529, well before my birth; it lasted less than a month and became known as the Siege of Vienna.

'For my sins,' the bartender said with a hearty laugh.

The beers arrived. I took a sip of the cool liquid and closed my eyes briefly while I savored the familiar, bitter taste. It brought back old memories, not all of them bad. The faces of dead friends rose in my mind.

Reid cocked an eyebrow. 'This is good.'

Oktav laughed. 'Better make the most of it. Mortals rarely get to enjoy this.'

Grun and I spent several minutes reminiscing about events during the siege. Despite the bartender's subtle questioning, I remained vague about my origins and whereabouts following the battle.

Grun finally leaned back in his chair and studied us with a thoughtful stare. 'I have a feeling you're not just tourists passing through, my friends.'

Reid and I exchanged glances.

'You're right,' I murmured.

'Why are you here, really?' said Grun.

I removed the daguerreotype from my coat and pushed it across the table. 'Do you know this man?'

The bartender's face grew shuttered as he inspected the faded picture.

'No, I don't.' He shoved the frame back toward me.

'He's a Bastian immortal,' I said in a low voice. 'I believe he's in Vienna tonight.'

The bartender's expression did not change.

'There are Crovir Hunters after him and his female companion,' I continued, unfazed. 'I suspect he'll be seeking shelter with his friends in the city.'

The chair rocked back on its hind legs as the bartender rose to his feet. 'I think you should leave,' he said coldly.

'Look, we're only trying to help,' Reid protested.

Grun frowned. 'You don't act like Hunters. On the other hand, I don't quite know what you are.' He indicated the door. 'I'm afraid I have to insist.'

We exited the tavern under the bartender's hooded gaze.

'He knows something,' said Reid.

'Yes, he does.'

'What d'you wanna do?'

I inspected the narrow lane. My gaze landed on a low building huddling in the gloom some fifty feet away. A faint light shone through the thick lead windows at the front.

'Fancy some coffee?'

The cafe proved an ideal place from which to watch the tavern. At two in the morning, the last patrons finally left the bar. Grun stood on the threshold and studied the street carefully before locking the door. Lights came on behind the windows on the first floor. A shadow moved across the glass. The lights went off moments later. Darkness shrouded the tavern. We waited ten minutes.

The door remained resolutely closed.

'Is there an exit at the rear?' said Reid after a while.

'Yes but it only leads to an enclosed backyard.' I scanned the frontage with narrowed eyes and was about to call it a night when I spotted a ghostly glow behind the small cellar window inches above the sidewalk. 'Damn!' I threw some coins on the table and raced out of the shop.

Reid followed on my heels. 'What is it?'

I skidded to a stop next to the tavern wall and squatted in front of the dark aperture below the building. 'I forgot about the underground passages!'

I closed my eyes and silently cursed my immortal mind while I sifted through memories hundreds of years old. My eyes snapped open.

I rose and bolted toward the canal.

Reid was a few yards behind me when I staggered down the embankment. A hundred feet south along the waterway, I came to a grille in the canal wall.

Reid stopped beside me. 'Isn't this the sewers?'

'Yes. It's also one of the ways into the tunnels.'

I studied the rusted bars for several seconds before grabbing a section of the grating. I pulled sharply. It came away in my hands.

'This passage has been here since before the Ottoman siege. I've used it a few times before.' I hesitated before stepping inside the hole.

Reid came through the opening after me.

'You've led a charming life, haven't you?' he muttered as water squelched beneath our boots.

Several feet in, we were engulfed in darkness. There was a soft rustle behind me as Reid reached inside his coat and pulled out the pen torch. The beam barely cut through the greasy gloom around us.

Deep beneath the cobbles and paving stones of Vienna lay an extensive and intricate labyrinth of tunnels, halls, crypts, and cellars that had been in existence since before the late Middle Ages; some had probably been there from the time the original Roman fortress of Vindobona stood on the site. In more recent history, parts of this underground city had been used as bunkers by the Germans during the Second World War.

The last time I was down here, the Turks were trying to blow up the walls around Vienna.

The temperature dropped as we ventured deeper inside the tunnels. The water level gradually subsided.

I stopped at the entrance of a side passage. 'I think this leads to the cellar under the tavern. If so, Grun would have come this way.'

Reid directed the torch downwards. Fresh black scuff marks appeared on the dry stone floor.

Grun moved surprisingly swiftly for a large man; it was another ten minutes before we caught up with him. By then, we were in the catacombs of St. Stephen's Cathedral.

Rooms stacked with bones and grinning skulls unrolled around us. We passed through crypts and vaults housing well-preserved, dusty caskets on low stone sepulchers. The air was cool but dry, courtesy of the ventilation shafts that had been built to create the steady underground climate necessary to preserve the ancient remains of those buried beneath the city.

An orange glow ahead finally alerted us to Grun's presence. We turned a corner and glimpsed the figure of the bartender outlined against the light of the flame torch he held in his hand. Reid directed the pen torch toward the floor and cupped the end in his palm to mask the beam.

Grun unlocked a grille door at the end of the corridor. He closed it behind him and started down a flight of stairs. We waited until his footsteps faded before moving forward. Reid inspected the keyhole in the grille and inserted a fine pin inside. There was a faint click from the lock mechanism.

Narrow stone steps spiraled into darkness beyond the door. They ended two floors below and gave way to a passage that gradually broadened. We followed it to a junction.

A thin stream of water coursed along the shallow grooves in the floor where the tunnel branched out into three corridors. A light dwindled at the end of the one on the far right. We headed after it.

The passage twisted and split several times over. More grille doors appeared in our path. Had it not been for the fresh tracks on the floor, we would have lost Grun's trail.

The footprints ended in front of an oak door along a stone corridor. A faded, double-headed eagle crest was engraved in the wall next to it.

I lifted a hand and slowly traced the shape with my fingertips, my heart sinking at the significance of the symbol.

'What is it?' said Reid.

'This is the coat of arms of the House of Habsburg,' I murmured.

Reid raised an eyebrow. 'And?'

'I think we're under the Hofburg Palace.'

He frowned. 'Judging from your expression, I take it that's a bad thing?'

'The Hofburg is the official residence of the President of Austria.'

'Ah.' A glum look dawned on his face. 'That's definitely bad.'

CHAPTER TEN

REID TRIED SEVERAL LOCK PICKS IN THE DOOR. THERE WAS A faint, undeniable clink after his fourth attempt. He pulled on the handle. The door refused to budge.

He scowled. 'There must be a bolt on the other side.'

I looked down the passage. 'Let's keep going.'

A second door appeared in the stone wall a hundred feet later. It had no lock.

The wooden bar behind it gave away after a few kicks.

'That's going to be a bit hard to explain if we come across any guards,' Reid muttered as he followed me across the threshold.

'It'll be the least of our problems if we meet any.'

I inspected the room we had entered. It was a rectangular cell with pale limestone walls and no other apparent exits. I crossed the floor and moved my hands over the textured surface of the stone blocks.

'What're you doing?' said Reid.

'Checking for a hidden door.'

His eyes widened. 'Seriously?'

'Buildings like these always had secret openings.'

A sigh left his lips. He joined me and started to run his fingers along the wall. 'I feel like I'm in a bad spy movie,' he muttered under his breath.

I smiled.

It took a few minutes to find the subtle oval depression in the stonework. I held my breath and pressed my fingers against the shallow indent.

A section of the wall swung inward with a low grinding noise.

Reid's eyebrows rose. 'Well, what'd you know?'

The opening was just about wide enough for one person to squeeze through, which was the way it had been designed; the cell was a safe room where the nobles who lived in the palace could hide if enemies ever attacked.

A corridor lay on the other side.

Grun's footprints had all but faded on the stone floor. We followed the dwindling tracks and came to an empty chamber. I stiffened when I saw the fresh cigarette butts littering the floor. A gas camping stove stood in a corner of the room. A flurry of footmarks smudged the dirt on the ground.

My pulse quickened. We were close.

We passed a further two rooms before reaching a door. Yellow light flickered through the thin gap at the bottom. A low rumble of conversation rose from the other side.

I motioned to Reid. He dipped his chin, drew the Glock, and stood to the side. I took a step back and kicked at the lock. It gave way almost immediately.

I crossed the threshold into the chamber beyond.

Oktav Grun turned and gaped. Two of the three figures seated at the small table behind him rose and reached inside their coats.

'I wouldn't if I were you,' said Reid. The tip of the Glock appeared next to my left ear as he aimed the gun at the room's occupants.

I registered the mattresses and camping gear against the wall on the right before directing a steady stare at Grun. 'Where are they?'

The bartender glared. 'How did you find me?'

I narrowed my eyes; I had just noticed the door in the rear wall. 'You're not the only immortal who's used these tunnels.'

The third figure at the table finally stirred. 'Oktav, who are these people?'

I studied the middle-aged man who had spoken. Piercing dark eyes dominated his rugged features. He was dressed in a sophisticated suit, and sported a trim beard and a mustache, both of which bore an elegant sprinkle of gray.

His tone, though slightly accented, was old-school aristocracy.

'My name is Lucas Soul,' I said coolly. 'I'm looking for a man and a woman who arrived in Vienna by train tonight.'

Grun gasped at my name; it was the first time he was hearing it.

Something flickered in the other man's eyes.

'The Crovirs tried to kill them at the Hauptbahnhof in Zurich earlier today,' I added, wondering whether I had imagined the flash of recognition.

A taut silence followed.

'Look, we just want to talk to them.' Reid lowered the Glock. 'They may be able to tell us why the Crovir Hunters are after him.' He cocked a thumb my way.

The man with the beard straightened. 'The Crovirs are after you?' he asked sharply, his dark gaze drilling into my face.

'Yes.'

From his tone and words I concluded he was also a Bastian immortal.

He exchanged a glance with Grun. 'I'm sorry.' He rubbed a hand down his face. 'I wish I could help, but I'm certain Tomas wouldn't want me to get you involved in this matter further.'

I frowned. 'Tomas?'

A sad smile flitted across the older man's face. 'I've already said too much.' He rose wearily from his seat. 'I'm afraid I must ask you to leave.'

'Hang on a minute—' Reid started.

The faint but unmistakable sound of gunshots suddenly shattered the stillness.

We froze.

'*Verdammt!*' swore the bearded man in German. A scowl darkened his face as he reached for the Beretta under his arm. 'How the devil did they find us?!'

His bodyguards drew pistols from inside their coats and fell into step behind him as he strode to the door at the back of the room.

'Oktav, warn the others!' he snapped over his shoulder. He hesitated when his gaze fell on us. 'You two, come with me!'

'Victor—' said Grun.

The bearded man glared at the bartender. 'I know you want to fight. But right now, the safety of our other friends is paramount!'

A muscle jumped in the larger man's jaw. He nodded grudgingly.

Reid and I left him standing forlornly by the table and ran out of the chamber after the three men.

A maze of underground tunnels lit by flickering flame torches unfurled on the other side of the door. Our shadows danced on the walls as we raced toward the noise of the gunfight.

The darkness finally lightened ahead. We emerged under a bridge beneath the streets of the city.

Stars shone next to a crescent moon in the sky beyond. Lights from the overpass cast a muted glow across the canal at the bottom of a flight of stone steps.

Some hundred feet to the right, a group of dark-clad men

chased after five fleeing figures. Muzzles flashed in the gloom. The gun blasts echoed against the walls of the water duct.

We were at the bottom of the stairs when two of the figures fell.

The man called Victor cursed. His steps quickened.

The Hunters at the rear of the pack turned at the sound of our footfall. Gunfire erupted around me as Reid and the three immortals engaged them.

I left my guns in their holsters and pulled the daisho from its twin sheaths, my heart pounding against my ribs.

Moonlight glinted on the edge of the katana as it hissed through the air. Two Hunters fell beneath the blade. A third man pulled a German longsword from beneath his coat.

He was good but nowhere near as skillful as Haus had been.

I pulled the bloodied katana from his still figure just as a scream tore through the night, the sound piercing my soul like a blade. I looked up, stomach knotting in fear.

The man from the daguerreotype had fallen to his knees. He clutched at his side and tried to rise to his feet.

'Grandfather!' shouted the woman I now knew as Anna.

She ran back to the old man, her eyes wide with horror, and wrapped an arm awkwardly under his shoulders. They stumbled forward.

My heart stuttered in my chest.

Two Crovir Hunters closed in silently thirty feet behind them.

'Go!' yelled Victor. 'We'll cover you!'

I raced toward the running figures, my boots splashing through bloodstained puddles. Bullets thudded into the Crovirs who blocked my path. Black-clad bodies fell around me.

My eyes never shifted from the retreating backs of Anna and the wounded man.

They had just entered the shadow of another bridge when

they stumbled and fell next to a stone buttress. One of the Hunters raised his gun and aimed at the old man's back.

I released the wakizashi, drew the Smith and Wesson, and fired.

The immortal cursed and clutched at his bleeding hand, the weapon falling from his grip. I reached him a moment later and swung the katana across his arm, carving a slash from elbow to wrist. He screamed and stumbled to the ground.

The second Hunter turned, pistol in hand. Out of the corner of my eyes, I saw Anna look around wildly. She grabbed a piece of driftwood from the ground and hurled it at the Hunter.

It struck him on the shoulder just as he fired. The bullet hissed past my ear.

The Hunter took aim once more. A gasp left his lips. His eyes widened before dropping to the blade in his chest.

I yanked the katana out. He fell with a thud.

'Behind you!' shouted Anna.

I twisted on my heels.

The other Hunter was back on his feet, gun in his uninjured hand. Blood dripped down his wounded arm as he took aim.

I was already running when the first bullet grazed my left cheek. The next two shots missed my head by inches. I jumped, pushed against the stone buttress, spun backward in the air, and kicked the weapon out of the immortal's hand.

He staggered backward and went to reach for the gun in his ankle holster. A soft grunt left his lips as the bloodstained katana slashed across his neck. He dropped to his knees, fingers clutching at the crimson jet spurting from the wound at his throat, before collapsing to the ground.

I snarled and stabbed the sword savagely in his chest. Blood roared in my head as I leaned over the still body, my breaths coming in rapid pants. There was a noise behind me.

'Help me,' said Anna.

Her voice cut through the fog of rage clouding my mind like a knife. The clamor of the ongoing battle finally registered.

I removed the katana from the Hunter's body and walked to where she knelt by her grandfather. The old man grunted when we lifted him under his shoulders and guided him to the flight of steps next to the bridge.

His eyes opened as we propped him against the canal wall. He looked at me blearily. 'Lucas?'

I hesitated, an eerie feeling of familiarity stealing over me once more as I studied his face. 'Yes.'

He blanched. 'What are you doing here?' He grabbed my hand and shifted as if to rise.

'Don't!' snapped Anna. She pressed her hands against the wound in his flank, a grimace crossing her face as she favored her right arm. Blood seeped between her fingers where they lay on the old man's clothes.

The scent of oranges drifted from her hair, drowning out the musty odor of mold coating the banks of the canal and the rank smell from the thin line of water coursing along its floor. It was too dark to discern the color of her eyes.

'I've been looking for you,' I said, dragging my gaze from her face.

The old man bit back a curse. 'I told you not to follow us!'

I clenched my teeth. 'The Crovirs are after me. I think it has something to do with you.' My eyes shifted briefly to Anna.

The old man froze. Horror clouded his features.

I raised an eyebrow when a stream of colorful Czech left his mouth.

'Damn that Vellacrus woman!' he hissed.

Footsteps sounded behind us. I rose, fingers gripping the handle of the katana.

Victor and his men rounded the corner of the buttress.

Reid followed behind them. He handed me the wakizashi and indicated his left cheek wordlessly.

I wiped away the trickle of blood coursing down my face.

'Is everyone all right?' Victor demanded.

'Grandfather's hurt,' said Anna. Though anger darkened her tone, I was the only one close enough to see the tremor in her fingers as she pressed them against the old man's wound.

'It's just a scratch,' her grandfather mumbled. Despite her stern protests, he slowly climbed to his feet.

Victor narrowed his eyes at the older man before studying the shadowy canal. 'We need to get you out of here.'

He pulled a cell from his jacket and dialed a number. A short exchange followed. 'Help's on the way,' he said after he disconnected.

Minutes unfolded slowly while we waited. Despite my best efforts, I found my gaze irrepressibly drawn to Anna time and time again. My eyes helplessly traced the contours of her features while I struggled with an emotion I could not put a name to.

I had never been so aware of another being in all of my lives.

Judging by the tense glances she cast my way, Anna was just as conscious of the electrifying vibe floating between us.

By the time a squeal of tires rose on the street above, the last crows were leaving the canal and disappearing in the sky.

One of Victor's bodyguards stepped out of the shadow of the bridge and stared up. 'It's Oktav.'

Victor straightened from where he leaned against the canal wall. 'Let's get you up these steps,' he told Anna's grandfather.

He placed an arm around the older man's waist, Anna supporting her grandfather on the other side.

'I can walk, you know,' the wounded man protested weakly as they started up the steps. Blood had soaked through the waistband of his trousers and sweat beaded his pale face.

Victor sighed. 'Will you stop being so stubborn?'

He turned to his men and indicated the fallen immortals

who had been protecting Anna and her grandfather. Some had started to stir. 'Get them.'

A car and a van stood waiting on the road alongside the canal, doors open and engines running.

Grun stepped out from behind the wheel of the Volkswagen Transporter.

'Marcus betrayed us,' the bartender blurted out. 'He killed Josef and Ollana.' He broke off, his breath leaving his nose in sharp bursts.

Victor went still, eyes turning wintry with anger.

Reid and I exchanged glances.

There was more going on here than the immortals' enduring attempt to kill me; the Crovirs had attacked the Bastians in an open and vicious manner. My sense of foreboding was growing darker by the hour.

'And the others?' said Victor finally.

'They're heading for one of the hideaways,' Grun replied.

'Good.' A muscle jumped in Victor's cheek as he watched the semi-conscious immortals being loaded into the rear of the van. 'We'll deal with Marcus later. For now, we have to get Tomas and Anna to a safe house.' He narrowed his eyes at Grun. 'Send word to the First Council.'

The bartender pulled a cell from his coat and made a call.

Victor helped Anna and her grandfather into the van before looking at Reid and me. He indicated the Skoda parked a few feet away. 'Get in the car.'

One of the bodyguards got in the front of the vehicle while Reid and I climbed in the back.

A man with red hair and a friendly countenance sat in the driver's seat. He gave us an amiable nod over his shoulder. 'Welcome aboard.'

We took off a moment later, the Skoda following the Transporter as it sped west across the city. I looked at the skyline above the rooftops. A lightening edge on the horizon heralded the imminent arrival of dawn.

I stared blindly out the window, my mind abuzz with questions. Events had taken an unforeseen turn; from what I gathered, Reid and I had stumbled into the middle of a conflict between the Bastians and the Crovirs. Yet, despite the incidents of the last few days, I still had no idea how it all fit together, especially my role in the whole affair. My eyes moved to the Transporter. One thing I was certain of: the people inside that van had some of the answers.

Anna's face rose in my mind. Something twisted inside my chest.

We had just passed a deserted park when a flash of movement caught my eyes. A black Honda Fireblade superbike gunned out of a side street and skidded alongside the Skoda. A second bike materialized on the other side of the car.

The two riders atop each of the sleek machines wore dark helmets and leather biker suits.

'What the hell?' muttered the red-haired driver. He frowned at the apparition in his wing mirror.

'Watch out!' shouted the bodyguard.

The figures riding pillion had pulled semi-automatic guns out of their jackets. They raised the weapons and fired at the Skoda.

Reid and I ducked a second before the windows shattered. Tempered glass rained down on our heads.

The Skoda swerved across the road, the red-haired driver cursing under his breath while he attempted to outmaneuver the two bikes. The roar of the Fireblades' engines suddenly rose in the night. I raised my head in time to see the bikes disappear after the van.

'Shit!' said the bodyguard.

I couldn't agree more. The Crovirs were after Anna Godard again.

'Go after them!' I barked.

'I'm trying,' the driver replied steadily. He glanced at a side mirror. 'I think one of their bullets pierced our fuel tank.'

I leaned out of the window and smelled gasoline a second before I spotted the thin, dark trail splashing onto the asphalt behind the car. Something else caught my gaze. I stared at the road. My eyes widened.

I turned and lunged across the back of the driver's seat. He swore as I grabbed the steering wheel from his hands and yanked it sharply to the right.

It was what ultimately saved us. The gray Humvee bearing down on us with its headlights off clipped the rear end of the Skoda and sent the car spinning uncontrollably across the road.

The red-haired driver hissed as the wheel twisted between his hands. Reid and I braced ourselves against the roof of the vehicle.

The Skoda crossed the center line, slammed sideways against the opposite curb, and rocked to a stop. I looked over my shoulder, heart thudding wildly.

The Humvee was heading straight for the van.

A sudden shout from the bodyguard made me look forward. Thirty feet ahead and closing on us was another Hummer. It did not look like it was intending to stop.

The Bastian driver shifted gears and slammed on the accelerator. The tires squealed shrilly. The acrid smell of burning rubber rose around us. The wheels finally gripped the asphalt seconds before impact.

The Skoda shot backward.

The bodyguard clipped a fresh magazine in his gun, leaned out of the passenger window, and fired a volley of shots at the vehicle. A bullet flashed against the Hummer's side mirror. Another cracked its windshield. A third one thudded into the front right tire, causing it to slow down.

The Bastian driver spun the wheel of the Skoda. The car

turned in a sickening lurch until we were facing the right way once more.

Up ahead, the Fireblades and the gray Humvee were closing in on Grun's Transporter. Gunfire erupted in the night. Bullets thudded into the rear doors of the van.

The Bastian driver scowled and changed gears. The Skoda lurched forward and accelerated.

Sharp pings rose from the boot of the vehicle. I turned and looked out the rear window. The Hummer was back on our tail. Gun muzzles appeared alongside the behemoth. Flashes followed.

I lifted the Smith and Wesson and leaned out of the window. Reid's Glock echoed the shots from my gun on the other side of the car.

'Aim for the engine!' I shouted. 'They've got run-flat tires!'

Our next bullets entered the front grille of the Hummer simultaneously. There was a bang from under the hood. A cloud of smoke billowed out the front of the truck. It veered across the road, mounted the pavement, and crashed into the facade of a bank.

Flames erupted from the engine and licked the underside of the vehicle. An alarm sounded shrilly as we sped into the night.

Up ahead, the Humvee was half a dozen feet behind the Transporter. It accelerated sharply and rammed the van. The Transporter swung toward the center line. The Fireblades moved around and tried to overtake it. Bullets scored the side doors of the Transporter.

'Hang on!' yelled the Bastian driver. He shifted gears once more, stepped on the gas, and rear ended the Humvee.

The shock jolted us forward and buckled the hood of the Skoda.

The Humvee barely jerked on its suspensions. It picked up speed again.

'Take out their tires!' yelled the Bastian driver. 'Just slow them down, *goddamnit!*'

Victor's bodyguard grunted. He heaved his upper body out of the window, gun in hand. Just then, the Humvee's loading door swung open.

We stared into the mouth of a rocket launcher.

'Oh crap!' The Bastian driver spun the wheel sharply to the left.

A flash bloomed ahead. The first grenade whistled past the hood of the Skoda and detonated on the road behind us.

The blast blew the rear window in and showered us with shards of glass. The Skoda shuddered and rotated uncontrollably across the blacktop. Its tailgate swung around and crashed violently against a fire hydrant. The engine sputtered and died.

We sat stunned for a couple of seconds. I raised my eyes to the Humvee.

It had slowed down. The grenade launcher was being reloaded.

'Move!' bellowed the bodyguard.

The Bastian driver turned the key in the ignition, his movements stiff. The car stuttered and stalled. He cursed and tried again. The engine sprang into life with a sharp, high-pitched screech. He shifted into reverse and started to pull away from the curb.

We were too late to avoid the second grenade. At the penultimate moment, gunfire from the Transporter caused the Humvee to swerve. The rocket-propelled projectile gyrated widely from its path and exploded several feet from the front bumper of the Skoda.

The world tilted as we were flung in the air. The car flipped twice. Metal crumpled and gave way against the asphalt. The Skoda landed on its roof and skidded some two hundred feet across the road in a shower of sparks, before finally grinding to a halt on the center line.

Buzzing silence resonated in my ears. The stench of gasoline was overpowering. I coughed and opened my eyes. My vision blurred. I blinked.

Blood dripped from a fresh wound on my scalp and obstructed my sight. I slowly looked around.

I was lying at an angle against the door. Reid lay heavily across me. He wasn't moving. A crimson trail oozed from a gash on his head.

'Reid,' I said, dazed.

Low groans rose from the front of the car. The bodyguard and the Skoda's driver shifted as consciousness returned.

Reid's eyes fluttered open. Relief flooded my heart.

'Are you okay?' I slid to the side to give him space.

'I think so.' He winced and gingerly touched the wound on his head. 'You?'

'I'll live.'

'Oh crap,' someone said dully from the front seat. It was the driver.

Alarm washed over me when I looked past him and saw what he had spotted. Smoke was curling up from the hood of the car.

'I vote we get our sweet asses the hell out of here!' shouted the Bastian immortal.

I twisted around and crawled through the shattered rear window of the car, broken glass and debris cutting into my skin. I pulled Reid out after me and reached for the driver's hand.

'Go!' the immortal roared, pale eyes blazing.

'Just give me your goddamned hand!' I barked.

He mouthed something rude and grabbed my wrist. The bodyguard followed behind him.

We were twenty feet from the car when flames ignited the liquid trail to the fuel tank.

The resulting explosion knocked us to the ground.

We lay stunned for a moment, the heat from the conflagration scorching our backs. I sat up and stared at the blaze.

The Skoda was a giant fireball in the middle of the road. Pale light filtered down from the skies beyond it and illuminated the empty lanes ahead; the Transporter and its pursuers had disappeared.

Fear stabbed through my gut. 'Did they make it?'

'Don't worry.' The Bastian driver wiped blood from his face and grinned. 'Victor Dvorsky is not one to let himself get captured that easily.'

The bodyguard nodded and rubbed the back of his head with a wince.

Sirens flared into life behind us.

The driver looked over his shoulder. 'We better get out of here.'

We headed down the road and turned onto a side street. A screech of tires erupted ahead of us; a police car appeared at the next junction and skidded to a stop sideways across the asphalt.

The Bastian driver clenched his teeth. 'Have I mentioned that this is turning out to be a shitty day?'

Two uniformed officers got out of the vehicle and unholstered their guns. They shouted a warning in German.

'This way!' yelled the Bastian immortal.

He turned and bolted for an alley on the left. We raced after him and emerged on a parallel road a moment later. Two police cars sat blocking the exits at either end.

The driver scowled. 'Follow me!'

He dashed across the asphalt and entered another narrow back lane.

The sirens blasting through the crisp morning air stopped abruptly. Footsteps and shouts broke out behind us.

Someone yelled 'Stop! This is the police!' in German.

We turned a corner and staggered to a halt. A brick wall loomed in our path.

The driver pointed at the gray shape to the side. 'The dumpster!'

We rolled the metal container to the wall, our grunts of effort punctuating the grating shriek of the wheels. We were over the top seconds later and landed in a dimly lit passage on the other side. We broke into a run.

A squad car braked in front of the mouth of the alley when we were fifteen feet from it. We stumbled to a stop.

'That's not good,' said Reid.

Scuffling noises and thuds rose behind us as uniformed officers appeared over the wall.

'Police! I repeat, put your arms behind your head and get down on your knees!' someone shouted in German, then English.

'Anybody see a way out of this?' said Reid.

'Nope,' muttered the Bastian driver. The bodyguard frowned and shook his head.

My hands balled into fists and I gritted my teeth. I had been so close to Anna Godard and the answers that I sought.

Reid sighed. 'Oh well. Better do as they say.'

We were rapidly surrounded by a group of policemen. They pushed us roughly to the ground, slapped cuffs on our wrists, and read us our rights before hauling us back onto our knees.

A shadow loomed in front of me. A pair of polished shoes appeared before my eyes. I looked up.

'It's irony, definitely irony,' Reid muttered at my side.

'Mr. Soul, Mr. Hasley,' Christophe Lacroix said with a fierce smile. 'We meet again.'

∼

CHAPTER ELEVEN

THE HEADQUARTERS OF THE FEDERAL CRIMINAL POLICE
Office, or the *Bundeskriminalamt* as it was known locally, was
located on the Josef-Holaubek Platz, in the Alsergrund district
of Vienna. It was close to the banks of the upper Danube Canal
and across the road from one of the campuses of the city's
university.

'That was quite a stunt you guys pulled back there,' said
Lacroix.

I remained silent.

We had been booked in and placed in separate interview
rooms beyond the secured doors of the station. An Austrian
Federal Police investigator stood near the back wall and
watched the proceedings with a carefully neutral expression
while the Frenchman interrogated me. I suspected there were
others behind the glass partition to my right.

Lacroix crossed the floor and took the seat opposite mine.
'Why don't we start at the beginning?' He had taken off his suit
jacket and rolled up the sleeves of his crisp white shirt. 'What
do you know about the murder of Professor Strauss?'

I looked at him steadily. 'Not a lot, I'm afraid.'

Lacroix's eyes narrowed. 'Would you care to elaborate on that?'

'We were looking for him, but we never found any traces of his whereabouts.'

'Were you at his address in the *11ème arrondissement* on Saturday night?'

I shrugged. 'Yes. He wasn't there at the time.'

The Frenchman raised his eyebrows, his expression incredulous. 'So what are you saying? That his body miraculously reappeared in his apartment after you left?'

I suppressed a sigh. 'I take it your forensic pathologist concluded he had been dead for several days?'

Lacroix did not reply.

'You should be able to confirm that we were in the States at the time.' I rested my arms on the table and leaned forward. 'We did not murder Hubert Strauss,' I stated emphatically. 'The men who did are still out there.'

'Are these the same men who allegedly tried to kill you in Boston?' Lacroix retorted.

I sat back in the chair. 'I see you've been talking to Detective Meyer.'

Lacroix snorted. 'Not just him. The FBI in Washington is also keen to have a little chat with you and Mr. Hasley.' He glanced at his watch. 'They should be here in about nine hours.'

I looked down at my hands, struggling to mask my anxiety and anger. Our time was fast running out.

Despite the reassurances of Victor's bodyguard and the Bastian driver, I had no idea whether Anna Godard had fallen into the hands of the Crovirs. That lack of knowledge alone made me want to tear down the walls of the station and go on a rampage.

One thing I was certain of: the Crovirs would come after me again.

'The people you're dealing with will not wait that long to intervene,' I said.

Lacroix stiffened. 'Is that a threat, Mr. Soul?'

'It's a friendly warning.'

It was Lacroix's turn to be silent. 'What about Gif-sur-Yvette?' he finally said.

I took a deep breath and forced myself to relax. 'We went there to look for information on Strauss.'

'And the gunfight?'

A hush fell across the room.

'Why do I get the feeling you're going to tell me it was those "invisible" men again?' Lacroix added cynically.

'You found the four-by-fours?'

Lacroix shrugged. 'They were empty.'

'Well, you did say they were "invisible".'

The Frenchman glared at me before looking at the papers in front of him. 'You were also involved in the incident at the Hauptbahnhof in Zurich.'

I looked to the man at the back of the room. 'That's not strictly within your jurisdiction now, is it?' I murmured to Lacroix.

The Frenchman opened his mouth to reply. The Austrian officer interrupted him. Lacroix rose and strode to the other side of the room. A murmured exchange followed, during which the word "procedure" was repeated several times in German.

'It seems we're still waiting for Zurich City Police and Swiss Interpol to get here,' the Frenchman spat out.

The Austrian investigator gestured to someone behind the glass partition.

The door opened and a couple of uniformed officers appeared to escort me back to the detention center. I stopped on the threshold of the interview room and looked at Lacroix.

'Like I told your uncle, things are not as they seem,' I said quietly before I was led to my cell.

Reid was ushered in the lockup opposite mine several minutes later.

'Yo,' he said. There was a fresh dressing on his head. He winced and massaged the back of his neck gingerly.

'Yo yourself.' I observed his gaunt expression with a pang of guilt. 'How're you holding up?'

Reid grimaced. 'I've been worse.' He patted his jacket, paused, and sighed. 'Damn, they took the cigarettes.' He leaned against the wall and crossed his legs, hands jammed in his pockets. 'So, you found anything interesting?'

'The FBI's on their way from DC.' A wave of weariness washed over me. I sat on the bench. 'You?'

'They didn't find any bodies in the Hummer or at the canal. They were very interested in the amount of empty shell casings and blood they found at the scenes, though.'

Silence fell in the narrow corridor that separated our cells.

'The Crovirs will come for us,' I said in a low voice.

Reid cocked an eyebrow. 'Here?'

I nodded.

He rubbed his chin and made a face. 'You're right. Considering what they've done so far, that wouldn't surprise me.'

The door to the cellblock opened. The sounds of a scuffle followed. Victor's bodyguard and the driver of the Skoda came into view.

They were pushed roughly inside the cells next to us.

'Damn Stapos,' muttered the bodyguard after the officers left.

'Austrian State Police,' I translated at Reid's puzzled expression. 'They're kinda like the local secret service.' I studied the two immortals. 'It's about time you told us your names.'

The bodyguard wiped his bloodied mouth with the back of his hand and carefully moved his lower jaw from side to side.

'I'm Bruno,' he said gruffly. He indicated the driver. 'That's Anatole.'

The red-haired immortal nodded amiably.

'Reid,' said my partner from across the way.

'Lucas,' I murmured.

'We know who you are,' said Bruno. 'The immortal who can kill other immortals.'

An awkward hush followed.

Reid frowned. 'He wouldn't have to if you people just left him alone.'

I remained quiet while I tried to gauge the two immortals' moods. We would need their help if we were going to get out of there.

Anatole chuckled. 'Give him a break, will you?' he told the bodyguard. 'He could've finished you off if he'd wanted to. And quite frankly, with that shitty attitude of yours, I wouldn't blame him.'

Bruno grunted and lapsed into silence.

I came to a decision.

The door to the cellblock opened half an hour later. Several armed officers appeared. They were led by the Austrian investigator who had been in the interview room with Lacroix.

'You are being transferred to the Staatspolizei headquarters,' the man stated while we were handcuffed and removed from the cells. 'The orders have just come through.'

The lines around the Austrian investigator's mouth were strained. He avoided meeting my eyes.

I looked at Reid and the two Bastian immortals. They acknowledged my stare with brief nods. This was going to be our one and only chance to escape.

We were escorted out of the detention center and marched through the building. We passed an evidence room and an armory before reaching the security door to the station's main reception.

A familiar voice greeted me across the floor. 'Hello, Lucas.'

I stopped and stared at the man who had spoken.

Mikael Olsson had hardly changed in the decade since I had last seen him. Steely gray eyes studied me coolly from beneath a familiar fringe of dark hair. His tall and lanky frame was more muscular than I recalled.

A group of men crowded silently behind him, hooded eyes calmly observing the officers around them.

'You know this guy?' murmured Reid.

A muscle twitched in my jaw. 'Yes. That's Olsson.'

Reid stiffened.

The Austrian investigator was speaking to the sergeant at the desk when a door slammed open on the far side of the lobby. Lacroix stormed out of the passage beyond and marched up to the desk.

'What's going on here? Why are the prisoners being moved?' barked the French detective.

The Austrian investigator's expression grew shuttered. 'I have received orders from my superiors. These men are to be placed in the custody of the State Police.'

'Why?' said Lacroix. 'And by whose authority, exactly?' The Frenchman had gone red in the face.

Olsson took a step forward. 'I'm afraid that information is on a need-to-know basis.'

Lacroix turned and studied him from head to toe. 'Who the hell are you?'

Olsson smiled and held up a badge. 'Like he said, we are Staatspolizei.'

'These men are not from the State Police.' My voice resonated across the marble floor. I looked at Lacroix. 'They are the ones who tried to kill us.'

A strained silence fell across the lobby. Frowns appeared on the faces of some of the uniformed Austrian officers.

Olsson chuckled. 'Come now, these men are desperate. They're obviously lying.' The laughter did not quite reach his eyes.

The handcuffs at my wrists jangled as I pointed out three men behind him. 'Check their guns. The one on the right should match ballistics from Gif-sur-Yvette. The other two were at the Hauptbahnhof yesterday.'

Olsson's smile faded. 'Enough of this nonsense,' he said in a hard voice. 'We have a letter here from the Federal Ministry of Interior with instructions for you to transfer these men into our custody. Just hand them over.'

It was the wrong tone to take. The Austrian investigator frowned.

Lacroix straightened. 'What's the rush?'

Olsson sighed.

I tensed and rose slightly on the balls of my feet.

'Oh, there's no rush,' my former partner said calmly. He reached inside his coat and whipped out a gun.

I threw myself against Lacroix and carried him to the floor just as the first shot rang out.

The bullet from Olsson's semi-automatic missed the Frenchman's head by inches and thudded into the oak counter above us.

I grabbed Lacroix's weapon from his shoulder holster, twisted, and fired a volley of rounds at Olsson. He grunted and jerked backward.

I was behind the desk a second later, Lacroix's gun still gripped in my hands. Reid and the two Bastian immortals dropped down beside me.

The crack of bullets rose around the lobby as the Crovirs engaged the Austrian policemen. Distant crashes rose elsewhere in the building as officers converged on the noise of the gunfight.

'We need to get to the evidence room!' I said urgently. 'My swords are in there!'

Reid grabbed a paperclip from a table and started to work his way through our handcuffs.

The desk sergeant had been shot in the chest. A young man in uniform cowered next to him, hands clamped over the bubbling wound.

'If you want to live, give me your gun!' I ordered harshly in German.

The officer stared at me, petrified. I extended my hand brusquely. He gulped and passed his firearm across with a shaking hand.

I grabbed the weapon and tossed it to Reid. 'On the count of three?'

Reid and the Bastians nodded.

We rose from behind the desk and raced for the door to our right. Half a dozen Austrian officers lay dead or wounded around the reception. The Crovirs had fared better in terms of casualties, although I suspected they wore bulletproof vests under their suits.

I gritted my teeth, rage surging afresh through my veins.

Rounds scored the floor behind us. Anatole grunted and stumbled.

The security door slammed open a second before we reached it. A dozen officers in combat gear spilled out from the corridor beyond. We flattened ourselves against the wall and slipped inside a second after the last man crossed the threshold.

The hallway was blessedly empty. I headed for the evidence room and shot through the security lock on the door.

The katana and the wakizashi were on a shelf in the second aisle. Our guns, holsters, and Bruno's cell were in a box next to them.

'We could escape through the back,' said the bodyguard as he pocketed the phone.

Anatole looked up from tying a strip of cloth he had torn from his sleeve around the bullet wound on his thigh. Blood was already seeping through it.

I frowned. 'The Crovirs will slaughter everyone in this building if they don't find us in the next few minutes.'

Reid came back in the room. 'Armory door was wide open.' He threw us a Kevlar vest each and magazines for our guns. 'Look what else I found.' He grinned and held up a couple of Steyr AUG assault rifles.

'Nice.' Bruno caught the one Reid tossed at him.

'It's like Christmas come early,' said Anatole with a weak grin.

I finished loading fresh magazines into my guns and hesitated, my gaze swinging between the bodyguard and the driver.

'There's no need for all of us to stay. The two of you could—'

'Stop right there.' Bruno held a hand up. 'Dvorsky will have our heads if we abandon you now.'

Anatole nodded. 'He's right. The boss gave us strict orders to look after your sorry asses. Besides, it's been a while since we've seen this much action.' He snorted. 'We can't let you guys have all the fun!'

I returned his smile darkly. 'Just try and keep up.'

The gunfight was in full swing when we emerged in the lobby seconds later. I spotted Lacroix behind a concrete pillar to the left. Blood dripped down the Frenchman's arm; he had found a gun from somewhere and was shooting at the Crovirs.

Four of them lay on the floor, apparently dead from shots to the head. I knew better.

I left the guns in the holsters on my thighs and drew my swords. The stutter of the Steyr AUGs filled the room behind me.

Two of the fallen Hunters groaned and pushed themselves up. Horrified shouts erupted from the Austrian officers when the pair slowly climbed to their feet. There was a gasped '*Nom de Dieu!*' from Lacroix.

By then, I was already halfway across the floor.

The katana carved the air with a silken sound. The first Hunter fell again. I twisted on my heels and drove the wakizashi into the heart of the second Hunter. He folded silently at my feet, a puzzled look on his face.

'Lucas!' Reid shouted.

There was movement behind me. I ducked.

The tip of Olsson's longsword missed my neck by inches. He swore when the katana carved a deep cut on the underside of his arm.

'I didn't know you were a swordsman.' I straightened. Blood dripped from the edges of my blades. I moved and blocked a bullet with the katana.

'There're a lot of things you don't know about me,' said Olsson with a twisted smile.

'You're right.' The sword shuddered in my hands as further slugs struck it. I had to know. 'Why, Mikael?'

Olsson hesitated, guilt flashing across his face. It was replaced by a sneer. 'Because you're the only one who stands in our way! And because the man who killed my father holds you dear to his heart!'

He brought his sword around in an arc.

My eyes widened. I broke his move with the daisho, my mind reeling from his words. Olsson grunted. His knuckles whitened as he pressed down with his blade.

Bullets struck my left flank. Though they hit the vest, I still hissed at the stinging pain. My knee gave way beneath me. Olsson grinned as I was slowly forced to the floor.

There was a flash at the edge of my vision. By the time Olsson turned, he was already too late.

Reid leveled the Glock and shot him point-blank in the neck.

The longsword clattered onto the polished floor. Olsson's eyes flared in shocked surprise, his hands grappling desperately at the wound in his throat. Crimson spurts escaped between his fingers. He dropped to his knees and thudded face down on the floor. A dark pool spread out beneath him.

'Let's get the hell out of here!' Bruno shouted from the exit.

He held a bleeding Anatole under the shoulders. The Bastian driver had acquired a second gunshot wound to his lower abdomen.

I scanned the lobby. The Crovirs were down. A crow flew through the open doors, its shrill screech shattering the deadly silence. Another appeared near the ceiling and spiraled down to the marble floor, before skipping onto the body of a dead Hunter.

The Austrian officers hesitated, eyes swinging nervously from us to the black birds. Reid and I moved toward the exit.

'Stop!' Lacroix yelled behind us. A warning shot went off above our heads.

The crows screeched and flapped their wings. A third bird materialized through the doors.

I stopped and turned. 'I suggest you let us leave. They'll come after us again. If we stay, all of you will die.'

Lacroix scowled, the gun in his hand aimed unwaveringly at us. Blood oozed from a cut on his face and the wound on his shoulder.

One of the fallen Hunters coughed and blinked. A second man groaned.

Lacroix and the Austrian officers were still gaping at them when we headed out of the building.

'You could have finished him off,' Reid observed as we bolted down the steps of the police headquarters.

I knew he was referring to Olsson.

'Yes, I could have. But first, I need answers.'

I still didn't understand what Olsson had meant, nor did I know to whom he had alluded. I had already dismissed Pierre Vauquois as a possibility. To my knowledge, that left no one else.

We followed the bodyguard and the wounded driver across the road to the gloomy interior of a parking garage under the university building. Gunshots erupted behind us just as we entered the shadows. We started to run.

Some fifty feet ahead and to the left, an elderly gentleman was locking the door of his Volvo estate. He looked up at our footsteps. His eyes grew wide when Reid lifted the Glock and leveled it at his face.

'The keys, please!' my partner snapped.

Confusion washed across the old man's face.

Bruno repeated the order in German. Anatole leaned heavily against the bodyguard; the immortal had turned an ashen color and was bleeding profusely from his wounds.

The Volvo owner's hand shook as he passed the keys across. They dropped from his grasp. Reid cursed and leaned down to pick them.

The bullet missed him by a foot and thudded into the old man's shoulder. He cried out and staggered to the ground.

I turned and fired at the dim figures some hundred feet away. A panicked scream rose from elsewhere in the underground car park.

Reid finished unlocking the estate and threw the keys at me. 'You're the better driver!' he shouted.

I helped Bruno load Anatole in the back seat while he propped the injured car owner against a concrete pillar. A young woman cowered behind a van a few yards away.

'You, come here!' Reid beckoned.

She blanched, her eyes dropping to the gun in his hand. She hesitated before crawling across the narrow gap between the vehicles.

'Here, apply firm pressure!' Reid grabbed her hand and pressed it against the old man's wound. The young woman nodded tremulously, tears spilling over and coursing down her face.

Shots pinged on the hood of the Volvo. I started the engine and engaged the transmission. 'Reid!'

He turned and dove inside the car. I stepped on the gas.

The wheels spun madly before gripping the asphalt. The smell of burning rubber filled the air as the car shot forward.

A Crovir Hunter stepped in our path. Flashes erupted from the muzzle of his gun.

'Hang on!' I jerked the wheel sharply.

The Volvo's bumper caught the immortal across the legs. He landed on the hood with a sickening crunch and rolled off to the side. Further shots thudded into the car. The passenger window cracked.

'Get us out of here!' shouted Reid.

'I'm trying,' I retorted between gritted teeth.

The Volvo skidded around a corner and grazed a row of cars in a shower of sparks before barreling down an empty lane. The exit appeared in a flood of daylight at the opposite end.

Four figures emerged from the shadows on either side.

I floored the accelerator.

We crashed through the security barrier in a hail of gunfire. Bullets slammed into the boot of the car. Spider web cracks appeared in the rear window.

A tortured squeal of brakes suddenly rose from the left. I looked around. My stomach dropped.

A tram was coming up the road; we were directly in its path.

I spun the steering wheel to the right. Metal shrieked as the Volvo made contact with the flank of the carriage and scraped alongside it for some fifteen feet. The left wing mirror crumpled and disappeared under the tramcar. Half a dozen shocked passengers gaped through the windows while I pulled away.

I swerved around a fire hydrant and sent the car juddering back onto the road.

A trio of black sedans appeared in the rearview mirror.

'Reid,' I said urgently, my gaze shifting to the busy traffic ahead.

He glanced in his side mirror. 'Gotcha.'

He rolled the cracked window down, leaned out of the estate, and fired a series of shots.

The front right tire of the leading car went out in a burst of fragmented rubber. It pitched sideways, flipped onto its roof, and careened toward the center line in an explosion of sparks. The second vehicle swung around it and crashed into a truck in the other lane.

The third sedan drove past the wrecks, clipped the bumper of a van, and kept on coming. Police sirens tore the air in the far distance.

A bridge appeared up ahead. The lights were red at the end of a queue of stationary vehicles.

Reid slid back in his seat. His eyes widened when he saw what lay in front. He glanced at me. 'Tell me you're not thinking of—'

'Hang on!' I yelled.

I ignored Reid's and Bruno's shouts, swerved onto the verge, accelerated, and shot across the junction between the contra flow. A blare of horns erupted around us. It was followed by irate yells and the ricochet of bullets bouncing off the back of the Volvo.

I angled the car into the right lane and overtook a truck.

The black sedan stayed on our tail. Seconds later, the rear window acquired another crack from a bullet.

'Goddamnit!' yelled Bruno.

He pushed Anatole down on the seat, twisted around, smashed the tempered glass clear with the butt of the Steyr AUG, levered the rifle through the gap, and fired.

I glanced at the rearview mirror at the sound of an explosion.

The rounds had penetrated the front grille of the sedan and

ignited something under the hood. The car braked and slewed to a stop in the emergency lane. Figures staggered out of the vehicle in a billow of black smoke.

I wondered whether Olsson was among them.

The bridge disappeared behind us. I looked over my shoulder at Anatole.

'How's he doing?' I asked anxiously.

Though I had known the Bastian for only a short time, I liked him. Besides, I did not wish to be responsible for the death of yet another person. I had enough blood on my conscience as it was.

'Not so good,' said Bruno. He observed the buildings flashing outside the window with a troubled expression. 'Head north. I know a place where we can hide.'

～

CHAPTER TWELVE

THE BASTIAN SAFE HOUSE WAS A HUNTING LODGE DEEP IN THE
woods around Hollabrunn, some twenty-five miles outside
Vienna. We drove to the hotel in Landstrasse and swapped the
Volvo for our Audi before setting off.

Anatole drifted in and out of consciousness for most of the
drive up. By the time the car rolled to a stop on the pinecone-
covered clearing outside the cabin, his breathing had turned
shallow.

We carried the wounded immortal inside the lodge and laid
him on a couch in the front room. Bruno brought in logs and
kindling from the porch and lit a fire in the hearth. He emptied
the bag of supplies he had picked up from a chemist near Landstrasse; rolls of bandages, a sewing kit, a disposable scalpel, and
a couple of bottles of pills slipped onto the surface of the coffee
table.

'Get the bullets out and stitch him up,' he told me curtly.
'He'll live if he makes it through the night.' He turned and
headed for the front door.

'Where are you going?' said Reid.

Bruno paused with his fingers on the handle. 'I need to get

in touch with Victor.' He indicated the cell phone in his hand. 'There's no reception here. I'll have to make the call from a phone box.'

'There's a public telephone in the woods?'

'No. It's about an hour's walk away.' His eyes shifted to Anatole before he left.

Reid did a perimeter check around the hunting lodge while I searched the rooms. I discovered a bottle of gin at the back of a cupboard in the kitchen and was pouring a generous amount of it down Anatole's throat when he entered the cabin.

I followed the alcohol with painkillers and antibiotics.

'Isn't that a bit much?' Reid indicated the half-empty bottle of liquor.

I threaded a needle and turned to the semi-conscious immortal. 'He's going to need it.'

By the time Bruno returned some two hours later, Anatole was sleeping soundly in front of the fire.

'They made it to one of the hideouts.' The bodyguard crossed the floor with an armful of logs and set them by the grate. 'Victor's coming to meet us. He'll be here tonight.'

We made a meal from the cans we found in the larder. Bruno unearthed a dusty bottle of whisky from a hidden stock I had overlooked and passed it around.

I finally broke the silence that had befallen us. 'Do you know why the Crovirs are after Anna Godard?'

'No,' Bruno replied with a shake of his head. 'Victor received an urgent request for help from Tomas Godard late yesterday afternoon. They arrived at the Westbahnhof in the evening. We took them straight to the hideout under the Hofburg.' He gazed into the flames. 'We got word that a group of Crovir Hunters were asking questions about the Godards a few hours later. We decided to move them to another safe house. That's when you guys turned up.'

'Grun mentioned a name at the canal last night,' said Reid. 'Someone called Marcus?'

Bruno's face hardened. 'Marcus Pinchter. He's a Bastian noble and a member of our Second Council. He works for Victor.'

I rolled the glass in my hands. 'Why would he betray you?'

'I honestly don't know,' said the bodyguard.

'And Tomas Godard?'

Bruno observed me for a silent moment. 'I guess there's no harm in telling you.' He swallowed a mouthful of whisky. 'Godard is the oldest surviving member of one of the most ancient families of Bastians in existence today.' He gave me a levelheaded look. 'He is true nobility, if you know what I mean.'

The meaning behind his words sank in.

'You mean he's a pureblood?'

The bodyguard nodded.

Reid frowned. 'What's a pureblood?'

'It's an immortal who can trace his genealogy all the way back to the very origins of our races,' I replied.

Bruno shifted under my unrelenting stare. 'Godard used to be the Head of the Order of Bastian Hunters. He abdicated his position in the fifteen hundreds, for reasons unknown to immortals outside the First Council. Victor's father, Roman Dvorsky, was elected the next Head of the Hunters.'

'Is Victor the current leader?' I asked.

'No,' said Bruno. 'Victor's the Head of our Counter Terrorism Section. Most of us believe he will be the next Head of the Hunters though. Roman is still alive, if somewhat frail.' He grimaced. 'It was several decades before the full effects of the Red Death manifested themselves in him.' He leaned forward and threw another log onto the flames. 'In the eyes of most Bastian Hunters, Victor is our de facto leader, even if he has not officially been sworn in by the First Council yet.'

Anatole stirred on the sofa and mumbled something in his sleep.

'Godard mentioned another name last night,' I said curiously. 'Who is Vellacrus?'

Bruno scowled. 'Agatha Vellacrus is the Head of the Order of Crovir Hunters.' Amber liquid splashed inside his glass as he poured in more whisky. 'She's a pureblood and a nasty piece of work, if I say so myself,' he added with a snort. 'If it was up to her, the immortal war would still be going on to this day.' He caught the wary glance I exchanged with Reid. 'What?'

'Several members of the Crovir First Council attended a secret meeting in Washington a few weeks ago. A fortnight after that, a Crovir Hunter made contact with us in Boston.' I hesitated. 'Forty-eight hours later, he killed me.'

Bruno's eyes widened at my words.

'Twenty-four hours after that, he killed him again,' Reid added drily.

Bruno looked suitably impressed. 'How many is it now?'

I knew what he alluded to without him having to clarify the question. 'Sixteen.'

A low whistle escaped the bodyguard's lips. 'That's not good.'

'No, it isn't.' I sighed. 'I would like to get to the bottom of whatever's going on before my final death.'

The logs crackled and hissed in the hush that followed.

'I'm only on my tenth,' said Bruno. He glanced at the unconscious driver. 'Anatole here's on his eighth.' He made a face. 'He's turned into a bit of a pacifist in the last couple of centuries.'

'I heard that,' murmured Anatole.

Bruno straightened. 'Hey. How're you feeling?'

'Like shit,' said the immortal. He opened his eyes and sat up slowly. A groan escaped his lips. His gaze alighted on the bottle on the table. 'Here, pass me the whisky.'

'I don't think you should be drinking,' said Bruno. 'You already had half the gin.'

'What are you, my mother?' retorted Anatole. 'Besides, that was strictly for medicinal purposes. Now shut up and give me the bottle.'

Dusk had fallen across the forest when the roar of an engine finally rose in the distance. Bruno crossed the room with his gun in hand and peered through a gap in the curtains.

'It's Victor,' he said, shoulders visibly relaxing.

Headlights appeared between the trees. Moments later, a black Volkswagen minivan rolled to a stop next to the Audi. The passenger door opened.

Victor Dvorsky stepped out. There was a bandage around his left wrist and a nasty bruise on his face.

'You guys ready?' he called out.

'Yes,' said Bruno. He closed the front door behind us.

We headed down the porch steps.

Victor peered at Anatole. 'You look like hell.'

'Thanks, boss,' muttered the Bastian driver. 'You don't look so hot yourself.'

Dvorsky's gaze shifted to Reid and me. 'Put your stuff in the van. We're leaving the car.'

We emptied the Audi and climbed inside the minivan. The vehicle turned and started back up the path that led out of the woods.

'Where we headed now?' said Reid.

'Vilanec,' said Victor from the front passenger seat.

'Oh. Where's that?'

'It's in the Jihlava District,' said Victor, 'in the Czech Republic.'

Pinecones and twigs snapped loudly under the wheels of the van in the silence that followed.

'We sure travel a lot, don't we?' Reid told me woodenly.

'Consider it your first European tour,' I said.

He scowled. 'Anyone got a smoke?'

It was another half hour before we crossed the border into the Czech Republic. The van skirted around the Podyji National Park and headed north.

'How's Godard?' I said after a while.

Victor glanced at my reflection in the rearview mirror. 'He'll live,' he said with a grunt. 'He's a tough old man.' His tone clearly discouraged further conversation.

I ignored it. 'Did he tell you why the Crovirs are after his granddaughter?'

Victor sighed. 'I'd rather Tomas did the explaining. He was hoping to spare you from the Crovirs, but you're in too deep for him to put it off any longer.'

It was my turn to be quiet while I tried to decipher the meaning behind his words. 'Do you know a man called Mikael Olsson?' I said finally.

Victor thought for a moment. 'I can't say I've heard the name before,' he replied. 'Why do you ask?'

'He's an old friend who's now working for the Crovirs. He tried to kill me in Boston a few days ago and posed as an officer of the Austrian State Police at the Bundeskriminalamt this morning.'

Victor scrutinized me in the mirror. 'Does he bear a grudge against you?'

I shook my head. 'Not that I was aware of.' I looked out the window as we drove past a hamlet. 'You and Godard seem to be good friends.'

Victor snorted. 'You could say that. Tomas Godard is my godfather.'

I was still brooding over this shocking revelation when we reached the outskirts of Vilanec. The van turned down a country lane outside the sleepy village and headed west across a series of dark fields. The land gradually rose up ahead. A wooded hill appeared on the skyline. The road was soon replaced by a rutted dirt track.

Aside from the eerie glow of the eyes of the wild animals that fled the glare of the headlights, the forest seemed uninhabited. Two miles later, the trees thinned out.

A clearing appeared at the end of the track. It was fringed by the woods on three sides, with a dark ridge soaring behind it to form the crest of the hill.

A house stood in the lee of the gray rock face. The limestone walls looked pale under the light of a crescent-shaped moon. Dark windows reflected the star-studded sky.

Victor suddenly stiffened. 'Stop!' he barked.

The driver slammed on the brakes. Pebbles peppered the underside of the van as it juddered to a halt at the edge of the clearing, jolting us all forward. Anatole swore behind me.

Victor frowned. 'Something's wrong.'

Unease flooded my mind. 'What is it?' I scanned the woods outside the windows of the vehicle.

'I told Tomas to turn off the porch light if there was any sign of trouble.' He took the Beretta from his coat and checked the magazine.

I examined the house through the front windshield of the van. The lantern above the front door was dark.

'I could've sworn Marcus didn't know about this place,' Victor muttered.

The words had barely left his lips when the windows on the first floor blew out. The white glow of the explosion bloomed brightly in the night and shot through the roof, blasting tiles and part of a stone chimney toward the sky. The shockwave rocked the van on its suspensions.

We sat stunned for a moment before scrambling for the doors.

Burning bricks, scorched wood, and smoldering debris drifted down around the clearing. Flames erupted on the ground floor of the house. Glass popped and cracked inside the building as further explosions shook its foundations.

'We need to get out of here!' Victor took a step toward the van.

I grabbed his arm, stopping him in his tracks. 'What about the Godards?' I snapped.

'There's a hidden passage in the basement. If Tomas detected the Crovirs' presence in time to warn us, he would have gotten out through there.'

The conflagration engulfed the house. Heat from the flames washed over us.

Despite the immortal's reassuring tone, I could not stop the icy lump of fear forming in my gut.

'Where would they have gone?' I asked doggedly.

'Not far. They'll probably lay low for a while and catch up with us later.' Victor scrutinized the woodland. 'We need to leave. The Crovirs must be close.'

I hesitated; although it pained me to admit it, I had no choice but to trust the Bastians. I turned to cast a final glance at the burning building.

A faint flash erupted from the trees to the east of the clearing. My eyes widened.

'Get down!' I shouted.

A second later, a rocket-propelled grenade smashed into the side of the van and detonated. The pressure waves from the explosion sent us tumbling across the pinecone-covered track. Hot shrapnel and blazing fragments erupted from the wreckage and rained down from the sky. A tire hurtled out of the fiery wreck and rolled toward the trees, leaving a flaming trail in its wake.

I pushed myself up to my knees, my ears ringing from the blast. Blood dripped past my eyes where a jagged shard had slashed the flesh on my forehead.

Reid groaned and climbed dazedly to his feet.

A muffled curse sounded to our right. The driver of the van rolled desperately in the dirt, his legs engulfed in flames. Victor staggered unsteadily toward him.

Gunshots rang out from the trees. I looked over my shoulder and saw figures emerge from the woods next to the house. Muzzles flashed in the darkness.

A bullet slammed into the dirt by my hand. I dropped to my back, fingers on the Smith and Wesson, and shot the Crovir Hunter crouching some twenty feet away in the grass.

'*Move!*' Victor shouted.

He hauled the wounded driver upright and dragged him into the tree line to the west. Bruno and Anatole followed, spent rounds from their guns dropping soundlessly to the ground as they fired at the Crovirs.

I grabbed Reid's arm and pulled him after the fleeing Bastians.

Dead leaves and twigs snapped beneath our feet as we entered the forest. The footsteps and shouts of our pursuers soon rose behind us.

The woodland thickened, the gloom beneath the crowded trees deepening with each passing second. We stumbled and tripped over invisible roots and burrows, the undergrowth snagging at our clothes and limbs.

Gunfire erupted on our left. Reid grunted and clutched at his arm. I drew the Glock and fired blindly in the night. More shots whistled through the air from the right and scored a tree as we darted past it.

Up ahead, Bruno cried out and lost his footing. He clamped a hand on the fresh bullet wound on his thigh. Anatole draped an arm around the bodyguard's waist and dragged him forward, their breaths leaving their lips in hoarse gasps.

Fear drenched my body in a cold sweat. The shadows between the trees were drawing closer, the enemy flanking us on all sides; we were being herded inside a closing circle from which there would be no escape.

'We need to split up!' I called out to Victor.

He cast a quick glance around and nodded. We divided into pairs and headed off in separate directions.

I looked anxiously at Reid's bleeding arm as we continued north. 'You okay?'

'Yeah! The bullet went through the flesh!'

Another explosion rocked through the night. It was followed by a bloom of brightness between the trees behind and to the right. Hungry flames painted the sky above the burning house with an orange glow. I clenched my teeth.

The light also revealed the figures closing in on us.

Shots rang out behind us. Reid looked over his shoulder, grabbed my arm, and dragged me down in a thicket. We lay frozen, struggling to mask our gasps. Footsteps thundered past a few feet away. Reid peeked through the low branches of the bushes. He gripped the Glock and motioned to me.

We rose and fired at four Hunters. The men fell with hardly a cry. By the time their bodies struck the ground, we were already running.

Muzzles flared repeatedly in the gloom. Bullets peppered the trunks of trees and showered us with fragments of wood. A splinter sliced across my scalp. I blinked blood out of my eyes and focused on where my feet were landing.

Though only minutes had passed since the first explosion tore through the safe house, exhaustion had started to creep through my body. I sensed Reid's movements had also grown sluggish. This was hardly a surprise, considering the events of the last week. Still, although we were both functioning at over eighty percent of our abilities, I knew we desperately needed to be closer to a hundred if we were to make it through the night.

The darkness lightened ahead, distracting me from my grim

reflection. The trees thinned out. A glade materialized out of the gloom.

We burst into the open space, our breaths coming hard and fast as we raced for the cover of the tree line two hundred feet away. I suspected the same thought had just crossed Reid's mind: if the Crovirs found us now, they would shoot us down like fish in a barrel.

Halfway across the clearing, Reid gasped and fell. I skidded to a halt on the muddy, leaf-covered ground and stumbled back toward him.

He lay on his back in a shallow puddle of inky water. I reached him in time to see blood bloom across his shirt from a bullet wound. Air froze in my lungs.

Reid blinked. He lifted a hand to his chest and stared at his crimson fingers. I dropped to my knees by his side. His blank gaze shifted to my face.

'Damn. This is definitely *not* good.' His eyes fluttered closed.

'No,' I whispered brokenly.

I dropped my guns and pressed my hands against the bubbling hole in his ribcage, disbelief numbing my senses. His breathing grew labored, air rattling in and out of his lips in shallow pants. I felt and heard the faint whistle beneath my fingers. I pushed down harder.

Heat exploded on my right flank.

A shocked grunt escaped my throat. I was already reaching for the guns when the second bullet hissed through the night and grazed my forehead. I blinked fresh blood out of my eyes and twisted on my knees.

A man walked out from under the trees to the west of the clearing. As he crossed the ground toward me, he put away the gun and suppressor in his hand and reached for the sword at his waist.

I gritted my teeth and climbed to my feet. Wet warmth

coursed down my side and leg; I didn't have to look to know I was bleeding heavily. I drew the katana from its sheath and held it in a double-handed grip.

The stranger stopped a dozen feet from where I stood, swaying slightly.

'We meet again, half-breed,' he said.

I scrutinized the figure in front of me and blinked to clear blood from my lashes. Hundreds of years of instinct told me this was not a man I dared look away from.

The stranger was tall and lean. Shoulder-length, ash-blond hair gleamed under the shafts of moonlight drifting through the clouds marching across the sky. A scar carved a jagged path from the corner of his right ear to his mouth. Despite the radiance that bathed the clearing, it was too dark to fathom the color of his eyes.

Though I could not recall ever meeting the man before, an eerie sense of recognition coursed through me. I pushed the troubling feeling aside and focused on his feet. I knew they would betray his next move. Already, my vision was starting to blur.

I almost missed the first swing of his blade and lurched back awkwardly. The edge of the sword glinted as it whispered past my face. The flow of blood from my flank doubled.

Our blades met a heartbeat later. Metal clashed as I parried his blows. Mere seconds passed before I found myself forced back a step. Despite the haze of pain and the blood loss that dulled my senses, I recognized his expert swordsmanship.

The stranger continued his relentless attack, a mocking smile dawning on his face. While I could feel rivulets of perspiration trickling down my back, he had barely broken a sweat. His expression grew gleeful when I stumbled. A moment later, I was down on my knees.

I raised the katana and blocked the fatal blow in time. A

sharp sting erupted across my shoulder where his blade had cut through flesh.

'Give up,' he growled. He pressed down with his sword, teeth gleaming in the gloom as his lips parted in a feral snarl. 'You know you're going to die, half-breed!'

I saw Reid's chest rise and fall shallowly out of the corner of my eyes. A spasm of guilt and anguish racked my body, almost paralyzing in its intensity. Tears rose in my eyes. He was going to die.

A wave of unrelenting rage surged through me at the thought of the immortals who had brought us to this. My knuckles whitened on the handle of the katana. A grunt left my lips. I rose to my feet.

I was unprepared for the ring of blackness that closed in around me. I shook my head dazedly and blinked in time to catch the glint of the blade.

His sword entered my chest just beneath my right ribcage. I froze, eyes locked on his triumphant grin in dull incomprehension. My gaze finally dropped to the metal embedded in my flesh. He stepped forward.

I gasped and stiffened as scalding pain tore across my body: the sword had gone straight through my chest and out my back. A gush of frothy blood rose in my throat and spilled past my lips, choking my breath.

The stranger raised a booted foot to my thigh and pulled out the sword.

The blade left my body with a sickening wet noise. I stood stock still for a moment before falling to my knees once more. The stranger grabbed the back of my bowed head and leaned down, his lips stopping an inch from my ear.

'And now,' he hissed, spit flying from his mouth and striking my bloodied cheek, 'in these final seconds of your long and abominable life, I shall tell you the name of the man who killed your parents and who is about to end your loathsome existence!'

A crazed grimace washed across the stranger's face; it flickered distortedly as a veil of darkness clouded my vision. 'Tell your mother and father that Felix Thorne says hi!'

Moonlight shone on the edge of his sword when he raised it above his head.

I looked past him at the star-filled heavens, a strange sense of calm and acceptance washing over me as I faced my inevitable fate. Though I was grief-stricken at having led Reid to an untimely death and having been the cause of so many others dying, I knew I had done my utmost to protect the ones I cherished.

My one remaining regret on leaving this world was not having had the chance to get to know Anna Godard.

The blade pierced my heart in a single savage blow. My vision dimmed. The pain and coldness shrouding my body faded. As the last breath left my lips and I thudded to the forest floor, an image of my parents rose before my open eyes.

∼

PART TWO: RESURRECTION

CHAPTER THIRTEEN

FOR A LONG AND IMMEASURABLE STRETCH OF TIME, THERE was only darkness and a feeling of absolute weightlessness. I drifted through an endless space, unaware and nonexistent. At some undefined moment during my everlasting sleep, I became conscious of an all-encompassing presence floating around me, cocooning me in warmth. An overpowering feeling of peace washed over me and I found myself crying. Except I was no longer an "I" and I had no body to cry with.

Was this Heaven or was this Hell? Or yet still, was it the anteroom where my final fate awaited me even now?

Then came the voices. They were faint but insistent, echoes in a vast and watery tunnel. Muted words drifted tantalizingly in and out of earshot. Someone spoke quietly in Czech.

Slowly, steadily, I started to perceive my own consciousness. It was dim and ill defined, but nevertheless there. It waxed and waned for an eternity before fading once more. I sank back into dark oblivion and experienced a strange sense of loss.

Something soft and warm glided over my face. I opened my eyes.

A sea of green hovered above me. I blinked and became

aware of the tears that clouded my vision. The greenness resolved into a pair of pale, olive-colored irises, flecked with a thousand gold and brown specks. They were framed by thick lashes and long, luxuriant chestnut curls.

'Hi,' said Anna softly. She sat back, the sun cross pendant glinting at the base of her throat.

'Green,' I mumbled, the word spilling out before I could stop it.

Her brow knotted in a frown. 'What?'

'Your eyes. They're green.' My voice sounded weak and raspy even to my own ears.

Her lips curved in a smile that dimpled her cheeks. 'Yes. They are,' she acknowledged with a chuckle.

The sound of her laughter prickled my skin with a wave of awareness. Memory returned in a surge of stark images. Coldness gripped me.

'I died,' I said bluntly.

Anna's expression sobered.

Another frozen still rose in my mind. 'Reid!'

I pushed up on my elbows and gasped when pain painted a dozen fiery trails across my body.

There wasn't an inch of me that did not seem to be hurting.

'Don't!' Anna placed her hands on my shoulders and lowered me to the bed. 'You might reopen your wounds.' A tired smile crossed her face at my stricken expression. 'Reid is fine. He's resting in the next room.'

Unspeakable relief washed over me at her words. Reid was alive. As was I, incredibly enough. But how? A horde of questions buzzed through my brain.

I looked around and asked the most pressing one. 'Where are we?'

Sunlight streamed through gauzy white curtains framing a tall window to the left. It illuminated the faded wallpaper covering the walls of a bedroom and sparkled off the crystal chandelier hanging from the elaborately corniced ceiling. Cobwebs populated the distant corners. The furniture was sparse and utilitarian; whatever there was of it looked antique Bohemian, old but in good condition.

'We're in a safe house outside Prague,' said Anna.

She poured some water from a carafe on the bedside table, lifted my head carefully off the pillow, and brought the glass to my lips. I sipped, then gulped the cold liquid, suddenly conscious of my raging thirst.

'Not so fast,' she admonished and took away the glass.

I settled back in the bed and gazed blindly at the ceiling. My mind was clearing. A single thought now occupied it, far ahead of the queue of others.

'That was my seventeenth death.' My eyes shifted to Anna. She looked away, her expression troubled. An uneasy silence fell between us. 'What happened?'

She rose from the bed and stepped to the window. I stared at her profile and the elegant line of her neck while she spoke.

'When grandfather and I realized that the Crovirs had found us, we started a fire in the safe house and escaped through the underground passage in the cellar,' she said quietly. 'It took us to the woods on the other side of the hill.' She glanced at me. 'When we heard the explosion and the shooting, we knew Victor had returned with Reid and you, and that you were engaged in a fight with the Crovirs. We came to look for you afterward.'

I digested this information for a moment. 'What of Victor and the others?'

'They all made it, but not without sustaining injuries.' She turned then and stared me straight in the eye, her gaze unflinching. 'When we found the two of you, Reid was almost dead. You had no detectable pulse. By the time Bruno returned with a car, you were breathing again.' She hesitated. 'You're absolutely positive that *was* your seventeenth death?'

'Yes,' I replied flatly.

Footsteps sounded outside the room. The door opened to reveal Victor Dvorsky.

The Bastian noble's eyes widened when he saw that I was awake. 'You're up.'

There was a fresh dressing on his forehead and a bandage around his hand. He was favoring his right leg.

'How long have I been out?' I pushed back the covers and tried to sit up again. This time, I was successful.

I swung my legs off the bed. A wave of dizziness hit me. I leaned heavily on the edge of the mattress.

That was when I saw the bandages encircling my chest and flanks.

'Two days,' said Anna. 'You lost a lot of blood.'

I reached for the glass of water with a shaky hand and grimaced when the movement stretched damaged muscles.

Victor leaned against the doorjamb and watched me closely. 'How are you feeling?'

'I've been better.' I struggled to mask my anxiety at Anna's words. Considering the events of the last week, two days was a long time to lose. 'Although, technically, I shouldn't even be here.'

'True,' said Victor guardedly.

A figure loomed behind him.

Reid's left arm was in a sling. The outline of dressings was visible beneath his shirt.

A smile tugged at my lips when I saw the cigarette at the corner of his mouth. He looked a bit pale but seemed his normal self.

'I heard voices,' he said with a grin.

Anna's eyes narrowed when she saw the cigarette. She crossed the floor and snatched the roll from his lips.

'I removed a bullet from your chest barely forty-eight hours ago. The least you could do is not smoke!' she hissed.

Reid looked unrepentant. 'You do realize this will only delay my recovery, don't you?'

'How, exactly?' Anna retorted.

'By not letting me smoke, you're causing me undue stress. I'm sure I read somewhere that stress slows down wound healing,' said Reid, deadpan.

Anna rolled her eyes and opened her mouth for what was likely going to be a scathing riposte when movement outside the room interrupted her.

'What's going on?' said Tomas Godard.

The old man seemed to have aged a decade since I last saw him.

'Your granddaughter's infringing on my rights,' Reid explained.

'She's your doctor. You should listen to her,' said Godard with a distracted expression. His eyes never left my face. 'Besides, you owe her your life. She gave you blood.'

Reid's eyes widened. He stared at Anna. 'You did?'

Her cheeks colored.

'Oh.' Reid looked stunned.

Anna squared her shoulders. 'Right, all of you leave, *now*. He needs to rest.'

She shooed the men out of the room and paused on the threshold. 'There's a bathroom across the corridor. The clothes in the wardrobe should fit you.' Her eyes softened. 'Come down when you're ready.'

I watched the door close behind her. My skin still burned where she had touched me.

The light outside was fading when I finally made my way along a corridor to the head of a grand staircase. Already, I could feel strength flowing back in my limbs.

The new safe house was a manor. From what I had glimpsed through the window of my bedroom, it was situated on a deserted estate. I stopped on a landing and examined the paintings lining the wood-paneled walls of the entrance hall. It was a deliberate distraction; my mind was not quite ready to deal with the overwhelming subject of having survived my seventeenth death.

I crossed the foyer at the bottom of the stairs and followed the sound of voices down a dim passage to a kitchen at the back of the house. There was a lull in the conversation when I appeared in the doorway.

Reid, Victor Dvorsky, and the Godards sat at an old, scarred walnut table dominating an extensive flagstone floor. A fire crackled in the hearth next to them, the flames casting golden, flickering light across the whitewashed walls.

Reid drew out the chair next to him.

'Where are Bruno and Anatole?' I said as I took the seat.

'They're out getting provisions,' said Victor.

An awkward hush followed.

I sighed. 'So, are we going to get to the point or are we going to indulge in some small talk first?'

Victor leaned back in his chair. Reid unearthed a cigarette from somewhere and struck a match lazily. Anna turned and gave him a dark look.

A low chuckle broke the silence. 'You always were impatient, even as a child,' said Tomas Godard. 'In that respect at least, you resemble your mother.'

I froze, shock coursing through me as I stared at the blue eyes so alike to mine. The strong feeling of foreboding that had lingered at the back of my mind since I first met Tomas Godard suddenly crystallized into a cold certainty. I knew this man. Though I could not recall his features, I felt that I had known him for a long, long time.

'Who are you?' I said in a low voice, almost afraid to hear the answer.

Godard's shoulders sagged. He suddenly looked incredibly old. 'I am your grandfather.'

Anna gasped. 'What?'

Though I sensed the sudden tension running through him, Reid remained silent at my side.

Victor watched me wordlessly. From the lack of surprise on the Bastian noble's face, it was evident he knew the facts of the matter.

I sat still for some time, Godard's words ringing in my ears. Although my whole being resonated from his revelation, I was convinced that he spoke the truth.

'Your mother, Catarine, was my eldest daughter,' said Godard. He looked at his granddaughter. 'Anna's mother, Lily, was my youngest child.'

'How—' Anna started, her expression troubled. She stopped, visibly struggling for words. 'Why have you never spoken of this before? I thought mother was an only child!' She could not mask the accusing tone in her voice.

A sad light appeared in Godard's eyes. 'I've kept this secret for so long, I'm afraid that it has become a force of habit over the years.' He reached out and touched her face with gentle fingers. 'Besides, the knowledge would only have brought you pain.'

'What do you mean?' Anna's voice rose. Anger and grief darkened her irises to a cloudy sea green. 'In what way would knowing that I had—' she glanced at me, 'a family have hurt me?'

Silence followed her tormented words.

My hands fisted under the table. 'I take it she doesn't know about the half-breed thing?' I said bitterly. I was surprised at the anger surging through me.

A pained expression washed across Tomas Godard's face.

Victor frowned. 'We don't like to use that term.'

'Why not?' I retorted. This time, I was unable to hide the fury in my voice. Reid laid a hand on my arm. 'After all, it's the reason my parents were murdered and I've been hunted all my life! Why be coy about it?'

'I don't understand,' whispered Anna. She stared from me to her grandfather, her face deathly pale.

Tomas Godard closed his eyes briefly. 'Five hundred years ago, well after the last days of the Red Death, Catarine fell in love with a highborn Crovir noble. They met at one of the balls organized jointly by the immortal societies to foster kinship between our two races following the end of the war.' He glanced at Victor with a troubled expression. 'That noble's name was Balthazar Thorne.'

I flinched. 'My father's name was Slovansky.'

Godard shook his head. 'Slovansky was the name your parents adopted when they went into exile.' He looked down at his hands. 'Despite my protests, Catarine and Balthazar married secretly in the year following their first meeting. As immortals, they recognized their destined soulmate in each other and were determined to never be apart from that time forth. You were born forty years later, in 1560, in Prague. When the immortal societies found out about your existence, a warrant was issued for your capture and execution.' He turned to Anna. 'You know of the old law that prohibits the union between a Crovir and a Bastian?'

Anna nodded. 'I've always thought it an archaic rule,' she said stiffly. 'The only function it appears to serve is to separate our two societies further.'

A sad smile crossed Godard's face at her words. 'Yes, I thought so too, from that time onward.'

His gaze shifted to Victor again. The latter was frowning at the table.

'With both the Crovir and Bastian Hunters after them, Catarine and Balthazar had no choice but to go into hiding,' Godard continued. 'They fled to the Carpathian Mountains. Nine years passed and they managed to stay out of sight. On their tenth year in hiding, the Hunters finally found them. By the time Victor told me they were on their trail again, it was too late. When we got there, Catarine and Balthazar were already dead.'

'Weren't you the Head of the Bastian Hunters at the time?' I said, still doubtful.

'No. I gave up that position on the day you were born.' Godard observed me with a tortured expression. 'I could never order the murder of my own daughter and grandchild.'

'Grandfather,' Anna whispered. She placed her hand over his.

'It was my father who issued the decree on the Bastian side,' said Victor curtly. 'He received a tip from the Crovirs as to the whereabouts of your family.'

'But...the old man said you tried to stop the Hunters,' said Reid with a puzzled frown.

Godard bestowed a forlorn gaze upon Dvorsky. 'Victor loved Catarine. And I believe he still does to this day.'

Victor cleared his throat. 'Look, I wouldn't go that far. That woman used to bully me.'

'She was a hundred years younger than you,' said Godard.

'She had a sharp tongue on her,' Victor retorted.

Godard smiled. 'True. Had Balthazar not stolen her heart, I had hoped the two of you would marry one day.'

Victor's ears glowed bright red. 'Stop talking nonsense, old man.'

'You were there when my parents died?' I said at last.

The rage that had threatened to overwhelm me had abated. In its place was a cauldron of mixed emotions. Memories of that snowy day in the Carpathian Mountains rose afresh in my mind.

'Yes,' said Victor. 'We got there after your first death. Tomas and I took care of the rest of the Hunters before you woke up.'

A dozen questions clouded my mind. I gazed at my grandfa-

ther and asked the one that troubled me the most. 'Why did
you leave me?'

'Victor and I debated this time and time again,' said
Godard. 'We always arrived at the same conclusion. If you had
remained with me, the Hunters would undoubtedly have found
you again. Though it was the most difficult choice I have ever
had to make in my immortal life, you had a much better chance
of survival on your own, out there in the world of humans.'

'I made sure you at least got out of the mountains and
reached the nearest village safely,' Victor said gruffly.

An incident from that time suddenly came to me. 'The
wolves?' I asked.

As I made my escape from the mountains, a lonely and
frightened ten-year-old, I had been trailed and almost attacked
twice by a pack of wild wolves. They disappeared unexpectedly
after the third day.

Victor's lips curved in a faint smile. 'It took a while to get
rid of them. I nearly gave myself away the second time.'

I observed him silently, unable to voice the feelings that
choked my throat. My eyes moved to Godard. 'Did you know
where I was all these years?'

'Sometimes,' said Godard. He grimaced. 'I always heard of
your deaths at the hands of the Hunters. When it became
evident that you did not pose a threat to the immortals, Victor
and I persuaded both Orders to call off the hunt. In exchange, I
promised never to make contact with you again.'

I digested this information silently. I now knew the reason
why the Hunters' attempts to kill me abated a century ago. I
recalled his words at the Hauptbahnhof and finally understood
their meaning.

'Is that why you didn't want me to get involved in whatever
it is that's going on here?'

'Yes,' said Godard. A scowl washed across face. 'Of course,
that was before I knew the Crovirs were after you again.'

Anna rose and turned on the lights. Night had fallen outside.

'The man who killed me said his name was Felix Thorne,' I said after a while, still struggling to come to grips with the revelations of the last hour. 'Is he related to my father?'

Godard's eyebrows rose. 'Felix was there that night?'

'Yes.'

Victor and Godard exchanged troubled glances.

'He's your uncle,' said Victor. 'And the Crovir Head of Counter Terrorism.'

I stiffened.

'They're getting bold,' murmured Godard. 'For Felix to join a hunt is practically unheard of.' He turned to me. 'Agatha Vellacrus had three sons. Their names were Cecil, Felix, and Balthazar Thorne. Of the three, only Felix is still alive.'

Another jolt of shock darted through me. 'You mean Vellacrus is my grandmother?'

'Yes,' Godard replied. 'Although she *has* tried her best to keep it a secret from both immortal societies. There are only a handful of us still alive today who know the truth.' He sighed. 'I will never understand how she gave birth to someone as gentle and kind as your father.'

A door slammed at the front of the house, startling us. Bruno and Anatole entered the kitchen moments later, their arms laden with carrier bags. They paused when they saw us.

'Hey, you're up,' said Bruno. He glanced at me awkwardly and put the bags on the countertop.

'You gave us all quite a shock when you started breathing again,' said Anatole.

'Anatole,' Bruno admonished.

Anatole shrugged, unrepentant. 'What? It's true. I mean, the guy survived his seventeenth death. No immortal has ever done that before.'

I looked at Tomas Godard. 'He's right.'

The old man's expression reflected my own perplexity at the most staggering fact in this whole affair so far. 'I'm afraid I don't have the answer to that question,' he said. 'I am just as surprised as everyone else.'

'Does it have anything to do with the fact that I can kill other immortals?'

Godard shook his head. 'I honestly don't know.'

'Anyone hungry?' said Anatole in the silence that followed.

Bruno glared at him.

'What? We still gotta eat, right?'

CHAPTER FOURTEEN

THE MANOR HOUSE WAS OWNED BY VICTOR'S FAMILY AND stood, as I had suspected, on a large estate a few miles outside Prague. Once a popular entertainment venue for the Dvorskys, it had been abandoned since the end of the Second World War and now mostly served as a hideout for the nobles.

I stared at the moonlit trees lining the driveway to the house and caught a glimpse of Anatole patrolling the grounds; Bruno was guarding the rear of the manor. A scattering of leaves still clung to the bare branches high above the ground. Autumn was well and truly here. I turned from the window and faced the room.

We were in a study on the ground floor of the mansion. A fire hissed in the hearth at the head of the room.

'How did you know Strauss?' I asked Anna. 'And what were the two of you working on?'

'Hubert was a Professor in molecular genetics,' Anna replied. 'We met twenty-five years ago, when I was working at the UPMC in Paris. At the time, we were both doing research in potential genetic therapies for cancer.'

'So you *were* trying to find a cure for cancer?' said Reid.

Anna shook her head. 'No, not a cure, as such. We were attempting to—well, control the disease, really.' She ran her hand through her hair. 'If we could affect the rate at which cancer cells replicated, we would be able to extend the life of a patient to such a time when a cure might be available.'

'Why did you leave Paris?'

'I received an invitation to work at the FGCZ ten years ago,' said Anna. 'I was promised my own lab and as many research assistants as I wanted. It was too good an offer to refuse. Even Hubert agreed.' A sad smile crossed her face. 'Even though I left the UPMC, we kept in touch. After all, we were still working in the same field and shared common interests.'

'Then he received the grant from GeMBiT,' I murmured. All the pieces of the puzzle were almost there. I just couldn't see how they fit together yet.

'Burnstein approached him directly,' said Anna. 'Hubert was surprised. It seemed the scientists at GeMBiT Corp had been keeping an eye on his research for some time.'

'What was it again?' said Reid. 'Advanced cell—'

'Advanced cell cycle control and DNA transposition. Hubert was attempting to manipulate genetic material to create an "off" switch to down regulate cancer cell production.'

'Slow down cell production and you control the cancer,' I said.

She nodded. 'Exactly.'

'What happened?'

Anna closed her eyes briefly. When she opened them again, I saw the answer to my question in their green depths. 'He succeeded.'

Stunned silence descended on the room. Subconsciously, I think I had known what her reply was going to be even before she uttered the words. The potential ramifications of such a find were truly staggering; whoever owned the rights to the discovery would be raking in billions every year.

At that notion, a different thought crossed my mind.

'It can't be what this is really about.' I frowned. 'The Crovirs have more than enough money to buy the entire European continent. They couldn't have been interested in Strauss's research just for the financial gain.'

'It sounds like a big enough reason to me,' said Reid. 'And the *entire* European continent? You're kidding, right?'

'I'm afraid he isn't,' said Victor.

Reid paled.

'I have another snippet of information for you,' added Victor. 'Frederick Burnstein is not just any Crovir—he's the Head of their Research & Development Section and a member of the First Council.'

Somehow, this latest news hardly came as a surprise.

I observed Anna thoughtfully. 'It still doesn't explain why the Crovirs are after you. Or why they're trying to kill me again.'

Anna hesitated. 'You're right. Hubert discovered something else. Something far more staggering than a cure for cancer.'

Reid grunted. 'What could be a bigger find than a cure for cancer?'

'That's the thing. I don't know,' she said, frustration evident in her tone. 'I lost contact with Hubert before he could tell me. His last email indicated that whatever the discovery was, it would change the world as we know it forever.'

'You were helping him?' I asked after some time.

Anna dipped her head. 'Hubert wanted someone outside GeMBiT to validate his work. I guess the only one he trusted to do this objectively was me.'

I raised my eyebrows. 'Did Burnstein know he was sharing research information with you?'

'No,' Anna replied. 'Our messages to each other were always encrypted.'

The flames in the hearth popped and crackled while I

absorbed this new piece of information. 'Why did Strauss open a bank account in Zurich?'

Anna's expression became troubled. 'Two months ago, out of the blue, Burnstein visited Hubert in Paris. He wanted access to his latest research data. This was just after Hubert made the major breakthrough. From what he told me, Burnstein was quite forceful. Hubert got scared and contacted me.'

'Was that when he went into hiding?'

'He stalled for time as long as he could,' said Anna. 'When Burnstein sent some men to follow him, Hubert panicked and ran away.'

'Is that how they got your picture?' I asked.

Lines wrinkled her brow. 'What picture?'

'We found a photograph of you and Strauss on Burnstein's computer. You met in a restaurant, at night,' I explained.

'Oh.' Her expression softened. She smiled at her grandfather. 'Yes. That was before our trip to Italy.'

'Where did Strauss go?' said Reid.

'We have some mutual friends in the Rhône region,' said Anna. 'He was supposed to be staying at their farm until I returned to Zurich.' A sad light dawned in her eyes. 'He was going to join me there.'

'How did they find him?' I said.

'I can only guess that he went back to Paris or Gif-sur-Yvette for some reason or another. The Crovirs must have been watching both addresses.'

'Did you know Burnstein was an immortal?'

'No,' said Anna, shaking her head vigorously. 'It was only after Hubert disappeared that I discovered GeMBiT Corp was owned by a Crovir noble. I called Grandfather for help shortly after our return from Italy.'

'How did you end up on the run?' said Reid.

It was Tomas Godard who replied. 'When I found out the Crovir First Council was plotting something big in Europe, I suspected it might be linked to Burnstein's recent interest in Hubert and the latter's disappearance. Anyone else involved in the matter was bound to be in danger from the Crovirs.'

'The day after I got back from Italy, someone tried to break into my house,' Anna added quietly. 'Grandfather took me into hiding that very evening.'

Stillness fell over the room once more. I suddenly remembered something.

'Here, I believe this is yours.' I took the daguerreotype from my jacket and handed it to her.

Anna's eyes widened. She took the frame from my grasp. 'I thought I'd lost this.' She showed the picture to Godard.

'My goodness,' said Godard. 'I remember that day.' He smiled. 'It was raining. You had just turned ten.'

'Yes.' Anna chuckled. 'I was so bored on that trip, I must've driven you crazy.'

Envy stabbed through me as I watched them. Shocked at the unexpected emotion, I turned and met Reid's shrewd stare. I flushed self-consciously.

'What was in the safety deposit box in Zurich?' Reid asked Anna as she gazed warmly at the daguerreotype.

Her head snapped up at his words. 'How do you know about the safety deposit box?'

Reid shrugged. 'We've been doing our own research.'

Anna frowned. 'You went to the bank?'

'Yes,' I said.

'And they let you see details of the account?' she said, aghast.

'They had to for Interpol Agent Petersen and FBI Agent Barnes,' drawled Reid.

Anna looked slightly mollified. 'After what happened with Burnstein in Paris, Hubert and I decided it would be best to keep his research findings somewhere secure. We opened the Zurich account shortly after.'

'Wasn't his latest discovery in there as well?' I said, puzzled.

'No. He didn't include it in those papers.' Anna hesitated. 'I think he was too afraid to write it down.'

I removed Strauss's battered journal from my pocket. 'Will this help?'

Anna gasped and shot out of her chair. 'Where did you find this?' She touched the journal reverently, her fingers lingering on the cover.

'At Gif-sur-Yvette,' I replied, trying not to inhale the heady scent of oranges drifting from her skin. 'He hid it inside a staff locker in the building.'

Anna took the diary from my hands and leafed through the last few pages. Her brow knotted.

'Did you find something else with this?' she said, rifling hastily through the rest of the journal.

'Yes. There was a memory stick.' I grimaced. 'I'm afraid we lost it when we were getting away from the Crovirs.'

'What's wrong?' Victor asked Anna.

'Hubert encrypted the last twenty pages of the journal,' she explained in a dispirited tone. 'The cipher must be on the memory stick.'

My stomach sank. 'Haven't you used the same ones in the past?'

Anna shook her head. 'No. We changed them all the time. Part of the challenge was decoding them.' She scrutinized the final pages of the journal. 'I've never seen this one before. It looks like a stacked cipher.'

'What's that?' said Reid.

'It's a combination of different ciphers used together in a series,' said Anna. She stared blindly into space. 'It's quite diffi-cult to unravel.'

'Do you think you can decrypt it?' I asked.

'Given time, yes, probably.'

'How much time?' said Reid. "Cause I get the feeling we're running out of that precious commodity.'

Reid's words mirrored my own feelings. The trepidation that had been humming through my veins since the incident at the canal in Vienna had doubled when I heard what Strauss's research was about; I also sensed that speed was now of the essence in our race to find out what the Crovirs were up to.

Anna's gaze switched from the journal to Victor. 'I need a computer,' she demanded. 'And a couple of other things.'

I could practically see cogwheels turning behind her eyes.

'Write down what you require,' said Victor with a curt nod. 'We'll get the items for you.'

Five minutes later, she handed him a short inventory. Victor made a call on his cell and listed the articles Anna had requested to the person on the other end of the line. He disconnected and gave Bruno an address.

'Go to this place. They should have everything ready by the time you get there.'

The clock on the mantelpiece was chiming midnight when the bodyguard finally returned with a boxful of hardware.

'Do you need a hand?' I asked Anna as she started to unpack a laptop.

She cocked an eyebrow. 'Are you any good with this stuff?' She indicated the array of electronic equipment laid out across the mahogany desk in the study.

I shrugged noncommittally. 'I'm not too bad with them.'

Reid's muffled snort erupted from across the room.

Anna studied me for a moment. 'All right. I should insist you get some rest, but I could do with the help.'

Godard turned to Victor. 'Have you heard any news from your father?'

Victor shook his head. 'No. According to our intel, the Crovir First Council has denied all knowledge of any involve-

ment by any of their members in the incidents in Vienna and
Vilanec.'

Godard's jaw tightened. 'They're stalling for time. Has
Roman or another member of the Bastian First Council actually
spoken to Vellacrus yet?'

'She's currently unreachable,' Victor replied in a dry tone.

Godard stared at the flames in the hearth. 'She's playing a
dangerous game,' he murmured after a while. His anxious gaze
shifted to Victor. 'We all know the attempt on your life is
grounds enough for an official challenge to the Crovirs.'

'That doesn't sound good,' said Reid in the taut lull that
followed.

Godard sighed. 'It isn't. If the immortal war was to start
again, millions of humans would get caught in the crossfire.' A
scowl clouded his features. 'I'm not about to let six hundred
odd years of peace end because of that damn woman!'

'That won't happen,' said Victor with an adamant shake of
his head. 'Roman and the entire Order of Bastian Hunters will
be behind us. He's talking to the rest of our Councils as we
speak.' He paused. 'Besides, you forget we have friends among
the Crovirs.'

Godard hesitated. 'I hope you're right, for all our sake.'

'You should try and get some sleep,' said Anna. She walked
around the desk and placed a hand on her grandfather's arm.
'This is going to take some time.'

While the others retired for the night, Anna and I stayed in
the study and pored over the information in Strauss's journal.
Despite cross referencing the encrypted paragraphs with online
deciphering programs, including the ones used by the US
National Security Agency, we hit a dead end time and
time again.

'This is impossible,' Anna finally murmured just after two
am. She ran her fingers through her tousled hair, leaned back in
the chair, and closed her eyes.

I lifted the journal from the desk and randomly leafed through the encrypted pages. 'How did you usually come up with the ciphers?'

A sigh left Anna's lips. She opened her eyes and fixed me with a green stare. 'They were mostly about things we had in common. Places we'd been to, work we had done together, even the music we both liked.' A sad smile dawned on her face. 'It was a bit of a game for Hubert. He loved nothing more than coming up with the most intricate of ciphers.'

I ignored the prickle of jealousy that darted through me. 'Were the two of you involved in a relationship?'

Surprise flared in her eyes. For a moment, I thought she would not reply.

'We were, in the past.'

I looked down at the journal to mask my relief. Something caught my eyes on the last page. It was a small diagram in the margin I had not paid particular attention to before. I pointed it out to Anna.

'What's this?'

Anna studied the sketch. 'That's a drawing of an Okazaki fragment,' she said. 'It's a short section of genetic material created during DNA replication,' she explained at my puzzled expression. A tired chuckle left her lips. 'He liked to doodle.'

I straightened, unable to shake the feeling that I had just touched on something significant. 'I think I saw something similar earlier.'

I thumbed back over the previous pages. Seconds later, my hands stilled on the journal. I tapped a finger over another drawing at the edge of the paper. 'Here.'

Anna's eyes slowly widened. 'It isn't similar. It's an exact mirror image of the other one!'

We looked at each other with rising excitement.

'He drew them at the start and end of the encrypted pages,' I said.

Fifteen minutes later, after carefully piecing together the twelve pairs of Okazaki fragments scattered across twenty pages of text, we had the first cipher. It took another half hour to uncover the other two.

'He used a combination of a polyalphabetic substitution, a transposition, and a date-shift cipher based on the first, middle, and last encrypted pages,' Anna murmured in an awed voice.

We stared at the three algorithms scribbled on a sheet of paper.

'Is that common?' I knew a little about the art of cryptography from my previous involvement in wars over the last four centuries.

'No. Even a professional cryptanalyst would have struggled with this. Had you not spotted the significance of the Okazaki fragment, we would have been at this for days.' She looked at me gratefully.

I was suddenly aware of how close we sat. I rose to hide my unease and offered to make coffee while she deciphered the encrypted data.

It was well past four in the morning when Anna reached the last page of Strauss's diary. I watched her writing grow slower while she double-checked her work. She finally stopped and put the pen down carefully.

'Dear God,' she said in a shaky voice. 'No wonder he didn't want to put this on paper.'

Anxiety knotted my stomach as I studied her pale face. 'What is it?'

Anna glanced at me with a distracted expression. 'Remember the "off" switch I was talking about?'

'You mean the one that can slow down cancer cell production?' I said.

She nodded.

'What about it?'

'Hubert found an "on" switch,' Anna said flatly.

I frowned, unable to grasp the significance of her words. 'What does that mean?'

Anna's eyes reflected the fear in her voice. 'It means he discovered a way to control the cell cycle.'

'When you say control the cell cycle...' I trailed off as understanding began to dawn. I felt my blood grow cold.

'If what is written here is true, he has uncovered the Holy Grail of science,' declared Anna. 'He's made a genetically modified cell that can never die.'

'Immortality,' I said numbly.

Anna shook her head. 'No, not just immortality as *we* understand it. At the rate at which this cell would be able to replicate, it means true immortality.'

I inhaled sharply. 'You mean, beyond seventeen deaths?'

'Yes.' A frown clouded her face. She turned to the desk and rifled through the papers from the Zurich deposit box. 'But there's something I don't understand.'

'What?' I mumbled, still trying to absorb the staggering implication behind Strauss's research findings.

'Hubert used a sequence of techniques both of us have worked with in the past,' Anna explained in a puzzled voice. 'The only difference between the experiments would have to be —' She froze. 'Oh, no.' The blood drained from her face. She stood abruptly.

'Anna?' I rose from my seat as she ran from the room. Her footsteps faded on the stairs.

I was still standing there when she returned moments later, a metal flask clasped in her hands. My eyes widened. 'Is that—'

'Yes. From that day at the Hauptbahnhof,' Anna replied breathlessly. 'This is what Helena was bringing me.'

'What is it?'

Anna opened the canister and carefully removed a vial from it. I stared at the crimson liquid inside.

'Is that blood?'

'Yes.' Anna's gaze shifted to me. 'I have to get to a lab.' Her voice was edged with desperation.

'Why?' I said. Something was tugging at the back of my brain. A cold suspicion trickled through my thoughts as I examined the glass tube in her hand.

'I need to test this sample,' said Anna.

I opened my mouth to voice another question.

She raised a hand and stopped me. 'Please! I just have to do this. It's the only way I'll know for sure.'

I studied her stricken expression for some time before turning to the computer. 'What kind of lab do you need?'

CHAPTER FIFTEEN

AT FIVE IN THE MORNING, THE PRAGUE INSTITUTE OF
Molecular Genetics was dark and deserted. We broke into the
building through a side door and went in search of the Functional Genomics and Bioinformatics department.

Reid and Bruno took up guard duty outside the room while
Anna and I entered the premises.

'How long will this take?' I said, flicking on the overhead
lights.

'An hour and a half, two at the most.'

Anna crossed the room briskly, her face brightening as she
studied the array of machines humming quietly on the countertops; already, her eyes held a faraway gaze. She slipped on a pair
of gloves and removed the vial of blood from the metal canister.

She transferred a few drops into a smaller tube and turned
to me. 'Can I have your sword?'

I stared at her, nonplussed.

'I need a sample of my blood,' she explained. I lifted the
wakizashi from my waist and passed it across reluctantly.

She nicked the side of her thumb with the edge of the short
blade and dripped several scarlet droplets into a second vial. I

removed a Band-Aid from the first aid kit next to the sink and wrapped it gently around her finger. She stiffened slightly at my touch.

'Thank you.'

'You're welcome.' I took a seat in the corner of the room and ignored the tingling heat in my hands while I watched her work.

Anna moved from one complicated apparatus to another, her movements swift and confident. All the while, a tiny frown wrinkled her brow.

I looked out of the window, unsettled as always by the complex feelings her presence engendered; if Reid had been in the room, he would no doubt have been wearing a sickening leer.

Forty minutes later, Anna lowered herself onto the chair next to me.

'Now we wait,' she explained at my questioning gaze.

The next hour passed at a snail's pace while the machines hummed quietly. The sun had just peeked above the horizon when Anna finally lifted a sheet of paper from the printer attached to an instrument.

She stared at the data crowding the page. 'It's done,' she said in a flat tone.

We exited the campus moments later and headed back to the estate.

Anna remained subdued during the drive back, her green eyes staring blindly at the landscape outside the window. I remained silent by her side, certain my suspicions about the vial of blood would prove to be correct.

Victor and Godard were waiting for us when we entered the foyer of the mansion.

'Well?' said Godard anxiously. 'What is this all about?'

Anna had refused to answer any questions when we roused

the rest of the household several hours ago to organize our expedition to the Prague Institute of Molecular Genetics.

'You had better sit down,' she said dully.

We gathered in the kitchen. Anna took the seat at the head of the table and removed the metal canister out of the bag she had clutched with white-knuckled fingers during our return trip. Her hands shook slightly when she placed the container in front of her. She took a deep breath and started to talk.

'Six months ago, I sent Hubert a sample of blood to use in his experiments. I am certain it's this particular specimen that helped provide the last breakthrough in his research.' She hesitated. 'You see, Hubert's discovery was...immortality.'

Shocked gasps echoed around the room.

'*What?*' Victor barked.

'Hubert created a genetically altered cell that can replicate forever,' Anna stated.

'You mean—' Godard started.

'Yes,' Anna interrupted with a somber expression. 'He made a cell that can never die.'

A stunned silence ensued.

'No wonder the Crovirs are stirred up,' Victor finally murmured.

My eyes never left Anna's face. Although I knew the answer, I still had to ask the question.

'It was your blood, wasn't it?'

She met my gaze unflinchingly. 'Yes.'

Godard stared at her, aghast. 'Why on Earth would you—' He stopped and swallowed convulsively.

A mirthless chuckle left Anna's lips. 'Why did I give him a sample of my blood? Well, they do say the best scientists experiment on themselves.'

'Hang on,' said Reid. 'Surely, this isn't the first time immortal blood has been used in some kind of research or another. Burnstein sounds like the kinda guy who would've tried something like this already.'

'You're right.' Anna sighed and rubbed her temples. 'I've sent Hubert several samples of blood from other immortals in the last few years. I've even used some in my own research.'

'But it never worked before,' I said.

'No.'

Victor grew still. 'What are you saying?'

'It's my blood!' Anna snapped. 'There must be something in my blood that—that finally made the experiment work, somehow!'

Godard went pale at her words. He glanced at me with an unreadable expression.

I frowned. 'That's why the Crovirs are after you. Burnstein must have found out Hubert used your sample in his research.'

Anna shook her head vehemently. 'Hubert didn't know it was my blood. Even if he knew, he would never have betrayed me.'

'I'm not saying he did. That information could've been somewhere in his lab.'

'If the Crovirs don't know the blood was yours, then they must be after you to find out whose it was,' said Victor. He observed Anna guardedly. 'Did Strauss know you were an immortal?'

'No,' Anna replied, her tone adamant. 'But I'm sure he must have suspected something. After all, I've hardly aged in the last twenty-five years.'

'What now?' said Reid after a while.

'We need to determine exactly what the Crovirs are intending to do with this knowledge,' said Victor in a hard voice. 'Burnstein must be working directly with Vellacrus. Only she or Felix could have rallied so many Hunters in such a short time.'

Godard's gaze shifted from Anna to me. 'It doesn't explain why they're after Lucas though,' he said in a troubled voice.

Olsson's words suddenly rose in my mind. I had been puzzled by them at the time and still was to a certain extent.

'Mikael said I was the only one who stood in their way.'

'In the way of what though?' said Victor. A frustrated sigh left his lips. 'Enough of this! Let's see what the First Council has for us.' He rose and strode out of the room, cell phone in hand.

The back door opened. Anatole strolled in.

The immortal was no longer limping.

'Right, we got eggs for breakfast, and look what I caught us for lunch.' He grinned and lifted a pair of dead pheasants. The grave mood permeating the room finally made an impression on him. 'What's with the gloomy faces?' His smile faltered. 'Did someone die?'

Bruno sighed. 'Just give me the goddamned eggs.'

Victor returned moments later, a thoughtful look on his face. 'I just spoke to Oktav. They caught Pinchter in Suben. He was trying to cross the border into Germany.'

'That shifty bastard,' Anatole muttered.

'They're taking him to Linz.' A dark smile curved the Bastian noble's lips. 'I'm sending the two of you to collect him,' he told Bruno and Anatole.

The bodyguard and the driver exchanged meaningful glances.

Victor's eyes narrowed. 'You're not allowed to rough him up.'

Anatole sighed. 'Jeez, you really take all the fun out of this job.'

Victor patted him on the shoulder. 'Don't worry. It doesn't mean I'll stop you from doing so once he's here.'

Anna straightened in her seat. 'You're going to torture him?' she said stiffly.

Victor grimaced. 'Not exactly. But we need answers.'

Godard scowled. 'They're trying to kill you and Lucas. I wouldn't mind having a go at the man myself.'

'That's the spirit, Gramps!' Anatole punched the air with his fist. He sobered at Victor's expression. 'Sorry, boss.'

The two immortals left the manor a short while later. The sound of the Transporter's tires grinding across gravel gradually faded in the distance.

I studied the dark circles under Anna's eyes. 'You should get some rest.'

'So should you.' A guilty expression flashed across her face. 'I should check your wounds first though.'

I nodded.

We left the kitchen and headed upstairs to my room. I sat on the edge of the bed and shrugged out of my shirt. My bruised and torn muscles were mending fast. The fiery pain of the day before had turned into a dull ache.

Anna knelt before me and gently took down the dressings that covered my ribcage.

'They're almost healed,' she said, surprise evident in her voice.

Her fingers fluttered over my skin while she examined my injuries. She paused over a faint scar next to my birthmark and looked at me questioningly.

'That's from last week,' I explained stiffly. A different kind of heat was spreading through my body at her touch.

Her gaze shifted. 'And this one?'

I glanced at the recent bullet wound she indicated. 'Last week as well, I'm afraid.'

She smiled. 'You've been busy.'

The now sweetly familiar and intoxicating scent of oranges wafted from her hair and the skin on her nape inches from my face. Something tightened in my gut. I bit back a groan, muscles clenching under her hand.

Anna looked up. Whatever she saw in my face made her rise abruptly to her feet. 'There's no need for further dressings.' A dark flush tainted her cheekbones. 'Just be careful you don't reopen your wounds.'

I stared at the door long after she had gone as I waited for my racing pulse to slow. Finally, I lay down on the bed and closed my eyes.

I now knew what the emotion was that I felt for Anna Godard.

It was desire.

The fact that we were related through our lineage should have made this feeling an aberration. Yet, nothing had ever felt as right in any of my lives as the startling connection between us.

I thought of the long history of immortal and human nobilities and how close relationships had been common practice for millennia to preserve the bloodlines of dynasties and maintain bonds between sovereignties.

Even though I was bone-tired, sleep proved elusive. A dozen questions still raged through my mind. What did surviving my seventeenth death mean? Would I survive my eighteenth death? And the ones after that? And who had Olsson meant when he said the man who killed his father held me dear to his heart? Was that man Tomas Godard? What were the Crovirs planning to do with Strauss's research findings?

Sometime around noon, I drifted into a light slumber.

The sun was sinking toward the horizon when a noise finally woke me. I blinked at the orange light pouring through the curtains and sat up slowly. The sound of a commotion came again.

It had originated from the ground floor of the mansion.

I gathered my swords and guns, and left the room.

Angry voices erupted from the foyer as I approached the stairs. I paused at the top and studied the scene below.

Bruno and Anatole stood in the middle of the dimly lit vestibule. They held a man between them, their fingers clasped in an iron grip around his upper arms. A black canvas hood covered the stranger's head and face. Anatole reached out and tugged the cowl off. The man blinked in the light.

The stranger was short and sported a ferret-like face. Blood trickled from his broken nose and split lip, staining the white shirt under his jacket. His hands were tied behind his back.

'What is the meaning of this—*this transgression?*' he roared, struggling in his captors' grasp. 'If you don't release me right now, the First Council will hear of this!' He glared at Bruno and Anatole.

'The First Council already knows,' said an ominous voice. 'In fact, as Head of Counter Terrorism, I don't even need their approval to arrest you, Marcus.' A shadow detached itself from the wall.

Marcus Pinchter looked around. 'Victor.' The color drained from his face. His gimlet eyes hardened a second later. 'Does Roman know about this?'

'Not only does he know, he thoroughly approves,' said Victor with a grim half-smile. 'After all, you tried to kill his only son and successor.'

The man swallowed convulsively. 'It wasn't me, it was the Crovirs,' he mumbled. 'And they weren't trying to kill you. They were only after the woman.' His nervous gaze flicked to Anna, who stood watching impassively from the doorway of the study. Godard appeared behind her.

Pinchter took a step back. 'What—what are you doing here?'

'You mean you didn't know when you betrayed us in Vienna?' Victor snapped. 'Anna is Tomas Godard's granddaughter.'

'No.' A hunted expression dawned on Pinchter's face. 'I swear to God, I didn't know! The Crovirs never said—' He broke off, his lips pressed in a thin white line.

Victor scowled. 'So you *do* admit to helping the Crovirs?'

Pinchter clenched his teeth and remained mute.

I started down the stairs.

Pinchter looked up at the sound of my footsteps. His eyes widened. '*The half-breed?* But that's impossible! You died! Felix Thorne himself—'

I stopped at the foot of the staircase and watched Pinchter expressionlessly.

'"Felix Thorne himself killed you". Is that what you were about to say?' Victor said silkily in the taut silence that followed. 'The interesting thing is, he did. And, as you can see, the "half-breed" survived his seventeenth death.' He glanced at me with hooded eyes. 'It's our little secret for now.'

He crossed the foyer and placed an arm casually around Pinchter's shoulders. 'Now you, my dear man, need to share some of your own secrets with us. Bruno and Anatole have volunteered to keep you company while you divulge these pearls of wisdom to me.'

'I can't,' Pinchter said flatly. 'Vellacrus will have my head on a plate if I say any more than this.'

'Look at it this way,' Victor said icily. 'You *will* die, here, today, if you don't tell me what I need to know.' He paused. 'However, if the information you provide us with turns out to be useful, I promise I'll do my best to keep you from the clutches of that woman.'

'That's impossible!' Pinchter retorted. 'You have no idea what you're up against this time. Vellacrus is—' He stopped and clamped his lips shut once more.

Victor patted Pinchter's back in a friendly manner and motioned to Bruno and Anatole. 'Fear not, Marcus. You'll talk. I promise you that at least.' He headed down the corridor that led to the kitchen and opened the door to the cellar. 'Down here if you please, gentlemen.'

Pinchter's protests faded as he disappeared below ground. The door closed softly behind the four men.

Cigarette smoke wafted past my head. I looked over my shoulder.

'He's a scary man,' said Reid, strolling down the stairs.

Godard sighed. 'He needs to be. He's the future leader of the Bastians.'

An hour later, footsteps rose outside the study. The door opened and Victor strode in.

'This is taking too long,' he said, frustration evident in his tone. He rubbed the bloodied knuckles on his right hand absent-mindedly.

Anna looked away, a muscle twitching in her jawline.

'Can we help?' said Reid mildly.

Victor looked at us. His gaze focused on me. 'Yes, I think you can, actually,' he said after a moment.

The cellar under the mansion was large and cool. Racks of dust-covered wine bottles occupied a generous portion of the extensive floor and bare light bulbs cast a yellow glow on the brick walls.

Pinchter sat tied to a chair in front of a table at one end of the vaulted space. Bruno stood silently behind him. Anatole leaned against the wall to the side, a frown darkening his normally jovial countenance.

Pinchter's face was a bloodied pulp. His nose was broken in at least two places and his left eye was swollen shut. His right wrist was twisted at an odd angle.

Undaunted, the little man spat out a broken tooth and sneered.

'What now, Victor? You're going to set the rest of your dogs loose on me?' He glared at us out of his bloodshot right eye.

'Just let me shoot him,' muttered Anatole.

Victor shook his head. 'No, that would be far too easy. I

have a better idea. I'm going to leave you in the hands of the "half-breed", as you like to call him.'

My eyes narrowed at the Bastian noble's words.

Pinchter's widened. 'You wouldn't dare!'

Victor smiled coldly. 'Oh but I would.'

Pinchter glanced at me and snorted. 'He couldn't do anything even if he wanted to. Look at him!' An ugly grimace crossed the man's lips. 'You know as well as I do that he has never attacked an immortal in cold blood. All he ever does is run!'

Reid took a step forward. I put a hand on his arm and felt the rigid tension running through him.

'It's all right,' I said quietly, my eyes never leaving Pinchter's battered face.

The little man smirked. 'See? Your half-breed is nothing but a coward! Every Hunter knows it. How such a weakling could come from the bloodline of Tomas Godard—' He broke off abruptly.

A hush fell across the cellar.

'The tip of this blade is exactly an inch from your heart,' I explained in a low and measured tone.

Pinchter gulped. His frozen gaze drifted to the wakizashi partially embedded in his ribcage.

'I believe you're aware of my abilities?' I added in the same neutral voice.

The little man nodded frantically.

I was surprised at how calm I felt. The anger that had been burning inside me for days had all but melted away.

In its place was another, stronger emotion.

'You're right,' I stated, more to myself than to him. 'So far, I have only ever killed to defend myself.' I watched understanding begin to dawn on the man's startled face. 'I think I'm beginning to grasp why Vellacrus wants me out of the way.'

I nudged the blade slightly. The immortal gasped. Blood seeped onto his shirt.

'It's because I truly am the only one who can stop her. I believe that's what Mikael meant when he said those words to me.'

The expression in Pinchter's eyes confirmed my suspicions. I leaned forward. Pinchter moved back in the chair as far as his bonds allowed him.

'Thank you. It makes sense now. I've been running for a long time.' My voice hardened. 'I won't anymore.'

Minutes later, Reid and I followed Victor into the study.

'Well?' Godard observed our grim faces anxiously.

'Vellacrus is gathering all the Crovir Hunters,' Victor announced flatly. 'They'll be in Europe tonight.'

~

CHAPTER SIXTEEN

Roman Dvorsky was an older and thinner version of his son. Though disease had ravaged his immortal body and added lines to his face, he walked with a confident step born of a natural leader.

'Victor.' He crossed the foyer and hugged his son.

'Father,' Victor murmured back.

The Head of the Order of Bastian Hunters looked around the foyer. 'It's good to see you looking so well,' he told Godard. His gaze shifted. 'And this must be your granddaughter.'

Anna nodded an acknowledgment and returned the older man's stare steadily.

The dark eyes so similar to Victor's finally fell on me. I was subjected to a long and penetrating stare. 'Lucas Thorne.'

I frowned at the name. 'I prefer Soul.'

Stony silence descended on the lobby. Roman Dvorsky watched me with an inscrutable expression. 'Soul it is then. I guess I owe you a long-overdue apology.'

Victor's father had not travelled alone; the Dvorskys' estate was swarming with Bastian Hunters. They arrived in a large convoy of transporter vans and SUVs earlier that day and were busy setting up a security perimeter around the grounds.

I had been receiving guarded looks for most of the morning.

'Bet they make you feel twitchy, huh?' said Reid.

He leaned against the window frame next to me and gazed outside. We had retired to the study while Roman Dvorsky and the other members of the Bastian First Council gathered in the kitchen for a meeting. The lawn in front of the mansion was crawling with immortals.

'I guess they're on our side now,' I said.

Reid shifted and stretched his wounded arm. 'Well, they do say the enemy of my enemy is my friend.'

I had a feeling the majority of the Bastian Hunters out there would not be subscribing to a similar viewpoint.

'How's your chest by the way?' I glanced at the outline of the dressing beneath his shirt.

'Much better than I thought it'd be,' said Reid. 'The doc said I'm healing fast.' He made a face. 'Though she still hasn't given up on getting me to stop smoking.'

I smiled.

The door opened behind us. Bruno appeared on the threshold.

'The boss is asking for you.' He hesitated. 'Mr. Roman is who I mean.'

I looked at Reid. He shrugged. We turned and followed the bodyguard to the back of the manor house.

Several Hunters stood to attention next to the windows and doors of the kitchen. A couple of them visibly stiffened when I entered the room.

The Godards and the Dvorskys were already seated at the table. A number of unfamiliar faces occupied the chairs around them.

'I've updated the Council members about recent events,'

said Victor. He indicated the empty seat at the end of the table. 'Come, join us.'

I crossed the floor and took the chair. Reid leaned against the wall next to me. He folded his arms, nodded amiably at the Hunter beside him, and assumed a bored air.

An uneasy hush filled the room.

It was broken by a stout man with the expression of a bulldog.

'Look here.' The immortal turned to Roman, distaste twisting his lips. 'Do you really expect us to work together with this—*half-breed?*' He gestured vaguely in my direction.

Godard went rigid. Anna placed a hand on his arm. She was also frowning.

'I will not have you speak so of my grandson,' said the former leader of the Bastian Hunters.

'I mean you no disrespect, Tomas,' said the stranger coolly. 'However, you have to admit that your grandson's existence flies in the face of the conventions of our society.'

A sigh left Roman Dvorsky's lips.

'All right, everyone calm down.' He turned and addressed the man with the bulldog face. 'We've already gone over this, Costas,' he said in a patient voice. 'Soul came off our wanted list a long time ago. We have no grief with him.'

'Still, to have someone like him share a table with the most senior members of the Bastian Councils is deplorable, not to mention a clear breach of our rules,' grumbled the man named Costas.

There was a grunt beside me. 'Who made those rules?' said Reid.

Costas's gaze shifted past me. He scowled at my partner. 'And you are?'

'A friend,' said Reid. 'For now.'

'The affairs of immortals do not concern you, human,' the Bastian immortal stated dismissively.

Reid struck a match and lit a cigarette. He ignored Anna's glare and nonchalantly blew a couple of smoke rings toward the ceiling.

'Correct me if I'm wrong,' he drawled, 'but it seems to me that the "half-breed" and the "human" pretty much saved your immortal asses in the last few days.'

Costas snorted. 'I heard you nearly got yourself killed.'

'Well, I gotta admit, when it comes to dying, you have the advantage over me,' Reid said steadily.

'It's okay,' I said quietly. I turned and observed the faces around the table. 'Let's get something clear,' I said, making no attempt to hide the coldness in my voice. 'I have no love lost for you or most other immortals, be they Crovir or Bastian. As far as I'm concerned, you can continue to have your petty disputes for the rest of eternity.' I frowned. 'Unfortunately, the current situation concerns us all. This is a matter of survival, pure and simple. *You* need *me*. And for the time being, as much as I hate to admit this, it appears that I need you.'

I leaned forward and rested my elbows on the table.

'Whatever Agatha Vellacrus is plotting, she believed that I was the only one who could stop her. That's the reason the Crovir Hunters have been after me for the last two weeks.' I glanced at my grandfather. 'And I hear that for Felix Thorne to personally come out on a Hunt is practically unheard of.'

The man next to Roman stiffened. 'Thorne is here?'

'Yes,' Victor's father replied wearily. 'He killed Soul a few days ago, outside the safe house in Vilanec.'

'And it was his seventeenth death at that,' Anatole said cheerfully. His eyebrows rose at Victor's expression. 'What?' he asked with an innocent shrug.

Bruno sighed and shook his head.

'We were trying to keep that fact a secret for as long as possible,' Victor explained stiffly.

'Oh.' Anatole pulled a face. 'Sorry boss, but half the men out there know about it already.' He cleared his throat. 'Won't be long till the other half finds out either,' he added under his breath.

Costas had gone red in the face.

'Impossible!' The Bastian noble shot out of his seat, the chair clattering to the floor. 'You're lying! There's no way he could have survived his seventeenth death!' He turned to Roman. 'This is a grotesque farce, Roman! I demand that you—'

'Costas is right,' the man on the other side of Tomas Godard interrupted. 'No immortal has ever lived beyond seventeen deaths.'

'Soul did,' said Victor above the furor that followed. Dvorsky's voice had an edge of steel to it. 'I was there.' He waited until the rumble of voices died down. 'And you forget. No one in our history has the ability he has.'

The other Council members shared guarded glances.

'How is that possible?' said Costas finally.

One of the Hunters pulled his chair up.

He sat down slowly, a stormy expression still clouding his face.

'No one knows the answer to that question,' said Victor. He glanced at me and hesitated. 'But I think we should hide this fact from the Crovirs for as long as possible. If they believe Lucas is out of their way, they will get bolder. And they may let their guard slip.'

The man next to Roman leaned forward. 'What do you have in mind?' he said, eyes shining.

The Council members stared at Victor expectantly.

He looked at his father. The leader of the Bastian Hunters nodded.

'First and foremost, we must protect Anna Godard,' said Victor. 'She appears to be a crucial component to Vellacrus's plan. We cannot let her fall into the hands of the Crovirs at any cost.'

Anna stiffened at his words. 'Wait a minute. That's going a bit far!' she protested.

'My dear, as much as I dislike admitting it, Victor's right,' said Godard. 'I would hate to think what that woman would do to you if she had you in her grasp.'

'So what, I'm just supposed to hide and let others get killed because of me?' Anna retorted. 'That makes me feel so...useless!'

'You're not,' I said quietly. 'If we find out what Vellacrus is up to, you may be the only one who can put a stop to it.'

With Anna's knowledge of Strauss's research, I was confident she would get to the bottom of what the Crovirs were plotting and find a solution to the problem. As I was rapidly discovering, she was too stubborn to resist a challenge.

'All right,' Anna muttered. 'But no pointless heroics, okay?'

I smiled in response.

'That's not the entire plan, is it?' said Costas incredulously. 'Surely we do not need the whole Order of the Bastian Hunters just to keep one woman safe?'

'No,' said Victor. 'There's more.'

'Vellacrus arrived in Prague last night,' said Roman. 'She wasn't alone. Almost the entire Order of the Crovir Hunters came with her.'

Shocked murmurs broke around the table at this news.

'The Crovir First Council will be meeting this evening at Kazimir Benisek's mansion,' Roman continued. 'Victor and I are intending to drop in for a visit.'

Stunned silence followed this statement.

'That's suicide,' the man next to Roman said dully.

I watched Victor and his father with a frown. The Council member was right. What the Dvorskys were proposing was madness. I caught the glint in Victor's eyes and relaxed slightly.

'No, Grigoriye. Suicide would be going in without a plan,' said Victor.

He gestured to Bruno. The bodyguard stepped up to the table and spread a map across the surface. A series of high-definition satellite and surveillance photos were pinned to it.

'Roman and I will go in through the main gates of the compound with an appropriate-sized escort,' the Bastian noble continued, pointing at a section of the map and a corresponding picture. 'We'll have a team of Hunters waiting here, here, and here,' he indicated three spots on the periphery, 'in case there's any trouble.'

He straightened and looked around the table.

'The aim is simple, gentlemen. We want to surprise and confuse the Crovirs. They will not be expecting this.' He observed the various expressions of incredulity washing across the faces of the other Council members with a small smile.

'Roman and I will pretend to be passing through Prague on our way to Budapest,' he added, unperturbed. 'Vellacrus will not dare do something to us in the open, not in front of the entire Crovir Council. And you forget—we have allies among the Crovirs. Not everyone in their ranks wishes to see another immortal war.'

'And what exactly are you hoping to achieve with this hare-brained move?' said Costas after a while, his face bearing a look that managed to combine disbelief with disgust.

'Well, I doubt Vellacrus will just come out and tell us the details of her plans,' drawled Victor. 'No. We're just the decoy.'

Grigoriye frowned. 'The decoy?' he repeated, his puzzled countenance mirroring the others around the table.

'Yes,' said Victor. 'While we distract Vellacrus and the Council, another team will infiltrate the mansion to collect information about what the Crovirs are plotting. Benisek is Felix Thorne's chief intelligence officer. I'm certain there'll be a lot of data in that place.' He tapped a finger on the blown-up photograph of the manor. 'This team needs to be small—three, four men at the most. They will have to be in and out of there before we leave the estate.'

He scrutinized the faces in the room. I was hardly surprised when his gaze found mine.

'I propose Lucas, Reid, Bruno, and Anatole,' said Victor. 'They worked well together in Vienna.'

A grin lit up Anatole's face. 'Now we're talking!'

Anna scowled. 'That sounds too risky.'

'On the contrary,' said Victor, his eyes never leaving my face. 'If anyone can overcome the Crovir Hunters, it's Soul. So, what do you say?'

I watched the immortal for several seconds.

The plan was bold and utterly foolish; the chances of us making it out of the Crovir compound unscathed were slim at best. Still, I could not shake the feeling that our time was running out. We had to get some answers fast.

'I'm in.'

Victor's gaze shifted to my side. 'Hasley?'

Reid looked at me questioningly. I shrugged, indicating that the choice was his to make.

He stepped away from the wall and crushed the cigarette butt in an ashtray on the table. 'Ninety-nine-point-nine percent chance of getting captured or killed. Zero-point-one percent chance of success,' said the former US Marine. 'What's not to like?'

Victor nodded with a satisfied expression. 'It's settled then. We leave at dusk.'

The Bastian Council broke up and vacated the room in a low rumble of murmurs. I rose and stopped by Anna's chair.

'Do you have some time to spare?' I said in a low voice.

An idea had been taking shape in my mind for the last two days. The time to see it through was now or never.

'Yes. By the sounds of it, I'm about to have plenty of that

precious commodity on my hands soon enough,' she said, rolling her eyes.

'Good. Come with me.'

Anna looked puzzled but followed me nonetheless. I led her out through the back door and headed for the woods at the rear of the mansion. Her eyes widened when we came to a shooting range.

'What are we doing here?' she said guardedly.

I removed the Glock from the holster on my hip and checked the magazine. 'You need to learn how to use a gun.'

I knew from talking to Tomas Godard that Anna had never handled a firearm in her life. Sullen silence followed my words. I looked up into a stormy green gaze.

'Why?' Anna said stiffly.

I watched her carefully while I tried to figure out the quickest way to convince her that this was a necessity. 'If you can defend yourself, less people will have to die protecting you.'

A flush darkened her cheeks. She glared at me and extended her hand commandingly. 'Give me the gun!'

Some time later, one of her shots finally struck the edge of the target board.

Anna lowered the Glock and bit her lip. 'All right, what am I doing wrong?'

I suppressed a smile and walked up behind her. As with everything else she came across, it seemed that once Anna Godard made her mind up to do something, she was deter-mined to be excellent at it.

'Here.' I closed my hands over the back of hers and lifted them gently. 'Put your fingers high on the back strap.'

'Like this?' said Anna, correcting her grip.

'Yes,' I replied, glad my voice did not betray my inner turmoil; the smell of her hair and the touch of her skin were threatening to flood my senses. 'Bend your knees more. Relax your elbows. Got your sights?'

Anna nodded.

'Take a deep breath. Exhale. Now squeeze the trigger.'

The next two shots echoed loudly around the range. The bullets thudded into the scoring rings inches from the center of the board.

'That was good.' I stepped back and quietly let out the breath I had been holding.

Anna checked the magazine like I had taught her.

'It seems wrong, shooting bullets into people,' she said after a while, her hands stilling on the gun. She looked at me quizzically. 'Did you know I was one of the first female surgeons in France?'

I shook my head.

She smiled. 'Of course, in those days my male colleagues at the University of Paris were not too impressed that a woman had dared invade their exalted ranks.'

'Why did you leave medicine?' I said curiously.

'Because I realized I could make a greater impact on its future if I dedicated my life to research.' She raised the gun and fired another couple of shots at the target. 'How's that?'

She turned and stared at me when I didn't reply. 'Lucas?'

'Er, good. That was…better,' I murmured, trying to still the pounding in my chest.

There was a noise behind us.

Someone cleared their throat in a deliberate attempt to gain our attention. I closed my eyes briefly, already suspecting who it was going to be.

'Am I interrupting something?' said Reid in a suspiciously syrupy voice as he stepped onto the range.

'No.' Anna flushed and glanced from him to me. 'Lucas was just showing me how to use a gun.'

'Was he now?' said Reid.

I avoided his calculating gaze. 'Reid's a great shot,' I told Anna. 'Why don't you stay and practice with him?'

I turned and headed for the trees.

'Why? Where're you going?' Reid called out.

I touched the handle of the katana. 'I haven't used the swords for a while.'

I could feel his narrowed eyes on my back as I exited the range. I turned east and walked to a deserted clearing half a mile from the manor. I removed the long blade from its scabbard and started to work through the basic steps of kendo.

In the distance behind me, the sound of shots carried faintly on the wind.

I had built up a healthy layer of sweat when a voice suddenly came from between the trees.

'Those are some good moves you've got there.'

～

CHAPTER SEVENTEEN

I LOWERED THE KATANA AND STUDIED THE FIGURE STANDING in the shadows on the edge of the clearing. 'Thank you. I had a good teacher.'

'Yes, I know,' said Roman Dvorsky. 'Miyamoto Musashi was an excellent swords master.'

I straightened, my attention now totally focused on the Head of the Order of Bastian Hunters.

'I never met the man myself,' said the older man. He stepped out of the shade.

I tensed when I noticed the two-handed longsword he carried.

'But I have to admit, I've always wanted to spar with someone who knew the art of Niten Ichi-ryu.' Roman Dvorsky strolled to the opposite end of the glade and turned to face me. 'Shall we?'

I considered the immortal's inscrutable face for timeless seconds before slowly drawing the wakizashi from my waist.

'I will not go easy on you,' I warned in a low voice.

'It would be an insult if you did,' Roman retorted mildly.

Though the clearing stood a good distance from the manor

house, the sounds of our clashing blades soon drew an audience. Out of the corner of my eye, I saw Reid and Anna pause in the midst of a group of Bastian Hunters on the edge of the tree line. Reid lit a cigarette and inhaled lazily.

Despite the growing crowd, I could feel Anna's gaze on me as if it was a dazzling beam of light cutting through inky darkness.

Victor appeared and propped himself against the trunk of a maple tree. He watched the fight with a neutral expression.

There was no time to study the other faces gathered around us; the older man's sword had just missed my left eye by an inch.

Roman Dvorsky fought with a grace and deftness that belied his frail appearance. He countered my moves strike for strike, almost anticipating where my blade would fall next. Time and time again, the tip of his sword came within a whisper of my skin. In the end, I had to draw on all the knowledge and skills taught to me by my Edo master to get one over the leader of the Bastians.

'Touché,' Roman said in a strained voice. He stood frozen in the middle of the clearing, the edge of my katana over his heart. 'However, I think you will find my blade is also touching your chest.'

'Look lower.'

The immortal's eyes moved to where the wakizashi hovered over his right femoral artery. 'Well done,' he said grudgingly.

I stood back and lowered the swords.

The older man relaxed. 'I'm surprised you lost to Felix Thorne. You're as skilled as he is.'

'I'll be more prepared next time.'

The silence suddenly registered. I looked around.

Some sixty Hunters lined the perimeter of the clearing. Among them were the Bastian nobles who made up the First Council. Many of the immortals wore frowns. Others looked strangely thoughtful.

Tomas Godard stood slightly to the side, his face full of a nameless emotion. He turned without a word and walked back toward the mansion. Anna cast an apologetic glance at me before taking off after him. The rest of the Hunters and the Bastian nobles slowly dispersed.

Victor and Reid walked out from beneath the trees.

'That was quite a show,' said Victor.

Roman leaned on the longsword. 'Your old man still has it in him.'

Victor chuckled. 'I never doubted it.'

Roman looked at me curiously. 'By the way, that's an interesting design you have on your katana.'

I glanced at the engraving. 'Miyamoto was fascinated by my birthmark. He had it carved into the blade.'

Roman watched me with an inscrutable expression before nodding.

I looked questioningly at Reid.

'I don't think you need to worry about the lady,' he drawled. 'She's a scarily fast learner.'

Sundown came too fast. As we made our final preparations, I finally cornered Godard on the stairs of the manor house. 'There's something I need to ask you.'

'Yes?' said Godard.

'Do you know a man by the name of Mikael Olsson?'

He frowned. 'No, I can't say that I do. Why?'

I told him about Olsson and the circumstances behind his apparent death in Boston ten years previously, as well as his recent appearance in my life.

'I knew a Johan Olsson once,' said Godard after a thoughtful pause. 'He worked for the Order of the Bastian Hunters during the 1600s. I was still an advisor for the First Council at the time. As I recall, he was one of the immortals who perished at the Second Battle of Khotyn, during the Great Turkish War.' A sigh left his lips. 'I'm afraid many of us lost lives during our conflicts with the Ottoman Empire.'

I thought of my own gruesome deaths during the Battle of Vienna. The irony that both my grandfather and I fought on the same side during those tumultuous years and yet were unaware of each other's presence did not escape me.

'Were you at Khotyn at the time?'

Godard shook his head. 'No. Although I helped High Commander Sobieski coordinate the battle, my presence was needed in Lwów. The King of Poland had died only the day before.'

An unexpected wave of relief washed over me at his words. Olsson's assertion was evidently misguided. 'Thank you.'

The blue eyes so alike to mine widened slightly. 'You're welcome,' murmured Godard.

We left the manor house when the last of the light was draining out of a red sky.

A group of fifty Hunters were staying back to guard the Godards. As the convoy barreled down the driveway, I caught a glimpse of Anna at the window of the study.

'How are you doing?' said Reid after a while.

We were in the back of a van, along with Bruno, Anatole, and four other Hunters. The immortals were chatting among themselves.

I finished fitting a suppressor to the Smith and Wesson. 'I'm fine.'

'Really?' Reid countered. 'So, you're telling me that finding out that you have a grandfather and a cousin who are still alive, that you're probably truly immortal in every sense of the word, and that your long-lost grandmother is trying to kill you, is *not* freaking you out?'

'Well, to be honest, the bit about my grandmother kinda sucks.'

A crooked smile dawned on Reid's lips. 'All right,' he said, shaking his head. 'You know where I am if you wanna talk.'

I nodded gratefully.

Kazimir Benisek's manor house was located on eight hundred acres of land north of the village of Drhovy, in the Příbram District twenty-five miles outside Prague. The plot was enclosed by an impressive stone wall topped with barbed wire fencing. Beyond it, a further half-mile of dense woodland lay between the boundaries of the property and the extensive lawn that fronted the mansion. A pair of thick, wrought iron gates with ornate latticework barred the entrance to the grounds. To the left of it, a metal plate read "Private Property: Trespassers will be prosecuted" in Czech. A driveway lined with rows of well-established evergreens bisected the lawn neatly before ending in a graveled forecourt.

We entered the estate from the northwest. Thermal images taken just before we left the safe house had indicated that that section of the property harbored the least number of guards and had almost no surveillance cameras. There was also a cool breeze blowing in from the south that would help mask the sounds of our approach.

The land at the rear of the mansion was taken up by extensive manicured gardens dotted with Roman sculptures, arbors, and stone seats. The gardens stretched down a series of shallow terraces to an orchard and a small, artificial lake rimmed on three sides by trees.

We paused in the gloom beyond the still waters and waited for the signal.

At exactly seven pm, there was a flurry of activity around the property. Dozens of figures left their posts on the grounds and hurried toward the mansion. Startled voices rose to the dark skies.

The Dvorskys had arrived at the gates.

We used the cover of the shadows and moved silently up the

incline. Seconds later, we dropped down by a water fountain set in a circular stone terrace.

Bruno lifted the iron grating behind the water feature and exposed a narrow hole in the ground. We climbed down the metal ladder beneath it and descended into darkness.

There was a faint click. The beam from Bruno's torch cut through the murk and cast a ghostly glow on damp, moss-covered stone walls.

Anatole grimaced. 'This place stinks.'

We were in an underground service tunnel that ran all the way beneath the gardens. From the plans of the estate that Victor had procured, it led to one of four cellars underneath the mansion.

Bruno nudged something with the edge of his boot. 'There's a dead rat.' He moved the beam around. 'Make that a lot of dead rats.'

'Great,' Anatole muttered. 'I hate rats.'

We headed south along the passage, occasionally crossing thin bars of pale light streaming through narrow grilles in the roof. A quarter of a mile later, the tunnel ended at a locked, rust-colored metal door.

'We're here,' I said quietly in the microphone pinned to my Kevlar vest.

The earpiece in my ear crackled.

'You're good to go,' said a voice after several seconds.

When the first commercial satellites were launched into space in the nineteen sixties, the Bastians and Crovirs privately acquired dozens of the machines and placed them in orbit all over the world. The cluster of Bastian satellites above Europe was currently tracking the movement of anything with a heat signal within a two-mile radius of Benisek's property. To make life less complicated for the Bastian technicians monitoring the area, the Dvorskys, the Bastian Hunters on the ground, and our team of four all carried a transmitter with a specific thermal reading.

Bruno cut through the lock on the door with a small blow-torch, oiled the hinges, and carefully pushed it open. Cool air washed over us. The darkness beyond hinted at a large space. He crossed the threshold and directed the torch beam in a grid pattern across the shadows.

Wine racks appeared in even rows that extended to a low ceiling. On the left, an entire wall was stacked high with beer barrels. Bottles of expensive spirits glowed briefly in the torchlight.

We were halfway down the middle aisle when Anatole rocked to a halt and stared into the gloom.

Bruno froze. 'What is it?'

'Damn.' Anatole pointed at a crate. 'That's a whole case of Chateau Latour 1886!'

There was a pregnant pause. Bruno muttered something under his breath and started walking again.

'Oh, come on!' hissed Anatole, trotting after him. 'Do you *know* how much a bottle of that would fetch on the open market?'

We reached a thick, iron-plated oak door at the other end of the cellar.

'You're still good to go,' said the voice in my ear.

Reid picked the lock; we could not risk using the blowtorch with the smoke alarms in the cellar. My fingers gripped the handle of the katana when the door swung open. Darkness and silence greeted us on the other side.

We exited the basement and ascended shallow stone steps to a deserted corridor at the rear of the mansion.

Muted voices rose south of our position. From what we had seen of the thermal images before we entered the property, the Crovir First Council was gathered in the reception rooms at the front.

'Take the service stairs fifteen feet to your right,' murmured the voice in my earpiece. 'It should take you to the first floor.'

We turned and headed swiftly along the passage to a flight of carpeted steps. We were almost at the top when the voice barked an abrupt 'Stop!' in our ears.

We froze in the gloom.

'There're four bodies heading your way, two from above and two from below,' the voice said tensely. 'They're not friendlies.'

I signaled to Reid and Bruno. They headed back down the stairs.

Anatole and I ran up the last steps, guns in hand. We had barely pressed ourselves into the shallow recesses on either side of the door when it opened. Two Crovir Hunters stepped over the threshold.

They never heard our shots.

We dragged the bodies to the cellar and found Bruno and Reid tying up the other two Hunters.

Bruno glanced from me to the still immortals. 'You could finish them off with your sword. That will leave less of them for us to contend with.'

I finished securing the man at my feet with a pair of cable ties before rising to my full height.

'I have never killed in cold blood.'

The Bastian immortal observed me for a beat. 'All right.'

We disposed the Hunters of their weapons and headed swiftly up the stairs to the first floor of the mansion. According to the blueprints, Benisek's study was located on that level.

I glanced at my watch.

Fifteen minutes had elapsed since we entered the service tunnel under the gardens. With each precious second that passed, our chances of successfully completing our mission grew smaller.

My earpiece crackled again just as we entered the corridor

at the top of the steps. 'Three bodies moving toward you from the front of the house. ETA ten seconds.'

'Thanks,' I murmured, studying the passage we stood in.

Thick curtains framed the French windows lining one aspect of the gallery. Crystal chandeliers dangled from the high, ornately corniced ceiling and shed a muted light across the oil portraits adorning the walls.

We slipped in a shadowy alcove a moment before the doors at the end of the gallery swung open. Two Crovir Hunters crossed the threshold. A third man appeared behind them.

Bruno sucked in air through his teeth. 'This is our lucky day.'

'Why?' I muttered.

'That's Kazimir Benisek.'

~

CHAPTER EIGHTEEN

I STARED AT THE MAN IN THE WHITE EVENING SUIT.

Benisek was short and overweight. A silver beard crowded the lower half of his face, partly masking his thick jowls. The upper half was a mass of red wrinkles surrounding a pair of rat-like eyes.

He unlocked a door halfway down the passage and stepped into the room beyond. He turned and murmured something to the Hunters before closing the door behind him. They took up guard position outside the room.

I signaled my intentions to the others. They nodded. I stepped out of the alcove and strolled toward the guards.

The man on the right spotted me first. His eyes narrowed and he reached for the gun at his waist.

'Hi.' I plastered an engaging smile across my face. 'I'm with the Bastian escort. I'm kinda lost. Could you guys tell me how to get to the main hall?'

Recognition dawned in the second Hunter's eyes. 'Wait a minute, aren't you—'

'Wrong answer,' I said.

Bullets whispered past me and hit them in the chest.

We caught the Hunters' bodies before they hit the floor and tied them up in a bay beneath the French windows. We were back at the door seconds later.

'There's a man in the room in front of us,' I said in the mouthpiece. 'Is he alone?'

'Yes,' replied the Bastian tech. 'I'm getting a high heat signal from that place. Looks like he has a lot of hardware up and running in there.'

We found Benisek seated behind an oak desk in the middle of a large study. A row of monitors flickered on the wall in front of him; beneath them, stacks of slim hard drives rose from the floor, their faint hum almost inaudible.

Benisek's eyes never left the screens when we locked the door behind us.

'I thought I said I wasn't to be disturbed!' he barked, fat fingers flying over the ergonomic keyboard beneath his hands.

When this did not elicit the desired response, he finally looked in our direction. His hands froze on the keyboard. The rat-like eyes widened.

'Hello,' I said with a cold smile. 'I believe you know who I am.'

'You! But—but—you're dead!' stammered Benisek. 'Thorne killed you!'

'Funny how everyone keeps mentioning that. As a matter of fact, he did. I have to point out that the guy doesn't exactly play fair though.'

Fear dawned in Benisek's eyes. His fingers moved. A second later, he yelped and clutched at his hand.

A faint trail of smoke curled from the suppressor on Reid's gun. 'I wouldn't touch anything if I were you,' he told Benisek in an affable voice.

'You'll never get out of here alive!' shouted the fat man while Bruno and Anatole dragged him from the chair to a couch in a corner of the room. 'Vellacrus will have you—hmmff, hmmff!'

'There!' Anatole stepped back and admired his handiwork. 'That's much better, isn't it?'

Benisek scowled behind his gag.

I took the seat he had been forcibly evicted from and studied the monitors on the wall.

'Can you work this?' said Reid.

'There's only one way to find out.' I looked at my watch. Another five minutes had passed since I'd last glanced at the dial.

Benisek had been in the process of transferring all the files on the hard drives to an off-site server; this was likely a security measure against the unexpected presence of the Dvorskys in the mansion. Fortunately, he had already entered the primary password to access the mainframe. The folders, however, were still in code; they would have to be decrypted before they could be moved.

I scrutinized the lists on the screens. Which ones did I need to access? My gaze shifted to the bound man on the couch. Benisek did not look like he was in a mood to cooperate and we hardly had time for harsher persuasive measures.

'What's wrong?' said Reid.

'The data's encrypted. I don't know what I'm looking for.'

'Can't you just download all of it?'

I shook my head. 'There're hundreds of folders. It would take too long.'

I eventually found the original encryption file hidden deep beneath clever layers of programming; whoever had installed Benisek's security system was good. All I had to do now was decipher the code.

'You probably don't want to hear this, but there's a whole boatful of unfriendlies heading your way,' said the voice in my ear.

Bruno and Anatole moved to the door.

I typed "GeMBiT" into the password box. There was a beep

from the machines; the words "Access Denied-Incorrect Password" appeared on the screens. I tried "Crovir", then "Thorne" and "Vellacrus" unsuccessfully. A series of unhappy high-pitched sounds rose from the speakers.

Sweat beaded my forehead. I had one more chance to get it right before the system locked me out. If that happened, I would have to reboot and start all over again. This was not an option under the current circumstances.

'Those unfriendlies are almost on top of you,' interrupted the voice through the earpiece. A strained pause followed. 'By the sound of things, Roman and Victor have overstayed their welcome. They're getting ready to leave.'

I yanked the receiver out of my ear, closed my eyes, and shut out the noise around me. Seconds passed. Three, then five and eight.

At ten, I opened my eyes and typed "Immortality".

The screens flickered. Lists of decoded folders streamed down the monitors. There was a muffled scream of rage from Benisek.

My fingers fluttered over the keys while I grouped all the files containing the words "GeMBiT", "Burnstein", "Strauss", and "Godard". I sent the data through to the Bastians' secured server and made a copy on a memory stick. As I moved to shut down the hard drives, a folder at the bottom of one of the screens drew my gaze. It was titled "Red Death". I copied it and exited the system.

'We have about a minute before the Dvorskys exit the building,' said Bruno from the door.

I pushed back from the desk. 'I'm done.'

The doorknob turned and rattled.

'Kazimir, are you in there? Open the door,' someone said through the woodwork.

Coldness gripped me. I knew that voice. I placed the receiver back in my ear and carefully rose from the chair.

'Are Roman and Victor out of the building?' I said softly in the mouthpiece, my gaze not shifting from the doorway.

Reid frowned at my tone.

'They're walking to the cars,' came the reply. 'Seriously, you guys need to move. There's an unfriendly right outside the room.'

I slid the daisho from my belt. 'I know. It's Felix Thorne.'

Reid and the two Bastian immortals stared from me to the door; behind us, Benisek's struggles doubled in effort.

There was a buzz of static from the earpiece. 'Shit,' muttered the Bastian tech.

Anatole grimaced. 'He said it.'

'Is he alone?' I watched the doorknob turn again and tried to quiet the rapid thuds of my heart.

Mixed in with dread at the inevitable battle that now faced us was an unexpected sense of anticipation; I was looking forward to meeting Thorne again. In fact, I could hardly wait.

'Yes. But there are others close by.'

'How many?'

'I count ten signals within twenty feet of your position,' came the solemn response.

'Okay. Thanks.'

'Do you need back-up?' the tech asked hesitantly.

I looked at Reid and the two Bastian immortals. They shrugged.

'We'll be fine,' I said in the mouthpiece. 'Just make sure Victor and Roman get through those gates safely.'

'Will do.' The tech paused. 'And Soul?'

'Yeah?'

'Good luck.'

I smiled. 'Sure.' I took the earpiece out, crossed the study, and turned to observe the others. 'When I open this door, I want you to run.'

Reid's eyes widened. 'What?'

'Hey, look here—' Anatole started in a disgruntled voice.

'None of you stand a chance against Thorne.' Silence followed my words. I could tell from their aggravated expressions that they knew this to be true and were not pleased about the fact. 'We haven't got time to argue. Here, catch.'

I threw the memory stick at Reid.

He palmed the device and glared at me. 'So what, you're saying you're gonna fight all of them?'

'No. Just Thorne. The others are yours.'

Bar a change of clothes, Felix Thorne was exactly as I remembered him. His tall frame was covered in a black evening suit and his ash-blonde hair gleamed under the light of the chandeliers. Chilly, gunmetal eyes widened slightly when he saw me.

I stepped out in the corridor. 'Hello, Uncle.'

There was movement behind me as the others exited the room.

Thorne barely looked at them. Dark pupils dilated wildly within a sea of wintry gray. The thin lips pulled back in a sneer.

'How is this possible? I watched you die.'

'I'm afraid no one knows the answer to that yet,' I said in a steady voice.

Thorne peered over my shoulder at Benisek. He scowled. 'What have you done?'

I shrugged. 'Nothing much. I just wanted to say hello. After all, we *are* family.'

An ugly expression distorted the immortal's features. 'You are no relative of mine, half-breed!' he hissed.

A savage smile tugged at my lips. I finally recognized the feeling coursing through my veins; it was what a hunter probably experienced when he was closing in for the kill.

The whine of bullets rose behind me as Reid and the Bastians engaged the Crovirs. I ignored the sound of the gunfight and glanced at Thorne's waist.

'I see you have your sword with you.' My smile widened, which only seemed to infuriate Thorne further. 'Would you care for a rematch?'

The Crovir noble glared at me. 'I killed you once.' He removed his blade from its sheath. 'I can kill you again!'

His first move was so fast I barely blocked his blow. I grunted and took a step back.

'I see you've improved,' Thorne said in a condescending tone. 'Still, you have far to go before you can hope to defeat me, *boy*.'

'You forget, *Uncle*. This time, I'll fight you without the benefit of bullet wounds,' I retorted.

Thorne's eyes narrowed.

The next seconds were a blur of movement. As with our previous battle in Vilanec, the Crovir's speed verged on the supernatural. Our blades clashed again and again, sparks rising from the gleaming steel edges.

The tip of Thorne's sword hummed past my face. I dropped to my heels, twisted, and brought my leg around in a sweeping kick. He jumped backward.

I rolled toward him, rose to one knee, and thrust the wakizashi upward. It slipped an inch past his guard and scored a gash across his chest.

A shocked grunt escaped Thorne's lips. He raised his hand and fingered the cut.

'You'll regret this,' he snarled, staring at his bloodied fingers. He touched the scar on his right cheek absent-mindedly and left a crimson trail on his pale skin. 'Your father marked me once.' A sadistic grin dawned on his face. 'He paid for it with his life.'

A wave of blind rage shook me to my core; it took all my self-control not to rush the immortal there and then. I inhaled deeply and forced my fingers to relax on the handles of the daisho. My feet shifted into the basic stance of kendo. I felt my heart rate slow down.

'Let's do this.'

A growl ripped from Thorne's throat as he lunged toward me. I blocked his first blow. He attacked again. I blocked his second, then his third blow. His eyes narrowed into silver slits.

He struck over and over again, the tip of his sword slicing through the air in nearly invisible moves. With every swing of the blade, his breathing grew more erratic.

I deflected his strikes with an ease that enraged him to no end.

That was when I realized something astounding. I was faster and stronger than he was.

Before I could assimilate this shocking observation and ponder whether it had something to do with surviving my seventeenth death, the doors at the end of the gallery opened. A murmur of muted voices washed over the threshold from the front of the mansion at the same time a figure in an ice-blue evening gown stepped through.

My heart stuttered in my chest. I knew without a doubt that I was looking at Agatha Vellacrus.

The woman's silver-white hair was coiled in an elegant bun at the back of her head. Diamonds dangled from her ears and draped across the base of her throat, the gems catching the light and fracturing it into a thousand brilliant sparks. Her face was pale and ancient as the stars.

Set within it were gray eyes an identical shade to my father's. But whereas Balthazar Thorne's eyes had been smoky and warm, hers were as cold and bleak as the depths of space.

She stopped and studied us with a frown. 'Felix? What's going on?'

Thorne never looked away from me.

'Why, don't tell me you don't recognize him, mother!' he spat out. 'It's your grandson, the half-breed!'

The words had barely left his lips when he swung his sword round in a double-handed grip.

I broke his attack with the katana and forced him back a step. My gaze shifted to the woman in the doorway. Her mouth was pinched in a bitter expression.

'You said you killed him,' she said in a voice devoid of emotion.

'I did!' Thorne retorted. The woman's frown deepened.

Until that moment, despite what I had been told by my grandfather and Victor Dvorsky, I had clung to a slim hope. The Bastians had to be wrong; how could the woman who gave birth to my father want me dead? The very thought struck a discordant chord deep within my soul.

At that very instant, the moment passed and the sliver of hope shattered into a million shards that pierced my heart with blinding pain. I should have blinked back tears. Instead, my vision had never been clearer.

I moved.

The katana slid along Thorne's sword and entered his chest in a single blow. The immortal grunted, his gray eyes widening in shocked incredulity.

There was a barely audible gasp from the woman at the end of the passage.

I pulled the blade out of Thorne's ribcage and watched him fall to his knees. Blood blossomed across his shirt and dripped onto the expensive Venetian carpet. He coughed and took a rasping breath, a stream of red bubbles staining his lips.

'I could kill you now,' I said dispassionately. 'But I won't.' My gaze shifted from him to the woman in the blue gown. 'Not until I get to the bottom of whatever it is that you're up to.'

I turned and walked away, my steps even and my grip steady on the handles of the daisho.

Reid and the Bastians had cleared a path to the cellar. I

stepped over the bodies of fallen Crovirs and caught up with them in the service tunnel under the gardens.

Reid blinked when he saw me and slowly lowered the Glock aimed at my chest. His gaze skimmed over my swords as I sheathed them. He loaded a fresh magazine into the gun. 'You ready?'

'Yes.' Voices rose in the distance behind us. 'Let's go.'

We were almost at the lake when the first wave of Crovir Hunters reached us. A staccato of gunshots erupted around the gardens. Bullets sang through the night, peppering the ground at our heels and raising clumps of soil and grass. Deadly shards erupted from the statues that populated the gardens.

I turned, dropped to one knee, raised my guns, and squeezed the triggers rapidly. Reid staggered to a stop at my side, the shots from his Glock echoing mine. Shadowy shapes fell in the darkness; more appeared to replace them. I rose and followed Reid to the woods.

We entered the shelter of the trees in a hail of gunfire and raced for the boundary of the estate, our breaths pluming the chilly air with pale puffs. A crescent moon shone brightly in the clear autumn sky, its light bathing the woodland in a silvery glow. Heavy footsteps thudded behind us as the Crovirs gave chase.

We got to within a hundred feet of the outer perimeter wall when the second wave of Hunters blocked our path. Shooting erupted from all around. We dove inside a nearby thicket and took cover behind the trunks of some young poplar and black locust trees.

'I hate to say it, but this isn't looking good!' Reid exclaimed.

I inspected the terrain, pulse racing anxiously. There were no visible exit routes.

Bullets thudded into the undergrowth around us. Chips of bark and plant debris rapidly clouded the air.

As I contemplated drawing the Crovirs away from the

others long enough to give them a chance to escape, a gust of wind blew leaves and twigs down onto our heads. The sound of rotors followed a moment later.

A beam of light cut through the night and danced across the ground close to where we hid. I squinted upward and blinked dirt out of my eyes.

A black chopper appeared in the sky and pulled up sharply above the treetops. The cabin doors opened. Two rope ladders dropped down and swung violently in the down-draught.

'What are you waiting for?' shouted the voice in my earpiece. '*Get on!*'

We rose, ran the few steps to the ropes, and jumped. Gunfire crisscrossed the air around us. They were echoed by the stutter of machine guns from above. Shots riddled the forest floor and the bodies of several Crovir Hunters. The rest retreated under the cover of the trees.

The helicopter rose and banked sharply to the left, the four of us still clinging to the rope ladders. We were over the wall of Benisek's estate within seconds.

I reached the door of the aircraft's cabin behind Reid and was pulled inside by someone.

'Thanks!' I gasped and looked up into Costas's grim face.

'Don't mention it,' grumbled the Bastian noble. 'Someone had to get your sorry asses out of there.'

Grigoriye smiled faintly from the opposite side of the aircraft.

I was just starting to get my breath back when the co-pilot passed me a headset.

'Are you guys okay?' someone barked in my ears. It was Victor.

I looked at the others. Except for some scratches, everyone appeared to be in one piece. 'Yes, we're fine.'

An audible sigh came across the connection. 'I'm glad to

hear it. We stalled for time as long as we could. I think Vellacrus suspected something.'

My eyes moved to the darkness outside the cabin window.

'I met her,' I said quietly. The numbness that had shrouded me since my encounter with Thorne and Vellacrus was starting to fade.

There was a hush from the headset. 'Did she say anything to you?' Victor asked finally.

'She watched me fight Thorne.'

This time, the silence was short-lived. 'Did you kill him?' The tension in Victor's voice was mirrored in the strained looks on the faces of the immortals inside the helicopter.

I hesitated. 'No. I wounded him.'

Bruno glanced at me with a troubled expression. I felt the unspoken question in the air.

Victor was the one who voiced it. 'Could you have?'

I leaned back in the seat and stared blindly at the roof of the helicopter. 'Yes.'

This time, Victor's sigh was barely perceptible above the noise of the rotors. 'I'll see you back at the house.'

～

CHAPTER NINETEEN

GODARD WAS WAITING FOR US IN THE FOYER OF THE mansion.

'We heard what happened from the Bastian Hunters,' he said gruffly when we walked through the doors. He strode across the floor and pulled me roughly into his arms.

I stiffened in his embrace.

If the older man noticed, he didn't give any indication of it. He stood back and looked me over with a worried expression.

'Are you all right?'

'Yes. I'm fine.' I looked over his shoulder and saw Anna smiling from the doorway of the study.

'We have the data you sent,' she said.

'Good,' I said with a nod. 'Have you looked at it yet?'

Anna shook her head.

'We were waiting for you.'

A group of Bastian Hunters entered the hall behind us. Roman, Victor, Costas and Grigoriye were in their midst.

'Well done.' Roman smiled. 'For a moment there, I thought you weren't going to make it.'

'So did we,' said Reid. 'You never told us about the helicopter.'

Victor grinned.

'It was Costas's idea. He thought it might come in handy.'

The Bastian noble scowled in the face of our stares. 'They were nearly at the wall anyway,' he muttered, his ears reddening. 'So, we looking at this data or what?'

We gathered in the study a moment later. The Bastians had been busy in our absence; the room now resembled the control deck of a modern warship.

'These are the folders you sent us,' said the Bastian tech seated behind three keyboards. He was working several monitors simultaneously, his glasses reflecting the light from the screens; a large projector screen took up half the wall ahead of him. 'They were encoded with another layer of encryption, but we managed to decipher most of them.' He clicked on a mouse. 'Here's the first file.'

We stared at the information on display.

'That's the data from Hubert's latest research,' Anna said impatiently. 'We know this already.'

'Okay.' The Bastian's fingers moved over the keys. 'Here's the second one.'

A familiar image filled the screen. It was the black and white photograph of Anna and Hubert Strauss from Burnstein's computer. More data streamed down the display.

The tech whistled softly.

'I have to say, they got a helluva lot of info on you, Miss.'

Anna's expression darkened.

'They even have details of the Zurich account.'

'They probably hacked into the bank's computer system,' I said thoughtfully. 'According to the Head of Accounts, no one else had asked to see it.'

'All right, let's look at the next file,' said Victor.

Burnstein's folder contained financial information about his corporation and the various projects the company was involved in. The one on Strauss chronicled the progress of the scientist's research and held detailed background information on him and his colleagues.

The one entitled GeMBiT was still encrypted. It took a short while to decipher the code.

The Bastian tech finally leaned back from the keyboards. 'That's the best I can do.'

We studied the screen. It was filled with reams of scientific jargon. I saw Anna stiffen. I tensed.

'What does it mean?' said Victor. He had also picked up on Anna's mood and looked warily from her pale face to the projected data.

Anna was quiet for a moment.

'May I?' she asked the Bastian tech. She gestured to the keyboards.

'Be my guest,' said the immortal.

Anna took the seat he vacated. She reached for the mouse and scrolled down the pages on the display.

'If I'm correct, this is a program of GeMBiT's principal areas of activities as planned by Burnstein over the next few months.' Her tone was strained as she read out the details. 'The first stage appears to be aimed at manufacturing a number of transfusions of the genetically modified cells from Hubert's research for use on test subjects in their labs in Washington.'

Lines creased Victor's brow. 'Transfusions?'

'The process is very similar to stem cell transplant,' Anna explained. 'You can introduce cells that have the ability to evolve into different types of tissues into the body of a patient to carry out specific functions.'

A sick feeling formed in the pit of my stomach. I suddenly knew what the Crovirs were planning to do. 'Like making someone immortal?'

Anna's eyes moved to me.

'Yes.'

A muscle jumped in Victor's cheek. 'What's the next step?'

'If the trial works, they plan to mass produce the serum.'

The significance of her words finally started to dawn on everyone else in the room. Restless murmurs rose from the Bastian Council members.

'Are they planning to give this transfusion to the Crovirs?' asked Victor.

Anna's fingers moved on one of the keyboards. Lists appeared on the display.

'Not all of them. Just the people on here.'

We stared at the projection screen. There were some five hundred names on it. I frowned when I saw Olsson's halfway down the sixth list.

It was Roman who spoke next.

'That's most of the nobles and other significant figures in Crovir society, as well as two hundred Hunters or so,' said the Bastian leader. 'Basically, anyone who supports Vellacrus is on that list.'

'How generous of her,' murmured Grigoriye.

A vein throbbed on Costas's forehead. 'If she does this, she will—' He stopped, visibly struggling for words.

'She will have a truly immortal army at her feet,' Victor continued icily. 'One that would be eternally loyal to her and do her bidding, no questions asked.'

'It will only lead to another war.' Godard sat down heavily in an armchair, his face gray. He stared at Roman. 'There'll be no stopping the Crovirs this time. They will wipe us out from the face of the Earth!'

Roman remained silent, his expression grim.

Reid interrupted the somber hush. 'Let me get something straight—can they actually do any of this without Anna's blood?'

We all looked at Anna.

'No, they can't,' she replied quietly. She turned and studied the rest of the information on the screen. Her eyes suddenly narrowed.

'What is it?' I said.

'There's something on here I don't understand. They mention a vaccine that is to be administered a couple of weeks prior to the start of the transfusion process.' She looked at me with a puzzled expression. 'I have no idea what it's for.'

An image flashed through my mind. I thought of the last file I had downloaded from Benisek's hard drives.

Dimly, I heard Victor say, 'Is there no mention of it anywhere else?'

Anna shook her head. 'No. Not that I can see, anyway.'

I felt my blood grow cold as I recalled the title of the folder.

'Reid, you got that memory stick?' I said in a voice that sounded strangely detached even to my own ears.

Anna went still at my tone. 'What's wrong?'

'There was another file on Benisek's computers. I didn't have time to send it through.'

I took the USB device from Reid and plugged it into one of the hard drives. A box opened up on the screen. I scrolled down the list of files and clicked on the one titled "Red Death".

For once, the data was not encrypted.

Silence fell across the room while we examined the information streaming on the display. Even though most of it was in scientific terminology, the essence of the thing was horrifyingly clear.

'Dear God.' Anna's fingers rose tremulously to her face. Her whispered words echoed the palpable dread in the air.

'What is it?' Reid studied the fearful expressions around the room with a frown.

'Being the only human here, I take it you've never heard of the Red Death?' said Victor.

'No,' said Reid. 'Enlighten me.'

'Seven hundred years ago, at the time the Black Death was sweeping through Europe and killing millions of humans, another highly contagious and fatal disease called Red Death wiped out more than half the population of immortals on Earth.'

Reid's eyes widened.

'Wait. Are you talking about the *plague?*'

Victor nodded.

'Yes. Although the bubonic plague killed many humans, it did not affect us immortals.' His lips pinched in a bitter smile. 'We had our own version to contend with.'

'The Red Death was an extremely contagious form of a viral hemorrhagic fever,' Anna explained. 'Once infected, the end came within a matter of days. And that wasn't the worst of it.'

Reid's eyebrows rose. 'It wasn't?'

'No. The worst part was that most of those who survived became infertile.' Anna looked around the room. 'To this day, we are still nowhere near the number of immortals that existed prior to the plague.'

'What exactly is Vellacrus planning?' said Godard. He rose from his seat and stepped forward with a purposeful stride, his walking stick striking the floor forcefully.

Anna turned back to the monitor.

'From the information here, it seems Burnstein and his team isolated a strain of the virus sometime last year.' She frowned. 'And they've been busy trying to modify it since.'

'Modify it?' Costas grunted. 'How?'

Anna scrolled down the screen.

'It looks like they genetically reengineered it.'

The Bastian Council member scowled.

'Why?'

I glanced from the complex information on the monitor to Anna's pale face, a cold sweat breaking across my brow.

'To make it more deadly,' she said dully, confirming my suspicion. A gasp left her lips a moment later.

'What's wrong?' I took a step toward her, tension humming in my veins.

'This can't be right,' Anna whispered.

The only sound in the room for the next few seconds was the clattering of her fingers on the keyboard. Her hands finally stilled. She sat back in the chair.

'Anna?' said Godard. He placed a hand on her shoulder.

Anna's voice, when it came, was low and horror-struck.

'This virus has the ability to cross species.'

'Cross species?' our grandfather repeated. 'What do you mean?'

Understanding exploded in my mind. An icy chill ran down my spine.

'It can infect humans? Non immortals?' I said stiffly, staring at her ashen face.

I knew the answer even before she returned my gaze unflinchingly and nodded once. Shocked murmurs erupted around the room.

Victor pointed at the screen.

'Do they know this?' he barked.

'You mean the Crovirs?' A mirthless chuckle escaped Anna's throat. 'They intentionally designed it that way.'

There was a moment of stunned silence.

'Vellacrus is mad!' snarled Victor. 'If this virus is set loose—'

'Not only will it wipe out the immortals,' Anna interrupted bitterly, 'it'll take out more than half of the world's human population with it.'

'What's she hoping to achieve by this?' asked Reid in a deadly voice.

'No one knows the working of that woman's mind,' mumbled Godard. 'This only goes to show how crazed she has become over the centuries. Even the Crovir First Council appears to have no control over her!'

I thought of the woman I had met earlier that evening and felt my blood run cold at his words.

'She must be stopped,' Roman asserted, his tone edged with steel.

The ensuing silence was broken by a hesitant voice.

'I'm sorry to point out the obvious here, but didn't someone just mention a vaccine?' asked Anatole.

'Yes.' Anna scrolled down the screen. 'It seems they're still in the process of manufacturing it.'

'Do you think you could make another one?' I said, voicing the unspoken question in the air.

A frustrated sound left her lips.

'I'm afraid it's an area I know little about,' she said. 'I would need the help of experts in the field of Cellular and Molecular Microbiology, not to mention Immunology.' She watched us with a defeated expression. 'Even if I could get my hands on a sample of the virus, it could take weeks, if not months to produce another vacc—'

She stopped abruptly. Excitement flared in her eyes. She turned to the keyboard. The monitor flickered and data from a scientific website appeared on the screen.

'There *is* this relatively new technique called reverse vaccinology. It uses the pathogen's genetic information instead of the usual method of culture to identify immunogenic antigens that can be targeted for vaccine development.' She looked up into our blank expressions. 'It could halve the time taken to produce a vaccine,' she explained animatedly.

'So, we have to destroy this virus, steal the vaccine, or make a new one,' Victor stated with a heavy frown.

'Don't forget. We also need to stop them from getting their hands on Anna,' said Godard. 'Their plan of true immortality won't work unless they have a sample of her blood.'

Victor directed a questioning stare at his father. Roman hesitated before nodding. Victor turned to the other Bastian Council members.

'We should talk to Reznak.'

I frowned at the unfamiliar name.

There was a stir among the nobles; some glanced at each other uneasily. It was Costas who spoke.

'That old fox?' he scoffed. 'What makes you think he'd be willing to help us after all these years?'

Victor sighed. 'The man is barely a hundred years older than you. And we've kept in touch over the years. Besides, he was a key figure in forging the truce that ended the first immortal war. I doubt he would want to see a second one.' He paused. 'I'm sure he's not the only Crovir who will want to stop Vellacrus.'

Costas grunted. 'Still, I never thought I'd see the day when a member of the Bastian First Council would request assistance from a Crovir.'

Roman's eyes narrowed at the noble's words. 'There is far too much at stake here for our pride to get in the way, Costas. We're talking about the mass genocide of an entire race of immortals.'

'Let's not forget about the puny mortals,' drawled Reid.

Roman dipped his head solemnly. 'You're right. I apologize.' His eyes moved to the window. It was still dark outside. 'I propose we get some rest. If I'm correct in my assumptions, I believe we shall hear from some of the Crovir Council members themselves by morning.'

Roman Dvorsky's prediction turned out to be unerringly accurate. Too restless to sleep after the events of the previous twenty-four hours, I was standing at the window of my bedroom and watching dawn break across the land when a knock sounded at the door. It was Victor.

'Reznak just called,' he said without preamble. 'He wants to meet. I thought you should come along.'

I nodded and gathered my weapons.

The door to Reid's room opened when we strolled past it. He stood on the threshold and yawned. 'What's up?'

He stiffened when he took in our attire and the swords at my waist.

'We're going to see the Crovirs,' said Victor.

'If he's going then so am I,' said Reid, cocking a thumb my way.

Victor arched an eyebrow at me. I shrugged. He sighed.

The sun was washing the landscape in shades of gold when we stepped out onto the porch. The grass on the lawn still bore the fading whiteness of an overnight frost and the chill in the air hinted at the approaching winter.

Costas and a group of Bastian Hunters stood waiting on the graveled driveway. We climbed aboard three SUVs and headed out of the estate.

The meeting point was the ruins of a medieval castle several miles south of Prague. Situated on a low knoll between two villages, it was enclosed by a mile of woodland. The only way to reach the site was up a narrow, rutted track lined with undergrowth and crowded by trees.

Branches scraped noisily against the doors and underside of our vehicle as the driver negotiated the incline. Up ahead, fresh tire marks were visible in the mud. The path leveled off after a few minutes and the SUVs pulled to a stop in front of a waterlogged field.

The brow of the hill was dotted with the rubble of what was once an extensive fort. Some moss-covered stones showed signs of quarry activity and the grass bore faded lorry tracks. From behind the trees and bushes punctuating the wild heather emerged a group of men.

We exited the vehicles and made our way across the field toward them.

'Dimitri.' Victor bestowed a small nod of acknowledgment upon a middle-aged man in a dove-gray suit at the head of the group. 'It's been a while.'

Had he been wearing black like the immortals around him, Dimitri Reznak would still have stood out from his entourage. Although he was an inch shorter than Victor, he was heavier set in the shoulders and legs. His full lips, straight wide nose, and strong jaw suggested a Slavic ancestry. Deep set eyes glittered beneath a pair of bushy eyebrows.

'Yes, it has.' Reznak stepped forward and hugged Victor warmly. 'You still owe me a game of chess from last Christmas. And whatever happened to that bottle of whisky you promised me?'

Victor rolled his eyes. 'I don't recall saying any such thing.'

Reznak chuckled. His amused gaze shifted beyond Victor's shoulder. 'Hey Costas. The years haven't been kind to you.'

The Bastian Council member scowled. 'As rude as ever, I see,' he mumbled.

'You just bring out the best in me.' Reznak's eyes moved to my face. His smile faded. 'I see you brought Soul with you.' The Crovir noble's tone remained light as he addressed Victor. 'Should I be concerned?'

Victor sighed. 'If I wanted to kill you, I'd do it with my own bare hands.'

Reznak grunted.

'Lucas has a deeply vested interest in this matter,' Victor continued. 'A group of Crovir Hunters have been after him again in the last two weeks.'

Reznak grimaced. 'I have to say, my section doesn't exactly have a lot to do with that.' He paused. 'Who's the human?'

'I'm with him,' said Reid, indicating me. 'It's the eyes, isn't it? It's gotta be the eyes,' he added under his breath.

'That was quite some stunt you guys pulled last night,' Reznak told Victor. 'It took Vellacrus by surprise.'

I stiffened at his words. There was something I needed to know. 'How's Thorne?'

'He'll live.' Reznak observed me with an inscrutable expression. 'I'm amazed you didn't finish him off.'

'I had my reasons.'

His eyes narrowed slightly. 'Let's walk, shall we?'

~

CHAPTER TWENTY

'Last night was the first we heard of Vellacrus's grand plans concerning the immortality serum and the new strain of the Red Death virus. Judging by the reactions of the Council members in the room, some already knew the broader details of the scheme.' Dimitri Reznak frowned. 'The rest of us were horrified, to say the least.'

'You're on the list,' said Costas.

Reznak raised an eyebrow.

'You mean the one containing the names of the hallowed few upon whom Vellacrus has chosen to bestow the gift of true immortality?' he said mockingly. 'Trust me, it will give me no joy to be one of her army of eternal followers. Life as an immortal is long enough.' He grimaced. 'And can you imagine me swearing fealty to her, like in the old days?' He removed a cigar from the inside pocket of his coat, lit up, and inhaled deeply. 'To be honest, there are times when I really look forward to the final death.'

The ensuing silence was broken by the squawking of a pair of crows as they lifted off the ground ahead of us.

'She must be stopped,' Victor stated flatly.

'I couldn't agree more,' muttered Reznak.

'Who else will help?'

The Crovir noble was quiet for a beat. 'I know of at least two other First Council members, as well as several in the Second Council and the Assembly, who will want to see her plans fail,' he said finally. 'Their men are loyal to them, as are mine.' He hesitated. 'To be honest, some of us have been thinking it was time to put an end to Vellacrus's rule. Her actions will undoubtedly lead us to another immortal war. She never wanted the original truce in the first place, but since she wasn't the leader of the Order of Crovir Hunters at the time, she couldn't influence that decision.' A humorless laugh escaped his lips. 'It looks like she's about to get her wish.'

'Still, she has many faithful followers,' said Victor.

Reznak nodded. 'Yes, she does. Half of them do so out of greed and a hunger for power. The other half are just too afraid to stand up to her. But if another potential leader was to come to the fore and challenge her...' He lapsed into silence.

Victor smiled faintly. 'Are we in the presence of her proposed replacement?'

Reznak shrugged.

'Who knows what the future holds,' he said, a shrewd light gleaming in his eyes. 'But no, I really wouldn't want that kind of responsibility. It would distract me from my main interests,' he added on a more serious tone.

He stopped in his tracks and turned to face me.

'However, the question still remains, Lucas Soul. If and when the time comes, will you have the courage to end it all? Will you be able to kill your own kin in cold blood?'

The wind picked up, causing ripples to course across the heather. Dead leaves and twigs snapped and swirled around our feet in an unruly dance in the expectant silence that followed.

The Crovir noble's question hardly surprised me. After last night, I knew the Bastians shared the same concern. Up until yesterday, I had had similar doubts. Then, for the umpteen time in the last eight hours, I recalled the look in Agatha Vellacrus's eyes.

'Yes,' I said in a cold and steady tone.

Reznak's stare persisted for several more seconds. A grunt left his lips and he turned to Victor with a strangely satisfied expression.

'The vaccine is being made at our lab in Germany,' he said. 'Burnstein had the virus flown across from the States a month ago. From what Vellacrus revealed to us last night, they're probably days away from the final product. The next step will be to carry out a short, accelerated trial on a group of volunteers to identify any significant side effects. Once she gets the all clear from Burnstein's scientists, Vellacrus will start the inoculation program.'

We reached the crest of the hill. Reznak stopped and studied the landscape stretching to the village drifting out of the morning mist in the distance.

'One more thing. Vellacrus intends to put all the resources of our Councils into hunting down Anna Godard. Wherever she is, she won't be safe for long.' He looked at Victor. 'Pinchter is not the only Bastian willing to betray you for the gift of true immortality. There will be others eager to work with Thorne and Vellacrus.'

Victor's eyes narrowed. 'Do you have names?'

Reznak shook his head. 'Vellacrus isn't that trusting. I believe only she and Thorne know the identities of the possible traitors in your midst.'

Victor was quiet for some time. 'Tell us about Germany.'

We were back at the estate an hour later. The air had lost its wintry chill and the sun was warm on my face when I stepped out of the SUV. I followed the others inside the mansion, my mind still buzzing with the information Reznak had shared with us.

The foyer was crowded and noisy. The Bastians were getting ready to leave; Victor had called his father on the drive back and updated him on the outcome of the meeting.

Anna crossed the hall toward me. 'Is it true? The Crovirs may only be days away from completing the vaccine?'

I nodded. Her eyes darkened.

Victor came up behind her. 'We need to move you to another safe house.'

Anna glanced at him distractedly. 'Yes, I know.'

'The equipment you asked for will be there.' Victor stopped a passing Hunter in his tracks and handed him a piece of paper. 'Here, give this to the techs. They're the codes for the Crovirs' satellites.'

He turned back to Anna. 'We've located five Bastian and four human scientists specializing in the areas you asked about. They should be making their way to the compound as we speak.'

Godard appeared beside Anna and laid a hand on her shoulder. 'It'll be all right, child. I won't leave you.'

Anna wrapped her fingers over our grandfather's.

'Get me something from that lab,' she said in a low voice, her eyes never leaving my face. 'Without a sample of that virus or the vaccine, we won't have a chance in hell of stopping the Crovirs.' Her narrowed gaze shifted to my left. 'And you, make sure he's okay.'

'Yes ma'am,' said Reid.

The Godards headed for the front doors just as the sound of rotor blades rose from outside. I frowned when I saw the black chopper landing on the lawn.

'How many men are you sending with them?'

'From here on it'll be Costas and Grigoriye,' Victor replied.

I startled and opened my mouth to voice a protest.

Victor put a hand up to silence me. 'The helicopter will take them to an abandoned airfield a few miles from here, where they'll take a jet to their final destination. The Bastian Hunters guarding the safe house won't have a clue who they're protecting. And the fewer people know about it, the better.'

His words made sense. Still, I could not quiet the feeling of dread in my gut; I hated the thought of being separated from the Godards.

I strolled out to the porch and watched them leave, my sense of unease unabated. Anna's grim face disappeared from view as the helicopter rose toward the sky.

I was still standing there a while later when Victor spoke behind me.

'You ready?'

I turned and looked around. 'Your father?'

'He's talking to the Bastian Councils as well as our Assembly,' said Victor. 'Not everyone believes Vellacrus has such a terrible plan in motion. Now that we have some evidence, it should be easier to convince them that action needs to be taken.'

He looked over his shoulder. Roman walked past one of the windows in the study; he was talking on his cell and frowning.

'We have to gather as many troops as we can.' Victor directed a somber gaze my way. 'I fear we will need them all at the end.'

Victor's words were still ringing in my ears when we crossed the border into Germany several hours later. According to Reznak's intel, the Crovirs' research facility was located in a forest outside the town of Amberg, in the state of Bavaria. By the time the convoy of SUVs reached the heavy woodland surrounding the facility, a group of local Bastian Hunters had completed a preliminary recon of the site.

'This is a map of the area,' said the leader of the team as he led us inside a makeshift tent. The immortal, whose name was Friedrich, pointed at the printouts on a foldable table. 'And these are the corresponding satellite images from an hour ago.'

We studied the pictures in silence. I exchanged a troubled glance with Reid. This was not going to be a walk in the park.

'How deep is this thing?' Victor finally said, fingers tracing the thermal outline of the subterranean structure that dominated the ground-penetrating radar satellite imagery.

'Our best estimate? About two thousand feet,' said the Bastian Hunter. 'And that's just the first level.'

Anatole whistled softly and earned himself a dark look from Bruno.

Friedrich indicated the pictures. 'From what we deduced, the labs are located at the very center of the structure, here and here. The rest of the facility consists of a score of specially designed ventilation shafts, four security rooms, a canteen, a gym, and the administrative and living quarters for the staff.' He looked at Victor. 'We've patrolled the perimeter and can confirm the number of guards is accurate.'

A bleak smile crossed Victor's face as he stared at the heat signals crowding the images. 'Vellacrus has already increased security. Somehow, I'm not surprised.'

'Going overland undetected is going to be virtually impossible,' continued the Bastian team leader. 'Even if we disable their satellites, they'll shoot us down before we get within spitting distance of the main elevator shaft. Luckily, we may have found an alternative route to get inside.'

One of his men handed him a roll of paper. He unfolded it across the tabletop.

I pushed aside the feelings of trepidation I still harbored about the Godards. 'What're we looking at?'

Friedrich glanced at Victor. The Bastian noble nodded. The Hunter cleared his throat.

'It's a mining map of the area. This entire forest is located above the remains of an old coal mine. You probably passed the main gates on the way here.' He tapped the paper. 'We've identified three other access points into the facility; here, here and here. Two of the tunnels are being guarded by the Crovirs. The third one isn't.'

Victor frowned. 'What's the catch?'

'The tunnel collapsed,' said Friedrich. 'Not completely, obviously,' he added at our expressions. 'There's about twelve feet of rubble blocking the entrance. Beyond that, it looks clear all the way to the central structure.' His fingers moved across the thermal images. 'There are too many shafts and side passages for a security team to be able to cover practically, even with the added number of guards. And they have to have safety exits for the facility. This tunnel leads to one of them. We've already confirmed that they have no cameras down there.' He hesitated. 'There's a strong possibility that the rest of the tunnel is unstable. It may explain why they seem unconcerned about guarding it. However, I believe it's our best chance of getting in and out without being detected.'

Victor raised his eyebrows at me. 'Lucas?'

I considered the map and the satellite images on the table for a moment. 'He's right.'

Victor nodded. 'I concur.' He turned to Friedrich. 'Leave half the men on the surface. We might need them for backup.'

Friedrich's team had used their time well. When we reached the site of the abandoned tunnel, the men were unloading a micro digger from the back of a flatbed truck. Steel girders lay on the ground.

'We borrowed them from a local construction site,' said the Bastian Hunter by way of explanation at our stares.

'What's the steel for?' said Reid curiously.

'They're to support the tunnel entrance,' said Friedrich. 'We'll need an escape route if we get out of the facility alive.'

Anatole had gone pale. Bruno frowned at him. 'What's wrong?'

'You know how I feel about underground spaces,' muttered the red-haired immortal.

'We were underground at Benisek's mansion,' Bruno pointed out.

'Yeah, but at least I could see starlight and smell fresh air,' Anatole replied glumly. 'This is gonna be like that time in Rome. Remember? When we were in the catacombs? God, I hated that trip. The rats were the size of my arm.'

Bruno rolled his eyes.

The tunnel was clear for the first ten feet. Beyond that, an impenetrable wall of compacted earth, wood, and rock barred the way.

It took an hour for the digger to move the core of the debris. After the last support beam was fixed into place, we geared up and checked our weapons.

Victor was staying topside to cover us. He put a hand on my shoulder as I turned to follow the others into the passage.

'Be careful,' he said quietly. 'I'll be waiting for your return.'

I nodded and climbed through the ragged opening after Reid and the Bastians.

It was like stepping inside a tomb. The air was dry and choked with the dust stirred up by the excavation. The light from our torch beams washed over rusting roof bolts and girders supporting a low ceiling. Timber frames propped up sections of the walls. Some had given way, causing tiny landslides that revealed the bare rock underneath.

'You okay?' said Reid.

'Yeah, I'm fine.'

To be truthful, I was not particularly comfortable with confined underground spaces either. Months spent in the battle trenches during the First World War had seen to that. I also had a highly unpleasant memory from my time in Vienna in 1683, when I became trapped for several days in one of the city's tunnels after it caved in behind me. Had it not been for a fortuitous explosion from a nearby Ottoman mine, I would have been buried alive for the rest of the siege, along with the rats.

I took a deep breath and headed into the mine. Up ahead, Anatole muttered a short prayer.

A hundred feet in, we came to an open elevator shaft descending into pitch blackness. Friedrich shone his torch over the control box at the side and pulled a lever. Nothing happened. He opened the panel, changed the fuse and the battery, and tried again. A high-pitched roar erupted from the old electric motor. The gears engaged and the elevator whined into life.

A wire cage rose shakily past the corroded rungs of an emergency ladder. We stepped inside it and started a slow, rickety descent into the gloom. Two hundred feet down, abandoned galleries appeared off the central shaft.

'How far are we going?' Anatole eyed the tunnels being reclaimed by the shadows above us with unease.

'All the way to the bottom,' said Friedrich.

The lift stuttered to a stop some thousand feet below ground. Despite the glare of our torch beams, the darkness at the bottom of the pit had a suffocating, cloying quality that threatened to overwhelm the senses. I could hear Anatole's heavy breaths somewhere to my left.

'There had better not be rats,' the immortal murmured to no one in particular.

We exited the cage and made our way toward the tunnel straight ahead. More galleries branched off the passage and we passed several caved-in channels. Half a mile later, a faint whine rose in the distance.

'What's that?' said Reid.

'The fans in the south-west ventilation shaft,' said Friedrich. 'We're close to the facility.'

I removed the Glock from the holster on my thigh and nudged off the safety catch. Soft clicks sounded around me as the others did the same.

Tension spread through the group. A muted light appeared

in front of us. The soles of our boots struck concrete. The
darkness receded. Seconds later, we stopped on the edge of a
brightly lit, circular vertical duct.

The shaft was thirty feet wide, with smooth walls. Some
fifty feet below, the blades of a horizontal fan rotated lazily,
drawing air down from the surface. Other fans were visible
beneath it. I looked up.

The roof of the borehole was lost in shadows. Narrow
handrails rose on the east side of the shaft and disappeared into
the gloom.

'Oh boy,' said Anatole.

Friedrich holstered his gun and removed a pistol bow from
his backpack. He dropped to one knee, squinted through the
crosshairs of the telescopic sight at the passage on the opposite
side of the duct, and pulled the trigger. There was a soft thump
as the arrow carrying a zip line thudded into the concrete ceiling. Another Hunter drilled a hole in the roof above our heads
and screwed in a steel eyebolt before fastening the end of the
cable to it.

The Bastian team leader unhooked a carabiner from his
harness, locked onto the zip line, and winched himself over the
gaping space. We followed him across one at a time.

The tunnel on the other side extended another eighty feet
before ending at a rust-covered, airtight door. It took three of
us to twist open the stiff, circular wheel that sealed it shut. The
panel finally creaked and moved on its hinges.

We peered over the threshold into the bowels of a modern
elevator shaft.

Friedrich indicated the metal rungs that ran along the wall
next to the doorframe. 'Now we go down.'

Six hundred feet below, we reached a stationary lift cabin.
We continued past it and dropped to the bottom of the shaft
moments later.

A single access door stood in the north wall of the structure.

No sound escaped from the other side. I slipped the katana out of its scabbard and gripped the handle of the Glock tightly.

'Ready?' said Friedrich.

Anatole shrugged. 'As ready as we'll ever be, I guess.'

The Bastian Hunter grabbed the handle and pulled the door toward him.

CHAPTER TWENTY-ONE

A BOILER ROOM LAY BEYOND THE BASE OF THE ventilation shaft. Pipes rumbled and hissed on the walls and ceiling as we crossed it, eyes scanning the shadows above our guns.

A second door appeared on the other side. It led to a narrow, white concrete corridor with a metal staircase at the far end.

'The labs should be a couple of levels beneath us,' said Friedrich. He was staring at the security camera in a corner of the ceiling above the doorway. 'Are we good to go?' he murmured into the mouthpiece of his microphone.

'You're clear,' a voice replied in our earpieces.

The Bastian techs had used the access codes provided by Reznak to infiltrate the Crovirs' satellites and security networks and temporarily override the CCTV system inside the research facility with pre-recorded clips.

We moved to the stairs and headed into the bowels of the structure. Seconds before we reached the first landing, a door clanged somewhere above us. We flattened ourselves against the wall and froze.

Footsteps echoed on the metal steps. Another door opened and closed. We waited a moment before resuming our descent.

Two stories below the boiler room corridor, we came to a high-containment, stainless steel entrance. A glazed circular window sat in the top half of the metal panel. Beyond it was an empty corridor. I studied the airtight seals around the frame and the security panel next to the handle with a sinking feeling.

'That's not good,' said Reid.

'Can the Bastian techs get the access code from the Crovirs' security frames?' I asked Friedrich.

'No,' said the Bastian Hunter. He slipped a small rectangular device from his bag. 'The facility's security chief chooses the door codes individually.'

I stared at the electronic door opener in his hands. He moved to connect it to the security panel on the door. I placed a hand on his shoulder and stopped him.

'That'll take too long.'

Friedrich looked from the device to me. 'Do you have a better idea?'

'Yes. Does anyone have a wireless cell phone?'

The Hunters exchanged puzzled glances. Reid smiled.

Bruno hesitated before handing me his phone.

I flipped open the security panel, pulled out a pair of wires, and connected them to the application processor at the back of the mobile device.

'I thought you couldn't get a signal this far below ground,' said Anatole as they watched me work.

My fingers danced over the touch screen. 'Most modern mines have advanced digital communication systems. Even though this facility is old, it would surprise me if the Crovirs hadn't installed the latest technology for their labs.'

A low beep issued from the containment door. It hissed open. I disconnected the cell and returned it to Bruno.

Friedrich's eyebrows rose. 'I'm impressed.'

We moved soundlessly into the corridor beyond and reached a junction thirty feet in. Friedrich peered around the corner of the wall and drew his head back sharply. A low rumble of conversation rose close by before dying in the distance.

Friedrich indicated his men. 'We'll take the north lab. You guys take the south one.' He offered me his hand. 'Good luck.'

I hesitated; it was the closest I had ever gotten to a friendly gesture from a Bastian Hunter. I shook his hand. We parted ways, Reid, Anatole, and Bruno following behind me.

Minutes later, my earpiece crackled into life. Friedrich's voice came through.

'Does something strike you as odd?'

'Yes,' I said quietly. 'This place is dead.'

The underground facility was deserted. We had already crossed numerous corridors and rooms devoid of signs of life. The only sounds disturbing the tomb-like silence were the buzz from the overhead fluorescent strips and the hum of the vending machines.

'This place should be crawling with Crovirs,' said Friedrich. 'Something's off.'

We stopped at a crossroad and observed another pair of empty hallways.

'I think he might be right,' said Reid.

'Wait.' Friedrich's voice became tense. 'I see something.' There was a pause. 'We've reached the lab.'

I heard a muffled hiss, followed by a protracted silence.

'It's empty,' said Friedrich.

A chill ran down my spine at his words. 'What do you mean?'

'There's no one here,' he replied grimly. 'It looks like they left in a hurry. The place is a mess.' Rustling noises came across the earpiece. 'I can see a decontamination room. It must lead to another lab. I'm gonna check it out.'

I tried to quell the ominous foreboding growing inside me. 'Be careful.'

'Hey!' someone called out. I looked around.

Bruno had wandered to the end of the east hallway; he was staring at something in the adjacent corridor, his gun pointed downward. 'I found a dead guy.'

We joined him and looked at the body on the floor.

The man was dressed in a white, gas-tight decontamination suit complete with clamped boots, gloves, and a hood with a shattered laminated visor. The mode of death was unmistakably evident; there was a single bullet wound in the middle of his forehead. Rigor mortis had started to set in and he lay stiffly against a pair of high containment glass doors. A sign above the lintel read "UL 2".

Beyond the transparent walls, discarded instruments sat atop the work surfaces of a lab. Another set of glass doors stood in the wall on the other side of the room. A second body was visible through them.

I lifted the passkey from the dead man's waist and moved it across the access panel to the right. The doors beeped and slid open. We stepped inside the lab.

'What the hell is going on?' muttered Bruno.

I studied the array of complex equipment crowding the countertops. There was no sign of anything remotely resembling a hazardous, biological product-containment device, or a vaccine. My knuckles whitened on the weapons in my grasp.

'It's a trap.' I stopped in front of the doors leading to the inner room. 'Vellacrus must have known we were coming.'

'How? We only left Prague a few hours ago!' exclaimed Anatole.

'I can only think of two reasons.' I waved the passkey across the second security display and crossed the threshold into the next chamber. 'Either she's a tactical genius or someone betrayed us.' I stared at the second body and struggled to control the anger in my voice. 'If I was a betting man, I'd go with the latter option.' I squatted by the still figure.

The woman was dressed in a decontamination suit and had suffered a bullet wound to the chest. Her body had twisted sideways in her final death throes and her outstretched hand reached toward a stainless steel door to the left of the room.

'I take it these people weren't immortals,' Reid said behind me.

I straightened. 'No. They were probably hired from the nearest town.' I crossed the floor to the steel door and gazed through the oval glass port in the top half of the panel.

'What's through there?' said Reid. He joined me.

'It's an airlock chamber.' I scrutinized the gray space beyond. 'It must lead to a decontamination room and another lab.'

I used the passkey to open the door. There were sterile suits on the wall inside.

Reid started to climb into one of them. I turned and stared at him.

'What're you doing?'

Reid met my gaze with a frown. 'We're not having this discussion again. Just shut up and get in a suit.'

I exhaled loudly and looked to the doorway, where Bruno and Anatole stood watching us. 'See if you can find anything on the computers,' I told them. 'They may not have erased the hard drives.'

I closed the steel door and engaged the airlock. An ominous hiss sounded behind me as a second door opened. I left the daisho in the chamber and followed Reid into the decontamination shower.

Moments later, there was a sensation of pressure and air whistled from the room. The light on the next containment door changed to green and a panel slid aside. We entered a brightly lit sterile lab.

The facility was still functional. Lights glowed on the instruments thrumming on the counters lining the wall to our right, the steady buzz from the machines penetrating through the soles of our boots. A fridge with a glass door stood next to them. My heart sank when I noted the empty shelves inside.

A row of containment cages stood on a table. The bloated and bruised bodies of several dead rats lay inside.

'It's a good thing Anatole didn't come with us,' I murmured.

'Lucas.'

I turned and looked to where Reid stared.

A glass wall rose behind and to our left, separating the inner lab from yet another chamber. Inside it were three gurneys. Medical equipment crowded the space around the beds and overshadowed the bodies lying upon them.

The figures were still attached to life monitors and IV drips. The machines had been turned off.

I took a step toward the door in the middle of the wall.

Reid frowned. 'What are you doing?'

'They may still be alive.' I reached for the passkey at my waist.

'They look dead enough from here,' Reid muttered as he followed me into the second room.

The body on the first bed was that of a young woman. Several IVs were hooked to her arms and a central line dangled from her neck. There was a disconnected ET tube taped to her mouth.

'What the hell?' Reid moved to the second bed, his eyes widening in consternation. The body of a man lay in it. Tubes and wires dotted his arms and legs, and he was attached to an array of silent machines.

This time, the coldness that gripped me felt arctic.

Large, purple necrotic lesions covered the visible areas of skin on the two corpses. Dry blood coated their eyes and orifices. A macabre patchwork of rust colored stains darkened the sheets where they had bled from their IVs and lower gut.

'They were infected with the virus.' I was surprised at how calm my voice sounded.

Reid stared at the bodies. 'Why would they do that?'

'To see whether it worked.' I took a deep breath and suppressed the rage and dread that threatened to overwhelm me.

I moved to the third bed.

The last figure was also that of a man. His skin was covered in the same lesions as the first two. One of his IVs was attached to a working drip stand. A trail of blood had oozed out of his left nostril. As I watched, it trickled down his cheek. My eyes widened.

'He's still alive!' I moved to the side of the gurney and reached for the man's wrist. There was a faint pulse. I looked up and saw his eyelids flicker open.

The man blinked at me. 'Yanof? Is that you?' he murmured through dry, cracked lips.

It was obvious he could not see clearly through the visor of my suit helmet. Either that or he was delirious from his sickness. I hesitated before holding his hand gently.

'Yes, it's me,' I lied in a steady voice.

The man swallowed convulsively, a rasp escaping his parched throat. He lifted his head off the pillow and grabbed the front of my suit in a surprisingly strong grip.

'Burnstein tricked us, Yanof!' he hissed. 'He said he was going to give us the vaccine, but he injected us with the virus. You have to get out of here! Get out before it's too late!' He collapsed onto the bed, his chest shuddering.

Alarm tore through me. I leaned across the gurney. 'Listen! Is there anywhere else in the lab where they might have stored the virus or the vaccine? Please, tell me!'

The man's eyes closed. For a moment, I feared he had

passed away. A second later, his eyelids fluttered open once more.

'They took it all away,' he whispered. 'I saw them. There's nothing left!' He gasped. 'I heard Burnstein say...they were taking it to America.'

He took a final rattling breath and sagged against the pillow, his features slackening. I stared at the dead man for a moment before lowering his limp hand to the sheet and closing his staring eyes.

A blast boomed in the distance. The walls and floor of the lab shook violently. Plaster dust drifted down from the ceiling.

Reid and I stared at each other.

'What was that?' I barked in the mouthpiece.

There was a burst of static from my earpiece. Anatole's voice came through brokenly.

'Explosion—other lab—Friedrich and—trapped—we've gotta go!'

I scanned the room wildly, heart slamming a rapid tempo against my ribs.

'Listen to me!' I shouted in the mouthpiece, frantically opening the drawers on the medical trolleys. Reid watched me with a puzzled frown. 'I want you to leave right now. Rescue the others if you can, then get out of here!'

'What about you?' Bruno's overwrought voice came across clearly.

I finally found what I was searching for. 'We'll manage. Now go!'

I lifted the sterile needle and syringe out of a plastic wrapper.

Reid stared as I tied a tourniquet around the dead man's arm. 'What're you doing?'

'We need a sample of the virus.' I slid the needle under the man's skin. 'This is the next best thing.' Dark blood filled the syringe. I glanced at Reid. 'You should go too.'

His eyebrows rose behind the visor. 'What the hell makes you think I'm going to leave without you?'

I smiled bleakly and capped the needle. I located a secured biohazard container in the next room and sealed the syringe inside.

We were slipping out of the sterile suits in the outer chamber when a second explosion made the floor tremble beneath our feet. This one sounded closer.

I grabbed the daisho and ran out of the airlock after Reid. We raced past the dead scientists and started down the dust-filled corridor. We had just reached the junction when the roof caved in behind us. A cloud of plaster and brick dirt billowed past us.

We covered our mouths and noses with our sleeves and carried on. It was several minutes before we reached the intersection where we had parted ways with Friedrich and his men. In that time, more explosions rocked the foundations of the underground facility.

A shadow loomed in front of us.

'It's me,' said Bruno into the muzzles of our guns.

The Bastian bodyguard shifted the unconscious man across his shoulder. Anatole dragged another wounded immortal toward the containment door behind him.

I lowered the Glock. 'Is that everyone?'

Bruno shook his head. 'Friedrich's still back there.' He indicated the passage to the left. 'He's bringing the last of his men out.'

A sudden blast brought down part of the hall Reid and I had just exited. A single strip light shattered onto the rubble a moment later. The ceiling creaked ominously.

We rose to our feet and observed the mound of debris.

'It'll be faster if one of us helps them.' I turned and headed toward the lab where Friedrich and his men had been.

'This place is about to come down on our heads!' barked

Bruno. 'We should head back! Look, Friedrich's a Hunter. This is how we work. Besides, we can dig them out later. Victor will—'

'Victor will just have to understand!' I snapped.

The bodyguard scowled.

'Everyone suspects I might be truly immortal. Now's as good a time as any to test that theory,' I said.

The immortal looked unconvinced by my words.

I removed the biohazard container from my backpack and tossed it to Reid. He caught the metal flask in mid air and watched me with a puzzled expression.

'You need to go.' This time, my tone was resolute.

The canister sailed across the corridor and hit me in the chest. A grunt left my lips.

'You've gotta be kidding me.' Reid stalked past in a huff.

I sighed, slipped the container inside the pack, and followed in his footsteps.

'Where're they going?' said Anatole behind us.

'To save Friedrich,' Bruno replied bitterly.

I caught the immortal's faintly murmured words as we turned the corner. 'Goddamned bloody heroes.'

'He called us heroes,' I said after a while.

'Shut up,' said Reid.

There was another detonation elsewhere in the facility. The floor shuddered beneath our feet. We negotiated another two corridors before turning a corner and reaching an impasse.

A wall of debris obstructed our path. The billow of dust that had accompanied the collapse of the passage was only just settling.

'Wasn't this the way to the lab?' said Reid.

'Uh-huh.'

'Is there another way around?'

I looked over my shoulder with a sinking feeling. 'I don't think so.'

A noise drew my gaze to the rubble. There was a disturbance near the bottom. Dirt trickled out in a minor landslide.
Fingertips appeared in the gap.

Reid and I started to dig wordlessly. The hand became a
flailing arm. We grabbed it and pulled out the buried man.

It was Friedrich. Blood oozed from a jagged wound on his
grimy forehead. His left leg was twisted and looked broken in at
least two places.

The Bastian Hunter blinked at me. His eyes suddenly
widened. He tried to sit up and choked.

'One of my men was behind me!' he gasped between hoarse
coughs.

It was another minute before Reid and I dug out the second
immortal from the wreckage. The man had severe crush injuries
to his chest and legs and was barely conscious.

The whole corridor shook violently as another explosion
rocked the underground lab. The rubble shifted with a sinister
groan.

'I think now would be a good time to get out of here!'
said Reid.

We hauled the wounded men up and headed for the exit.

'Why did you come back for us?' Friedrich asked, his words
punctuated by painful grunts.

'We don't make a habit of leaving our men behind,' I
replied, panting.

The immortal seemed to consider this. 'That's all very altru-
istic and admirable but still, kinda dumb,' he muttered.

'Yeah, well, dumb's our middle name,' said Reid. I smiled.

We reached the passage to the steel containment door and
started up the stairs beyond. Four feet from the final landing, a
detonation tore through the open stairwell above our heads.

I looked up. My eyes widened. 'Run!'

Deadly debris smashed into the stairs seconds later.

We entered the boiler room in a thick billow of dust. The

ground trembled. Pipes burst, releasing jets of steam around us. Tremors shook the walls from the impact of the wreckage pounding the stairwell.

We were halfway to the door leading to the elevator shaft when another explosion brought most of the ceiling down on us.

Buzzing stillness followed. I blinked and coughed dirt out of my mouth.

I was lying on my back under a thin layer of rubble. A jagged piece of metal protruded from the ground inches from my left eye.

I rolled over and crawled to my knees. Friedrich groaned somewhere in the gloom.

Reid was climbing to his feet a short distance to my right. He shook his head dazedly, looked up, and froze.

'Hell. Talk about bad luck,' he said leadenly.

I followed his gaze. The weak glow of an emergency light revealed the mound of shattered concrete and metal blocking the access to the elevator shaft. I rose unsteadily and stared at the impenetrable barrier, anger and fear knotting my stomach.

'We're trapped,' Friedrich murmured.

I climbed across the rubble to the far wall and studied the obstruction with narrowed eyes; I was damned if a pile of bricks and mortar was going to stop us after all we had been through.

'There's a crack in the wall,' I said after a moment, tracing the jagged lips of the fracture with my fingers. 'We could blast our way through.'

Reid frowned. 'That could bring the whole place down on our heads.'

'Unless we decide to wait here in the hope that Victor will dig us out before the Crovirs blow this entire joint to hell and back, I don't see that we have any other options,' I retorted.

Reid held my eyes for long seconds. A sigh left his lips.

'That's all fine and dandy, but where are you gonna get your hands on explosives down here?'

My gaze switched to Friedrich.

The Hunter raised an eyebrow. 'How did you know?'

I shrugged. 'I suspected Victor would've instructed you to destroy the lab before getting out.'

The Bastian Hunter grunted. 'That was a good guess.' He reached inside his backpack and brought out a slim, rectangular block of C4.

It took several minutes to dig a trench in the debris on the opposite side of the room. I stuck the explosive inside the crack in the elevator shaft wall and joined the others behind our makeshift barricade.

'Ready?' I said tensely.

'Not really,' said Reid. Friedrich shrugged and coughed.

'Here goes.' I took a deep breath and depressed the switch on the remote control detonator.

A thunderous boom reverberated ahead of us. Fragments of plaster and concrete filled the room. The ceiling groaned.

I lifted my head from my arms and peered over the lip of the trench.

'Did it work?' said Reid.

The dust started to clear. A smile tugged at the corners of my mouth.

Reid rose on his elbows. 'Well, I'll be damned.'

The explosion had created a hole large enough for a man to pass through. We made our way across the uneven floor and crawled into the space beyond.

A few bricks had fallen to the base of the elevator shaft. It was otherwise intact. My heart sank as I looked from the wounded immortals to the metal rungs rising up the wall.

'It's a long way up,' said Friedrich. He met my gaze steadily. 'It might be best to leave us here.'

There was the sound of another distant explosion. A fine

blanket of dust rained down around us. I looked questioningly at Reid.

He shrugged. 'Hell, we haven't gone through all of that just to abandon them here.'

In the end, we secured the injured men to our harnesses and hoisted them up the ladder. By the time we made it to the hatch, my arms and legs shook with effort, and my breaths came in harsh gasps. Sweat dripped down Reid's pale face; he looked as exhausted as I felt.

We reached the ventilation shaft moments later and found the zip line intact.

Reid looked from the unconscious immortal in his arms to the tunnel on the other side. 'How're we gonna do this?'

Friedrich took a thin coil of climbing rope from his belt bag. 'Here. If you go over first, you can use this to pull him across,' he panted.

Reid crossed the ventilation shaft with one end of the rope while Friedrich and I secured the lifeless man to the cable.

'You're next,' I told Friedrich once the unconscious immortal had made it to the opposite tunnel safely.

The Bastian Hunter nodded and leaned heavily against the wall, sweat and blood streaming down his ashen face.

I attached him to the line, tugged on his harness to make sure it was secure, and watched anxiously while he winched himself to the other side. Reid grabbed him seconds later and helped him to the ground.

I had just locked myself onto the cable when a violent blast shook the walls around me. A jagged crack tore through the east side of the ventilation shaft. The ground shifted beneath my feet.

'Lucas!' Reid shouted from across the way.

There was no time to think. Heart thudding erratically in my chest, I launched myself across the gaping space.

Chunks of concrete pelted down around me as the walls

started to collapse. A grunt left my lips when debris hit the zip line. The wire suddenly sagged.

I looked over my shoulder, alarm twisting through my gut; the steel arrow was almost out of the ceiling.

'What the hell are you waiting for?' Reid barked. '*Move!*'

I needed no further prompting.

Six feet from the mouth of the tunnel, the arrow finally gave. I felt the abrupt slack in the line, grabbed it with both hands, and fell through empty space.

I slammed into the wall of the shaft. Air left my lungs in a stunned hiss. I slipped a couple of inches, the wire cutting into my palms.

A thunderous noise erupted above me. I looked past Reid's anxious face at the distant roof. My eyes widened.

The entire structure was caving in.

I placed my feet against the wall and started to climb at the same time Reid pulled frantically on the other end of the line. He grabbed my shoulders and heaved me inside the tunnel.

A large section of concrete and the twisted remains of a metal fan crashed against the space where I had been a second ago. I rose on my elbows and stared at the falling debris.

Reid scowled down at me. 'What took you so long?'

'I was admiring the view,' I said drily in between coughs. Further explosions rocked through the earth around us.

'Yeah, well, now's not the time to sit and reminisce about it.' He yanked me to my feet.

We pulled the wounded men upright and headed into the mine.

After what felt like a lifetime of obscurity and a silence that was only broken by the blasts from the underground facility and our increasingly labored breathing, a dim light grew in the distance ahead of us.

'We're almost there!' I gasped to Friedrich.

Sweat drenched my face and clothes, turning the dirt

coating my skin into grimy rivulets. My muscles burned from the strain of carrying the injured immortal.

The Bastian Hunter did not respond. His eyes closed and he slipped into unconsciousness once more. I grunted and lifted him under the shoulders, my gaze focused on Reid's back as I took one heavy step after the other.

The elevator shaft to the upper mine appeared in the gloom. A group of figures stood bathed in the glow of torches next to the wire cage. They turned at our footsteps.

Anatole grinned. 'You must have the lives of a thousand cats.'

Relief flashed across Bruno's face. 'I'll let Victor know you're safe. He'll be—'

His words were drowned by a rising rumble. I stiffened and looked over my shoulder.

Shadows shifted behind us. Violent tremors shook the floor of the tunnel.

'Go!' I shouted at Reid, my heart thundering inside my chest.

We raced the final twenty feet to the elevator shaft just as the roof of the passage collapsed behind us. I gritted my teeth and pushed Friedrich forward a second before debris hit my back. I stumbled and fell.

Darkness engulfed me as I was buried beneath a pile of rock and dirt. I lay stunned for long seconds before blinking and choking on a mouthful of dirt. I tried to move.

The rubble above me barely shifted.

Light suddenly stabbed through the gloom. A pair of hands reached in and dragged me out of my earthy tomb. I gasped and rolled over, air entering my parched lungs in giant gulps.

'For a minute there, I really thought you were a goner,' said Reid.

He was sitting on the ground a couple of feet away, his

breathing heavy and fast. Blood oozed from a wound on his head and the fresh scrapes on his knuckles.

The immortals were slowly climbing to their knees behind him.

I smiled weakly through the cloud of dust settling around us and grabbed Reid's hand. Something clattered to the ground as he pulled me upright. I turned.

The canister from the lab had slipped from my backpack.

Icy fear filled my veins when I saw the dent in the side of the container. The cooling liquid inside was already leaking through and stained the dirt a dark brown.

Reid reached down.

'Don't!' I shouted, stilling his hand.

His eyes widened. 'Lucas?'

I was surprised at the steadiness of my own fingers when I crouched and lifted the canister. I twisted the cap open and carefully removed the shattered remains of the inner holder.

There was a small fracture in the wall of the syringe. The split widened under my frozen gaze.

My heart slammed dully against my ribs. I looked from Reid and the frozen immortals to the cracking, blood-filled tube and the attached hypodermic needle. It took but seconds to reach the inevitable conclusion. There was only one thing I could do.

∼

CHAPTER TWENTY-TWO

'HE DID WHAT?!'

Anna's outraged shriek was audible even through several layers of insulated glass.

I grimaced and gazed through the sealed port at the section of the interior ceiling panel visible above me.

Victor drifted into my field of view. He was talking on his cell.

'Uh-huh,' he said while he studied me. 'How does he look? Guilty. No, no, he seems fine otherwise.'

A litany of Czech issued from the other end of the line; I recognized several choice expletives.

Victor brought the cell back to his ear. 'I'll get in touch when we land,' he said drily. He ended the call, his eyes never leaving my face.

'That was an extremely foolish thing you did.' His voice was muffled by the protective glass. 'Brave, but foolish.'

I shifted in my steel prison and remained silent.

We were on a private plane bound for the States.

After I injected myself with the contaminated blood and burned the remains of the syringe and needle, I sat in the twilight at the bottom of the mine and waited for Reid and the Bastians to return. It had taken them a couple of hours to locate a suitable high containment transport pod and the necessary equipment they needed to move me. During that time, I prayed fervently that I would get to see the Godards again.

Night had fallen by the time we reached the military airfield outside the town of Plzeň, fifty-six miles west of Prague. A C-40 Clipper stood waiting for us on the tarmac.

I watched the plane fill up with Bastian Hunters and crates of hardware before the container I lay in was hoisted onto the main deck.

'Where's Reid?' I said presently.

Victor glanced toward the back of the aircraft's cabin. 'I don't think he's ready to talk to you yet.'

'That bad, huh?' I grimaced. 'How many has he smoked so far?'

A wry light appeared in Victor's eyes. 'Five. And counting.' He disappeared from view.

Reid's irate face materialized through the glass window some time later. 'You're a jackass.'

I sighed. 'It was the only option available,' I explained for the tenth time. 'We couldn't afford to lose the virus.'

'That still doesn't change the fact that you're a jackass,' he retorted, a muscle jumping in his cheek. 'How're you feeling?'

'The injection site is a bit sore.' I glanced at the red halo surrounding the needle mark at my left elbow.

Reid went pale. 'Any fever? Headache?'

I shook my head. Another wave of remorse hit me as I studied his anxious expression. He rubbed his face and exhaled loudly.

'You should get some rest,' I said.

Reid glowered at me, opened his mouth to say something, stopped, and stormed off. One disadvantage about being confined to an isolation pod was that I could hardly follow people when they stamped away in a huff.

Anatole appeared a couple of minutes later. *And neither can I control the people staring in at me*, I thought tiredly.

The immortal was grinning. 'That was quite a show you put on for us.'

'It wasn't meant to be,' I said coldly.

Anatole's grin widened. 'The lady didn't sound very happy.'

I considered this for a second. 'No, she didn't, did she?'

'Look on the bright side,' said the immortal with a carefree shrug. 'The plague might kill you first. I wouldn't want to be in your shoes when she gets her hands on you.'

Strangely enough, this thought occupied my mind for the remainder of the flight.

We touched down somewhere on the US eastern seaboard six hours later. It was still early evening. A star-dotted night sky filled my field of vision when the pod was unloaded from the plane. It disappeared as I was lifted into the back of a truck.

'How are you doing?' said Victor above me while my steel and glass prison was securely latched into place.

'I'm fine.'

He looked relieved at my words. 'We're not far from the compound.'

Twelve hours had passed since I had injected myself with the virus. I wondered how long it would be before I started to experience symptoms of the infection. An image of the three dead, bleeding bodies in the Crovir lab flashed through my mind. I grimaced.

The truck's engine roared into life. It rolled across the tarmac and gathered speed.

A dim feeling of claustrophobia soon surfaced at the edge of my consciousness; my view was limited to the ceiling and the sidewall of the vehicle. Although I was aware that the truck was full of Bastian Hunters and that Reid and Victor were among them, I could not quell the unsettling sensation.

An hour passed. The truck started to climb.

The vibrations from the suspensions suddenly increased; we had left the main road. The gradient grew steeper, the ground more uneven. The pod rocked on its metal bed, jarring me along with it.

The truck braked briefly before setting off again. The land leveled out after a mile. We finally rolled to a stop.

Footsteps scuttled past and shadows played across the glass port. The doors of the truck opened, bringing a flood of light. From the way the vehicle suddenly rose on its wheels, a number of people had exited it. Muffled voices rose close by. The floor shuddered as someone approached.

A face appeared through the window of the containment pod. It was Anna.

Relief washed over me at the sight of her. Her eyes were red-rimmed and puffy; the rest of her features were dominated by a scowl. She said something in Czech. It did not sound particularly flattering.

Reid and Victor materialized next to her. Muted words reached me through the glass.

'Has he complained of any symptoms?' said Anna.

'Apart from some pain where he injected himself, no,' Reid replied.

'I can hear you, you know,' I said mildly.

'I'm not ready to talk to you yet!' she snapped. Movement outside the truck drew her gaze. She turned and spoke to an unseen person before addressing Victor. 'The lab's ready. Let's get him there.'

The pod was transferred to a trolley. I had a brief vision of a dark, star-speckled heaven before a lintel appeared above me. A series of fluorescent light strips followed. A hundred feet or so later, I was wheeled into a service elevator. The doors closed behind me.

They opened again seconds later somewhere underground. I was aware of a cavernous space as I was maneuvered across the floor. Victor appeared at my side.

'Where are we?'

'Inside one of our bunkers,' said Victor. 'Anna and the other scientists set up their lab down here. We thought it would be the safest place on the compound.'

I drifted past a high containment glass wall and was wheeled through a decontamination chamber and into an inner sterile room. The pod was lifted from the gurney and secured onto a metal-framed bed.

I was patiently studying the gray paneling above my head when I detected movement to my left. The bed slowly tilted upright by ninety degrees. A wall appeared in front of me. Several figures were visible behind the window that occupied the breadth of it.

Someone punched a code in the access panel on the side of the pod. Almost half a day after I first entered it, the door of my steel and glass prison hissed open. I stepped out onto a tiled floor.

Anna was the only other person in the room. She wore a white decontamination suit. Her green eyes regarded me steadily from behind a visor. 'Hi.'

'Hi,' I murmured. I studied the window ahead.

Men and women in white coats milled about the room beyond the glass. Victor and Reid stood in their midst. Tomas Godard and Roman Dvorsky appeared behind them.

'How are you feeling?' said Anna.

I dragged my gaze from Godard's stricken face. 'I'm okay.'

Anna carefully inspected me from head to toe. 'You haven't experienced any fever or chills?' she said insistently.

'No.'

She reached out and lifted my left arm in her gloved hands. Her fingers slowly traced the small red mark at my elbow.

'Of all the—' She stopped, her shoulders shaking, and punched me in the chest.

I grunted in surprise.

Someone chuckled behind the glass. I recognized Reid's laughter.

Anna handed me a hospital gown.

'Put this on,' she instructed curtly. 'There's a bathroom through there where you can change.' She indicated a steel door in a corner of the sterile chamber. 'Place your clothes in the plastic carrier inside and give them to me.'

I was poked and prodded by Anna and the other scientists for the next hour. They took samples of my blood and swabs from my throat and the injection site on my arm before attaching me to a series of monitors.

I sat on the edge of the bed and scrutinized the array of equipment around me. 'Is this strictly necessary?'

Anna paused at the door; she was the last one to leave the room. 'Yes,' she snapped.

'Oh.' My stomach grumbled loudly in the silence that followed. I made a face. 'Could I at least have something to eat?'

Her expression softened. 'Sure.'

The meal was hot and filling. Anna returned and took another sample of blood from my arm.

'Any idea how long I'm going to be in here?' I asked patiently.

It was a while before she answered.

'I don't know.' Her eyes met mine steadily. 'So far, all your observations are stable.' She bit her lip. 'We should know within the next twenty-four hours if you develop any symptoms. The incubation period is quite short.'

I digested this information with a sinking feeling. 'Can you make a vaccine from the samples you've taken from me?'

Anna nodded, her face brightening. 'It might take some time, but it's feasible.' She glanced over her shoulder at the wall that separated us from the outer lab. 'I can't tell you how relieved Grandfather is that you're okay.' She stared at me. 'Were you aware that our grandmother died during the first plague?'

My gaze shifted from her to the room beyond. Another ripple of remorse fluttered through my conscience. 'No. I didn't know that.'

No wonder Godard had looked so shaken.

A sad smile flitted across Anna's face. 'We've only just found you. We can't lose you now.' She turned and left the room.

I closed my eyes and lay back on the bed, her words playing over in my mind.

It was another four hours before the fever started. By then, a pounding headache was already hammering at my temples. Chills soon racked my body and sweat soaked the bed sheets beneath me.

I started to drift in and out of consciousness, barely aware of the people entering and leaving the room. At one stage, I opened my eyes and saw Anna at my side.

'Hang in there,' she said shakily, glancing at the monitors above me. Her face was ashen behind the visor.

Next to her, someone was injecting a straw-colored liquid into my IV.

The tone of her words alarmed me more than anything happening to my own body. I blinked moisture out of my eyes and tried to focus on her face.

'It's all right,' I stammered, my teeth chattering uncontrollably. 'I'll be okay.' I was stunned at the weakness of my voice.

'No, it's not!' Anna's eyes glistened wetly.

It took all of my willpower to reach out and take her gloved hand into my own shaking one. 'I'm going to be fine.'

Her fingers curled around mine. A single tear spilled down her face. My eyelids fluttered closed and I sank into oblivion.

The fever broke thirty-six hours later. How I lasted until then, I was not sure myself; the details were more than a little hazy. Apart from a sore head and some general grogginess that hung around for most of the next day, I was back to my normal self.

It was another twenty-four hours before Anna returned to give me the news.

'Your body mounted a response in the form of an elevated white cell count. Otherwise, all the other parameters have stabilized.' For the first time in days, her eyes were bright with barely concealed excitement. 'I've got the results of your latest tests.'

'What is it?'

'It's over.' Anna smiled at my puzzled expression. 'The infection. It's gone.'

My eyes widened. I was unsure I had heard her correctly. 'Gone?'

Anna nodded.

'Completely?' I said insistently.

'Yes. There's no trace of active disease.'

I digested this incredible fact slowly. 'How is that possible?'

Anna hesitated. 'I—I don't know.'

I observed her troubled expression. 'Did you manage to isolate the virus?' I said finally.

'Yes. And it's definitely the one Burnstein was working on. You already have significant levels of protective antibodies in your blood.'

'That's good, isn't it?'

'It is.' Anna's tone was wary. 'It's also incredibly fast.'

The meaning behind her words sank in. Coldness spread through me.

'You think this has something to do with surviving the

seventeenth death?'

It was her turn to be quiet. 'Yes, I suspect it does,' she eventually murmured. Her eyes grew shuttered. 'You may be truly invincible after all.'

I stared at the floor, uncertain how I felt about that statement.

'Am I still contagious?' I said distractedly.

'No. The virus is no longer detectable in your blood stream or your swabs. This is the final all clear.'

I looked up. 'Does this mean I can get out of here?' I asked, unable to mask the hope in my voice.

Anna smiled. 'Yes.'

The first person to greet me was Reid. Godard and Victor followed closely on his heels.

'How do you feel?' said my partner.

'I'm okay.' More than anything, I was relieved to be out of the containment room.

Godard pulled me toward him and engulfed me in a tight hug. I stiffened for a moment, before relaxing in his grip.

'You're a very silly boy,' the old man said gruffly. 'Silly, but brave.'

'Yeah, I get that a lot,' I murmured. I ignored Reid's knowing grin and turned to Victor. 'Any news on Burnstein and the Crovirs?'

'Burnstein's holed up in DC, along with the rest of Vellacrus's scientists,' he replied. 'It appears they have another research facility there.'

An image of the tower we had followed the CEO of GeMBiT Corp to on Pennsylvania Avenue flashed in my mind. Our trip to Washington felt like a lifetime ago.

'And the vaccine?'

Victor's expression hardened. 'They've completed the trial. Reznak called a few hours ago. Vellacrus started the inoculation yesterday.'

Shock darted through me. I was stunned at the speed of events. Only three days had passed since we broke into the Crovirs' lab in Germany. 'That's not good.'

Victor sighed. 'No, it isn't.'

I looked around the lab, aware of the curious stares of the scientists and several Hunters. 'Where's your father?'

Victor exchanged a meaningful glance with Godard.

'In Europe,' he said in a low voice. 'The Councils and Assembly are proving more difficult to persuade than we originally anticipated. We suspect some of them are deliberately delaying the process.'

I studied him for a moment. 'What's the plan?'

'I'm glad you asked. Walk with me.'

Half an hour later, I stood back from the table that dominated the crowded operations room in the main lodge of the Bastian compound.

'Vellacrus will no doubt have a significant number of Crovir Hunters guarding that place.' I inspected the satellite and surveillance photos of the Pennsylvania Avenue sky rise pinned to the board on the wall. 'How many men have you got?'

'Enough to do the job,' said Grigoriye.

I watched the Council member steadily. 'I doubt that. You'll need to leave a considerable fraction of your army behind to guard the Godards. You won't have a large enough number to defeat the Crovirs.'

Costas frowned. 'You'll do well not to question your superiors, Soul.'

A strained silence followed the Bastian noble's words.

'You forget,' I said quietly. 'I'm not a Hunter.'

Costas half rose from his seat, his face red. 'I will not—'

'Enough!' Victor interrupted harshly. Costas settled in his chair with a disgruntled expression. 'Lucas is right. We'd be lucky to breach the front door with our current numbers.'

'I have a suggestion,' said Reid from where he leaned against the wall. He rolled a cigarette between his fingers. 'Christophe Lacroix.'

Mutters rose around the table. The Bastians glanced at each other in confusion.

'Who's this...Lacroix?' said Costas.

I stared at Reid. 'That's gonna require some leap of faith from the man.'

His lips curved in a wry smile. 'After what he witnessed in Vienna, he'll be begging us for a piece of the action.'

I smiled back. 'Solito?'

Reid shrugged. 'We owe him. Besides, the more the merrier.'

A strangled sound escaped Costas's lips. 'Will one of you tell us what the hell you're talking about?' he roared.

Reid and I explained our involvement with the FBI and the French detective. Costas and Grigoriye listened with mounting skepticism. Victor watched us silently.

'Do you seriously expect us to enlist the help of humans in the affairs of immortals?' Grigoriye eventually said with a frown. Reid's eyebrows rose. 'Present company excluded, of course,' the Bastian added grudgingly.

'Humans have as much at stake here as immortals, although they're yet to be aware of that fact.' I glanced at Victor. 'They could tip the balance in our favor.'

Costas sneered. 'Are you suggesting we reveal the affairs of our race to a bunch of—of mortals? You think we're suddenly going to get friendly with them, after thousands of years of keeping them out of our business?' He turned to Victor. 'This is preposterous!'

'After what went down at the Hauptbahnhof and in Vienna, I would be surprised if they didn't suspect something already.' I gazed unwaveringly at Victor. 'It's your decision. Reid and I trust these men.'

Victor held my eyes for several seconds. 'Call them,' he said finally.

It was almost midnight when we ended our negotiations with the FBI and Interpol. Lacroix was taking a chartered flight from Paris with some twenty agents from Europe, the Swiss and Austrians having been all too keen to offer their assistance. Solito's boss promised us another eighty men, including two SWAT teams from the local Metropolitan Police. Homeland Security and the CDC had been placed on high alert.

'You have friends in high places,' I told Victor while the room slowly cleared. I had listened while he spoke with various senior officials at the Pentagon and in the White House, and found myself strangely unsurprised by their discussions. 'We didn't really need to contact Lacroix and Solito, did we?'

A dark smile crossed the immortal noble's face.

'Let's just say the top brass like to have good grounds to offer us their assistance. The events in DC and Europe are more than enough reason to justify this operation under the counter terrorism act.' Victor paused. 'The few mortals who know of our existence are extremely wary of us, understandably so. After all, we've shaped the course of human history for almost two millennia.' He sighed. 'Neither side wishes to see a war between our races, us more so than the humans. That's why we have observer status at the UN and maintain close ties with the political leaders of the world.'

'I'm sorry to interrupt, but has anyone given any thought to the mortals who'll be working with us on the ground?' said Grigoriye. The Bastian Council member hovered in the doorway, a frown on his face. 'It won't be easy to hide the abilities of our kind from them. They're bound to talk.'

'Not if we spread the rumor that the Crovirs possess new, technologically advanced body shields and a fast-healing serum that confers an unnatural ability to survive otherwise mortal wounds,' said Reid. 'Your men will just have to be extra careful. Besides, the FBI will probably give us body vests.'

Costas snorted. 'Good God, I never thought I'd see the day when an immortal would have to wear human armor!' He stormed out of the room.

Victor looked at his watch. 'We have eight hours before we leave. I suggest we all get some rest.'

I had been given a guest room at the back of the lodge. I grabbed a quick bite, showered, and climbed into bed. The mattress was soft and more comfortable than the one I had been forced to lie on for the last three days. Still, although I felt physically drained, sleep proved elusive once more. I stared at the ceiling for what felt like hours before drifting off.

A sound woke me some time later. A soft breeze was blowing in through the open window. Light from a nearby security lamp flickered through the swaying curtains and cast moving shadows across the walls of the bedroom.

There was a creak from the doorway.

I lifted my head off the pillow and gazed at the figure standing there. Surprise washed over me. 'Anna?' I sat up, alarmed. 'What's wrong?'

She crossed the floor silently, bare feet sliding over the dark wood. Her eyes were unreadable in the gloom. She stopped at the side of the bed and pulled the covers back before crawling into the space next to me.

'Don't speak.' Her voice was a bare whisper in the night.

Her lips covered mine a heartbeat later, her hair a silky curtain falling around my face.

I froze for a moment, too shocked to move. Then, all thoughts of resistance were drowned by the hunger that had been raging inside me since the very moment I first set eyes on her. I raised my hands to her head and deepened the kiss with a low groan.

∾

CHAPTER TWENTY-THREE

She was gone the next morning. I blinked at the ceiling. Distant sounds came through the bedroom door as Victor's men prepared for the day's mission.

Memories from the night flooded my mind. The softness of her skin under my fingers. The velvety taste of her mouth beneath my lips. The strength in her warm, supple legs as they clung to my hips. The intoxicating heat of her body. Her quiet, breathless moans as she arched beneath me. Her nails clawing at my back. And throughout it all, the heady smell of oranges that infused the space around us, flooding me in her scent.

Someone rapped sharply on the door, startling me.

'You up?' said Reid from the other side.

'Uh-huh.' I sat up and swung my legs off the bed, trying to suppress the sensual images still flashing past my eyes.

'Get your butt moving. We leave in forty minutes.'

A column of SUVs and vans stood waiting in the driveway at the bottom of the porch when I walked out of the lodge moments later. I stopped as I got my first daylight look at the Bastian compound.

The complex was positioned near the summit of a peak,

surrounded by a thick oak and pine forest. The land fell away in
carefully carved terraces that accommodated a collection of
buildings and underground entrances, all of them artfully
camouflaged to blend with the green and brown background.
Guards with automatic firearms patrolled the grounds.

I caught a view of blue skies and a distant range through a
gap between the trees, the peaks crowned in wisps of thin
clouds and fading morning mist.

'We're in Virginia, in the Blue Ridge Mountains,' said Reid
at my side. He lit up, inhaled deeply, and blew out a smoke ring.
'Impressive, isn't it? Victor tells me they've had this place for
over sixty years.' He smiled faintly. 'It's bigger than the FBI's
training grounds in Quantico.'

The Bastian convoy was getting ready to move. I watched
Costas and Victor climb inside one of the trucks. Victor spoke
to Grigoriye briefly through the open window; the Council
member was staying behind to guard the complex, along with
some eighty Bastian Hunters.

Footsteps sounded behind me. Godard appeared at my side.
'Be careful,' he said and handed over the daisho.

My fingers closed over the familiar handles. 'Thank you. I
will.' I slipped the blades into my belt. 'Say goodbye to Anna
for me.'

The drive to DC took a little over two hours. The tension
inside the vehicle rose perceptibly as we drew closer to the city.
Shortly before eleven, we rolled into a deserted parking lot
close to the Washington Circle Park.

Lacroix and the FBI were already there.

Solito's boss was a burly Texan called McCabe. A frown
darkened the man's features as he shook hands with Victor.

'I have direct orders from the Oval Office to follow your
instructions to the letter.' He chomped down on a cigar stub. 'I
don't know who you are, Mister, but if you put the lives of my

men in jeopardy, there'll be hell to pay, whatever the Attorney General says.'

'Same here,' said Lacroix coolly.

A polite smile crossed Victor's lips. 'Rest assured that our organization will do the utmost to prevent any such misfortunes.'

Lacroix's eyes shifted to me briefly. 'You wouldn't want to tell us the name of this organization of yours, by any chance? It appears to have a great deal of influence with Heads of States on both sides of the Atlantic.'

Costas grunted. 'That's none of your concern. You know far too much as it is.'

Discontented mutters arose among the agents behind McCabe and Lacroix.

'Not exactly a people person, is he?' murmured Reid.

My lips twitched despite the anxiety humming through my veins.

Victor sighed. 'There are sound and valid reasons why we must keep our identities a secret from you,' he said, looking the FBI chief and the Frenchman firmly in the eye. 'I'm afraid that to say more would indeed, as Costas states, reveal too much.' He turned to the surveillance photos of the Pennsylvania Avenue sky rise spread across the hood of a vehicle. 'In any case, your men won't be going higher than the tenth floor.'

'And why is that?' Lacroix challenged.

Victor glanced at him. 'Because we have more experience dealing with these people than you do,' he said curtly.

The Frenchman looked unconvinced.

A Bastian tech passed a handful of pictures to Victor.

The immortal spread them over the FBI surveillance photos. 'These are the latest thermal satellites images we have of the tower.'

'Wow.' Solito's eyebrows rose. 'Those look a helluva lot better than ours.'

The tech who brought the images grinned. 'Oh, we're using the latest in laser satellite technology.' His expression sobered at Costas's stare. He cleared his throat and retreated silently in the background.

'How did you guys get your hands on that kind of money?' said Solito.

Silence fell across the parking lot. The FBI analyst observed the crowd of unsmiling faces. 'Forget I asked,' he muttered.

'Most of their men will be in the top four floors of the building,' said Victor, pointing at the pictures. 'That leaves about forty guards watching the access to the underground garage and the ground floor, as well as the dozen others spread out above.'

He looked at McCabe and Lacroix. 'We need you to handle the guys on the ground while we get to the lifts. Tell your men to aim for the head. Their body armor will protect their other vital points.' He ignored Lacroix's frown. 'Are your SWAT teams in place?'

'They are,' said McCabe with a nod.

'Good. Let's move.'

The day before, we had debated long and hard between a slow and subtle infiltration of the Crovirs' defenses versus a fast and hard approach. We all voted for the latter tactic, convinced that shock and the element of surprise would work in our favor.

As the cavalcade drew closer to the sky rise, Reid and I fastened FBI vests over our clothes and checked our earpieces.

'You ready?' said my partner while he loaded a magazine into the chamber of his Glock.

'Not really.' My fingers slid over the reassuring weights of the blades at my waist. I looked at Lacroix. 'Good luck.'

The Frenchman nodded curtly.

Our convoy squealed to a halt in front of the Pennsylvania Avenue tower. We opened the rear doors of the van and spilled out onto the asphalt. McCabe's men surrounded the building and started setting up a security perimeter.

We ran onto the sidewalk and fired at the facade of the main foyer. The glass wall shattered in a rain of glittering fragments. The shards crunched loudly beneath our feet as we stepped through the gaping frames.

Figures appeared around the lobby. I holstered the Glock and unsheathed the swords. Two Crovir Hunters fell beneath my blades a moment later.

'Head for the lifts!' Victor shouted to my right.

I nodded and raced along the concourse toward the bank of elevators.

Lacroix's agents and McCabe's men entered the building just as dozens more Crovirs charged across the floor. Gunfire erupted around the lobby, the echoes deafening in the vaulted space.

The first elevator pinged a moment before I reached it. My stomach lurched. I skidded on the polished floor.

'Get down!' Reid yelled behind me.

I dropped to the ground a heartbeat before the metal panels opened to reveal five Crovir Hunters.

Reid and Lacroix emptied their guns into the men before they had a chance to raise their own weapons. I jumped to my feet and lifted the daisho, blood thundering in my ears.

The blades slashed all too readily through the flesh of the immortals.

We heaved their bodies out of the lift and stepped inside. Bullets from the foyer struck the doors as they closed after us. The elevator started to rise.

'If one of you is intending to say something patronizing like "You shouldn't be here", save your breath!' Lacroix snapped while he reloaded his gun.

Reid and I exchanged glances.

'Wasn't gonna say a word,' muttered my partner as he shoved a fresh magazine into the Glock.

The lift opened on the fourth and seventh floors. We left a

trail of bullets in the corridors beyond and the bodies of the Crovir Hunters who stood in the way. Distant explosions reached our ears as we neared the tenth floor.

The battered elevator doors slid aside with a tortuous creak. The lift opposite opened a second later. Victor, Costas, Bruno, and Anatole crouched inside, their guns raised.

We stared at one other and listened to the deadly silence in the corridor outside.

Anatole poked his head around the corner of the lift door. A bullet whined through the air and struck the metal frame, raising sparks inches from his face.

'Whoa!' said the red-haired immortal while Bruno dragged him backward. A grin lit up his face. 'Looks like they're home after all, boss.'

A frown clouded Costas's face. 'What's he doing here?' he hissed in a loud whisper, gesturing pointedly at Lacroix.

I shrugged noncommittally. Lacroix muttered something rude under his breath.

Victor studied the interior of the elevator. 'Looks like these lifts don't go any higher without a security pass.'

I inspected the control panel next to me. 'You're right.'

'It shouldn't come as a surprise, really. I guess we're going to have to make our way on foot from here on.' A smile played across the immortal noble's face.

Even though my heart was racing inside my chest, I found my lips curving upward. 'Sure looks like it.'

'On the count of three?' said Victor.

I nodded and took a deep breath.

Bullets riddled the air and ricocheted off the walls when we charged out of the lifts. Ceiling lights shattered, showering us with slivers of glass and metal. Plaster dust clouded the air.

Reid grunted when a slug struck his vest. I gripped my blades and moved.

We paused seconds later in the clearing smoke and observed

the still bodies around us. Further explosions rocked the foundations of the building. Doors slammed in the distance. Footsteps pounded the floor and drew closer.

'Go!' shouted Victor. He indicated the fire escape at the end of a passage beyond a junction. 'We'll hold them back!'

I turned and raced toward the fire door. It opened just before I reached it. I stabbed the man crossing the threshold. My eyes widened as he fell to the floor.

The Hunters behind him raised their guns.

Shots sang past my ears from behind, the draft from the bullets ruffling my hair. The Crovirs jerked violently and dropped to the ground. Reid, Lacroix, and Costas materialized at my side.

'What're you waiting for, an invitation?' snarled the Bastian noble.

I leapt over the fallen immortals and started up the stairs beyond. Halfway to the next landing, the sound of gunfire rose from the lower levels of the tower. I glanced over the banister and caught a glimpse of the first wave of Bastian Hunters as they made their way up through an army of Crovirs four floors below.

Something hot stung my face. I looked up and saw the Hunter above me take aim once more.

Reid shot the immortal in the head.

'You're bleeding again,' he said, inserting another magazine in the Glock.

I wiped away the sliver of blood where the bullet had grazed my cheek.

'It's a distressing habit of yours,' he continued as we raced up the steps. Costas and Lacroix had already plowed through several Hunters on the landing above. 'Anna will undoubtedly kill me if I let you hemorrhage all over the place, so please try not to do so.'

I smiled. 'Right.'

We reached the eleventh floor only to find it abandoned. Empty storage rooms lined the massive space. It was evident from their state that they had recently been cleared.

I lifted a scrap of paper from the ground and studied it with a frown; it was a label for a box of medical equipment.

'We can't be far from the research facility.'

The labs were on the next story.

Several figures dressed in white decontamination suits worked swiftly inside the network of interconnected glass chambers that occupied the floor. They were clearing the work-tops and packing steel canisters inside transport boxes.

Some twenty Crovir Hunters stood between us and the closest room.

I clenched my teeth, knuckles whitening on the handles of the daisho.

There was a noise from behind. I looked over my shoulder and watched a dozen Bastian Hunters step through the fire door. Blood oozed from their wounds. Their breaths left their lips in harsh pants.

They straightened when they saw the Crovirs. Scowls dawned on sweaty, red-streaked faces. Fingers tightened on the handgrips of guns.

'Oh boy,' muttered Reid, mirroring my own thoughts.

Flashes of light and smoke filled the air as gunfire exploded around us.

I ducked and weaved through the wave of surging Crovirs. Crimson rivulets soon dripped from the edges of my blades and splashed across the floor and walls as the daisho slashed repeatedly through skin and flesh.

Behind me, Reid and Lacroix emptied their guns and reloaded.

Halfway across the complex of labs, I saw movement out the corner of my eyes.

Burnstein was racing toward an exit to the east. Two scientist in sterile suits followed behind him, each with a pair of silver cases in hand.

I wheeled around and headed after them.

I was ten feet from the doorway through which the three men had disappeared when half a dozen figures materialized before me. In addition to guns, these Crovir Hunters wielded swords.

'You're not getting through us, half-breed!' one of them barked.

I scowled and widened my stance.

The daisho sang at the tips of my fingers, the steel edges glinting coldly under the light of the fluorescent strips. A sword grazed my back. Another sliced across my cheek.

I dropped to the floor a heartbeat before metal slashed across the space where my head had been. I spun and kicked out, taking out the three remaining Hunters. The wakizashi flashed through their ribcages in rapid succession.

I stepped over the dead men and entered the stairwell. A second group of Hunters appeared on the steps above me. Frustration gnawed at my insides; with every second that passed, Burnstein got farther away, along with the virus and the vaccine.

I sheathed the wakizashi and held the katana in a double-handed grip.

Bullets scored the ground and pinged off the metal banister as I bolted up the stairs. A couple of slugs struck my vest. I grunted and forged ahead, the sword carving a lethal path through the smoke-filled space.

I reached the next landing and opened the fire door. My heart thudded in my chest. I threw myself to the side.

A grenade shot from the rocket launcher shouldered by the Crovir Hunter fifteen feet ahead skimmed the air inches from my flank and detonated against the opposite wall. I hugged the floor and covered my head as debris riddled the stairwell. Something slashed across the back of my left hand. Bricks and chunks of concrete thudded around me.

Gray billows choked the air in the aftermath of the explosion. Ears still ringing from the blast, I used the cover of the dense cloud and crawled through the doorway.

Gunshots erupted ahead of me. The shadows shifted.

I sheathed the swords and raised the Smith & Wesson in a steady grip, my finger on the trigger.

'It's me,' said Victor.

Anatole and Bruno appeared next to him in the clearing haze. The body of the Crovir Hunter with the grenade launcher lay on the ground behind them.

'We found a pass for the lift,' said Anatole. He observed the wreckage of the stairwell with a grin. 'You've been busy.'

'Have you seen Burnstein?' I said urgently, climbing to my feet.

'No,' said Victor. 'We just got here.'

We found a second exit on the opposite side of the building.

'They've cleared the labs,' I said when we stopped in front of the fire escape. 'Whatever they've got, they're carrying inside some silver cases.'

Victor looked over his shoulder in the direction of the damaged stairs. 'Our friends will have to find another way up.'

I nodded and opened the door.

The staircase on the other side was ominously silent, the gunfire from the floors below barely audible through the concrete walls. We started cautiously up the steps to the final landing.

A single door stood at the top. It was made of reinforced steel. No noise escaped from beyond it.

As Anatole reached for the handle, a familiar whine suddenly reached my ears.

'Wait!' I hissed.

Understanding dawned on Victor's face. 'Get down!' he yelled.

We threw ourselves to the ground just as the door buckled and splintered under the force of a rocket-propelled grenade. Lethal shards filled the air when it separated from its hinges and smashed into the stairwell. Dust and smoke darkened the space around us.

We darted through the distorted frame onto the thirteenth floor. Muzzles flashed ahead of us. I swapped my gun for the daisho.

Elevators pinged on our right as we worked our way through the clearing cloud, dodging shots and blades from a crowd of Crovir Hunters. The lift doors opened to reveal a horde of Bastian Hunters. Reid and Lacroix were among them.

A storm of bullets erupted across the room. The pungent smell of gunpowder filled the air.

The Crovirs came in waves, washing over us in seemingly countless numbers. I raced through them, my heartbeat steady and the bloodied blades whirling in my hands. My eyes never left the doors on the other side of the floor.

I reached them just ahead of Victor and Costas.

'Stand back!' Victor shouted.

The two nobles raised their guns and shot through the lock. We pushed the doors open.

In the room beyond, Felix Thorne turned and smiled.

The south section of the tower was taken up by an executive suite with a panoramic floor-to-ceiling glass wall offering a distant view of the Washington Monument and the Potomac River. French doors stood open in the middle of the transparent facade.

I froze.

Beyond the suite was a rooftop with a helipad. Burnstein and his scientists were already halfway across it. A pair of twin-engine Bell 222 helicopters descended from the skies and landed in front of the men.

Thorne held my shocked gaze for a heartbeat before walking out onto the terrace to join them.

Blood thrummed furiously in my veins.

'We mustn't let them leave!' I shouted above the noise of the rotors.

'Right!' Victor retorted grimly as he studied the Crovir Hunters who stood in our way.

It took far too many precious seconds to carve a path through the wall of immortals. By the time I ran out onto the rooftop, Thorne's helicopter was lifting off. I sheathed the swords and drew the guns at my hips.

Bullets scored the concrete at my feet. I hit the ground, rolled to one knee, and squeezed the triggers rapidly. Thorne disappeared from view, his helicopter rising toward the sky.

I looked to my left. Burnstein had just finished loading a pair of silver cases onto the floor of the second Bell helicopter. I rose and raced toward the aircraft.

The Crovir's eyes widened when he saw me. He scrambled inside the cabin and reached for the door. A cry of pain left his lips when a bullet whistled past me and struck his hand.

'Lucas!' Reid yelled behind me.

'*Go!*' Burnstein screamed in the direction of the cockpit. The Bell 222 rose from the ground.

I holstered the guns and jumped.

My fingers grazed the starboard skid and closed around it. The helicopter pitched slightly. It corrected itself before continuing its ascent. I looked down.

My mouth went dry.

The sky rise dropped rapidly away beneath me. Reid and Victor became distant frozen figures on the rooftop.

I gripped the metal runner with both hands and hauled myself up onto my elbows with a grunt of effort. A faint noise reached my ears above the clatter of the rotors and the rush of blood in my head.

It was the sound of someone cocking a gun.

I glanced up, swore, and swung my body to the left, losing my right hold on the skid.

A volley of bullets missed me by a hairbreadth when Burnstein emptied the magazine of his pistol in my direction. I reached for the Smith and Wesson and fired inside the cabin, the tendons in my left arm screaming with tension while I hung from the belly of the aircraft.

A scream of rage erupted from within the helicopter. I smiled savagely, holstered the gun, renewed my grip on the landing gear, and pulled myself up.

The din of an approaching helicopter suddenly rose on my left. I caught a glimpse of a large black and silver UH-1 chopper with the words "FBI" blazoned in white on its side. I was inside the cabin of the Bell 222 a second later.

I almost fell out again when a bullet slammed into my vest. I gripped the edges of the door, ignored the cowering scientists to my right, and staggered across the floor toward Burnstein.

Both his hands bore gunshot wounds. Despite this, the Crovir noble was frantically trying to reload the weapon on his lap. He raised it just as I reached him and froze.

The tip of the wakizashi dented the skin at the base of his throat.

'Don't,' I said coldly.

A fierce grimace crossed Burnstein's face. His finger flexed on the trigger. A gasp left his lips.

Below the wakizashi, the katana had pierced his heart.

As his eyes turned dull, the blast from a rocket-propelled grenade caused the aircraft to swerve violently.

I hit the wall of the cabin with my back and cursed. The FBI helicopter had fired at the Bell 222 in an attempt to force its pilot to land.

I sheathed the swords and was reaching under the dead man's seat for the silver cases when dazzling brightness bloomed next to the aircraft.

The UH-1 exploded in a giant ball of fire.

The shockwaves from the detonation wrapped around the Bell 222 and sent it spinning on its axis. Alarms sounded from the direction of the cockpit. The pilot swore.

I found myself on the floor, the handle of a case in each hand. I crawled to my knees and stared through the open starboard door in dull incomprehension.

The Roosevelt Island was a splash of autumnal reds and yellows against the dark waters of the Potomac River below. A hundred feet away, Felix Thorne sneered at me from the second Bell helicopter. The Crovir Hunter crouched on one knee next to him finished reloading the rocket launcher on his shoulder.

Burnstein's pilot must have seen the other aircraft, for the helicopter suddenly dove sharply. My stomach lurched. The river grew alarmingly close, then disappeared; we flew low over a busy highway.

Buildings materialized ahead of us. The pilot pulled up abruptly.

Seconds later, a missile left Thorne's helicopter and exploded about a dozen yards from the tail rotor of the Bell.

The aircraft rotated violently. The pilot cursed again. The shadow of a sky rise loomed on our left.

The rotors struck the wall of the glass tower. Silver shards rained inside the cabin as the helicopter scraped alongside the building.

I glanced over my shoulder in time to see another grenade leave the rocket launcher in the second Bell helicopter. Heart hammering wildly against my ribs, I grabbed the silver cases and leapt through the port door.

~

CHAPTER TWENTY-FOUR

'Wow,' said Anatole. 'You are one crazy bastard.'

I winced while a paramedic cleaned the cuts on my face.

I was sitting on a curb some thousand feet from the waters of the Potomac. Half an hour had passed since the Bell helicopter had crashed into a tower next to the Lee Highway. The area of Rosslyn next to the Curtis Memorial Parkway had been closed to traffic. Flashing lights from the county's fire trucks reflected in the glass facades of the buildings across the road.

A few yards away, McCabe was attempting to pacify the Arlington District Two police commander. By the sound of their raised voices, things were not going well.

'Here,' said someone above me.

I looked up and took the Styrofoam container proffered by Reid. A familiar scent reached my nostrils above the rich aroma of coffee wafting from it. I raised my eyebrows. 'Bourbon?'

'Uh-huh.'

'Where'd you get it from?'

'A bar up the road,' Reid replied. He took a sip from his own cup.

The paramedic tending to my wounds glared at us.

'I'm about to give you a strong painkiller,' he told me in an admonishing tone. 'I don't think you should be drinking alcohol!'

I sighed. 'I'm fine, really.'

The second paramedic grunted. 'You just jumped from an exploding aircraft into the twelfth floor of a skyscraper. You should be dead.'

'Yeah, I get that a lot.' I ignored their scowls and lifted the container to my lips.

I paused when I saw the man coming up behind them.

'Can you walk?' said Victor.

I nodded and shrugged off the blanket around my shoulders before rising to my feet.

'Thanks,' I said to the gaping paramedics.

'Hey, we need to take you to the hospital to get checked out!' one of them stuttered. 'I'm sure you broke a couple of ribs. And you probably have a hairline fracture under that gash in your head!'

'They'll heal.' I turned to follow in Victor's footsteps.

We headed past the smoking wreckage of the Bell 222 and walked to a black van parked further down the road.

Costas was already inside; the Bastian noble was inspecting the contents of the silver cases at his feet.

'It's the vaccine,' he said gruffly when we climbed into the back of the vehicle.

My heart sank at his words. 'The cases that went with Thorne must have held the virus.'

Victor pressed a hand on my shoulder. 'You did a good job. We'll be able to help millions of people with this.'

My hands fisted at my side. 'Not if they release the virus in the coming days. Anna said it might take a couple of weeks for humans and immortals to develop protective levels of antibodies against it,' I explained with mounting frustration. 'Considering what they've been capable of to date, it wouldn't surprise me if they decided to unleash the plague earlier than planned. Besides, Burnstein wasn't stupid. The Crovirs are bound to have samples of the vaccine elsewhere.'

A somber silence ensued.

'We have to move fast,' said Victor, his tone troubled.

Costas frowned at him. 'You should contact Roman.'

The blare of a phone interrupted us. Victor looked at the number on his cell. His eyes narrowed.

'Dvorsky here,' he said curtly into the mouthpiece.

A cold foreboding filled my veins when I saw his expression change.

He disconnected a few seconds later and stared at me blindly, his face pale. 'The Crovirs have taken the Blue Ridge compound.'

Icy fear drenched my body in sweat.

It was another half hour before we were able to leave Arlington. In the end, it took a private phone call from the Vice-President himself to stop the county commander from arresting us.

'McCabe's not too pleased about you taking the bodies away,' said Lacroix. He watched me climb in a transporter van after Reid. 'I have to admit, neither am I.'

'It's for the best,' I said distractedly.

The Frenchman observed me for a silent beat. 'This isn't the end of the matter, is it?'

I hesitated. 'No, it isn't. But I'm afraid we can't involve you further than this.' I masked my mounting agitation and looked at him steadily. 'We got Burnstein at least. He was the main player behind the incidents in Europe.'

Lacroix frowned. 'Yes, but he wasn't the leader, was he?'

I shook my head.

He studied me for a while longer before releasing a sigh. 'Well, good luck.'

I nodded briskly. 'Will you be talking to your uncle sometime soon?'

Lacroix smiled faintly. 'Yes. I'll be sure to tell him the man he trusted as a friend for so many years is not a criminal after all.'

With the convoy doing over a hundred miles an hour, the return to Blue Ridge took less time than our outward journey. The Bastian Hunters inside the van remained silent for the entire trip, their expressions bleak under the dirt and blood still caking their faces.

We spotted the first columns of smoke when we were still two miles out from the compound.

'Shit,' said Anatole, staring through the windscreen.

The metal gates guarding the entrance were hanging off their hinges when we pulled up to them. By the looks of the distorted steel plates, rocket grenades had been used to force entry into the complex. We drove through and carried on up the hill.

The first bodies appeared a moment later. We passed three burning SUVs, their deformed carcasses testimony to the fierceness of the battle that had raged in our absence. Fires blazed in most of the outbuildings, the flames licking dangerously close to the surrounding trees.

It was a scene of utter devastation.

We found the largest group of Bastian Hunters at the top of the rise.

Bombs had churned up clods of earth and dug craters into the ground around the main lodge. The walls of the building were riddled with bullet holes. Flames engulfed the upper levels while black smoke billowed from broken windows and the rooftop. Glass cracked and shattered inside.

It was apparent from the destruction that this was where the Bastians had stood their ground as the last line of defense against the enemy.

We exited the vehicles with our guns in hand, even though it was evident the Crovirs had long departed the premises.

A muscle jumped in Victor's jawline as he stared at the burning building. 'Damn it!'

'You said it, boss,' muttered Anatole.

There was a groan from the porch. One of the fallen Bastians opened his eyes. He blinked slowly at the smoke-filled sky.

Victor ran up the steps and crouched by his side. 'What happened?' he asked harshly.

The Hunter licked his lips. 'They came from nowhere,' he whispered. 'There were so many—' He broke off, rasping coughs racking his frame. A trickle of blood escaped his mouth.

I gripped the Smith and Wesson so tightly that my fingers blanched. 'The Godards?'

The wounded man looked at me in a daze. 'The Crovirs took them.' His gaze shifted to Victor. 'It was Grigoriye. He let them in.' His words were barely audible above the muted explosions from inside the building. 'The man leading the Crovirs was called...Olsson.'

I froze at his words. Victor's eyes widened. Stunned silence fell across the porch.

'Grigoriye betrayed us?' Costas's eyes were expressionless.

'Yes,' the Hunter replied hoarsely.

'Are you sure?' said Victor insistently.

The man coughed again and nodded. Cries echoed across the grounds as more Bastian Hunters returned to consciousness.

Victor rose and surveyed the ruins of the compound.

'Tend to the wounded,' he ordered quietly. 'And put out those fires.'

It was another half hour before we managed to piece together the events of that morning. At approximately the same time we started our assault on the Pennsylvania Avenue tower in DC, vast troops of Crovir Hunters led by Olsson had descended upon the Blue Ridge compound in Virginia. From the Bastian Hunters' accounts, it appeared Grigoriye had disabled the surveillance and communications systems minutes before the Crovirs arrived. The enemy's targeted movements across the grounds suggested they had had access to detailed maps of the complex.

The Bastian Hunters had been caught completely off guard.

'We're online,' said a Bastian tech. His fingers clattered over the keyboard of the onboard computer in the back of one of the vans. 'They crashed the system, but we've managed to regain access to sixty percent of the network.'

'Good,' said Victor. 'Contact the Council.'

The monitor flickered a moment later. A room appeared on the screen.

Coarse, exposed bricks lined the curved walls of the chamber. The stones were a faded yellow and adorned with swords and shields bearing coats of arms. A sculptured oak table stood in the middle of a flagstone floor. Some twenty figures were seated around it.

By the frowns on their faces, they were not pleased with the interruption. I recognized Victor's father and several Council members I'd met in Prague.

'How did things go in Washington?' said Roman Dvorsky.

'We were partly successful,' Victor replied. 'We have the vaccine, but Thorne got away with the virus. Burnstein is dead.'

Roman was silent for a beat. 'Did you suffer many casualties?'

'Nothing that won't heal,' Victor retorted. 'There's something urgent you need to know, hence my call. The Crovirs attacked the Blue Ridge compound in our absence.' He glanced at Costas, who stood stiffly next to him. 'They had help.'

Shocked murmurs rose from the Bastians around the table.

'It was Grigoriye,' Victor continued. 'They took Anna and

Tomas Godard. They also destroyed our lab and stole the samples of blood she had been working on to find an alternative cure for the Red Death.'

'You mean Soul's blood?' said Roman, his face ashen.

Victor nodded.

'But you have their vaccine, don't you? Then surely it doesn't matter,' said the Council member seated to Roman's right.

'I'm afraid it does matter a great deal. The Crovirs have already started their inoculation program,' Victor explained. 'Even if we were to give the vaccine to every immortal and human in the world today, if they choose to release the virus in the next week, millions will still die.' He stood back from the screen. 'And you're forgetting the most important thing. They now have Anna Godard in their hands. If we don't stop them soon, Vellacrus's plan will become a reality in a matter of weeks.'

Unease filtered through my consciousness at the troubled look in Roman Dvorsky's eyes.

'About that,' said the Bastian leader, his voice tinged with evident distaste. 'There are some among us who believe we should attempt to negotiate a pact with the Crovirs.'

Stony silence descended inside the van.

'What?' Victor said stiffly. Costas's face tightened in a stormy expression beside him.

'I know,' Roman murmured apologetically. 'I'm only expressing the views of a few members of the First and Second Councils.' His tone hardened. 'We still have to vote on it, of course.'

Costas leaned toward the monitor.

'What is this going to achieve?' he snarled. 'Vellacrus will never agree to a treaty between our races. That woman wants to exterminate us once and for all!' His eyes narrowed. 'Are some of you so willing to forgive and forget the atrocities she has committed against our kind?' he hissed. 'Are you so eager to bow to her for a chance to taste true immortality that you would ignore the fact that she tried to kill our next leader only days ago?' His voice rose to a roar. 'And you dare call yourselves Bastians?!'

Victor placed a hand on the immortal's shaking shoulder. 'It's all right, Costas.'

'It would be wise to listen to Victor and Costas,' said the Council member next to Roman. 'I will not have you doubt our allegiance to our race so easily, Costas, although I understand why you would think that way.' His narrowed eyes darted to several faces around the table. 'I for one will definitely be voting against the idea of a pact and for swift and aggressive retaliation.'

Victor watched the figures on the screen. 'When will we have your decision?'

'Tomorrow at the earliest,' said Roman. 'The Council members would like to consult with the nobles under their command.'

I stepped up to the terminal.

'That's too long.' I did not bother to hide the resentment in my voice. Further mutters arose from the Bastians on the screen and frowns clouded several faces when recognition dawned. 'With or without your help, I'm going after them.'

'We'll have an answer for you soon enough,' snapped a Council member. 'And do you really think you can take the entire Crovir army on your own, half-breed?'

'He won't be alone,' Costas retorted. He glanced at me. 'And I guarantee you that all the Bastians here today will follow him without a second thought.'

'We'll be mobilizing as soon as we know where they've taken the Godards,' said Victor.

Roman nodded gravely. 'I trust your judgment. Do what you think is best.'

The screen went blank.

Anatole let out a low whistle. 'Wow, you sure told them.' He gazed at Costas in wide-eyed admiration.

The Bastian noble glared at him. 'This doesn't mean we're friends,' he said gruffly in my direction before storming out of the vehicle.

'Sure,' I murmured, studying the disappearing figure.

Victor grimaced and patted me on the shoulder. 'Don't take it personally. It took me two hundred years to get him to exchange Christmas greetings.' He turned to the Bastian tech manning the onboard computer. 'We need to call in some favors. Is the system fully functional yet?'

The tech nodded. 'Yes, as of a minute ago.'

'Good,' said Victor. 'I want you to contact this number on a secure line. Put it on speaker phone once you get through.'

Static echoed around the interior of the van when Dimitri Reznak answered the call a couple of minutes later.

His voice came through brokenly. 'What happened in Washington?'

'We got our hands on the vaccine. Unfortunately, Thorne got away with the virus.' Victor frowned. 'Where are you?'

'Egypt,' said Reznak, his voice fading and crackling.

Victor's eyebrows rose. 'On Crovir business?'

'Not quite. Just indulging in one of my pet projects.'

'Does it have anything to do with matters at hand?' asked Victor.

'I'm not sure,' came the enigmatic answer.

'The Crovir Hunters stormed our compound in Virginia. They took Anna and Tomas Godard. Do you know where they are?'

Silence rose from the speakers.

'Dimitri? Are you there?' Victor asked sharply after a moment.

'Yes,' came the quiet reply. The Crovir noble sounded perturbed. 'That's the first I've heard of it.'

Victor hesitated. 'Do you think she suspects you?'

'No. Vellacrus is renowned for keeping her cards close to her chest. This is likely to have been a last-minute strategy. She doesn't need the approval of the First Council for urgent tactical decisions.' Static erupted across the line again. '—find out what I can—get back to you—'

The transmission ended abruptly. Victor stared at the speakers.

'Are our satellites back online?' he said after a while.

'Yes,' said the Bastian tech.

'Good. I want you to start tracking all known Crovir facilities around the globe. There's bound to be a lot of activity on the ground if they're detaining the Godards in one of them.'

Dusk was falling across the mountains when I entered the building that housed the lab. Foam from fire extinguishers coated the floor and walls, turning the ash and soot into muddy slush. I made my way to the service elevator and went down to the bunker.

Glittering fragments crunched under my feet as I crossed the floor to the outer room.

Bullets had damaged the equipment Anna and the scientists had been using. Documents lay scattered across the worktops, most shredded beyond recognition by volleys of rounds and debris.

I stopped in front of a workstation and trailed my fingers across the back of Anna's chair.

'We'll find them,' said Reid behind me.

I kept my back to him, afraid to speak. My hands clasped the edge of the seat tightly while I stared into the isolation chamber where I had lived as a virtual prisoner for three days.

The familiar scent of Pall Mall clouded the air. A smoke ring drifted past my ear. 'She's quite a lady, isn't she?'

'Yes, she is,' I murmured. I turned to Reid. 'Anna and I,' I started hesitantly, 'we—'

He raised a hand. 'Stop right there. I know what you're gonna say. A blind man would have guessed what was going on between the two of you.'

I hesitated. 'And it doesn't disgust you?'

Reid shrugged. 'You've been around for hundreds of years. And it's not as if you grew up in the same crib. Besides, I think the normal rules of morality have to be bent slightly for immortals, a bit like for royalty.'

A wave of gratitude washed over me. 'Thank you.'

A companionable silence fell between us.

'Never thought I'd hear the bulldog defend you,' Reid said after a while.

A smile crossed my lips despite my inner turmoil. 'Neither did I.'

Footsteps sounded behind us. We turned and watched the figure striding across the floor of the bunker.

'Victor wants you,' said Bruno.

∼

CHAPTER TWENTY-FIVE

'Reznak called.'

We were on the ground floor of the lodge. The Bastians had recovered some of the equipment from the operations room and were busy setting up camp in the kitchen.

I ignored the bustle around us and studied Victor intently. 'And?'

'The Godards are in Europe.'

I took a step forward. 'Where?'

There was a flicker on one of the smoke-stained walls. An infrared, night-vision satellite image appeared on a projection screen. A Bastian tech brought the shot into sharp focus.

We inspected the grainy picture silently.

'They're on an island in the Mediterranean Sea, somewhere between Sardinia and Sicily,' said Victor. 'The only reason we know its location is because Dimitri gave us the exact geographic coordinates.' He glanced at me. 'It doesn't appear on any maps of the area. In fact, according to the US Geological Society and the European Federation of Geologists, it doesn't exist.'

'It sure looks real to me,' muttered Reid.

The island was a fortress. A jagged ring of rocks surrounded the rugged landmass, churning the dark waters around it into a roiling, foaming death trap. A few night birds danced and swirled above the silver spray. White-topped waves surged and crashed against the sheer, three-hundred-foot-high cliff walls soaring vertically above the sea. Tendrils of scrub clung to the bare rock face.

A castle stood on the summit of the bluff. A nightmare concoction of towers, rooftops, and terraces, it sprawled across the prominence like a scar on the land and was enclosed by hundred-foot-high, towering brick ramparts. Narrow courtyards and labyrinthine paths intersected the extensive grounds in front of it. Barred casement windows glimmered in the dark, the leaded glass reflecting the glare from the security lights around the perimeter of the monstrous citadel.

Dozens of figures guarded the walkways topping the walls. Scores more patrolled the ground.

The place was swarming with Crovir Hunters.

'Reznak and the rest of the Crovir Councils have been summoned to the island,' said Victor. His expression hardened. 'Vellacrus is intending to make an example of Tomas. He will be the first Bastian to be exposed to the Red Death in more than six hundred years.'

Numbness spread through my limbs at the Bastian noble's words. 'When does she plan to do this?'

'Not for a day or so, at least. She'll have to wait until all the Council members are gathered on the island.'

Victor's eyes moved briefly to Costas's stony face. 'One out of the other three Crovir First Council Heads has pledged to help Dimitri stop Vellacrus and Thorne, as have several members of their Second Council and Assembly. They each command about a hundred men.'

Reid grimaced. 'So, what you're saying is, we're kinda outnumbered three to one.'

'We wouldn't be in this position if the Bastian Councils stopped sitting on their hands and did something!' Costas snapped.

Victor turned a steady gaze on him. 'Roman *will* persuade them.'

'When? By then it might be too late!' Costas exhaled loudly and rubbed his face. 'I'm sorry. It's just that—'

Victor crossed the floor and put his hand on the Bastian noble's shoulder. 'The friends who betrayed us will be made to atone for their treachery,' he said coldly.

A hunted look flitted in Costas's eyes. 'Seven hundred years. That's how long I've known Grigoriye. You would think after all that time I'd know the man inside out.'

A hush followed his tortured words.

'From what we witnessed earlier, there are others in the Bastian Councils who want to imitate his actions,' said Victor.

'They will have to answer to my blade if they do!' Costas growled.

My nails dug into my palms. 'When do we leave?'

'We can be airborne in two hours.' Victor walked to a table on which a map of the Mediterranean Sea was spread out. 'But first, we have to consider the small matter of logistics.'

We left the compound within the hour, the convoy of SUVs and vans traveling swiftly through the night to the private airfield where we had landed days previously.

Victor and Costas spent the drive making a number of long transatlantic calls.

A cold wind was blowing in from the Virginia coastline when we arrived at the airstrip. The C-40 Clipper stood waiting in the glare of a dozen halogen floodlights.

Shadows soon danced across the gray fuselage as the aircraft was loaded with weapons and hardware. Many of the Bastian Hunters were still recovering from their recent injuries and some moved more slowly than others.

Forty minutes after reaching the airfield, we were in the air. It was a nine-hour flight to our destination. Victor finalized the details of our operation and ordered everyone to get some rest.

Despite my bone-deep exhaustion, sleep proved unsurprisingly elusive once more. I stared out of the window next to my seat, my mind filled with images of Anna and our grandfather from the previous week. My fingers unconsciously tightened on the armrests, my emotions fluctuating from anger and frustration to fear at their fate. Clouds glowed in the moonlight beneath the belly of the plane; occasionally, a break in the white blanket afforded a glimpse of the dark waters of the Atlantic below.

'Can't sleep?' someone murmured beside me.

I looked to my left. Reid had moved up the aisle and taken the seat opposite mine.

'No.'

He watched me steadily. 'We'll get them back. You have to believe that.'

I sighed. 'I know.'

He shrugged. 'Look on the bright side. Half the immortals on the planet are no longer trying to kill you.'

I smiled and leaned against the headrest. My gaze shifted to the dark sky outside. Memories of the night before flashed past my eyes once more.

It felt like a lifetime ago since I'd held Anna in my arms.

Sometime before noon the next day, we landed on a military airfield in the south of Sardinia. I stepped off the plane onto hot, cracked asphalt and looked around.

The base was teeming with officers from the Italian Air Force. A dozen transport and fighter planes as well as a pair of combat search-and-rescue helicopters stood parked on the tarmac. The C-40 Clipper earned a few curious stares as the Bastian Hunters started unloading the plane.

Cloud-wreathed peaks rose to the west of the base. Two

dots appeared above the shimmering foothills of the mountain range.

Seconds later, a pair of F-16 fighter jets boomed overhead and disappeared in the azure skies to the east.

A smoke ring blew past my ear. 'That's a sight you don't see every day,' said Reid.

I looked at the cigar in his hand.

'Oh, this? I got it from Costas.' He grinned at my expression. 'The bulldog's bark is definitely harsher than his bite.'

We headed toward a hangar where Victor and Costas stood in conversation with a tall, distinguished-looking, gray-haired man in uniform.

'This is Major Vincenzo. He's the commander of the base and an old friend,' said Victor by way of introduction.

Shrewd eyes studied us from beneath a pair of thick, white eyebrows. 'Are these the men you want me to coach?'

'There are six others,' said Victor. He signaled to a group of Bastian Hunters hovering close by.

Surprise darted through me when I spotted a familiar face. 'It's good to see you again.'

Friedrich nodded an acknowledgement. His injuries appeared to have healed and he walked with barely a limp. 'Victor thought my skills might come in handy.'

The major observed him critically. 'How many jumps have you done before?'

'Twenty,' said the German Bastian Hunter.

Vincenzo's gaze shifted to the sky framed by the hangar doors. 'We've got six hours left till sundown. Come with me, gentlemen.'

We followed him to a DHC-6 twin otter plane standing on the tarmac a short distance away. Several figures loaded bags full of gear into the rear of the fuselage. The turbo engines roared into life as we reached the aircraft.

'Get in,' ordered the major. 'We'll go through basic drills in the air.' He hesitated. 'Have any of you performed accuracy landings before?'

Bar Friedrich, everyone shook their head.

Vincenzo sighed. 'Well, we'll have to see what we can do.'

'Oh boy,' Reid muttered as we climbed inside the plane.

The light was fading fast when we made our final descent to the base hours later.

I stepped off the aircraft and gazed at the kaleidoscope of orange and pink streaks arching across the horizon to the west; though my heart still raced and my limbs shook from the intensive training we had just received, I was aware that time was fast running out for the Godards.

The major was the last man to exit the plane. He dropped onto the tarmac while his officers wrapped up the equipment we had used during our exercises.

'That was good work. You're all fast learners. I can safely say that none of you are likely to kill yourselves after what we've just put you through.' A guarded look appeared in his eyes. 'As to what happens after that, I'm not in a position to comment.'

We returned to the hangar assigned to the Bastians. The brightly lit confines were a hive of activity. A line of army trucks and jeeps stood at the ready at the doors of the building; the Hunters were getting ready to leave.

A command center had been set up in a corner of the vast space. The lights from the monitors cast shadows on the faces of the people gathered around the terminals.

Victor looked around at our footsteps. 'How did it go?'

'He said we wouldn't die,' Reid replied.

Victor smiled. 'Coming from Carlo, I would take that as a compliment.'

I stared past him at the flickering screens. 'Are we ready?' I asked, unable to conceal the edge in my voice.

Victor nodded. 'Yes. Dimitri and the remaining Council members arrived on the island an hour ago.' He glanced at his watch. 'They'll have the radar-jamming devices set up by twenty-hundred. Costas and I will be heading for the port in fifty minutes. You should get some rest before you leave.'

Although I felt drained from our flight drills, I was too tense to follow his advice.

I found a deserted spot at the edge of the airfield and practiced with the swords under the rising moon. It took all my concentration to quell the nervous tension building inside me. A warm breeze blew in from the sea and flicked the droplets of sweat beading my face and arms onto the tarmac.

The Bastian convoy thundered past moments later. Anatole waved from behind the steering wheel of the leading SUV. Victor dipped his chin stoically from the seat next to him.

They were on their way to the city of Cagliari, some ten miles south and to the east on the Sardinian coastline.

Footsteps soon rose behind me. 'You almost done?' said Reid.

'Yes.' I lowered the daisho and slowly sheathed the blades.

'Good. We should get some food.' Reid grimaced. 'I hate to think what might happen if we eat too close to take-off.'

I smiled and followed him to the hangar.

Two hours later, at exactly 21:00, we finally left the base.

The refueled DHC-6 climbed steadily in an easterly direction, its twin engines filling the interior of the fuselage with a steady drone that would have made conversation difficult even if any of us had been in the mood to talk. Not that we could have easily, what with the face masks delivering the one-hundred-percent pure oxygen we needed to inhale to flush out nitrogen from our bloodstream and reduce the risk of decompression sickness associated with our high-altitude, low-opening jump.

Two of the major's lieutenants had accompanied us on the flight. As instructed by them, I spent most of the ninety-minute journey concentrating on my breathing and checking Reid for signs of hypoxia and hyperventilation.

'If I'd known I'd be doing a HALO jump soon, I would have quit smoking months ago,' said Reid in a low voice.

I peered at him anxiously. It was difficult to see his expression through the glass visor of his helmet. 'How're you feeling?'

'I could do with a smoke,' came the dull reply.

I muttered something under my breath and settled back in the seat.

A crackle of static echoed in my earpiece.

'We're fifteen minutes from the drop zone,' said the pilot. 'Check your gear.'

We rose and went through the safety drill we had been taught under the keen eyes of Vincenzo's lieutenants.

Another voice came over the comm line a moment later. 'Hey, can you guys hear me?' It was the Bastian tech at the base.

I observed the series of nods around the fuselage. 'Yeah, we hear you.'

'Victor called. Reznak's men are in place. They've secured access to the external security cameras and the radars. You're good to go.'

There was a further crackle from the earpiece.

'ETA five minutes,' warned the pilot.

'Good luck,' the tech added quietly.

I switched on the portable oxygen bottle on my back, disconnected from the central console, and checked my flow meter.

One of the lieutenants opened the loading door on the port side of the aircraft. Cold air rushed inside the hold.

'On five,' he shouted, signaling with his fingers.

I followed Reid to the exit and switched on the night vision goggles beneath my helmet. The wind whipped at my jumpsuit as I stepped off the plane. Seconds later, I was in free-fall.

The HALO jump was from thirty thousand feet. I tucked

my arms by my sides and angled downward. The island appeared as a green shadow in the waters ahead and to the left, the image strangely stark under the ambient moonlight. I turned toward it and kept my breaths slow and steady.

The audible altimeter soon sounded in my ears, indicating that I had reached a terminal velocity of 170 mph.

The fall lasted a thrilling two minutes. At the two-thousand-feet signal, I reached behind my back and pulled out the pilot chute from the bottom pocket of the container strapped to my body. There was a tug as the bridle lifted the deployment bag holding the main parachute. The canopy unfolded above me, suspension lines feeding steadily through the slider.

I braced myself for the sudden deceleration and reached for the steering toggles. One hundred feet below and to my right, Reid's parachute swooped toward the rapidly enlarging landmass. I headed after him.

We landed on the rooftop of one of the towers seconds later. I hit the ground with a soft thud, pulled out the wakizashi, and cut away the lines before the chute could drag me over the edge of the terrace.

There was movement out the corner of my eyes.

I ducked and stabbed a Crovir Hunter in the chest. The immortal crumpled, his gun falling out of his hand. I caught it before it struck the stonework and lowered the lifeless body to the ground.

There was a noise behind me. I looked over my shoulder. My stomach dropped.

I turned and ran toward the two figures struggling silently near the northeast parapet.

The men fell from the tower a second before I reached them.

I dove forward, slammed the tip of the blade in a groove between the slabs, and slid over the edge with an outstretched arm. My fingers closed over flesh.

I came to a juddering stop with half my body suspended over empty space. The silence beneath me was broken by a thump.

'That was close,' Reid murmured.

He swung from my grasp, his feet dangling over the hundred-foot drop. I pulled him up with a grunt and glanced at the dark shape of the Crovir Hunter lying at the base of the building.

Waves boomed against the rocks at the bottom of the cliff. No cries of alarm sounded in the night. Our landing had gone undetected.

'Everyone okay?' I whispered in my transmitter, studying the adjoining rooftops. A series of affirmative responses sounded in my ears. Friedrich gave us a quick wave from the next building and disappeared in the gloom.

Reid and I removed our flight gear before heading for the door tucked in a corner of the tower. A dimly lit stairwell lay on the other side. I stopped at the top of the steps and looked over the banister.

A further four landings were visible below. Silence rose from the lower depths of the turret.

We moved soundlessly down the spiral staircase and reached an iron-plated oak door at the bottom. Faint voices came through the wood.

'On three?' Reid mouthed.

I nodded, slipped the Glock from the holster on my hip, checked the suppressor, and moved to the side of the doorpost.

Reid's bullet struck the lock with a dull, metallic twang. The door crashed open on his first kick. He stepped out of the way while I turned and dropped to one knee. I raised the gun and fired.

My shots took out the first two Crovir Hunters. Light from the naked bulb on the ceiling glinted on the edge of the wakizashi as it spun through the air and thudded into the neck of the third man. His hand slipped from the handle of the door on the other side of the chamber as he collapsed to the ground.

I retrieved the short sword while Reid unscrewed the light bulb from the ceiling. We crossed the darkened room to the second door. He twisted the handle. It opened silently.

We were faced with a walkway at the top of one of the castle walls. A bank of clouds had moved in from the west and was drifting past the moon, causing shadows to dance across the stonework. Cold air whipped over the rampart from the sea on the left. To the right, a parapet overlooked a dark courtyard a hundred feet below.

Two Crovir guards stood next to another tower at the end of the path. Smoke curled up from the cigarettes in their hands. A chuckle drifted in our direction.

Darkness and the rush of the wind helped mask our approach. We were ten feet from the men before they noticed us. They jerked convulsively when our bullets struck them. The sounds of their bodies hitting the ground were muted by the crash of the distant surf.

An empty room lay through the doorway of the second tower. Narrow, leaded windows looked down onto an enclosed courtyard. We headed for the exit on the opposite side.

Halfway across the floor, I froze in my tracks.

Reid stiffened. 'What is it?'

I stared at the bench tucked beneath the windows. 'There are three glasses on that table.'

The words had barely left my lips when a gasp sounded to the right. I turned and saw the third man disappear through a door concealed in the shadows.

I was the first one over the threshold. Up ahead, the Crovir Hunter raced along a dim corridor, his figure darting between the bars of moonlight streaming through the windows lining the left wall of the gallery. A brightly lit archway stood at the end of the passage.

Reid's shot whistled past me and caught the man on the leg. He stumbled and started to fall.

It was all I needed.

I dove and tackled him to the ground a dozen feet from the opening.

We landed hard on cold, bare stone. The Hunter rolled out from under me and reached for his gun. He froze when the edge of the wakizashi touched the skin at his throat.

'Do you know who I am?' I said in a low voice while Reid relieved him of his weapon.

The Crovir Hunter dipped his chin and winced when the short blade drew a drop of blood from his flesh.

'Where are the prisoners?' I asked harshly.

'I don't know what you're talking about,' the immortal retorted.

I leaned down until my face was mere inches from his. 'Anna and Tomas Godard. Where are they?' I said between gritted teeth.

The man gulped. A thin, crimson line coursed down his neck and stained the collar of his shirt. He opened his mouth to reply.

Voices rose through the brilliant arch ahead.

∾

CHAPTER TWENTY-SIX

REID AND I GRABBED THE CROVIR HUNTER AND PULLED HIM into the shadows next to the door. I kept the wakizashi pressed against the immortal's throat and narrowed my eyes. His breath left his lips in a low sigh and he nodded with a defeated expression.

Snatches of conversation reached us when footsteps drew closer to the doorway.

' —the chamber ready?'

'Yes, sir. We've set it up as per your instructions.'

'Good. And the woman?'

'Our scientists are still working on her. As expected, she's not cooperating. They think —'

The rest of the exchange was muted when the voices went out of earshot. Rage stirred inside my veins. I took a step forward.

Reid placed a hand on my shoulder and stopped me in my tracks.

The first voice had belonged to Felix Thorne.

I drew a slow breath and turned a flinty stare on the Crovir Hunter. 'Where's your central command room?'

The immortal's eyes widened. 'You'll never get there in one piece!'

'I didn't ask for your opinion,' I snapped.

Reid sighed. 'Just show us to the nearest computer,' he told the Hunter.

The man guided us through the archway to a room some thirty feet down an adjacent passage. Reid reached for the door handle.

Five seconds later, we had disposed of the two guards inside.

Reid handcuffed our reluctant guide to the radiator on the wall. Fear filled the immortal's eyes when he observed the dead men on the floor.

I removed a USB stick from inside my jumpsuit and plugged it in one of the ports at the back of the computer terminal on the table.

'We're in,' I said in my transmitter.

A buzz of static overlaid the Bastian tech's voice when it came over the earpiece. 'That's great! Victor called. They're ten minutes from the island.'

I watched the screen flicker.

The device allowed the Bastians access to the Crovir fortress's mainframe and the security feeds inside the complex. Codes started to roll down the monitor.

'Here goes,' murmured the tech.

Video streams from dozens of cameras appeared on the screen. My eyes were drawn to one near the bottom right corner.

'Where is that?' I barked.

The tech zoomed in on the picture. Floor plans of the castle appeared next to the image. There was an audible intake of breath from the other end of the line.

'That room is in a secure facility two hundred feet below you,' he said in a low voice. 'It's inside the island.'

My heart pounded dully in my chest as I stared at the image

of Anna strapped to a metal gurney. A monitor above her head displayed her vital signs. There was an IV line snaking out of her left elbow to a stand holding a bag of clear fluid; her eyes were closed and her face deathly pale.

'Can you override the access doors to that unit?' I asked stiffly.

The Bastian tech was silent for a while. His voice finally came through the earpiece. 'No. And I'm afraid I've got more bad news.'

'What is it?'

'It seems they have a completely separate security system for that part of the complex. Even the camera feeds are controlled from a different subframe.' Frustration tinged his voice. 'The best I can do is get you to one of the elevators that goes down to that facility. After that, you're on your own.'

Reid and I exchanged troubled glances.

'Let the others know where we're headed,' I told the tech. 'My grandfather's bound to be there as well.'

We left the Crovir Hunter gagged and handcuffed inside the room and proceeded east along the corridor. All the while, the image of Anna's lifeless face burned at the front of my mind.

The tech guided us to an alcove in the south wall of a tower two floors below, where a metal door stood framed between a set of heavy curtains.

'This is as far as I can take you,' said the Bastian. 'The lift is through that door. There are five Crovir Hunters between you and the elevator.'

'Thanks.' I holstered my gun and lifted the daisho from my waist. 'Are the others here yet?'

'They've just reached the dock under the island,' replied the tech.

I glanced at Reid. In addition to the Glock, he also held a Beretta pistol in his hand. 'What about Friedrich and his team?'

'They're almost at the main command center.' Static travelled down the line. 'Reznak and his men haven't got control of the subframe security yet. Once you guys go through that door, the Crovirs will soon know we're on the island.'

'Okay,' I murmured. 'Warn Friedrich and the others.'

'Will do,' said the tech. 'Good luck.'

I looked at Reid. 'Ready?'

He shrugged. 'Not really.'

My fingers tightened on the handles of the blades. I dipped my chin.

Reid shot through the lock on the door. I kicked it open and moved out of the way. He stepped inside the room, took out the cameras near the ceiling, and fired rapidly from both weapons.

I dove after him, hit the floor, and rolled. Shots ricocheted off the edges of the daisho as I leapt to my feet. I weaved the blades around, my steps quick and measured. The tips of the swords gleamed with blood. Crimson sprays splattered the ground and walls.

Ten seconds later, I reached for the swipe card on one of the bodies and moved to the lift.

'Lucas,' Reid warned.

I looked to where he stared. The numbers on the indicator panel above the elevator had started to glow; the cabin was moving up.

We shifted to the sides of the steel doors a moment before they opened.

Olsson stepped out. He froze in his tracks, his eyes widening as he took in the bloody scene. His hand was halfway to his gun when the katana arced through the air and stopped a hairbreadth from his throat. He went still.

'Hello, Mikael,' I murmured. I was surprised at how composed I sounded.

'How did you—' Olsson broke off when a bullet sang past his ear.

Reid lowered the Glock.

The Crovir Hunter at the back of the elevator slid to the floor, his eyes turning dull beneath the fresh bullet wound in his forehead. His finger slipped from the control panel and his arm swung lifelessly next to his body.

A shrill alarm tore through the room. It was undoubtedly being transmitted to the rest of the complex.

Reid grimaced. 'Well, they were gonna find out about us soon anyway.' He indicated Olsson with the Glock. 'What do you wanna do with him?'

Olsson stood watching us stiffly, his eyes blazing with anger.

'He might prove useful as leverage.' I removed a cable tie from my backpack and closed it around Olsson's wrists.

Reid frowned. 'And if he doesn't?'

'We can always use him as a shield.'

Reid brightened. 'I like that.'

I pushed Olsson inside the lift and turned him to face the doorway. I touched the wakizashi to the pulsing artery in his neck. 'You're going to take us to Anna and my grandfather.'

'Like hell I will!' he barked.

'I don't think you understand.' I nudged his skin with the tip of the short blade. 'I will kill you if you don't do as I say.'

A mocking chuckle left Olsson's lips. 'Go ahead. You have no idea what these people are capable of, do you? Besides, Tomas Godard deserves to die!'

I scowled. 'My grandfather was not responsible for your father's death.'

'Yes he was!' shouted Olsson. Blood appeared on his neck as he strained against the wakizashi. 'He ordered the Bastians into Khotyn!'

The alarm was loud in the silence that followed.

'Your father was a soldier, Mikael,' I said. 'He knew what he was getting himself into.'

Olsson glared at me. 'Go to hell, Soul! I'll never help you, so you might as well kill me now!'

I watched him for a moment. 'Not yet, Mikael.' I pressed a button on the control panel. 'Not while there's a chance that we could still use you.'

The doors closed. The cabin started to move.

The sound of shots soon rose from the inner depths of the island.

'Looks like they started the party without us.' Reid grimaced and scratched the end of his nose with the Glock. 'Damn. I could really do with a smoke.'

'For a mortal, you sure are taking things lightly!' Olsson spat out.

Reid watched him steadily. 'You know, if Lucas doesn't shut you up soon, I swear I'm gonna shoot you myself.'

The noise of gunfire grew louder. One hundred and sixty feet after we started our descent, the elevator opened onto a scene of chaos.

Bullets crisscrossed the smoke wreathed air of a large vestibule ahead. Victor, Anatole, and a dozen Bastian Hunters had taken cover behind a makeshift barricade to the left of the lobby.

Some twenty Crovirs stood at the opposite end, semi-automatics singing in their hands.

'Take him!' I shoved Olsson toward Reid, sheathed the swords, and drew my guns.

I stepped out of the lift.

Time slowed. I breathed steadily while I emptied the magazines into the enemy. Ten seconds passed. I reloaded the guns. A stray bullet grazed my cheek. Another nicked the top of my left ear. One struck my body vest. I finished sliding the fresh clips into place and raised the weapons once more, my stride unbroken.

The final shell casings clattered to the floor a moment later.

I blinked through the clearing haze and observed the bodies covering the vestibule.

There were footsteps behind me.

'Well, that seems to be it for the time being.' Victor stopped at my side and changed the magazine in his gun. 'Though I'm sure there'll be plenty more where they came from.'

The Bastian Hunters started to divest the fallen Crovirs of their weapons.

'You look like shit,' Reid told Anatole.

'Traveling in a sub is not exactly my favorite mode of transportation,' the ashen-faced immortal muttered. 'Give me the high road anytime.' A gleam appeared in Anatole's eyes when he looked past Reid. 'Why, look who we have here. We meet again, asshole.'

Olsson stood nursing a wounded leg, a scowl darkening his face.

I cocked an eyebrow at Reid.

He shrugged. 'One of his own men shot him. Go figure.'

'Anna and your grandfather are somewhere through there.' Victor indicated the steel doors at the end of the lobby. 'Costas and Bruno are covering the lower floors to the dock. I don't know how much longer they'll be able to stall the Crovirs. Reznak and his men are still inside the main fortress.'

Faint explosions from above punctuated the end of his statement. 'And Friedrich?'

'He's fighting his way into the command room with the help of one of the Crovir nobles,' said Victor. 'Once they're in, we'll be able to get the rest of our men on the island.'

While we had been making our way to the Crovir fortress by air and by sea, Roman Dvorsky had finally contacted his son with the Councils' decision; the rest of the Bastian army was on its way from Europe to assist us.

I feared they would be too late. The expression on Victor's face mirrored my own doubts. I suppressed the dread coursing through me and turned to study the doors blocking our path. A complex security display stood to the left of the metal panels.

It was going to take more than an access card to get us inside the core of the Crovir fortress.

My eyes rose to the ceiling.

Victor followed my gaze to a large, square panel. 'What are you thinking?'

'From the floor plans I saw earlier, there's a ventilation duct right above us. It leads inside the facility.' I frowned. 'It won't be practical for all of us to go that way.'

I glanced from Olsson to the security panel next to the doors. It was similar to the one I had in my apartment in Boston.

'I suspect Mikael's fingerprint and retinal scan will get you through there,' I told Victor. 'We'll create a diversion to give you a fighting chance.'

Reid linked his fingers into a foothold. I climbed onto his shoulders and unscrewed the paneling above our heads.

I was in the vent within seconds and pulled him up after me. Anatole followed.

'See you on the other side,' Victor said from below.

The passage inside the duct was hot and tight. We crawled silently along it and came to a grated opening in the floor some thirty feet later. I unbolted the cover and peered carefully out of the hole.

A crowd of Crovir Hunters stood before the steel doors at one end of the passage, their guns at the ready. An empty, white-walled corridor disappeared into the facility in the opposite direction.

I gripped the edge of the ventilation shaft and slowly lowered myself to the tiled floor. Reid and Anatole dropped down silently beside me.

The Bastian immortal removed the pair of Steyr AUG rifles strapped to his back and handed one of the weapons to Reid.

He pressed the safety button, grinned, and waved wildly at the Crovirs.

'Hey, assholes! We're right here!'

The Crovirs turned. Their eyes widened.

By then, our bullets had already struck ten of them. The steel doors opened. Victor and the Bastians rushed inside the passage.

Rapid footfall pounded the ground behind me. More Crovirs appeared from the direction of the facility.

'Go! We'll take the front!' Anatole shouted over his shoulder.

I turned to face the approaching wave of immortals. A heartbeat later, the daisho started its lethal dance through the air. A couple of bullets thudded into my body vest. Another skimmed past my right eye and grazed my temple. My steps did not waver as the blades carved into flesh again and again.

Half a minute later, we had secured the access to the underground facility.

'Don't stop! We'll cover you!' Victor yelled as a fresh surge of Crovirs arrived at the steel doors.

I nodded and started to run, Reid and Anatole on my heels.

More guards materialized in our path as we advanced inside the island. They fell swiftly beneath our bullets and my blades. White corridors unrolled before us, walls blindingly bright under the harsh fluorescent strips in the ceiling. All the while, the alarms echoed around us.

Biohazard signs started to appear overhead. We turned a corner and skidded to a stop in front of a pair of containment doors.

'The labs must be through here!' I gasped.

My stomach plummeted when I saw the security display next to the doors. I had never seen one like it before.

There was a noise behind us. A group of Crovir Hunters came into view at the opposite end of the passage.

Reid scowled. 'Hurry up and do your stuff!'

I unscrewed the panel while Reid and Anatole laid down cover fire. I grabbed a pen torch from my backpack and shone it on the microcircuits inside the unit. A sliver of sweat dripped over my right eye. I blinked, stuck the torch between my teeth, and raised the wakizashi. The blade sliced through two wires. I rapidly twisted the ends together.

The light above the lintel turned green. The doors opened with a hiss of escaping air.

'Let's go!' I shouted.

We crossed the threshold into a hall lined with glass walls. Figures in white biohazard suits were visible behind the sterile partitions. They looked up at the sound of the gunfire, their eyes widening behind their visors.

I turned and stabbed the wakizashi into the access panel on the wall. Sparks erupted from the unit. The containment doors closed on the approaching Crovir Hunters, their shots thudding dully into the reinforced metal.

Reid raised an eyebrow. 'That should buy us what, ten minutes or so?'

I dipped my chin briskly, jogged down the hall, and turned left at the second intersection.

From what I recalled of the map of the facility, Anna was being held in a room somewhere in that passage.

Doors opened as I sprinted down the corridor; I paid no heed to the scientists fleeing past me. Another containment door appeared at the end. My pulse quickened.

Seconds before I reached it, four Crovir Hunters shot out of an opening to the right.

I snarled and raised the daisho. The immortals barely had time to lift their guns before they fell under my blades.

I lifted an access card from one of the dead men and moved it over the security display next to the door. It glided open with a soft, pneumatic noise.

Two figures in sterile suits looked up from the computer monitor in the room beyond. I ignored them and looked around wildly. My eyes finally found the figure I was searching for behind a glass partition on the left.

'Open that door!' I barked, indicating the sealed entrance in the wall.

One of the scientists reached for the phone next to him. He froze when the barrel of a gun touched the back of his head.

'I would do as he says if I were you,' said Reid.

The second man gulped and rose to his feet. He crossed the room and typed a code in the security panel, his hand shaking. The door slid aside.

I moved past him into the sterile chamber.

Anna's eyes opened when I reached the side of the bed. Dark pupils dilated in an ocean of green. 'Lucas?'

'I'm here.' I struggled to keep my voice steady against the wave of emotions surging through me.

A smile tugged at her lips. 'I knew you'd come for us.'

I took in the dark circles under her eyes and the fresh bruises on her arms and legs. Rage replaced the joy inside my chest. With trembling hands, I undid the leather belts holding her down on the gurney before lifting her gently to my chest. 'Are you okay?'

'Yes,' murmured Anna. Her body felt fragile under the hospital gown. The sun cross pendant gleamed at the base of her throat. 'I'm just tired. They've taken a lot of blood from me.' She laid her head on my shoulder and closed her eyes. 'I thought I'd never see you again.' A tear slid down her cheek. 'I never got to tell how much I—'

'I know.' I was intensely aware of her heartbeat against my skin.

It felt like coming home.

CHAPTER TWENTY-SEVEN

THERE WAS A NOISE FROM THE DOORWAY.

'I hate to rain on your touching parade here folks, but I think we should get going.'

Anatole flashed an awkward grin over his shoulder, the Steyr AUG aimed toward the main door of the lab.

Anna stiffened in my arms. 'Grandfather!'

'We haven't found him yet.'

'I know where he is,' said Anna, her voice growing hard.

I turned and carried her to the door.

'Wait!' she barked when we crossed the threshold into the outer room.

I froze in my tracks.

'Put me down,' Anna commanded.

I hesitated before lowering her to the floor.

She took a few steps toward the scientist cowering behind the desk.

'Give me your gun,' she ordered, her eyes never leaving the man's face while she extended a hand toward me.

I glanced at Reid. He shrugged with an 'I'd-do-as-she-said-if-I-was-you' expression. I slipped the Glock from the holster on my hip and slowly placed it in her grasp.

The scientist's eyes widened behind the visor. A mumble of incoherent words left his lips when Anna raised the weapon and leveled it at his chest. Her arm moved as she fired the gun.

The bullet shattered the computer terminal next to the man. He cried out in shock and collapsed to the floor.

Anna turned to the second scientist and punched him on the jaw.

I stared at her. Anatole gaped. Reid grinned.

'They're lucky I didn't shoot them,' muttered Anna. She stormed past us.

We joined her in the passage outside and soon reached the intersection with the glass hall.

Anna indicated the passage on the left. 'This way.'

The labs had emptied in our absence, the scattered paperwork and overturned chairs testimony to the haste of the scientists' departure. We came to a fire exit. It opened onto an empty, stone stairwell.

'Up or down?' I asked Anna.

She frowned. 'Down. Definitely down. They brought us here by boat.'

The stairs ended at a thick oak door three floors below. The corridor on the other side looked to have been carved out of the very core of the island and was lined with bare rock. Flame torches sat in metal brackets on the walls, casting an eerie, yellow light over the passage.

This far down, the alarms resonating through the facility and the fortress above it were barely audible.

'Not that I'm complaining or anything, but we haven't seen anyone for a while now,' Reid murmured after we had crossed a series of deserted passages. 'I'm not sure whether to take that as a good sign or a bad one.'

Anatole and I glanced at one another.

'It's bad,' said the red-haired immortal with a firm nod.

'The Crovirs must be regrouping,' I said in a low voice.

Though I was elated to have found Anna, nervous anxiety was building inside my chest once more. Our battle was far from over.

'Yes, but where?' murmured Anna.

We got our answer sooner than we expected.

Forty seconds later, the corridor ended abruptly on a metal gangway. A vaulted roof appeared some twenty feet above us. The ground dropped away precipitously on either side of the narrow platform. A low rumble of voices rose from below.

We pulled back in the shadows near the opening and looked over the edge of the walkway.

An enormous atrium unfolded beneath us. Wide, circular terraces not dissimilar to those of a Roman amphitheater were spread out over its four levels.

Scores of Crovir Hunters with guns and swords patrolled the floors.

'The room where they took Grandfather must be somewhere down there,' said Anna guardedly.

A round, steel and glass cage on metal castors stood in the epicenter of the marble floor at the bottom of the arena. A crowd of Crovir nobles dressed in formal evening wear milled around it, heads bowed while they engaged in muted conversation.

The air was fraught with tension.

An icy premonition rose in my mind as I studied the cage. It was large enough to hold a man.

'No!' Anna whispered shakily. I saw my own horror reflected in her eyes.

Anatole frowned. 'What?'

Reid remained silent, his expression grim.

A hush fell below, drawing our stares. The voices of the Crovir nobles slowly died down; as one, they turned toward a doorway on the left. Footsteps emerged in the distance and grew closer. Several figures appeared over the threshold and crossed the polished floor.

Anna stiffened beside me. I gripped her hand tightly.

My eyes never left the man in the middle of the small procession.

Tomas Godard was led inside the room in chains. Although he looked gaunt and pale, the former leader of the Bastians walked with stiff pride within a circle of Crovir Hunters, his head held high and his limp more evident without the ivory-headed cane.

He stopped when he spotted a familiar face in the crowd. 'Grigoriye.' Sadness tinged Godard's voice. 'I never imagined that you of all people would betray us so.'

The Bastian noble held the older man's gaze and shrugged. 'I'm afraid we need to move with the times, Tomas. What Vellacrus is offering is the future. I would've been a fool to refuse her.'

'Still, I fear you have made a grave mistake,' said Godard. 'Vellacrus is not to be trusted.'

Grigoriye frowned.

A storm of murmurs broke across the chamber as more guards filed inside the room; it rose to fever pitch when Agatha Vellacrus and Felix Thorne appeared in the doorway. Although a good proportion of the Crovir nobles still bore anxious expressions, scattered applause erupted in the crowd.

A wave of rage flooded my body.

Vellacrus stopped at the head of the arena and raised her hand.

'My friends,' she said once the clapping dwindled to a stop. 'I am pleased to see you in such good spirits.'

It was the second time I had ever heard my grandmother's voice; it still sounded cold to my ears.

'Today is a special day for us Crovirs, for it is the start of a new adventure for our race,' Vellacrus continued, a zealous expression distorting her features. 'And what could be a more befitting beginning to this chapter in our immortal history than the death of one of our oldest and most hated enemies?' She indicated Godard with a hand. 'I present to you the former leader of the Bastian Hunters, Tomas Godard.'

Applause rose again at her words. Some of the Crovir nobles exchanged troubled glances.

'For such an esteemed adversary, one must reserve a truly unique death.' Silence fell once more at Vellacrus's words. The corners of her lips lifted in a chilling smile. 'Today, my friends, we shall watch the first of many Bastians die from the Red Death.'

Among the roar of approving voices that followed, one spoke up.

'Really Agatha, is now the time to be engaging in such dreadful theatrics? We've heard rumors that the Bastian army is on its way to this fortress. Shouldn't we be making plans to evacuate the island?'

The speaker was an elderly woman with pale blonde hair and sharp eyes. She stood her ground defiantly in the face of the critical stares around her.

'Sylviana is right,' said a distinguished middle-aged man next to her.

Mutters arose from the gathering. Several nobles nodded in agreement.

Vellacrus cocked an eyebrow. 'My dear Sylviana, to not wish to see the death of a Bastian could be interpreted as an act of treason against our race. Should I construe it as such?'

The Crovir noblewoman scowled. 'I will not have you question my loyalty to my race so readily, Agatha.'

Vellacrus stared at her with an unreadable expression. 'Good,' she said with a dismissive nod. 'Then we shall proceed as planned. Felix.' She turned to Thorne.

The guards removed Godard's chains. He did not put up a fight when he was escorted inside the cage. The door closed on him with a final, somber toll.

A guard handed Thorne a silver flask. The man who once killed me walked to the side of the glass prison and opened a small compartment built in the steel support. He placed the container inside it.

'With this, I hope to finally see the end of the Godards.' A bitter smile twisted the scar on Thorne's cheek as he gazed at the man inside the cage. 'Of course, I still need to take care of your delightful granddaughter and that bastard half-breed grandson of yours. Rest assured, I shall take the greatest pleasure in killing them both.'

At this, Godard's composure finally broke. He took a step toward the wall of his prison, a scowl clouding his face.

'Don't you dare lay a finger on them, you monster!' He turned to Vellacrus. 'If you have any feeling at all left in that cold heart of yours, Agatha, then let Anna and Lucas live!'

Vellacrus studied Godard impassively. 'My dear Tomas, why ever should I do that?'

She dipped her chin at Thorne. He pressed a button on the control panel in the metal frame.

The flask moved up into an airlock. A needle came down and perforated the rubber top of the container. There was a faint electronic hum when the liquid inside was aspirated into a glass tubing and started to move up a narrow pipe.

My heart raced against my ribs when I tracked the course of the conduit to a box in the roof of the cage. I slipped my bag off my shoulders.

Reid frowned. 'What're you doing?'

I removed a harness from the backpack, stepped inside the straps, and fastened them swiftly to my body. 'I'm going in.'

Anatole's jaw sagged. 'Are you mad?'

I tied one end of a climbing rope to the harness, looped the other to a carabiner, and turned to Anna. I cradled the back of her head with one hand and kissed her fiercely.

The heat of her body warmed my frozen core.

'I have to do this,' I whispered against her lips. I pulled back and stared into her eyes.

Anna nodded, her breath catching in her throat. She slipped the Glock in my hand and wiped a tear angrily from her cheek.

'Live,' she ordered stiffly.

I looked at Reid. 'Get off the island if you can.'

'Will do,' he murmured with a grimace.

I walked to the middle of the walkway, locked the carabiner onto the handrail, and climbed over. I took a deep breath and gripped the guns tightly in my hands before jumping off the edge of the metal platform.

As I plummeted head down toward the floor of the atrium, I dropped both arms and fired.

The bullets smashed into the ceiling of the cage a second before the liquid in the pipe reached the box in the roof. A fine mist rained down on Tomas Godard.

I squeezed the triggers rapidly, shooting round after round into the cracking glass.

It shattered seconds before I reached it.

I pulled up sharply, hurtled through the jagged opening, and landed in a crouch in the middle of the shard-strewn floor. I raised my head and straightened slowly in the shocked silence that followed.

Panic washed across the faces of the Crovir nobles beyond the glass wall. Terrified cries erupted around the arena. The Crovir Hunters raised their guns and fired at the cage.

'Stop!' Thorne roared. 'The virus is still inside!'

'Lucas?' Godard whispered behind me.

I unclipped the rope from my harness, shot through the lock on the door, grabbed my grandfather's arm, and pulled him out of the prison.

Chaos reigned inside the atrium as the Crovir nobles surged toward the exits; it was obvious from the fear thrumming the air that not all of them had received the vaccine.

A group of Crovir Hunters surrounded us. I holstered the guns and drew the daisho.

'Stay behind me!' I barked at my grandfather. He nodded reluctantly.

I shifted into the starting stance of kendo and raised the swords.

The blades flashed under the lights, blocking bullets and slicing through flesh. Three Hunters fell, then five and ten. Another wave appeared. A bullet slipped past my guard and thudded into my vest. Another grazed my thigh. I ignored the wound and took out four more immortals.

Gunfire erupted on the upper floors of the atrium just as the third wave of Crovirs materialized before me. I glanced up. The Bastians had arrived.

Victor soon entered the arena with Bruno and Costas. They fought their way across the floor and were with us in seconds.

'Glad to see you're still alive, old man!' Victor told Godard.

My grandfather smiled weakly.

Costas scowled. 'Where's Vellacrus?'

'She went that way with Thorne.' I indicated an opening to the left.

'Anna?' said Victor.

'She's safe. Reid and Anatole are getting her out of here.'

Godard sagged. 'Thank goodness for that,' he murmured.

I scanned the faces beyond Victor's shoulder. 'What happened to Olsson?'

'He escaped when we were making our way here,' came the grim reply.

'Have you seen Grigoriye?' asked Costas.

'Yes. He left with Vellacrus and Thorne.'

Victor hesitated. 'We have Anna and your grandfather. And

we've destroyed the labs.' He looked at me steadily. 'What we do next is up to you.'

Costas reddened. Before the Bastian noble could burst in a tirade of angry words, I spoke quietly. 'Let's finish this.'

'I agree,' said Godard darkly.

We left Bruno and the rest of the Bastians inside the arena and headed for the door through which my grandmother and uncle had disappeared. More Crovir guards blocked our path. They perished quickly at our hands.

Victor and Costas lifted swords from the dead men.

A pair of elevators appeared at the end of a corridor. The indicator panel on the left glowed as the cabin ascended into the fortress.

I frowned. 'There's a helipad on one of the towers.'

Victor looked at the second lift. 'They'll be expecting us if they see this one light up.'

I pressed the call button. The doors slid aside. I entered the cabin and studied the access panel in the ceiling.

'I have an idea.'

The elevator opened with a soft ping on the highest floor of the castle a short while later. Bullets riddled the interior.

I waited until the roar of gunfire died down before dropping my upper body through the hatch in the ceiling. My shots did not miss a single target.

I stared at the fallen Hunters through the clearing gun smoke before jumping inside the lift. I helped the others down.

We proceeded swiftly along a deserted corridor. A narrow, spiral staircase appeared at the far end. Ominous silence drifted from the turret above.

I poked my head past the opening of the stairwell and pulled back sharply. A bullet whistled past my ear and struck the floor by my feet.

'Looks like this is the only way up,' I said grimly.

Further shots pinged off the walls and the steps.

Costas moved toward the stairs. 'I'll go first.'

I put a hand on his arm and stopped him in his tracks. 'I'm the better shot.'

The Bastian noble glared at me for several seconds. 'Well, I can't exactly argue with that,' he muttered in a disgruntled tone.

I clipped a fresh magazine into the chamber of the Smith & Wesson and unsheathed the katana.

'Be careful,' warned my grandfather.

I nodded and stepped into the stairwell.

Bullets bounced off the blade as I raced up the steps, Victor and Costas at my back. I raised the gun and fired at the Crovir Hunters on the landing above.

Shots thudded into the rock next to me. Stone chips erupted from the walls and cut the skin on my face and hands. I blinked and kept going.

The last immortal fell under my sword a moment later. I crouched at the top of the stairs and scanned the hallway ahead. It was empty. We regrouped and headed silently down it.

Voices reached my ears after twenty feet. My knuckles whitened on the handle of the blade. I reached the end of the passage and turned the corner.

Shock immobilized my limbs. My breath froze in my throat.

A circular room crowned the top of the tower ahead. Lancet windows dotted its thick walls and looked out on what remained of the night. The sound of distant waves drifted from the ocean far below.

Agatha Vellacrus and Felix Thorne were almost at the other side of the chamber, Grigoriye close on their steps. A twin-engine Bell 222 stood waiting on a helipad in the middle of the terrace beyond an open doorway.

My heart thudded erratically as I stared at the other figures in the room.

Olsson was holding a gun to Anna's head a dozen feet to my left.

'I'm sorry,' she murmured brokenly.

Fear formed a hard lump in my throat as I met her tortured gaze. 'Reid?'

Olsson sneered. 'He's dead! I shot him and that other mongrel immortal!'

I was moving before he finished talking.

'Put your weapon down or I'll shoot her!' Olsson shouted. He stepped back and dragged Anna with him.

She struggled in his grip and glanced frantically to where Vellacrus and Thorne were disappearing through the exit. 'You have to stop them! They still have the virus!'

Victor and Costas charged across the room.

The wakizashi left my hand and spun through the air. It thudded into Olsson's right shoulder a heartbeat later. He gasped and stumbled against the wall. His finger moved on the trigger of his Colt. The bullet left the barrel in a flash of light.

It hurtled past Anna's head and struck the ceiling.

I lifted the Smith & Wesson and shot Olsson in the chest. Blood bloomed on his torso. His eyelids fluttered closed and he slumped to the floor.

Anna bolted across the room and fell into Godard's waiting arms. 'Grandfather!'

They hugged each other fiercely.

The sound of clashing blades erupted from the other side of the tower, where the two Bastian nobles had engaged Grigoriye and Thorne. There was no sign of Vellacrus.

I headed for the fighting men just as Grigoriye fell beneath Costas's blade. My eyes widened. I opened my mouth to shout out a warning.

Thorne's sword slipped past Victor's guard and pierced his abdomen. A stunned gasp left the Bastian's lips; he blinked and froze. Thorne pulled the blade out and moved to strike again.

The katana blocked the edge of his sword an inch from Victor's neck.

'This is between you and me, Uncle!' I hissed.

Costas moved to Victor's side and lowered the bleeding immortal to the floor.

Thorne glared at me. A twisted smile distorted his features. 'Indeed it is, *Nephew!*'

His blade glided up mine and curved toward my chest. I jumped back and grasped the katana in a double-handed grip.

Thorne attacked viciously, his sword missing my flesh by a hairbreadth time and time again as we danced around the tower. I fought back just as savagely, the katana singing through the air and blocking his every move.

Motion caught my eyes. A figure had appeared in the doorway to the terrace.

It was Vellacrus.

Gun in hand, she strode toward Anna and my grandfather where they knelt on the ground and tended to Victor. My lips parted on a cry that never came.

Steel flashed ahead of me. Thorne's blade hummed millimeters past my face. I ducked and dropped to the floor. He moved forward with a hungry expression and brought his sword down with a harsh grunt.

The blade glinted as it fell toward me. I rolled and felt sparks ignite against my skin when it struck the floor next to my head. Blood roared in my ears as I swung my foot around and kicked Thorne in the leg.

He staggered against the wall, a curse leaving his lips. He straightened, took a step forward, and rocked to a standstill. Gray eyes widened in dull incomprehension.

'No!' screamed Vellacrus from across the floor.

Thorne's gaze dropped to the katana buried in his chest.

Vellacrus's features crumpled in a mask of fury. She raised her gun and shot Godard in the back. The latter gasped and collapsed on the floor. Anna cried out in horror.

My head whipped round at a low chuckle.

'Looks like you still lose, half-breed,' Thorne gasped mockingly.

Rage darkened my vision. I yanked the katana out of his heart and watched him drop to his knees. He fell forward with a thud. Blood pooled in a growing crimson tide beneath his body.

I turned and strode toward my grandmother.

Vellacrus's hand shifted.

My eyes widened. I started to run.

Anna rose in front of our grandfather's still form and glared defiantly into the barrel of the pistol.

My heart leapt in my throat. Arms and legs pumping through air that suddenly felt too thick, I waited for the sound of the shot, knowing I would be too late to stop it.

It never came.

Agatha Vellacrus froze. Blood drained from her face.

'That necklace! Where did you get it?' she shouted, pointing the gun at the sun cross pendant on Anna's chest.

I staggered to a halt several feet from the frozen tableau.

Anna's necklace had fallen out of the top of the hospital gown. She raised a hand and touched the thick gold with the tips of her fingers. 'It belonged to my mother,' she retorted.

'Impossible!' barked Vellacrus. 'I gave Cecil that pendant on his eighteenth birth—' She stopped abruptly. Her eyes widened. She turned to Tomas Godard.

Our grandfather's eyes opened. There was a triumphant look in his blue gaze.

'You knew?' said Vellacrus, disbelief dropping the pitch of her voice.

'Yes,' Godard replied with more than a trace of satisfaction.

'Knew what? What is it?' said Anna. She stared in confusion from our grandfather to Vellacrus.

Godard turned his head toward Anna.

'I'm sorry, child,' he murmured, his expression sorrowful.

'What do you mean?' Anna whispered.

Godard coughed and took a labored breath. 'Do you recall how I told you all those years ago that I didn't know who your father was?'

Anna nodded tremulously.

Godard gripped her hand. 'I lied.'

'What?' gasped Anna. 'But—but why?'

A sudden intuition blasted through my consciousness. My heart thudded erratically inside my chest.

'Because your father was Cecil Thorne, Agatha's eldest son,' breathed Godard. Tears shimmered in his eyes.

Anna stared at our grandfather. 'That's—I—I don't understand!'

'Cecil and Lily met when Balthazar and Catarine were married.' Coughs racked Godard's thin frame once more, air leaving his throat in harsh rasps. A sliver of blood trickled past his lips. 'They kept their relationship a secret for almost two hundred years.'

Anna sagged on the floor, her expression stunned.

'Shortly after your birth, Cecil passed away. Your mother followed him to the grave two years later.' Godard raised a bloodied hand and touched Anna's face with shaking fingers. 'I'm sorry I never told you, child,' he whispered, anguish distorting his voice. 'After what happened with Lucas, I thought it best to keep your existence a secret.'

Realization dawned on Vellacrus's face. She glanced from Anna to me, her eyes wild. 'Then that means—'

'Yes!' hissed Godard. 'The precious blood you wanted, the one that would have made your plans come true? It was running through our grandson's veins all along!'

At these words, Agatha Vellacrus finally snapped. A savage cry left her throat and she leveled the gun at Godard's head.

Her finger never squeezed the trigger.

She turned slowly and stared at me for fathomless seconds.

My vision blurred when I looked into gray eyes that were a mirror copy of my father's.

It was the closest I had ever been to my grandmother.

I stepped back and pulled the katana out of her chest. She crumpled to the ground, anger clouding her face even in death.

My fingers loosened on the handle of the blade. The sword clattered to the stone floor.

I dropped to my knees by my grandfather's side, my heart hammering painfully inside my ribcage. Blood still poured from the wound in his back.

'How—' I whispered brokenly, glancing at Anna.

Tears pooled in her eyes and ran down her cheeks. 'He has already died sixteen times.'

Anna cradled our grandfather's head in her lap, the crystal drops landing softly on his face.

Tomas Godard blinked. A small smile stretched his lips.

'It's my time to go,' he said with a trace of relief. 'I've been waiting for this moment for so long.'

The blue eyes shifted to me, pupils dilating darkly as he beheld something I could not see. He reached out and squeezed my hand.

'I'm so glad we had this time together. I want you to know that I always loved...you.' The words left his lips on a sigh. His arm dropped to the floor.

Anna buried her face in his chest, her muffled sobs filling the room.

Numbness spread through me as I gazed at the man who had come to mean so much to me.

Victor reached across and clasped Godard's fingers tightly, his face pale with grief.

'We should—' Costas started in a gruff voice a moment later.

A gunshot blasted through the tower. I spun around, the

Smith & Wesson in one hand while my fingers closed on the handle of the katana.

Reid stood inside the entrance to the castle. He lowered the Glock with a wince and clutched at the wound beneath his left clavicle.

My gaze shifted to the far side of the chamber.

Olsson slumped against the wall, his eyes wide beneath the bullet wound in his forehead.

'I told him I was gonna shoot him,' Reid muttered.

Shocked relief washed over me, taking away some of the numbness. 'You're alive.'

Reid grimaced. 'Yeah, well, it'll take more than a bunch of immortals to get rid of me. Besides, someone has to watch your back.'

His face darkened when he saw the still figure between Anna and me.

Anatole appeared behind him. Blood oozed from a nasty wound in the immortal's right flank.

'What did we miss?' he asked with a grin. His expression sobered when he looked around the room. 'Oh. A lot, by the looks of it.'

Footsteps pounded the corridor outside the tower. Reznak and Friedrich rushed in with a crowd of Crovirs and Bastians.

'The rest of your father's army just arrived!' Reznak told Victor. 'We've secured the island!'

He stopped when he saw the bodies on the floor. A sad light dawned in the Crovir noble's eyes as he beheld Tomas Godard's unmoving form.

Victor pushed away the helping hands around him and slowly climbed to his feet, his fingers clasped to his abdomen.

'Make sure we destroy the virus,' he ordered. 'Vellacrus still had some with her.'

He joined me when I rose silently from the floor with the

body of my grandfather cradled in my arms. We walked out onto the rooftop, Anna on my other side.

Up ahead, the sun rose on a new day, pale fingers of light flaring across the horizon and turning the sea crimson. A dark spot appeared on the bright orb.

It grew rapidly as a flock of crows descended from the heavens.

~

PART THREE: RESOLUTION

EPILOGUE

THE SOUND OF AN ENGINE DISTURBED THE LAZY SILENCE OF the afternoon. I looked up from the paper in front of me and shaded my eyes with one hand. Cornelius's ears twitched. The cat raised its head from my lap and followed my gaze.

Sunbeams danced across emerald-green waters, the light almost blinding in its radiance. A breeze rippled over the ocean surface and raised an army of small, foam-tipped waves that crashed onto a white beach.

The roar of the motor grew louder. A black speedboat appeared around the head of the cove and headed for the jetty in the lagoon a few hundred feet to my left.

I lowered the cat to the ground before rising from the wicker chair and strolling to the edge of the veranda that fronted the two-hundred-year-old colonial house I now called my home.

'Anna?' I called out over my shoulder.

Soft steps sounded behind me.

'Yes?' Anna came out through the patio doors. 'Oh. Our visitors are here.' She smiled. 'I'll make some drinks.' She kissed me and disappeared inside the house.

'Did I hear someone mention the word "drinks"?' someone gasped on my right. Reid appeared around the corner of the house. 'Could I have a splash of whisky in mine?'

Sweat poured down his face and he breathed heavily from his run around the island. The golden retriever puppy panting at his side stopped in its tracks and turned toward the approaching boat. The animal's back visibly stiffened. It let out a series of sharp barks, its tail tracing frantic circles in the air while it jumped back and forth.

Reid grimaced and shook his head. 'I don't know whether that means "Stay off my island or I'll bite you" or "Please come and play with me". And who the hell names a dog Peanut?'

'I heard that!' Anna shouted through an open window.

The speedboat glided to a stop behind the hundred-foot luxury yacht already moored at the landing. A man jumped out and secured the vessel to the pier. A second man climbed onto the wooden jetty and looked around with evident interest.

The pair made their way up toward the house.

'This is a nice place you've got here,' said Dimitri Reznak as he climbed the steps to the veranda.

'Thanks.' I shook his hand briskly and turned to the man behind him. 'It's good to see you again.'

Victor Dvorsky hugged me and smiled. 'Same here.' He looked to my left. 'Hello, Reid.'

Reid nodded at the two men. Anna came out of the house with a tray of drinks.

Victor crossed the deck, kissed her on the cheeks, and took the tray off her. 'My dear, you look as lovely as ever.'

A month had passed since the death of Tomas Godard.

Ironically, Olsson's demise at Reid's hands had also been his final one.

Following the release of the Red Death on the Crovirs' island fortress, those who had been exposed to the virus were quarantined and successfully treated with an antiserum Anna made from a sample of my blood.

There were many changes in the immortal world in the weeks after the battle. Roman Dvorsky retired as the head of the Order of Bastian Hunters and passed the mantle on to his son without any objections from the Councils, though he continued in his role as a senior advisor. Dimitri Reznak was temporarily appointed the leader of the Order of Crovir Hunters until a suitable replacement could be voted in.

After the unprecedented menace posed by Vellacrus and her army of faithful followers, both immortal First Councils had committed to working closely together in an attempt to subvert any similar future threats. It said a lot for Victor's and Dimitri's influences that such an unparalleled agreement had been made in so short a time. There were many still among both factions who disapproved of this new alliance between the Bastians and the Crovirs. There would undoubtedly be challenges ahead for the two leaders, but so far, the fragile peace was holding.

As for Anna and I, we left Europe the day after we buried our grandfather's ashes in Prague. We spent a week in my apartment in Boston while we finalized the purchase of our new home, a private island in the Pacific Ocean.

The location was known to only six people: the Dvorskys, Pierre and Solange Vauquois, Reid, and now Dimitri Reznak.

Two days ago, Victor called to say that the Crovir noble wished to meet with us urgently; Reznak apparently had some important information to impart and he wanted to do it in person.

'Are you visiting for a while?' Victor asked Reid presently.

Reid shook his head. 'I leave tomorrow, I'm afraid. I have business to take care of in Boston. We've just taken on some new employees.'

The Hasley and Soul Agency had grown a fair bit in the last month. There were now three more detectives working full-time with Reid, two of them old friends from the police force. A larger office had become vacant in our building and we moved premises a week ago. We even had a new secretary; it was Mrs. Trelawney's daughter, Izzie.

Although I still co-owned the business, I had opted out of working in the field for the time being. Most of my tasks were currently research-based and I performed them more than adequately from the new state-of-the-art study in our home.

We had also started constructing Anna's new lab on the other side of the island.

'I see your scar has almost faded.' Victor indicated the mark under Reid's left clavicle.

'Yes, it has.'

Reid and I exchanged guarded glances.

Something else had started to become evident since before the final battle with Vellacrus's army; from the time that he received Anna's blood in Prague, Reid's wounds had all healed at an alarmingly accelerated rate. Although it was not yet as fast as an immortal's regenerative abilities, it was still greater than that of a human. Even more astounding was what was happening to the injuries he had sustained before the transfusion: his old scars were also slowly disappearing.

Anna assured us that such a thing had never happened on the rare occasions when a human had received immortal blood.

We had yet to tell Victor and Dimitri of this intriguing phenomenon.

I turned a questioning gaze on Reznak. 'Victor said you had something you wanted to tell us?'

'Indeed, I did, although I'm not quite sure where to start,' Reznak admitted with a grimace. He looked to the clear waters beyond the veranda and the puppy playing on the beach before turning to me. 'How much do you know of the history of the immortals?'

The question surprised me.

'Not a lot,' I said with a shrug. 'As far as I recall, our races appeared in Europe some time around the mid-tenth century BC. They seem to have been at war pretty much since.'

Reznak leaned back in his chair and watched me with narrowed eyes. 'What if I were to tell you that this was not always the case? And that we've been around since well before that time?'

'What do you mean?' I said after a short silence.

Reznak did not answer the question directly. 'What do you know about the Book of Genesis?'

I glanced at Anna. She appeared as puzzled as I felt.

'It's the first book of the Hebrew Bible and the Christian Old Testament,' I replied.

The Crovir nodded. 'Good. Do you have any knowledge of the specifics of the third and fourth chapters?' His eyes gleamed with a mysterious light.

'You mean the accounts of how Adam and Eve were banished from the Garden of Eden and the subsequent stories of their descendants?' said Anna with a faint frown.

Reznak smiled his approval. 'Correct again. Of course, there's more to it than that.'

Anna raised an eyebrow. 'There is?'

'Yes. You're aware that most of the Dead Sea Scrolls are kept in the Shrine of the Book, in Jerusalem?' said Reznak.

Anna nodded, green eyes shining with intellectual curiosity.

'As far as mortals are concerned, they're the oldest scriptures ever discovered that reflect the actual wordings of the Old Testament and the Bible,' added the Crovir noble.

A stunned hush fell across the veranda. The puppy yipped in the distance.

'What d'you mean, as far as "mortals" are concerned?' said Reid.

'It's exactly as it sounds.'

Anna inhaled sharply. 'Are you saying that *immortals* possess documents older than the Dead Sea Scrolls?'

Reznak did not reply immediately. Instead, he fixed me with a shrewd stare. 'Do you recall where I was at the time Victor called me, after the compound in Virginia was attacked?'

I frowned. 'Yes. You were in Egypt.'

Reznak stared blindly into his glass. 'The origin of our immortal races is a subject that has always fascinated me, even as a child.' A wry grimace flashed across his face. 'Although I've been the Head of our Immortal Culture and History Section for several centuries, I've spent a considerable amount of my own fortune before and during those years trying to satisfy my personal obsession with discovering where we truly came from.' He sighed. 'Ironically, the breakthrough I had been yearning for took place just after I discovered the whole unpleasant affair with Vellacrus and her scheme of true immortality. My team of archaeologists found a cave in Egypt, in the mountains of the Eastern Desert. It was deep underground, which explains why the contents we discovered within were so well preserved. What with recent events and the need to reorganize the Crovir Councils, you can appreciate that I've been otherwise occupied of late. It's only been in the last couple of weeks that I was able to start analyzing the materials we found.'

He met our gazes steadily. 'The discovery is broadly made of two parts. The first is a series of scriptures that narrate the origins of the immortal races. They have been dated to approximately three thousand years BC.'

My eyes widened at his words. I felt my pulse start to race.

Reznak looked from Anna to me. 'The second, and by far the most extraordinary finding, are the biological remains we found with the scriptures.'

'That's impossible,' Anna stated flatly in the silence that followed.

Reznak shrugged. 'The evidence doesn't lie. Victor has seen

the relics and can confirm my findings. We have of course moved the scriptures to a more secure location.'

The Bastian leader nodded at our questioning gazes.

'What are these...“remains” you've alluded to?' I said after a while.

Reznak's eyes darkened. 'Before I tell you about those, I must add that there were in fact *two* caves. The first one had unfortunately been ransacked when we discovered it. The second cave was located in a different rock formation.'

Lines creased Anna's brow. 'Have you found out who looted the first cave?'

Reznak shook his head. 'No. But I've got my best agent on it.'

He gazed at us with a guarded expression. 'The remains were a pair of hearts, embalmed in individual clay pots. I believe they belonged to the original Crovir and Bastian, although this is difficult to ascertain without the rest of their bodies. Crovir and Bastian were not just the names of our races. They were men born in the thirty-eighth century BC.'

He paused at our stares. 'I know. I found it hard to believe myself at first. The genetic analysis we've carried out on the hearts shows that they were most likely brothers, a fact which is also supported by the translations of the scriptures. The texts tell most of their story and that of their father before them, a man named Romerus.' He took a deep breath. 'Now, this is where we all have to take a leap of faith.'

'Really? I thought we did that a while ago,' said Reid dully.

'This one requires a lot more of it, I'm afraid,' said Reznak. 'According to the scriptures, Romerus was probably a descendant of Adam and Eve. We cannot confirm this, as part of the texts are missing.' He frowned. 'I suspect they were stolen from the first cave.'

The crash of the surf on the shoreline and the puppy's

playful barks were the only sounds that interrupted the heavy silence that followed.

An eerie premonition started to take shape at the back of my mind.

'Adam's descendants are said to have lived hundreds of years,' said Anna. 'Is that where the concept of immortality arose?'

'Possibly,' said Reznak. 'But I believe that Crovir and Bastian were truly special beings, born with abilities that even their forefathers had not possessed. The clues, although we have yet to fully analyze the information, are in their genes.' He shared a cautious glance with Victor before turning to Anna and me. 'This is where the two of you come in.'

Anna's eyes widened.

My presentiment grew stronger at his words. 'What do you mean?'

'I obtained a small sample of your blood before the research materials at the Crovir labs were destroyed,' Reznak told Anna. His gaze shifted to me. 'I asked Victor to do the same with yours. Don't worry,' he added hastily at our expressions, 'there isn't enough for anyone to attempt anything like what Vellacrus had planned. All I wanted was to study your genetic material.'

'Why?' I asked stiffly, although I had a suspicion what his answer was going to be.

'To compare them with the samples we found in the cave,' said Reznak. 'Victor and I have both personally researched the extensive genealogy of the noble families of our two immortal societies. As far as we can establish, the Godards and the Thornes were true purebloods in every sense of the word—Bastians and Crovirs descended from pureblood Bastians and Crovirs all the way back as far as our scrolls go. As you're probably aware, Bastians and Crovirs have successfully mated in the past, but—'

'Never a pureblood with a pureblood,' Anna said breathlessly, her eyes glazed with shock.

Reznak nodded. 'And not just any purebloods. Your parents were direct descendants of Crovir and Bastian,' he said solemnly. 'The molecular studies we carried out on your samples and the tissues we found in the cave confirm that you both possess the same distinctive genetic variations as the two original immortals.' He stared at me. 'We also found the alpha and omega designs that make up your birthmark in the scriptures from the cave in Egypt.'

His words confirmed my gut feeling. I suddenly felt lightheaded.

'That's—' Anna started after a while.

'The kind of news that requires several stiff drinks?' Reid interrupted, his face pale.

Reznak's expression grew inscrutable. 'The two of you are unique,' he said quietly. 'As far as I'm aware, there are no other direct pureblood descendants of Crovir and Bastian alive today. Agatha Vellacrus, Felix Thorne, and Tomas Godard were the last ones left.' He hesitated. 'I suspect that Anna would also survive her seventeenth death. And I believe she shares your other ability.'

Anna and I gazed at each other for long seconds. Her hand moved under the table. My eyes followed her fingers to the folds of her dress while my heart thudded dully inside my chest.

The other incredible secret we had kept from Victor Dvorsky and Dimitri Reznak was that Anna was pregnant. It had only been a couple of days since we found out ourselves. Reid was the only other person who knew.

Both Anna and I found it a miracle that she had conceived so easily, after our very first night together. As the implications of the Crovir noble's revelations sank in, I saw my own unease reflected in her green gaze; if we were this gifted because of our possible blood links with the fathers of our races, then what would our unborn child be capable of?'

I frowned at Reznak. 'What do you—'

'Want from the two of you?' the Crovir noble interjected. He smiled and shook his head. 'Nothing, really. I thought you deserved to know about this discovery as it concerned you directly. Victor agreed with me on this matter.'

'No one but the two of us know the details of what Reznak has told you today,' said Victor. 'The scientists working on the project had access to only part of the materials at any one time.' He observed us from hooded eyes. 'However, we did wonder what impact it would have on the immortal societies if we let the truth be known.'

'About us?' Anna's fingers clenched convulsively on her lap. I grasped her hand and squeezed it gently.

Victor shook his head. 'About the origin of our races.' He hesitated. 'And possibly about you.' He shared another glance with Reznak. 'Both of us think the Bastian and Crovir First Councils would benefit from having the two of you as members.'

I stared at Victor for a long time before rising from the table and stepping to the edge of the veranda. As I gazed out over the rippling surface of the ocean, a strange and unexpected feeling of calmness stole over me.

It was as if I could see everything clearly for the first time in my long and unnatural life.

I looked over my shoulder. 'And if we were to say no?'

'Then both Victor and I would respect your wishes unconditionally,' Reznak replied. 'Think it over. We're not expecting you to give us an answer straight away.'

I turned and smiled at him drily. 'I don't think we're likely to change our minds anytime soon.'

Anna looked relieved at my words.

'If that proves to be your final decision, then so be it,' Reznak said graciously.

The puppy bounded over from the beach and dropped a mouthful of wet seaweed at Reid's feet. It sat on its haunches, cocked its head, and gazed at the former US Marine with an expectant expression on its canine face.

'If you think we're playing catch with this, you've got another thing coming,' said Reid.

The puppy yipped.

Reid sighed. 'I told you Peanut was a bad choice of name for a dog,' he told Anna. 'It's made him stupid. Even the cat's laughing at him.'

Cornelius was eyeing the dog haughtily.

'No, he isn't.' Anna rose from the chair and petted the puppy on the head. Its tongue rolled out further and it whimpered in delight. 'Let me guess, you would've preferred something like Butch or Bud.'

She lifted the tray of empty glasses from the table. Cornelius curled around her ankles as she headed for the patio doors.

'What's wrong with Bud and Butch? Or Bob, even?' said Reid. 'What?' he added defensively in the face of our stares. 'Bob's a great name for a dog.'

'I don't think so,' said Anna, her tone emphatic. 'When you have a dog, you can call *it* Bob.'

Reid muttered something under his breath.

Anna rolled her eyes. 'Tell you what, we'll rethink Peanut.'

I smiled.

Reid brightened. 'Oh. Good.' A faint frown dawned on the former Marine's face at Anna's expression. 'Wait. What're you gonna call him in the meantime?'

'Dog,' Anna stated firmly.

Victor grinned. Reznak chuckled.

Reid's eyes widened in horror. '*D–Dog?!* Why, you might as well just shoot the poor bastard!' He stormed after her.

As the sun started to sink over the ocean, we followed them inside the house, the D-O-G included.

THE END

THANK YOU

Thank you for reading HUNTED.

I would be really grateful if you could consider leaving a review on Amazon, Goodreads, or other platforms where you buy your books. Reviews are vital for authors and all reviews, even a couple of short sentences, can help readers decide whether to pick up one of my books.

WANT FREE BOOKS AND EXCLUSIVE EXTRAS?

Join my reader list today for free books, exclusive bonus content, new release alerts, giveaways, and more.
  Go to the link below to find out more.

www.ADStarrling.com/free-download-offer

ACKNOWLEDGMENTS

To all my friends who helped make this possible. You know who
you are.

FACTS AND FICTIONS

Now, for one of my favorite parts of writing my books. Here are the facts and fictions behind the story.

Miyamoto Musashi

The 17th century samurai who taught Lucas the art of *Niten Ichi-ryu* did exist. He is the author of **The Book of Five Rings** and the founder of the *Hyoho Niten Ichi-ryu*, the "Two Heavens as One" or "Two Swords as One" style of swordsmanship. His grave still stands to this day in the Kumamoto Prefecture, on Kyushu Island, Japan. You can find out more about how Lucas met him in **Dancing Blades, a Seventeen Series Short Story**.

Genetics Labs

The Center for Molecular Genetics of the Université Pierre et Marie Curie, where Professor Hubert Eric Strauss works, is factual and is indeed located on the Gif-sur-Yvette campus outside Paris. The same goes for the Functional Genomics Center in Zurich and the Prague Institute of Molecular Genetics. The interior descriptions given of these three buildings are fictional.

Historical Wars

Bar the Immortal war, all the conflicts featured in the story are based on true historical events. Count Ernst Rudiger von Starhemberg successfully defended his city against the Ottoman invasion during the Battle of Vienna in 1683. Vienna does have a network of underground tunnels and crypts, parts of which were used by the Germans in the Second World War. The secret passage under the Hofburg Palace is fictional.

On-off Cancer Switch

The cell cycle and the genetics behind cell reproduction and death form the basis of cancer research and the development of appropriate drugs to cure or control the disease. Hubert Strauss's attempts to create an "off" switch to down-regulate cancer cell production is something that cancer research scientists have been trying to do for a number of years. I believe we will see this happen successfully for some cancers during my lifetime. The "on" switch is purely fictional.

Black Death

The Black Death of the 14th century is factual and was a bubonic plague caused by the Yersinia Pestis bacteria. The fictional Red Death of the same century was a viral hemorrhagic disease similar to the ones caused by the Ebola, Lassa, and Marburg viruses. It was highly contagious and deadly, with a short incubation period of 24-48 hours, and left most survivors infertile. Reverse vaccinology, the technique that Anna Godard used to create a vaccine against the new strain of the Red Death, is factual.

And that's it for the science and technology lesson folks! Want to check out more Extras? Then visit my website at <u>www.adstarrling.com</u>

ABOUT THE AUTHOR

AD Starrling's bestselling supernatural thriller series **Seven-teen** combines action, suspense, and a dose of fantasy to make each book an explosive, adrenaline-fueled ride. If you prefer your action hot and your heroes sexy and strong-willed, then check out her military thriller series Division Eight.

When she's not busy writing, AD can be found looking up exciting international locations and cool science and technology to put in her books, eating Thai food, being tortured by her back therapists, drooling over gadgets, working part-time as a doctor on a Neonatal Intensive Care unit somewhere in the UK, reading manga, and watching action and sci-fi flicks. She has occasionally been accused of committing art with a charcoal stick and some drawing paper.

Find out more about AD on her website

www.adstarrling.com where you can sign up for her awesome newsletter, get exclusive freebies, and never miss her latest release. You'll also have a chance to see sneak previews of her work, participate in exclusive giveaways, and hear about special promotional offers first.

Here are some other places where you can connect with her:

www.adstarrling.com
Email: ads@adstarrling.com

ALSO BY A. D. STARRLING

Hunted (A Seventeen Series Novel) Book One

'My name is Lucas Soul. Today, I died again. This is my fifteenth death in the last four hundred and fifty years. And I'm determined that it will be the last.'

National Indie Excellence Awards Winner Fantasy 2013

National Indie Excellence Awards Finalist Adventure 2013

Next Generation Indie Book Awards Finalist Action-Adventure 2013

Hollywood Book Festival 2013 Honorable Mention General Fiction

Warrior (A Seventeen Series Novel) Book Two

The perfect Immortal warrior. A set of stolen, priceless artifacts. An ancient sect determined to bring about the downfall of human civilization.

Next Generation Indie Book Awards Winner Action-Adventure 2014

Shelf Unbound Competition for Best Independently Published Book Finalist 2014

Empire (A Seventeen Series Novel) Book Three

An Immortal healer. An ancient empire reborn. A chain of cataclysmic events that threatens to change the fate of the world.

Next Generation Indie Book Awards Finalist General Fiction 2015

Legacy (A Seventeen Series Novel) Book Four

The Hunter who should have been king. The Elemental who fears love. The Seer who is yet to embrace her powers.

Three immortals whose fates are entwined with that of the oldest and most formidable enemy the world has ever faced.

Origins (A Seventeen Series Novel) Book Five

The gifts bestowed by One not of this world, to the Man who had lived longer than most.

The Empire ruled by a King who would swallow the world in his madness.

The Warrior who chose to rise against her own kind in order to defeat him.

Discover the extraordinary beginnings of the Immortals and the unforgettable story of the Princess who would become a Legend.

Destiny (A Seventeen Series Novel) Book Six

An enemy they never anticipated.

A brutal attack that tears them apart.

A chain of immutable events that will forever alter the future.

Discover the destiny that was always theirs to claim.

The Seventeen Collection 1: Books 1-3

Boxset featuring Hunted, Warrior, and Empire.

The Seventeen Collection 2: Books 4-6

Boxset featuring Legacy, Origins, and Destiny.

The Seventeen Complete Collection: Books 1-6

Boxset featuring Hunted, Warrior, Empire, Legacy, Origins, and Destiny.

First Death (A Seventeen Series Short Story) #1

Discover where it all started...

Dancing Blades (A Seventeen Series Short Story) #2

Join Lucas Soul on his quest to become a warrior.

The Meeting (A Seventeen Series Short Story) #3

Discover the origins of the incredible friendship between the protagonists of Hunted.

The Warrior Monk (A Seventeen Series Short Story) #4

Experience Warrior from the eyes of one of the most beloved characters in Seventeen.

The Hunger (A Seventeen Series Short Story) #5

Discover the origin of the love story behind Empire.

The Bank Job (A Seventeen Series Short Story) #6

Join two of the protagonists from Legacy on their very first adventure.

The Seventeen Series Short Story Collection 1 (#1-3)

Boxset featuring First Death, Dancing Blades, and The Meeting.

The Seventeen Series Short Story Collection 2 (#4-6)

Boxset featuring The Warrior Monk, The Hunger, and The Bank Job.

The Seventeen Series Ultimate Short Story Collection

Boxset featuring First Death, Dancing Blades, The Meeting, The Warrior Monk, The Hunger, and The Bank Job.

Mission:Black (A Division Eight Thriller)

A broken agent. A once in a lifetime chance. A new mission that threatens to destroy her again.

Mission: Armor (A Division Eight Thriller)

A man tortured by his past. A woman determined to save him. A deadly assignment that threatens to rip them apart.

Mission:Anaconda (A Division Eight Thriller)

It should have been a simple mission. They should have been in and out in a day. Except it wasn't. And they didn't.

Void (A Sci-fi Horror Short Story)

2065. Humans start terraforming Mars.

2070. The Mars Baker2 outpost is established on the Acidalia Planitia.

2084. The first colonist goes missing.

The Other Side of the Wall (A Short Horror Story)

Have you ever seen flashes of darkness where there should only be light? Ever seen shadows skitter past out of the corner of your eyes and looked, only to find nothing there?

AUDIOBOOKS

Hunted (A Seventeen Series Novel) Book One

Warrior (A Seventeen Series Novel) Book Two

Empire (A Seventeen Seres Novel) Book Three

First Death (A Seventeen Series Short Story) #1

Dancing Blades (A Seventeen Series Short Story) #2

The Meeting (A Seventeen Series Short Story) #3

The Warrior Monk (A Seventeen Series Short Story) #4

WARRIOR EXTRACT

PROLOGUE

November 1700. Battle of Narva. Swedish territory.

The little girl stared into the dead man's eyes, her expression steady and unflinching. All around her rose the cries of soldiers and the clash of swords, while cannons boomed on a distant hill, and the sharp reports of musket shots echoed across the banks of the nearby river.

The morning's blizzard had turned the battlefield into a gray and bloody mire. The snow and rain that had been falling steadily during the night had grown heavy at dawn, and visibility was worsened by vicious gusts blowing in from the west. When the wind shifted to the south at midday, it provided an unprecedented advantage for the eight-thousand-strong army of Sweden's King Karl the Twelfth. They had been able to advance virtually unseen on the significantly larger Russian contingent, which laid siege to the city of Narva in early November of that year.

Although tired and hungry after traveling across miles of treacherous back roads and countryside laid to waste by the invaders, the better-equipped and more experienced Swedes managed to get within fifty yards of the enemy's front lines without being detected and led a swift attack on two fronts.

After overcoming Russian General Veyde's and Prince Trubetskoy's men, they now marched for the troops on the adversary's left flank, which were under the charge of Duke de Cröy, the field marshal whom Tsar Peter I of Russia had left in charge of his army.

As he carefully made his way across the treacherous ground, Dimitri Reznak glanced at the bruised skies overhead. Though the worst of the storm had passed, heavy flakes still fell from the low clouds that covered the land in eerie twilight. Interspersed with rain and sleet, the snow melted rapidly in crimson puddles that dotted the plain, forming brief teardrops on the cooling skin of the hundreds of Russian and Swedish soldiers who had fallen since the start of the battle. Reznak frowned at the gruesome sight.

Given that he was an immortal who had witnessed countless wars and conflicts over the five centuries of his existence thus far, he knew he should have been immune to the spectacle of blood and gore that surrounded him. Yet, despite the fact that he and the two hundred Crovir immortals under his command were assisting the young Swedish King in his endeavor to keep the new territories his predecessors had acquired during Europe's bloody Thirty Years' War, Reznak could not help but feel overwhelmed by sadness at the needless loss of human life. Which was why he headed straight for the little girl when he saw her standing on the knoll in the middle of the battleground.

Although he hadn't expected to see a child in the midst of the war zone, Reznak was not surprised. Some civilians had still been trying to reach the safety of the fortified city when they were caught between the advancing armies, and those who had not succumbed to the fierce blizzard perished in the subsequent crossfire. He could only presume that the child had become separated from her parents during the ensuing chaos.

The chances of finding them alive, he knew, would be slim at best.

When he got within twenty feet of her, the little girl finally looked up. It was not the panicked, wild movement he had been anticipating. Instead, it was a slow and measured gesture. Reznak froze.

Her eyes were a clear gray, the irises wide and almost silvery in their sheen. Her skin, where it was visible beneath the dirty yet elegant ivory dress she wore, was an alabaster white. Thick, dark curls crowned her head and fell in waves to her shoulders, framing a surprisingly slim face and neck. She looked to be about eight years old and was without a doubt the most shockingly beautiful being he had ever seen.

Yet it was not her startling appearance that stopped him in his tracks; it was the look on her face that sent a sharp chill through his bones and a shiver down his spine, immobilizing his legs.

There was only one word to describe the expression in her eyes: fearlessness.

Pure and unadulterated, the feeling seemed to seep through her pores and emanate from the very core of her being, an almost palpable energy focused in a lance-like beam projected from her dark pupils.

That was when Reznak knew she was not human.

The little girl blinked. Reznak suddenly found that he could move again. His gaze drifted down to her right hand, where the handle of an ugly knife was clasped firmly between her slender fingers. Red droplets still gleamed wetly on the edge of the blade and dropped into an expanding pool by her bare feet. His eyes followed the crimson trail to the dead man lying inches from where she stood. There was a deep, linear wound on the left side of the soldier's chest; by the looks of it, she had stabbed him in the heart.

It would have taken the man less than a minute to die.

Reznak's gaze shifted to the girl. 'Hello,' he said gently in German, conscious of the weight of the sword at his waist. 'My name is Dimitri. What's your name?'

The little girl remained silent. He hesitated. Certain he would not get a reply, he repeated the question in the local Estonian dialect. He was shocked when, in a clear and low voice that was oddly devoid of emotion, she said, 'Alexandria.'

Reznak took a cautious step forward, his eyes never leaving hers. Her chin tilted as she stared up at him. 'Where's your mother, Alexandria?' he continued quietly in the same vernacular.

A faint frown dawned on her face at his words. 'I don't know,' she said.

Less than two hundred feet from where they stood, scores of soldiers fought to the death, their swords and daggers carving through the flesh and bones of their enemies. The harsh breaths of their nervous horses misted the cold air, while musket rounds peppered the ground around them.

Reznak took another step forward. 'Can you tell me where you came from?'

The little girl's frown deepened while she considered the question. 'I don't know,' she repeated.

It was then that he noticed the fresh blood matted in her hair. She had suffered a blow to the side of her head. His gaze dropped to the red finger marks on her arm. His eyes narrowed.

'Did that man hurt you?' Reznak asked stiffly, indicating the dead soldier at her feet.

Her chin dipped in a brief nod.

He stared at her for a moment before slowly squatting down. With his face level with hers, he carefully extended a hand. 'Would you like to come with me, Alexandria? It's not safe here.'

The little girl gazed at him silently. Undaunted, Reznak stood up and waited. She turned on her heels and stared through the thin veil of snow at the river and the city beyond it. The wind picked up and ruffled her hair.

He peered at the back of her neck curiously. Imprinted a scant inch beneath her hairline, in the very middle of her delicate spine, was a triangular mark—a trishula. Although generically shaped like a trident, the more intricate details of the design reminded him strongly of the weapons he had seen wielded by fearsome Asian warriors in battles past. It was not a tattoo. It looked more like a birthmark.

The knife thudded softly in the deepening snowdrift when the little girl opened her fingers. Still gazing at the battlefield before them, she raised her bloodied hand toward him. Reznak clasped it in his own and was surprised at how warm her skin felt.

'Are you my father now?' she asked calmly.

'No,' he said with a weak smile. He glanced at the top of her head. The dark curls shivered slightly in the wind. Beneath them, the child's body was as still as stone. 'Can I call you Alexa? Alexandria is a bit of a mouthful.'

She gave this some thought. 'Yes,' she said finally with a curt nod.

∾

Get the book now!

Warrior (A Seventeen Series Novel) Book Two

CPSIA information can be obtained
at www.ICGtesting.com
Printed in the USA
LVHW031750020623
748747LV00001B/90